D0646532

GP   1st 10ee

COPYRIGHT ©2002 MCSWEENEY'S QUARTERLY. All rights are reserved by MCSWEENEY'S, unless they are held by the authors in question, in which case those people are welcome to them.

This issue was guest edited by longtime *McSweeney's* contributor Paul Maliszewski. Paul had long ago been talking about a compilation he was putting together around the themes of fact and fiction, hoax and prank, truth and its variations. He thought it would make a great book. I thought it would make a great issue of this quarterly. He acquiesced, and here we are. I think this is one of the very best issues we've published, and it is entirely Paul's creation.

FOLLOWING IS A NOTE FROM PAUL MALISZEWSKI:

Most of the editing on this issue happened between February and July 2001, with the bulk of that work getting finished between April and June, with the bulk of that bulk only starting to look complete around the middle of June. Although, to be fair and honest, which I mean to be, I should just admit that I began talking to a few of the writers that appear here about their contribution as long ago as December 1999, if you can believe that. I couldn't believe it myself, but late last night—this was around four, when the birds in the pine trees outside my window were just then cranking up the bird noise—while I was trying to first identify and second tie up all loose threads and was just generally worried that I'd forgotten something crucial and obvious, something on the scale of accidentally leaving the baby on the roof of the car and starting to drive off, I came across the e-mail to prove it. December 1999. This admission says a lot probably about the speed at which I work.

In any case, all this stubbornness—I'll just call it stubbornness in the interest of more of that honesty—is currently housed comfortably enough with me and one mostly-black, polydactyl female cat that makes peep- and squeak-type noises instead of anything resembling full-blown meows. This is in a two-bedroom apartment in Durham, North Carolina. Polydactyl means she has more than the normal number of toes. The apartment is one part or unit of a multi-part, sprawling apartment complex with a color scheme of maroon and light gray. Durham is full of multi-part, sprawling apartment complexes almost but not quite like this one; however, only about six or seven or eight can boast of a maroon-and-light-gray color scheme.

It has started to get so warm here that I break a sweat before I get to the mailboxes just up the road. Sometimes this cat opens her mouth but no sound comes out.

There's a paved trail that begins across the street from the apartment complex and runs back and around and about this whole part of the city, which part has two names, both of which sound, at least to my ear, like names of nursing homes. I take walks on the trail most every day. I walk about three or four miles I guess. A few nights ago I was coming back from one of my walks. It was almost nine and starting to get dark. A guy from the well-known chain of pizza delivery places whose name does not need to be mentioned was just getting into his car. He tossed his keep-the-pizza-warm thing into the backseat, and that's when he saw me. "Hey, man," he said, "you get around." He shook his head to indicate how much he disbelieved the extent to which I get around. Now at first I thought he meant this as a joke, because the fact is—to be honest—I really don't get around all that much. I hardly get around anywhere. But then I realized that he had no way of knowing this about me, or even guessing, and so was probably just referring to my walking around a lot. He must see me walking around a lot. I said, "I guess I walk around a lot." He shook his head again, laughed, and got into his car, there really not being anything left for us to say. Since then, I've seen him a few more times. I'll be out walking and he'll be driving by, delivering pizzas, and when he sees me he honks his horn, and when I see him I wave, all of which leads me to conclude that I'm slowly becoming a character, or else gaining an unwanted reputation as the walking guy, and that if this continues, in a few months, more people will be referring to me namelessly, as, you know, the person who walks around a lot.

I keep several Durham/Chapel Hill/Raleigh phonebooks by my desk, mainly to use as phonebooks, secondarily to use as paperweights, but also to mine for good names, for characters or whatever. I'll typically select one phonebook, whichever happens to be closest, flip through it, scan a few pages here, skim a few pages there, until I spot a really good last name. I'll repeat that name in my head, sometimes saying it aloud. Then I'll just match that last name with what I consider a more fitting first name. This is almost endlessly fun. If you don't believe me, if you're skeptical, just try it. Sometimes I don't even have any immediate purpose in mind, no character in pressing need of a name.

One day, while looking pointlessly through a phonebook, I flipped too far too fast and ended up in the coupon section, where all the coupons are. The first coupon I read was for a carwash. The second was for an Italian restaurant. The third one I read was the keeper. That one was for a painting workshop, the coupon offering one free class to every person who brought in the coupon. Pretty good deal, I thought. The motto of the workshop was, "Learn To Paint Like The Old Masters." Now I cannot tell the extent to which I enjoyed imagining a class full of people learning to paint, some choosing to paint like, say, Renoir, others wanting to paint like Rembrandt. I tore the coupon out and leaned it against some books, where it has stayed. From time to time I'd pick it up to study, sometimes coming close to getting on the phone to see about joining the class or interviewing the workshop's teacher.

Q. What Old Master do people most want to paint like?

Q. I'm a complete amateur when it comes to painting. Which Old Master is easy or good for beginners to emulate?

But I never called. And I never dropped by the painting workshop. Instead I persisted in imagining that classroom full of students painting like Ingres or Vermeer or making a go of Leonardo. I knew what I'd learn by calling. Or I had a real good feeling what I'd learn. I suspected I'd hear that the motto was just some motto, and that nobody ever came to class to paint like an old master. They just came to paint. Hearing that, I would have been a bit disappointed. For me, the class is still full of earnest devotees, apprentice copycats, and devilishly clever art forgers, and for reasons I don't entirely understand, I like that a whole lot better.

McSweeney's is available at most fine bookstores, including these stores, all great booksellers and members of our McSweeney's 100 program. McSweeney's 100 stores are the best places to find McSwys publications, especially rare McSwys stuff, and to see McSwys authors on tour. To find out about the stores or how to join the program, more please visit our website.

A CLEAN WELL LIGHTED PLACE FOR BOOKS, San Francisco, CA; BIG JAR BOOKS, Philadelphia, PA; BOOK COURT, Brooklyn , NY; BOOK PEOPLE, Austin , TX; BOOK STALL NP/JL/DE2, Pittsburgh, PA; BOOKS & BOOKS, Coral Gables, FL; BOOKSHOP SANTA CRUZ, Santa Cruz CA; BROOKLINE BOOK-SMITH, Brookline, MA; BOOKSMITH, San Francisco, CA; BULL'S HEAD BOOKSHOP, Chapel Hill, NC; CANTERBURY BOOKSELLERS, Madison , WI, CASCO BAY BOOKS, Portland, ME; CODY'S BOOKS, Berkeley, CA; COLISEUM BOOKS, New York, NY; COLLEGE HILL BOOKSTORE, Providence, RI, COMMUNITY BOOKSTORE, Brooklyn, NY; DAVIS-KIDD NASHVILLE, Nashville, TN; DUTTON'S BRENT-WOOD, Los Angeles, CA; ELLIOTT BAY BOOK CO. M/NP/DE, Seattle, WA, EMERSON AND COOK BOOK COMPANY, Old Saybrook, CT; GALLERY BOOKSTORE, Mendocino, CA, GOTHAM BOOK MART M/NP/L, New York, NY; GREEN APPLE BOOKS, San Francisco, CA; HALCYON, Nashville, TN; HUNGRY MIND (RUMINATOR) NP/DE, St. Paul, MN, ICONOCLAST BOOKS, Katchum, ID; MIDNIGHT SPECIAL BOOKSTORE, Santa Monica, CA; MILLION YEAR PICNIC, Cambridge, MA; MOE'S BOOKS, Berkeley, CA, OLSSON'S BOOKS & RECORDS, Washington D.C.; ONE STOP NEWS, Washington D.C.; POSMAN BOOKS, New York, NY; POWELL'S BOOKS M/NP, Portland, OR; QUIMBY'S, Chicago, IL; RAINY DAY BOOKS, Fairway, KS; REGULATOR BOOKSHOP, Durham, NC; SHAMAN DRUM BOOKSHOP DE, Ann Arbor, MI; SMALL WORLD BOOKS, Venice, CA; SQUARE BOOKS, Oxford, MS; ST. MARK'S BOOKSHOP M/NP/L, New York, NY; TATTERED COVER, Denver, CO; THIS AIN'T THE ROSEDALE LIBRARY, Toronto, Ontario; UNIVERSITY BOOKSTORE - Madison, Seattle, WA, UNIVERSITY BOOKSTORE, Seattle, WA & Madison, WI; VERTIGO BOOKS , College Park , MD; WORDSWORTH BOOKS, Cambridge, MA; JOSEPH-BETH CINCINNATI, Cincinnati, OH; ROYAL BOOKS, Baltimore, MD, LIBRARY BOOKS, Baltimore, MD; BAILEY COY BOOKS, Seattle, WA; DIESEL, A BOOKSTORE, Oakland, CA; NANTUCKET BOOKWORKS, Nantucket, MA, CITY LIGHTS, San Francisco, CA; ATOMIC BOOKS, Baltimore, MD; HARVARD BOOKSTORE, Cambridge, MA; RAKESTRAW BOOKS, Danville, CA; JOSEPH FOX BOOKSHOP, Philadelphia, PA.

GENERAL EDITORIAL ASSISTANCE FOR THIS ISSUE AND WITH McSWYS GENERALLY was provided by the following volunteers, on whom we depend continually: Tanner Colby, Ted Thompson, Lee Epstein, Ross McSweeney, Aaron Belyaert, Krista Overby, Jason Kellermeyer, Allison Devers, Chad Albers, Nick Steele, Michael Hearst, Joshua Camp, Ben White, Mieka Strawhorn, Ian Jursco and, always, Eduardo de la Manzana. CONTRIBUTING EDITORS: Lawrence Weschler, John Warner. EDITORS AT LARGE: Sean Wilsey, Todd Pruzan. COPY EDITING: Chris Gage. WEBSITE MAN: Michael Genrich. WEBSITE EDITOR: Paul Maliszewski. STORE MAN: Scott Seeley. WEST COAST CHIEF: Barb Bersche. VICE PRESIDENT OF McSWYS OPERATIONS: Julie Wright. HEAD OF McSWEENEY'S OPERATIONS: Sarah Min. GENERAL McSWYS EDITOR: Dave Eggers. INTERIOR DESIGN HELP: Jennifer Broughton and Elizabeth Kairys. GUEST COVER DESIGNER: Elizabeth Kairys. GUEST EDITOR-IN-CHIEF FOR ISSUE 7: Paul Maliszewski.

NOTE: THIS JOURNAL HAS BEEN PROOFREAD. WE DID WHAT WE COULD.

Printed in Iceland by the Oddi Printing Company, Reykjavik.
(http://www.oddi.is/)

10 9 8 7 6 5 4 3 2 1

All title page illustrations by
Marcel Dzama, of Canada

LETTERS . . . . *From Karyn Coughlin, Steve Timm, Mark Honey, Randall Williams, Amie Barrodale,*
Gary Pike, James Wagner, Lynne Tillman, Colleen Werthmann, Kevin Guilfoile, Edna Mayfair, J. Robert Lennon. 8

ALEKSANDAR HEMON . . . . *The Kauders Case* 29

SAMANTHA HUNT . . . . *Discovery* 41

MICHEL DESOMMELIER . . . . *The Original of Laura* 45

JEFF EDMUNDS . . . . *After Laura* 55

JANET BLAND, RIKKI DUCORNET, ERIC P. ELSHTAIN, AMY ENGLAND, CARLA HOWL, CHRISTINE HUME,
CATHERINE KASPER, CYNTHIA KUHN, CHRISTY ANN ROWE, DAVID RAY VANCE . . . .
. . . . *Ubar: A Reference* 59

LAWRENCE WESCHLER . . . . *Convergences: Tina Barney Portraits* 73

BEN MARCUS . . . . *The Name Machine* 77

C. STELZMANN . . . . *Moran's Mexico: A Refutation* 89

RACHEL COHEN . . . . *The Fernando Pessoa Society* 99

JOSHUAH BEARMAN . . . . *Unnatural History, An Interview with Jacques Gauthier* 111

PAUL LAFARGE . . . . *Mrs. Ferris* 119

GILBERT SORRENTINO . . . . *Five Exhibits from Painting the Moon* 129

GABE HUDSON . . . . *Cross-dresser: The Written Testimony of Captain Jeffrey Dugan, 418th Squadron*
Bandit #573 133

JILL MARQUIS . . . . *Problem Set No. 1* 145

RICK MOODY . . . . *Inerrancy: An Interview with Dewey L. Johnson, IV* 149

J. ROBERT LENNON . . . . *Darts 'N' Laurels* 165

JONATHAN AMES . . . . *The Nista Affair* 169

STEVE TOMASULA . . . . *The Atlas of Man* 189

AMIE BARRODALE . . . . *Prospectus* 213

PATRICK BORELLI, KARYN COUGHLIN, BEN DRYER, DAN GOLDSTEIN, JOHN HODGMAN, MIKE JEROMINSKI, ERIK
P. KRAFT, WHITNEY MELTON, EUGENE MITMAN, CEDAR PRUITT, BRIAN SPINKS, BILL WASIK, JOHN WILLIAMS
. . . . *Volume 13: M* 219

KEVIN SHAY . . . . *searched the web for "conrad applebank"* 227

. . . . *This War Never Happened: An Interview with Sandow Birk* 231

SEAN WILSEY . . . . *The Egg* 243

MONIQUE DUFOUR . . . . *The Education of Uncle Josh* 251

hands, so I started cursing wildly, raving and screaming about the caves of Mexico and the firecrackers and the banging. After at least thirty seconds of concentrated insanity, I took a breath.

"Ma'am," Ms. Axelrod said, "You're speaking to a faculty member."

"Oh!" I gasped, and paused a second, as though centering myself. "I am so sorry. I would have never if I had known. You must forgive me, I —"

"You were speaking to one of my students. She was trying to sleep. You awoke her."

I couldn't believe it. There was no need to lie, here, I mean, Stephanie was being harassed and cursed at, so there was no call for saying she'd been woken up as well. In a way, it was great.

"I am so sorry, I didn't mean to wake her. I feel just awful, may I apologize?"

"Well, she's pretty sleepy."

"I'll just take one second, I want to tell her that I'm sorry..."

"Well... Okay." She handed the phone off.

"Hello?" Stephanie said.

What we're coming to now is one of my supremest and most glorious moments. I summoned up all my venom and hissed, "Why you little bitch."

Stephanie hung up. The next morning I slid into the bus seat behind Ms. Alexrod.

"Morning," I said. "Heard there was some trouble last night."

Alexrod told the story, but in her version, she came out like some sort of hero. Which makes me feel a little foolish. Not because I think her account is the correct one, but because

her vanity makes my stomach hurt with how it resembles mine.

Sincerely,
AMIE BARRODALE
BROOKLYN, NEW YORK

DEAR MCSWEENEY'S,
As you know I work at Kinko's, where I am the night-shift manager, and where I happen to be right now (time of writing). Earlier tonight I got into something of a heated argument with my entire crew about which was invented first, the wheel or the string. It was me against the rest of the night shift, with all them saying that the wheel is the fundamental invention of mankind, case closed. This is complete bunk. As I contended then and will argue more persuasively here, you need the string in order to produce something vaguely circular. Once you're Cro-Magnon man and you got that string, you're just a skip and a jump from the wheel, because you're already well on your way to deducing that a fixed length of string, when traced around a fixed point, makes one sweet circle.

Which brings me to my next invention, which while not circular is in fact spherical. I am proposing that we start manufacturing the first ever sit-inside globe.

The sit-inside globe is no mere bit of high-priced whimsicality offering no utilitarian benefits for anyone anywhere. The sit-inside globe is educational, which can sometimes be a form of utility. The sit-inside globe has the power to give the student of the earth the perspective of someone inside the earth. It is a rare perspective when you think about it.

Down the road, I would like to pursue with you the feasibility of making the first sit-on-the-surface globe, as a companion product. As I picture the sit-on-the-surface globe now, it would utilize a polyurethane seat with four legs that terminate in these sharpened points. Such a seat could be picked up and stuck into various pre-drilled holes in the surface of the globe, thus anchoring the chair and the student in the chair.

Best to you,
GARY PIKE
SYRACUSE, NEW YORK

DEAR GARY,
How did you get started with the inventing?
EDITOR

DEAR MCSWEENEY'S,
As a young boy I wanted nothing more than to become an inventor. I read voraciously certain pages from one book called *Meet the World's Greatest Inventors and Their Inventions*. It was the only volume I owned from what was apparently a whole *Meet the...* library of knowledge. My point is I wanted to invent several cheaply produced, disposable necessities that could cost folks a whole boatload of their money and keep them spending throughout their lives.

It was around this time that I developed and, to some extent, indulged my fascination with those orange blinking lights that construction crews put up around construction sites. How I marveled at those orange blinking lights that construction crews put up around construction sites. In a notebook I kept that was in actuality an old, unused accounting ledger, I wrote the following fateful words: "What makes the lights blink? How

do they continue to blink for so long? How long is that (in time)? Find way to capture blinking and make it power cars or something." The idea sort of trails off here, unfortunately, and that's the only page of my notebook I ever filled. As I recall, I had the idea to start keeping the notebook only because I had this one thought about the blinking orange lights. But then I never had another idea that I felt inclined to write down.

You must understand that the concept of a battery was lost on me. I thought of those lights as magical. I was what you would term a child. I didn't yet comprehend the fundamental logic of machines. To give you just one more example, I thought when I turned the family television off, every television everywhere went off.

As a student of the fifth grade I thought to marry a pair of gloves with the fingers cut off to ten of those rubber fingers that office people will wear when they're counting pages and don't want to keep licking their fingertips. Such a wedding would result in a new pair of gloves, called Nimble Fingers.

When I went through my puberty stage I thought of manufacturing and marketing a stick of deodorant slightly more than one-yard long and calling it the Metre Stick.

To this day I am proud of my early inventions. When I think of them, and I do, from time to time, I feel a great big smile start to come over my face and take possession of it, so that all I can do is grin and smile like that for a good minute or so. My early inventions demonstrate a certain pluck, a kind of resourcefulness, and a brand of curiosity vis a vis the world around me (then) that I admire still (now). Maybe it says something basic about me, but I am not very much embarrassed by owning up to any of this.

GARY PIKE
SYRACUSE, NEW YORK

MR. EDITOR:
She tells me of her dream. In the morning. Of a yearning to have a baby. In the dream, she is yearning, and feeling the discomfort of yearning. She feels she wants a baby, and the hospital says she has one. They give her an infant, but it is inside a plastic bag, like the kind one would use to transport snacks. As she tries to hold on to it, she is only able to squeeze more tightly, which causes a thick white paste to come out of the bag. She wants this baby. She wants to show it to the boyfriend-father, and she does. She holds up the baby in the bag to him, and she is excited. For now their life is centered, is here around the baby. She, however, as she's holding it, seems to push too hard at this point, and a larger amount—a serious amount—of the paste comes out of the bag. Settling on her hand. The boyfriend doesn't know what to do. The boyfriend had thought to say, This is not my baby, No baby of mine would ever be allowed to be placed in a bag, No baby of mine would look so much like you. The boyfriend avoids these reflections. He says, You know this is not a baby, right? This is a toy. Why have you delivered a toy to me? She does not believe him, she loves the baby. They decide to deliver the baby back to the hospital, as if returning a television. She says to them I don't know what happened. I tried. I tried so hard to be the mother I wanted to be, but he is just this now, pointing to the bag. She says, What can we do now? Can I get another? Are there more in there? They say, The father was right. They say, We were worried about you. We were worried that you were not the mother you reported to be. So, yes, we did give you a toy. We see now we were right about you, your hand strength, your voluntary mechanisms. We are glad to know you cared enough to seek us out, because we care for you.
Dutifully,
JAMES WAGNER
SYRACUSE, NEW YORK

DEAR EDITOR,
Oliver Teller (born Telkmariam) and I have lost touch. I know you sometimes facilitate this kind of thing and would appreciate your printing this letter.
Sincerely,
LYNNE TILLMAN
NEW YORK, NEW YORK

DEAR OLLIE,
It's been a long time. I think of you sometimes, and I know you think of me. I take a perverse satisfaction in that, even in the jaded ways you disguise me in your so-called fictions. I really don't care. But I just read your "manifesto against the past." No one "votes for guilt." I also have "funny mental pictures" of that mansion we lived in on the Hudson. It wasn't "haunted," except by an unghostly Timothy Leary. Everyone said he dropped acid there. Everyone said they used to have wild parties. Even back then the term wild parties bothered me. No one ever gave details.

You and I were the only non-psych students living in the mansion. You and they were older, graduate students, but they were all research psychologists and thought everyone else was crazy, so they devised experiments to prove it. There was that one sullen guy who worked with rats. He had a big room near mine. I used to look in as I passed it. He kept his shoes under the chair of his desk in a certain way, everything in his room had a specific order, and if his shoes were moved even a quarter inch, he went crazy.

Remember when he drove his car into a wall? Then he disappeared. Remember it's my past, too, you want to "throw into the garbage, to be carted away by muscular men and sent floating on a barge to North Carolina."

One night, you brought a friend home from Juilliard, a fellow student. If you recall, our dining room had dark walls and no electricity. We ate by candlelight — there were many candles in different states of meltdown on the long table. I can't remember exactly how many people were around the table that night. About ten, I think.

Before dinner, one of the research psychologists suggested it'd be fun to put blue vegetable dye in the mashed potatoes. Your friend wouldn't know. We'd act as if the potatoes weren't blue, just the usual white, and even though your friend might protest and insist that they were blue, we'd keep insisting they were white. None of us would relent. We'd just pretend he was crazy for thinking they were blue. We cooked this up in the kitchen. When you came in with him, someone took you aside and told you. You went along with it. Everyone has a streak of sadism, one of the psych guys said.

I can't remember who brought in the potatoes, we all participated, though, and then we all sat down around the big wooden table. The blue mashed potatoes were served in a glass bowl. Even by candlelight, they were bright blue.

We passed the food. When the bowl of blue potatoes reached your friend, he reacted with delight. Blue mashed potatoes, he said. Someone said, They're not blue. Your friend said, They're not? They look blue. Someone else said, No, they're not. You were sitting next to him.

The potatoes kept going around. Your friend said, again, They really look blue. Everyone acted as if nothing was happening. Your friend kept looking at the bowl. He became visibly agitated. He said, They look blue. Someone said, Maybe it's the candlelight. The flames have a bluish tinge. Your friend kept looking, squinting his eyes. Then he insisted, They look blue to me. Someone said, with annoyance, Would you stop it? They're not blue. Your friend turned quiet. He kept looking, though, and we all kept eating.

The coup de grace, I guess you'd call it, was dessert. In the kitchen, someone decided to dye the milk blue. The cake, coffee, and blue milk were brought to the table. We served the blue milk in a glass pitcher. No one said much as the pitcher went around the table. Your friend watched silently. When it came to him, he stared at the pitcher and poured the blue milk into his coffee. This time, he said nothing. Nothing. At that point, I ran into the kitchen. I couldn't control myself.

Later, you told him. After dinner, when you were alone with him, you told him. But I'm wondering, after all these years, did he ever forgive you? What happened to him? Does he still play the trombone?

You were good, Ollie. But somehow, in "regurgitating the past and moving on," I'm "the reckless prankster" whose "promiscuous heart" you broke. The only thing in that house you ever broke was your musician friend and crazy Roger's green plates.

Whatever,

LYNNE TILLMAN
NEW YORK, NEW YORK

MR. EDITOR:
I finally threw the bedsheet away from my body. What was this craziness! Three in the morning, and this noise going on! I was certain I would find a man in the middle of the street making the sounds of a duck. I went to the window but couldn't find him. Something or someone was down there. He was probably hiding in the lilacs. I made my way past the encyclopedias, put the slippers on, and grabbed the flashlight. Emerging, I went to my left, and found construction blocks and a hanging cable cord. The sound was continuing? I made my way around the house, flashing my neighbors' houses at times, almost by intuition. I wanted to let nothing go to chance. Everyone has to be considered a subject. I managed to somehow trap myself in a dog kennel, which I will admit is ridiculous, but the ivy had tricked me, and I became disoriented, briefly. I had meant to avoid it, but I found myself searching in it for the same reason one looks in the freezer for one's wallet. I got out, of course—I wouldn't be writing this, obviously—and continued to the other corner of my lot.

There was, last Thursday, a similar sound, I was remembering. I waved my beam over some bushes. I walked down the street. No one seemed to be present. Which is a safety issue. I had hoped someone would open her door, in the same outfit as me. I had hoped some misunderstanding could be elevated to a moonish puzzle. For the moon is a very strange thing. What is it doing there? No one asks these questions. I was raised to explain myself. That is what the moon should be doing. I realized soon enough that I would not find the man, but the very fact I knew this pushed me on. I assumed my assertiveness would be seen by this man, even if I couldn't see him. This kind of show was all I was hoping for. Seeing is very much overindulged. For one will get by well enough by being seen, and producing in the head of the other a proper distortion. I assume others are doing these things to me as well, because I know for a fact I am not a complicated man, so the scenarios involved in my seeing others naturally cause me to reflect on the veracity of their image and their painstaking imagery. This is, in short, why I leave my house. To deter, by thinking.

With conviction,

JAMES WAGNER
SYRACUSE, NEW YORK

DEAR EDITOR,
Five years ago, I played an angry gay teenager in a small coming-of-age film. The angry gay teenager ends up finding true love with a shy girl from the high school. The other characters were my character's mom; a young guy from my class (initially the crush-object of the shy girl) who has a heavy-duty affair with the mom; and the young guy's sister, a fashion model who becomes an ice-skating showgirl in Las Vegas.

The movie's dialogue was idiosyncratic and, it must be said, not very much like the way young people talk, but there were some genuinely poignant scenes. The mother-daughter competition and the young characters' sexual discoveries were treated with disarming frankness.

I needed a job. But I was also really fond of my character. She was the closest character to myself I'd ever played. Also, though nobody would guess from watching the movie, the action was ostensibly set in Minnesota, where I grew up.

Toward the end of the shoot, we worked on a scene set "four years later" (when the characters are age 22). My character and her girlfriend were at the showgirl's house in Las Vegas. Visually, the scene was an homage to the charming scene in that old movie "That Touch of Mink," where the two leading ladies chat while lying in single beds set at an L-shaped angle. Light streamed in from the windows of the showgirl's guest room, which was really in suburban Long Island. The beds were decked out in frilly white eyelet. A desolate Western magic-hour light streamed into the room, golden and sad, thanks to lavender filters, gigantic beige Japanese paper lanterns, and big silver bounce cards. In the scene, my girlfriend and I engaged in distracted small talk until I suddenly broke down and asked if she would list me as a beneficiary in her will. I quickly explained that my own mother had not listed me in her will, a fact I discovered in high school, when I had run an errand to this safety deposit box, only to discover the hurtful and bitter truth. The scene ultimately turns into this big profession of commitment and, by the end,

winds up being touching, in spite of how arcane it sounds.

I was having a hard time connecting to the whole safety deposit box thing. I could understand the whole hurt/left out aspect, but I had a hard time getting to the extreme vulnerability that the character seemed to need there and then. I just couldn't get past the safety deposit box part of it. It seemed so clinical.

As actors, my girlfriend and I were friendly enough, but we weren't what anyone would call soulmates. So in order to do the scene I had to do some emotional substitution. I found this thing, rather randomly, that had come up in my mind a few times.

I thought about this time when I was around eleven. My two sisters and I were with my Dad at a cabin in Wisconsin that my folks had rented for the summer. It was early October, and we had returned to bring home the last of our stuff, shut off the water, and close it up for the winter. It was Saturday morning, overcast, beyond brisk but just shy of cold. We were talking about what to eat for lunch. There were a couple of cans of Spaghetti-O's, which we wanted. My dad was concerned that there would either be too much or not enough—I can't remember which. My sister Ingrid and I got into a combative argument about which one of us could eat a whole can of Spaghetti-O's:
Ingrid: I can eat a whole can. I will.
Me: No you can't.
Ingrid: Yuh-huh, I CAN. I'm gonna.
Me: You never ate a whole can. No way.
Ingrid: I have so.
Me: WHEN?

My dad got up from where he was sitting, screamed, "God!" and lurched past us, letting the screen door slam behind him. Ingrid and I watched as he walked a few feet and stopped in front of the fence. He faced the fence and clenched his fists, his barrel chest heaving. He exhaled through his mouth, hissing, and shook his head. We glanced at each other, still mad, but mesmerized by Dad. He generally had a demeanor of gruff good-heartedness, but he was not to be messed with. He taught at a vo-tech school and had a lot of tough students—ex-cons, addicts, lost souls. His usual method of controlling other people's bad behavior was to wind his arm up like a pitcher and then pound his fist on the nearest available flat surface. He was intense and quick to anger, but this was the closest we'd ever seen him come to losing it.

After a few seconds I followed him out to the fence and stood behind him. He wouldn't acknowledge me. I kept saying, over and over, "Daddy, please, I'm sorry, I'm so sorry, I didn't mean it." And then, "Daddy, I didn't mean to make you mad, I'm sorry." But he wouldn't even look at me. He didn't wave me away or say a word. He just kept drawing in and expelling huge breaths. I freaked out. I was scared to go any closer to him, and began to cry. All I remember after that is somehow ending up in the tiny bathroom, sitting on the toilet seat, blankly staring at the crimp of the thin metal baseboard where it met the carpet. So I relived all of that while I did the big scene. It worked, but it was exhausting.

The coming-of-age film was screened for exactly one week at the Quad Cinema, a tiny art-house place on 13th Street, and was reviewed kindly by Steven Holden of the New York Times. I saw the movie once, at its small premiere in Los Angeles, with my then-manager, who hated it because he thought I looked fat in the love scenes. The movie was never sold for distribution or released on video. I don't even have a copy of it. All I have is a ten-minute sample I got during editing—just a rough-cut of the big scene and a couple of others. My then-manager refused to let me use the big scene in my reel because it was too sad, and also because in it, my nose is red from crying.

COLLEEN WERTHMANN
NEW YORK, NEW YORK

DEAR EDITOR,
For a while now, I've been thinking about a literary sort of experiment. Not really an experiment, I suppose, as there's no hypothesis to prove. Maybe it's more of a prank, although that would imply that someone's going to get embarrassed, and I hope that's not the case.

The idea is to write a very short story on paper that looks like one of those homemade posters folks tack up around the neighborhood to advertise sublets or plea for the return of a lost puppy. For instance, the story might be titled "BELOVED FAMILY PET!" and have a photocopied picture of a kitten in happier times at the top, but the story wouldn't be about a lost pet at all. It would be about the joy of love, or the sorrow of a bus crash, or the fear of a mummy seeking horrible vengeance. Whatever. Maybe not a mummy. At the bottom there would be a layer of tear-away paper fringe, each piece with my e-mail address.

Next, I'd make copies of this story-disguised-as-cry-for-help and staple them to telephone poles in my neighborhood and elsewhere around the city. Near one of them, perhaps, I could set up camp on a bench, with a sandwich and a Mountain Dew, and watch for a time. Nine out of ten people, I'm sure, would walk right by, certain it was just another poster for a lost pet. Only folks who approach it with genuine concern, specifically to learn more about the lost kitty, would discover, in fact, that it was something else.

Best,
KEVIN GUILFOILE
CHICAGO, ILLINOIS

DEAR KEVIN,
Why, exactly, do you want to do this?
EDITOR

DEAR EDITOR:
Why? I like the idea of this story existing out in the street, all over the city, pretending to be something else. I like the thought of people reading the story only after they've been tricked into it. I'm curious to know how many people, having fallen for the bait-and-switch, would take the time to write. I'm intrigued by the benign manipulation, luring people into reading short fiction by their concern for a kitten in peril. Will they be relieved to discover that the cat in question is really safe and dry, nesting on a bathrobe I threw carelessly across my bed, or will they be angry?
KEVIN GUILFOILE
CHICAGO, ILLINOIS

DEAR KEVIN,
That business about "the benign manipulation of luring people" makes me think you work in advertising. In advertising circles is there a word for what you're proposing? Is there something that advertising folks know that fiction-writing folks either don't know or don't, for whatever reason, spend much time thinking about?
EDITOR

DEAR EDITOR,
In advertising, the word for the "benign manipulation" of people is "advertising." But that's an interesting question. I think lots of people suspect that advertising creatives have all sorts of secret knowledge about psychology and mind control, which we routinely use to manipulate consumers to act against their own free will, as if Foote Cone Belding recruits its art directors from the School of the Americas. Maybe folks believe this because so much of television advertising is rooted in misdirection. The next time you're watching a program, count how many commercials at first pretend to be an ad for something else. I've done it in spots, too, and I wonder why that is. I think it's because the inversion of the viewer's expectations forces some into a response, good or bad, and the only reaction every advertiser fears, of course, is indifference. I suppose the same is true for writers. That's why I want to put the e-mail addresses at the bottom of the story. It's a call to action, just as the person is feeling relief or anger or surprise. Let it out! Write to me!
KEVIN GUILFOILE
CHICAGO, ILLINOIS

DEAR KEVIN,
Correct me if I'm wrong, but I also hear you saying that people who have sudden and sympathetic emotional reactions to lost cats and dogs may, in

fact, make better readers of your fiction than people who, say, walk into a bookstore expressly looking to pass their eyes over some fiction. Why is that?
EDITOR

DEAR EDITOR,
Not better readers, but different ones. Let's say we conducted the experiment in a different way. Suppose I created this story as described, but instead of posting it myself, around my own neighborhood, you published it here, with a note on the facing page suggesting that readers make copies of the piece and put them up around their own hometown. Now, in McSweeney's, it would appear as a short story written on a piece of paper that looks a little like a cat poster. That's precious. But if one reader tacks it up on a telephone poll, in Tampa or Toronto or wherever, it becomes a short story *pretending* to be a cat poster, and it will be read by passersby with a completely different set of eyes. An individual who first encounters the story here, where one would expect to see fiction and mischief and literary games and so forth, could never have the same reaction to it as a person who first encounters it on the street.

Here's a barely-related thought: In Chicago, no one visits the Art Institute without marveling at the Chagall or the Seurat, but I bet virtually all of those people, on the way back to their cars, would walk right past the Camera-sized Picasso in Daley Plaza and not even think to look up.
KEVIN GUILFOILE
CHICAGO, ILLINOIS

DEAR KEVIN,
You know how the nightstands of hotel rooms always have those little copies of the Bible? From time to time I think about publishing a little book of stories and having my father leave them behind in the hotel rooms, just tucked inside the nightstand, right next to the Bible. My father used to travel quite a bit, staying in his share of hotel rooms. I'd have to maintain a map of the world, inserting colored pushpins into the places where my father left the book of stories. Then I'd wait to hear from people. Of course, I always figure on hearing from people. Like you, I like that idea of someone coming across the writing completely by accident, of someone being just exhausted and opening the nightstand expecting exactly what they always expect: a room service menu, maybe a notepad, a couple of complimentary pens, some promotional postcards, and that old Bible. But this time it's a bit different. This time, there's this other book in addition to the expected book.

But what does it mean that we favor the surprised reaction of the unaware person to one who is more knowing?
EDITOR

DEAR EDITOR,
Honesty, maybe. Do you ever wonder how honest your own opinions about literature are? I mean, we read books in school and assume we should be reading them because a teacher swears they have value. We read books as adults and assume we should be reading them because the reviews were all so good, or some editor pre-approved them for us. A story found by accident, however, a story of unknown provenance, is a rare thing.
KEVIN GUILFOILE
CHICAGO, ILLINOIS

DEAR KEVIN,
I think it also has to do with the difference between being liked by people who already know us and being liked by complete strangers. I suspect everybody wants to be liked a little bit by complete strangers once in a while, you know?
EDITOR

DEAR EDITOR,
Now I'm starting to think I'm going to need more than one story, maybe involving the same characters, or maybe just using the same telephone poles. I'll put up a new story every week. New picture, new story, same poles. And I'm asking myself, what's the best kind of story to hang on a telephone pole anyway?
KEVIN GUILFOILE
CHICAGO, ILLINOIS

DEAR KEVIN,
Let's print your first telephone pole short story here, and if readers want to make their own lost pet posters, well, then, that would be just absolutely great.
EDITOR

DEAR EDITOR,
For you, my lost pet poster story is below.
KEVIN GUILFOILE
CHICAGO, ILLINOIS

ANSWERS TO SHANKS:

At 5:19, just before sunrise, Jerry retrieves a red ball ornament from a stack of Christmas boxes in his attic, places it among the barren stems of his neighbor's tomato plants, and flip-flops back across the wet lawn to a milky bowl of corn flakes on his patio. When Jerry was in his thirties, like Shanks is now, he thought retirement would bring him bottomless reserves of time. Instead, he now finds the hours constricted and the short days cheapened by inflation, doled out like a subsistence pension. He rises early and beds late, and, in the hours between, remains inactive, trying to stretch the time left by not spending it.

Before long, Shanks appears on his own deck, holding a coffee by the handle, his long, white legs exposed beneath blue and yellow running shorts that would have been comically out of fashion twenty years ago, when Jerry was making the second of three career changes. Jerry, camouflaged against the redwood furniture in a burgundy robe, retracts his neck and watches from behind a terra cotta hanging planter. He likes his neighbor; Shanks is affectionate with his wife and loves his kids and takes good care of his tools. His helpless persistence in the garden is endearing. When Shanks sees the lone red globe among the green and brown vines and stakes, he sets his coffee down and races back into the house, reappearing a moment later through the sliding kitchen door. He hops across the grass while forcing a tattered sneaker onto his right foot. Shanks takes the slow grade in three long strides and sidles awkwardly between garden rows until he's close enough to see an aluminum hook where the tomato's leafy crown should be. He hunches over and grabs his knees, holds there for a moment, and turns, knowing Jerry will be watching. Jerry raises his yellow breakfast bowl as a toast, and the old man and the young man laugh together, each thinking how nice it must be to have all that time to waste.

Dear Editor:

I am repeatedly struck by how often the letters people write to you affirm the presence of God in our lives. And it has occurred to me that living in N____, Illinois, in this moment in time is very much like living in the Bible of Moses and Aaron and Joshua, when the Lord talked to his people and told them how they were to behave. When people die on the busy interstate system that passes our little town, when their sports utility vehicles pile into concrete embankments or into trucks or other sports utility vehicles, I no longer think of it as tragic. I do not wonder how God could allow a family of five to perish on the side of the road on Christmas Eve. I am not confused by bad things happening to good people. Rather, these deaths affirm for me the idea that God has his elbow in the punch bowl, as my mother used to say, and that he has something big planned for us. The people of our little town are in for some big and very profitable surprises soon! I cannot say what these surprises might be, but if you doubt me, please, consider these parallels.

In the Bible, before the Israelites could inhabit the Promised Land, *all of them had to die*. True! None that exited Egypt with old Moses arrived. None! God smote them himself. Or he had them smoted. He submitted his people to defeats at the hands of their enemies. My favorites are the stonings because I like trying to imagine what that was like. And boy howdy weren't there a lot of them!

Of course, when God's will strikes close to home, it is much harder to accept, though accept it we must. Well, his will has struck close to home for me this last holiday season. It is my husband. My husband, Roy, who has been my loyal husband and our family's principal bread-earner for thirty-five years. Well, something is wrong with his head. I think the best description of it is that it has come loose. It may be that the muscles in his neck have simply been stretched by some inexplicable force to a degree where they no longer work to hold his head in place.

I had never realized before how heavy a head is! I would estimate (given my experience with my husband's head) that they weigh about ten pounds. The connection to his body is so stretchy, now, that I was actually able to pretty much just put it on our bathroom scale.

This all began Christmas morning after opening gifts. This is why I know that his condition has to do with God's divine will realizing itself on earth. Roy got tools for his shop in the basement. Large tools that required clamps. I think clamps may have something to do with this. Well, he went off to install them and I began to cook the cinnamon rolls. Then, around 10:30, he came up from the basement with the most awful grimace on his face. He clutched his head in his hands. I didn't realize it at that moment, but he was actually holding his head in place. This is where the clamps could be relevant.

Have you or your readers ever played with that toy that has a wooden ball with a hole in it attached by a string to a stick? And you flip the ball in the air and catch it with the stick? I believe that is the sort of relationship Roy has developed with his head.

Well, my question is this: can you tell me what has happened to my husband's head? And do you have an opinion about whether or not this is one of the strange ways that the Lord our God works in?

Sincerely,
EDNA MAYFAIR
NORMAL, ILLINOIS

DEAR EDITOR:
I brought a friend from out of town to a lecture at the college where I teach. The lecture was introduced by Terry, my college-where-I-teach friend and the person I would have attended the lecture with, had my friend from out of town not been visiting, nor Terry been introducing said lecture.

I became absorbed in the lecture, which was delivered by a letterpress printer. She was discussing her bizarre upbringing by backwoods intellectuals. At some point I became aware of a presence beside me, the presence of my friend from out of town: but by now I had forgotten that my friend was visiting, and I assumed the presence beside me to be Terry's, as it often is at such affairs. But then I saw the back of Terry's head, ten rows in front.

Before I remembered that the presence was my out-of-town friend's, there was a moment when I believed simultaneously that Terry was 1) beside me, and 2) ten rows in front of me. So, for that moment, there were two Terrys and no out-of-town friends.

In the next moment I realized my mistake and corrected my perception. But some remnant of the melding of my friends remains, and I can't look at or think of one of the friends without

being reminded of the other, or thinking that the two of them secretly know one another, in some secret and intimate way, even though they are, in fact, barely acquainted. I don't know if this is a good thing or not.
Sincerely,
J. ROBERT LENNON
ITHACA, NEW YORK

DEAR MCSWEENEY'S,
At home my desk is near a window that looks out across the driveway and into the street. Earlier today I saw (from this desk) a woman walk by carrying a hanging plant. Now because I sit at an odd angle with respect to the window and because there is not a little distortion caused by the window panes and maybe also because this woman was quite short and looked as if she was dragging her plant on the ground, my first thought was that the woman was really dragging a dog behind her. It looked painful and cruel. "What did this animal do?" I wondered. "Or is the dog dead?" But then, like I said, I saw it was only a hanging plant. My perception righted itself. Everything was fine again.

What I find interesting is once I realized that the plant was not a dog, I could no longer even imagine how I initially thought the hanging plant so closely resembled the body of a small animal dragged on a leash across the road in front of my window.

Would it not be quite good if we could invent a machine to allow people to see once again the thing they misperceived but would like to see again, either because they like the thing better when they misperceived it or believe the misperceived thing demands further study?

The other night I saw a couple sitting on a bench, one with an arm around the other one's waist. At first I could not see the two people separately. At first I saw a big boulder. I thought, "I don't remember any big boulder here." I was not standing in the spot where I expected to see a big boulder. Then I thought, "Oh, no, that's not any big boulder, that's a person with a humpback." But as soon as I was severely chastising myself for being insensitive to this person with a humpback and mistaking her for a big boulder of all things, the image resolved itself, and I perceived the poor person with the hump as in fact two people without humps, huddled together in the cold, maybe waiting for a bus or sharing their love with each other or what have you. By this time—and this transpired in mere seconds—I could no longer convince my mind to show me the person with the hump again. No matter how much I concentrated. No matter what angles I took or perspectives I sought. No matter what trouble I went through retracing my steps and trying to duplicate the conditions under which I first saw the woman and her hump. Never mind the big boulder—that was two perceptions distant and long out of reach.

Can this machine I'm proposing be constructed?

I believe it can.

To return to the woman with the dog that then became a plant, she stopped at the house next door to pick through some furniture the neighbors threw out the weekend before. I'd already seen the furniture and gone through it myself. Just three or four matching pieces of sectional chairs and a low-slung couch type of thing, made

with silver chrome arms and a maroon material. The woman picked up an L-shaped pillow that served as a backrest, looked it over, and then turned to walk in the other direction, with her hanging plant in one hand and her L-shaped pillow tucked under an arm. That pillow was vast, I tell you, more than large enough to stop any conversation.

GARY PIKE
SYRACUSE, NEW YORK

THE KAUDERS CASE

by ALEKSANDAR HEMON

1. VOLENS-NOLENS

I MET ISIDORA in college, at the University of Sarajevo, in 1985. We both transferred to the general literature department: she from philosophy, I from engineering. We met in the back of a Marxism class. The Marxism professor had his hair dyed hell-black, and often spent time in mental institutions. He liked to pontificate about man's position in the universe: man was like an ant holding on to a straw in a Biblical flood, he said, and we were too young to even begin to comprehend it. Isidora and I, thus, bonded over tear-inducing boredom.

Isidora's father was a well-known chess analyst, good friends with Fischer, Kortchnoy; and Tal. He reported from world-championship matches, and wrote books about chess—the most famous one, an item in every chess-loving household, was a book for beginners. Sometimes when I visited Isidora, she would be helping her father with correcting the proofs. It was a tedious job of reading back transcripts of chess games to each other (K e-4, R d5; c8-b7; etc), so they would occasionally sing the games, as if performing in a chess musical. Isidora was a licensed chess judge, and she traveled the world with her father, attending chess tournaments. She would often come back with stories about the strange people she had met. Once, in London, she met a Russian immigrant named Vladimir, who told her that Kandinsky was merely a Red Army officer who ran a workshop of anonymous artists and then appropriated their paintings as his own, becoming the great Kandinsky. In any case, the world outside seemed to be a terribly interesting place.

We were bored in Sarajevo. It was hard not to be. We had ideas and plans and hopes that, we thought, would change the small-city staleness, and ultimately the world. We always had unfinished and unfinishable projects: once we started translating a book about Bauhaus, never finished the first paragraph; then a book on Hieronimus Bosch, never finished the first page— our English was not very good, and we had neither dictionaries nor patience. We read and talked about Russian futurism and constructivism, attracted to the revolutionary possibilities of art. Isidora was constantly thinking up performances, in which, for instance, we showed up at dawn somewhere with a hundred loaves of bread, and made crosses out of them. It had something to do with Hlebnikov, the poet, as the root of his name: *hleb* was the common word for bread in many Slavic languages. We never did it, of course—just showing up at dawn was a sufficient obstacle. Isidora did stage several performances, involving her friends (I never took part) who cared less about the hidden messages of the performance than the possibility of the random passer-by heckling them in a particularly menacing Sarajevo way.

Eventually, we found a socialist-youth institution and, with it, a way to act upon some of our revolutionary fantasies. The socialist-youth institution gave us a space, ensured that we had no interest in getting paid, and made clear that we were not to overstep the borders of decent public behavior and respect for socialist values. A few more friends joined us (Gusa, living in London now; Goga, in Philadelphia; Bucko, still in Sarajevo). We adorned the space with slogans hand-painted on bed sheets sewn together: "The fifth dimension is being created!" was one of them, straight from a Russian futurist manifesto. There was an anarchy sign (and a peace sign, for which I am embarrassed now, but it was a concession to the socialist-youth people with hippie pasts), and Kasimir Malevich crosses. We had to repaint some of the crosses, as they alluded to religion in the blurry eyes of the socialist-youth hippies. This place of ours was called Club Volens-Nolens, a ludicrously pretentious name.

We hated pretentiousness, so the name was a form of self-hatred. Planning the opening night, we had fierce discussions whether to invite the Sarajevo cultural elite, idle people who attended the opening of boxes, and whose *cultureness* was conveyed by wearing cheap Italian clothes bought in Trieste or from smugglers working the streets. One proposal was to invite them, but to put barbed wire everywhere, so their clothes would be ripped. Even better, we could do the whole opening in complete darkness, except for a few stray dogs with flashlights attached to their heads. It would be nice, we agreed, if the dogs started biting the guests. But we realized that the socialist hippies would not go for that, as they would have to invite some socialist elite, to justify the whole project. We settled for inviting the elite, along with local thugs and people some of us grew up with, and generally people who had no interest in culture whatsoever. We hoped that at the very least a few fights might break out, bloodying an elite nose or two.

Alas, it was not to happen. No dogs, no bites, no fights—the opening was attended by a lot of people, who all looked good and behaved nicely.

Thereafter we had programs every Friday. One Friday, there was a panel discussion on alcoholism and literature with all the panelists drunk, and the moderator the drunkest of all. Another Friday there were two comic-book artists, whose drawings we exhibited. One of them got terribly drunk and locked himself in the bathroom and would not come out, as the audience waited. After a couple of hours of our lobbying and outright begging, he left the bathroom and faced the audience, only to holler at them: "People! What is wrong with you? Do not be fooled by this." We loved it. Then there was the time when we showed a movie, called "The Early Works," which had been made in the sixties and banned almost everywhere in Yugoslavia and never shown in Sarajevo, as it belonged to a group of movies, known as the Black Wave, which painted not so rosy a picture of socialism. It was one of those six-ties movies, heavily influenced by Godard, in which young people walk around junkyards, discuss comic books and revolution, and then make love to mannequins. The projectionist—who was used to showing soft-core porn, where narrative logic didn't matter—switched the reels, showing them out of order, and nobody noticed except the director, who was present, but tipsy. We organized a performance of John Cage music, the only one ever in Sarajevo, by which I mean we played his records, including one with a composition performed by twelve simultaneously screeching radios and another with the infamous "4:33"—a stretch of silence on the record supposed to provide time for the audience to create its own inadvertent, incidental music. The audience, however, consisting by this time mainly of idle elite, was getting happily drunk—we heard that music many times before. When the performer, who came from Belgrade, forgoing a family vacation at the peril of divorce, stepped in front of the microphone, the audience was uninterested. Nobody had asked him to perform Cage in years, so he didn't care. The few audience members who glanced at the stage saw a hairy man eating an orange and a banana in front of the microphone, performing, unbeknownst to almost everybody, the John Cage composition appropriately titled, "An Orange and a Banana."

It was irritating not to be irritating to the elite, so even on the nights when we just spun records, the goal was to inflict pain: Gusa, the DJ, played Frank Zappa and Yoko Ono screaming plus Einsturzende Neubaten, the fine artists who used chainsaws and drill machines to produce music, all at the same time and at a high volume. The elite was undeterred, though their numbers declined. We wanted them all to be there and to be there in severe mental pain. This concept, needless to say, did not fly too well with the socialist hippies.

The demise of Club Volens-Nolens (which I might as well confess means "willy-nilly" in Latin) was due to "internal differences." Some of us thought we had made too many compromises: the slide down the slippery slope of bourgeois mediocrity (the socialist version) clearly began when we gave up the stray dogs with flashlights. Before we called it all off, we contemplated having stray dogs, this time rabid, for the closing night. But Club Volens-Nolens went out with a whimper, rather than a mad bark.

We sank back into general ennui. I busily wrote self-pitying poetry, hundreds of dreadful poems, eventually amounting to one thousand, the subjects of which flip-flopped between boredom and meaninglessness, with a dash of generic hallucinatory images of death and suicide. I was a nihilist, living with my parents. I even started thinking up an Anthology of Irrelevant Poetry, calculating that it was my only hope of ever getting anthologized. Isidora wanted to assemble the anthology, but nothing came of it, although there was clearly irrelevant poetry everywhere around us. There was nothing to do, and we were quickly running out of ways to do it.

2. THE BIRTHDAY PARTY

ISIDORA'S TWENTIETH BIRTHDAY was coming up, and she—ever disinclined to do it the usual way—did not want it to be a booze-snacks-cake-somebody-fucking-in-the-bathroom thing. She thought that it should have a form of performance. She couldn't decide whether it should be modeled on a "Fourrieristic orgy" (the idea I liked), or a Nazi cocktail party, as frequently rendered in the proper movies of the socialist Yugoslavia: the Germans, all haughty, decadent bastards, throwing a lavish party, it being 1943 or so, while local whores and "domestic traitors" licked their boots, except for a young Communist spy who infiltrated the inner circle, and who would make them pay in the end. For some unfortunate reason, the Nazi party won over the orgy.

The birthday party took place on December 13, 1986. Men donned black shirts and swastikas and had oil in their hair. Women wore dresses that reasonably approximated gowns, except for my teenaged sister, who was cast as a young Communist girl, so she wore a girly Communist dress. The party was supposed to be set in Belgrade, sometime in the early forties, with all the implicit decadence, as seen in the movies. There were mayo swastikas on sandwiches; there was a sign on the wall saying "In Cock We Trust"; there was a ritual burning of Nietzsche's *Ecce Homo* in the toilet; my sister—being a young Communist—was detained in the bedroom, which was a makeshift prison; Gusa and I fought over a bullwhip; Veba, who lives in Montreal now, and I sang pretty, sad Communist songs, about fallen strikers, which we did at every party; I drank vodka out of a cup, as I was cast as a Ukrainian collaborator. In the kitchen we discussed the abolishment of the Tito cult, still running strong, and the related state rituals. We entertained the idea of organizing demonstrations: I would be looking forward, I said, to smashing some store windows, as some of them were ugly, and, besides, I really liked broken glass. There were people in the kitchen and at the party whom I didn't know, and they listened carefully. The morning after, I woke up with a sense of shame that always goes with getting too drunk. I took a lot of citric acid and tried to sleep, but the sense of shame wouldn't go away for a while, and, in fact, is still around.

The following week I was cordially invited over the phone to visit the State Security—a kind of invitation you cannot decline. They interrogated me for thirteen hours straight, in the course of which I learned that all other people who attended the party visited or were going to visit the warm State Security offices. Let me not bore you with the details—let's just say that the good-cop-bad-cop routine is transcultural, that they knew everything (the kitchen listeners listened well), and that they had a big problem with the Nazi thing. I foolishly assumed that if I explained to them that it was really just a performance, a bad joke perhaps, and if I skipped the kitchen demonstration-fantasies, they would just slap our wrists, tell our parents to whup our asses and let us go home, to our comfy nihilistic quarters. The good cop solicited my opinion on the rise of fascism among the youth of Yugoslavia. I had no idea what he was talking about, but strenuously objected to the existence of such tendencies. He didn't seem too convinced. As I was sick with a flu, I frequently went to the State Security bathroom—no keys on the inside, bars on the window—while the good cop was waiting outside, lest I cut my wrist or bang my head on the toilet bowl. I looked at myself in the mirror and thought: "Look at this dim, pimply face, the woozy eyes—who can possibly think I am a fascist?" They let us all go, eventually, our wrists swollen from slapping.

A few weeks later the Sarajevo correspondent of the Belgrade daily *Politika*—which was soon to become the voice of the Milosevic regime— received an anonymous letter describing a birthday party at the residence of a prominent Sarajevo family, where Nazi symbols were exhibited and values belonging to the darkest recesses of history were extolled. The rumor started spreading around Sarajevo, the world capital of gossip. The Bosnian Communist authorities, often jitterbugging to the tunes from Belgrade, confidentially briefed its members at closed Party meetings, one of which was attended by my mom, who nearly had a heart attack when she realized that her children were at the party. In no time letters started pouring in to Sarajevo media, letters from concerned citizens, some of whom were clearly part-time employees of the State Security, unanimously demanding that the names of the people involved in organizing a Nazi meeting in Sarajevo be released, and that the cancerous growth on the body of socialism be dealt with immediately and mercilessly.

Under the pressure of the obedient public, the names were finally provided: there was a TV and radio broadcast roll-call in January 1987, and the papers published the list the next day, for those who missed it the night before. Citizens started organizing spontaneous meetings, which produced letters demanding severe punishment; university students had spontaneous meetings, recalling the decadent performances at Club Volens-Nolens, concluding with whither-our-youth questions; Liberation-War veterans had spontaneous meetings, whereby they expressed their firm belief that work had no value in our families, and they demanded more punishment. My neighbors turned their heads away, passing me by; my fellow students boycotted an English-language class because I attended it, while the teacher quietly wept in the corner. Some friends were banned by their parents from seeing us—the Nazi-party nineteen, as we were labeled. Even some who had attended the cursed party avoided meeting the others, including my girlfriend. I watched the whole thing, as if reading a novel in which one of the characters—an evil, nihilistic motherfucker—carried my name. His life and my life intersected, indeed overlapped. At some point I started doubting the truth of my being. What if, I thought, I was the only one not seeing what the world was really like? What if I was the dead-end of perception? What if my reality was someone else's fiction, rather than his reality being my fiction?

Isidora, whose apartment was searched, all her papers taken, fled to Belgrade and never came back, but some of us who stayed pooled our realities together. Goga had her appendix taken out, and was in the hospital, where nurses scoffed at her, and Gusa, Veba, and I became closer than ever. We attended the spontaneous meetings, all in the vain hope that somehow our presence there would provide some reality, explain that it was all a bad joke, and that, after all, it was nobody's business what we did at a private party. Various patriots and believers in socialist values played the same good-cop-bad-cop games at those meetings. At a Communist Party meeting that I crashed, as I was not invited, because I was never a member, a guy named Tihomir (which could be translated as Quietpeace) played the bad cop. He yelled at me: "You spat at my grandfather's bones!" and then moaned in disbelief when I suggested that this was all just plain ridiculous, all while the Party secretary, a nice young woman, kept saying: "Quiet, Tihomir."

The Party, however, was watching how we behaved. Or so I was told by a man who came to our home, sent by the County Committee of the Party, to check up on us. "Be careful," he said in an avuncular voice, "they are watching you very closely." In a flash I understood Kafka. Years later, the same man came to buy some honey from my father (my father was, at the time, brazenly dealing honey out of our home). He didn't talk about the events regarding the birthday party, except to say, "Such were the times." He told me that his twelve-year-old daughter wanted to be a writer, and showed me a poem she had written, which he proudly carried in his wallet. The poem was really the first draft of a suicide note, as the first line read: "I do not want to live, as nobody loves me." He said that she was too shy to show him her poems—she would drop them, as if accidentally, so he could find them. I remember him walking away burdened with buckets of honey. I hope his daughter is still alive.

Eventually, the scandal fizzled out. When a lot of people realized that the level of the noise was inversely proportional to the true significance of the whole thing. We were scapegoated, as the Bosnian Communists wanted to show that they would nip in the bud any attempt at questioning socialist values. Besides, there were larger, far more serious scandals that were to beset the hapless Communist government. Within a few months, the government was unable to quell rumors about the collapse of the state company Agrokomerc, whose head, friends with Communist big-shots, created his mini-empire on non-existent securities, or the socialist version thereof. And there were people who were being arrested and publicly castigated for saying things that questioned Communist rule. Unlike ourselves, those people knew what they were talking about: they had ideas, rather than confused late-adolescent feelings. We had been our own stray dogs with flashlights, and then Animal Control arrived.

But for years after, I ran into people who were still convinced that the birthday party was a fascist event, and who were ready as ever to send us to the gallows. Understandably, I did not always volunteer information about my involvement. Once, up in the wilderness of a mountain near Sarajevo, while called up in Army Reserve, I shared the warmth of a campfire with drunken reservists who all thought that the birthday party people should have at least been severely beaten. I wholeheartedly agreed—indeed I claimed, perversely, that they should have been strung up, and got all excited about it. Such people, I said, should be publicly tortured. I became someone else, I inhabited my enemy for a short time, and it was a feeling both frightening and liberating. Let's drink to that, the reservists said.

Doubts about the reality of the party persisted. It did not help matters that Isidora did eventually become a downright, unabashed fascist. Belgrade in the nineties was probably the most fertile ground for the most blood-thirsty fascism. She had public performances that celebrated the tradition of Serbian fascism. She dated a guy who was a leader of a group of Serbian volunteers, cutthroats and rapists, known as the White Eagles, who operated in Croatia and Bosnia. She wrote a memoir entitled *The Fiancée of a War Criminal*. Our friendship ceased at the beginning of the nineties, and I keep doubting my sense of reality—maybe the fascist party was concocted by her fascist part, invisible to me. Maybe I didn't see what she saw, maybe I was a pawn in her chess musical. Maybe my life was like one of those images of the Virgin Mary that show up in the frozen food section of a supermarket in New Mexico or some such place—visible only to the believers, ridiculous to everyone else.

3. THE LIFE AND WORK OF ALPHONSE KAUDERS

In 1987, in the wake of the birthday party fiasco, I started working at a Sarajevo radio station, for a program geared toward younger urban people. It was called Omladinski Program (The Youth Program), and everyone there was very young, with little or no radio experience. I failed the first audition, in the spring, as the noise from the party still echoed in the station's studios, but was accepted in the fall, despite my mumbling, distinctly unradiophonic voice. I did this and that at the station, mainly writing dreadful film reviews and invectives against government idiocy and general stupidity, then reading them on the air. The radio heads gave the program considerable leeway, as the times had politically changed, but also because we could still easily take a fall, if need be, as we were all young nobodies.

What is important is that I was allotted three minutes a week, on my friends' pretty popular show, which I used to air my stories. The timeslot was called, "Sasha Hemon Tells You True and Untrue Stories" (SHTYTUS). Some of the stories I read on the air were shorter than the jingle for SHTYTUS. Some of them embarrassed my family—already thoroughly embarrassed by the birthday party—because I had a series of stories about my cousin, a Ukrainian, in which he, for example, somehow lost all his limbs and lived a miserable life, until he got a job in a circus, where elephants rolled him around the ring like a ball, night in, night out.

Around that time, I wrote the story, "The Life and Work of Alphonse Kauders." It was clear that it was unpublishable, as it made fun of Tito, contained a lot of lofty farts, and involved the characters of Hitler and Goebbels and such. At that time, most literary magazines in Yugoslavia were busily uncovering this or that national heritage, discovering writers whose poems would later become war songs. I broke up the story into seven installments, each of which could fit into the three allotted minutes of SHTYTUS, and then wrote an introduction for each—all suggesting that I was a historian and that Alphonse Kauders was a historical figure and the subject of my extensive and painstaking research. One of the introductory notes welcomed me upon my return from the archives of the USSR, where I had dug up revealing documents about Kauders. Another informed the listeners that I had just come back from Italy, where I was a guest at the convention of the Transnational Pornographic Party, whose party platform was, naturally, based on the teachings of the great Alphonse Kauders. A third introduction quoted letters from non-existent listeners who praised me for exhibiting the courage necessary for a historian, and proposed that I be appointed head of the radio station.

Most of the time, I had a sense that nobody knew what I was doing, as nobody listened to SHTYTUS, apart from my friends (Zoka and Neven, now in Atlanta and London, respectively) who generously gave me the time on the show, and the listeners who had no time to change the station as the whole thing was just too short. Which was okay with me, as I had no desire to upset the good cop or the bad cop again.

After all seven installments were broadcast individually, I decided to record the whole Kauders saga, reading it with my mumble-voice, still fondly remembered as one of the worst voices ever broadcast in Bosnia, and provided some historical sound effects: Hitler's and Stalin's speeches, Communist fighting songs, *Lili Marlen*. We broadcast the whole thing straight up, no breaks, for twenty-some minutes—a form of radio-suicide—on Zoka and Neven's show. I was their guest in the studio, still pretending that I was a historian. With straight faces and solemn voices, Zoka and Neven read the listeners' letters, all of which were phony. One demanded that I and people like me be strung up for defiling the sacred memories. Another demanded more respect for horses (as Alphonse Kauders hated horses). Another objected to the representation of Gavrilo Princip, the assassin of the Austro-Hungarian Archduke Franz Ferdinand, and asserted, contrary to my research, that Princip *absolutely did not* pee his pants while waiting at a Sarajevo street corner to shoot the Archduke.

With that, we opened the phone lines to listeners. I had thought that a) nobody really listened to the Kauders series, and b) those who listened found it stupid, and c) that those who believed it was true were potheads, simpletons and demented senior citizens, for whom the lines between history, fantasy, and radio programs were already pathologically blurred. Hence I did not prepare for questions or challenges or further manipulation of dubious facts. The phones, however, were on fire, for an hour or so, live on the air. The vast majority of people bought the story, and then had many a tricky question or observation. A physician called and claimed that one cannot take out one's own appendix, as I claimed Kauders had done, which obviously stands to reason. A man called and said that he had in his hand the *Encyclopedia of Forestry*—where Kauders was supposed to be covered extensively—and there was no trace of him in it. There were other questions, but I cannot remember them, as I had entered the trance of fantasy-making. I came up with plausible answers, never laughing for a moment. I inhabited the character completely, fearing all the while that my cover might be blown, fearing—as I suspect actors do—that the audience could see the real, phony me behind the mask, that my performance was completely transparent. I did manage to dismiss the fear of the good cop or the bad cop (probably the bad cop) calling in and ordering me to instantly come down to State Security headquarters. But the weirdest fear of all was that someone might call in and say: "You know nothing about Kauders. I know far more than you do—here is the true story!" Kauders became real at that moment—he was my Virgin Mary, appearing in the sound-proof studio glass, behind which there was an uninterested sound engineer and a few people sparkling with the electricity of excitement. It was an exhilarating moment, when fiction ruptured reality and then overran it, much akin to the moment when the body rose from Dr. Frankenstein's surgical table and started choking him.

For days, even years, after, people stopped me and asked: "Did Kauders really exist?" To some of them I said yes, to some of them I said no. But the fact of the matter is that there is no way of really knowing, as Kauders really did exist for a flicker of a moment, like those subatomic particles in the nuclear accelerator in Switzerland, just not long enough for his existence to be recorded. The moment of his existence was too short for me to determine whether he was a mirage, a consequence of reaching the critical mass of collective delusion, or whether he had appeared to let me know that my life had been exposed to the radiation of his malevolent aura.

My Kauders project was an attempt to regain reality. I had blissfully persisted in believing I was a real person until I became a fictional character in someone else's story about the birthday party. I wanted Kauders—a fictional character—to enter someone else's reality and spoil the party by becoming real. After finding myself on the wrong side of the mirror, I threw Kauders back into it, hoping to break it, but he just flew right through and ran off, no longer under my control. I do not know where he might be now. Perhaps he is pulling the strings of fact and fiction, of untruth and truth, making me write stories that I foolishly believe I imagine and invent. Perhaps one of these days I am going to get a letter signed by A.K. (as he, of course, liked to sign his letters), telling me that the whole fucking charade is over, that my time of reckoning has come.

DISCOVERY

by SAMANTHA HUNT

"SENATOR, THE PRESIDENT has asked for a word."

"Which one?" the Senator wondered. "He can't have 'senator.' I've gone flush with it. 'Senator' has lubricated my life," he thought then relaxed for a moment, having cleared that up. But then fidgeted with a start, "He can't have 'pulsar,' either. It's the only sexy word I get to repeat in publically funded conversations with young co-eds."

The Senator was assigned to a seat outside the cockpit area, a seat where his feet did not touch the ground. While he waited for the others to enter the shuttle, a young astronaut passed the Senator a device of transmission, not a walkie-talkie, not a phone, and the Senator understood. "Mr. President?" the Senator asked. "Mr. President?" he asked again, and caught a dry "e" in his throat. Preseedent. The young astronaut kept his eyes averted.

The muffled sounds inside the shuttle and the powerless traction of his weighty spacesuit reminded the Senator of a boy he'd known in grade school. The boy had been born with a debilitating muscle disease that made him soft and small. In order to make the condition clearer to the boy, doctors had explained the disease to him like this: "Son, it's as though you were born with pillows for legs." This failed to make anything clearer. The boy did not understand; instead, he imagined flushing himself down the toilet but didn't know the word for this. He lived.

"Mr. President?" the Senator asked for the third time, but the line had apparently gone dead. The young astronaut beside the Senator took the receiver and demanded, "Hello? Mr. President, do you read me? Copy? Over. Over. Over!" The cabin door was sealed.

"What had the president wanted?" the Senator wondered. "Maybe there's something wrong with the shuttle," he thought and bit the dry skin of his lips. "If something were wrong they wouldn't leave it up to the President to drop the news," he thought. "Perhaps the President had phoned to encourage a sense of American duty. Maybe he was planning to say, 'You're a beacon to the nation, a shining star in the universe.' Or the President might have said, 'Give those young tigers hell, pal.' Or maybe, 'Senator, don't tell the others, but I haven't been feeling too hot, some stomach thing the doctors can't decide what to call. Read me?'" The shuttle was ready. The Senator secured his helmet and prepared for liftoff.

"The President probably wants me to claim anything out there for us," the Senator thought. "Maybe he was calling to remind me of his wife's maiden name in case something new up there requires naming." At this the Senator sat up straighter. "What's wrong with my wife's maiden name?" he thought. Countdown.

Blast-off was noisy and upsetting to the Senator's constitution. Once the battering calmed down, a voice on his headset alerted him, "Senator, the citizens of Perth, Australia, have a message for you." From the window the Senator saw the lights of an entire city flash on, flash off, flash on. A beacon, a shining star.

He tried to remember the speech that would be expected on his return to Earth but couldn't. Instead he thought, "Down there God used the word to separate light and dark into meaning, into switches. Up here, what is the word? From my window I see space. I name it wind, but the word has lost its glue. Nothing sticks in space. I could name the galaxy after a china pattern, 'Reverie in Strawberry.' Nothing seems to hold here. I could name it after her. It is like her. See, then name, then try to forget for the rest of your life so that you can stay married, so that strangers continue to call you Senator," he thought.

*   *   *

HE REMEMBERED A conversation: "You are mine," he had told her.

She had looked up from the bed where she sat. "If you scientists are so smart, how come white glue dispensers always clog when there's still glue left inside?" she'd asked. She was young, as young as his daughter, young enough to still consider white glue.

"Please," he'd said to her neck, which was exposed and red after a shower. "I'll stop breathing if you are not mine."

"Five, four, three, two..."

"What?" he'd asked.

"Stop breathing when I get to one."

Copy? Over. Over.

*   *   *

OUT HIS WINDOW was the world. Separated from the word "word" by a tiny sliver of "L." If naming asteroids, stars and galaxies were called for there'd be no "L"s. This ruled out his last name. Fine. "L"s tended toward erosion more than the other letters. Think of it in lower case. It is a flake, a sliver that can slip away at night when everyone else is asleep.

He rested his head, catching his dry lip on the inside of his helmet. "Stars are boring in the daytime," he said to comfort himself. He could talk about light without using the letter "L."

*   *   *

HE REMEMBERED A conversation: "Lover, lover, lover," he had said but she shook her head no.

He bit the skin of his mouth. Come back, L. Read me? Over.

THE ORIGINAL OF LAURA
A FIRST LOOK AT
NABOKOV'S LAST BOOK

by MICHEL DESOMMELIER

"Le visage de l'amour est proche de celui de la mort. Laure avait ce visage-là. Sans pourtant qu'elle fût maigre on sentait ses os sous sa peau, ces mêmes os auxquels on devait atteindre lorsque l'on faisait l'amour avec elle."[1]

BACKGROUND

THE ORIGINAL OF LAURA, Vladimir Nabokov's final novel, had been in his head, nearly complete, for three years when, in 1974, a series of accidents and illnesses prevented the aging author from committing to paper, or rather, to index cards, "more than a patch or two of his bright mental picture."[2]

In December 1975, after a too brief convalescence following the surgical removal of a (benign) adenoma from his prostate, Nabokov announced that

---

[1] Jérôme Peignot, "Ma mère diagonale," in *Laure, Ecrits de Laure* (Paris: Chez Jean-Jacques Pauvert, 1971). This book, published at about the same time that Vladimir Nabokov conceived of *The Original of Laura*, may well have been known to him. Could Laure (the pseudonym of writer Colette Peignot, who died of tuberculosis in 1938 at age thirty-five) be the original, or one of the originals, of Laura? A much earlier and more likely possibility is, of course, Petrarch's mysterious Laura. According to the *Dictionary of Italian Literature* (Westport, Conn.: Greenwood Press, 1979), in 1327 Petrarch glimpsed for the first time "his hauntingly beautiful Laura, whose exact identity has never been established" (p. 393).

[2] Brian Boyd, *Vladimir Nabokov: The American Years* (Princeton, N.J.: Princeton University Press, 1991), p. 643. Subsequent quotes are from the same work, with page numbers in parentheses following the citation.

he was "returning zestfully to the abyss of my new novel" (653). Early in February 1976 he compiled a progress report in his diary: "New novel more or less completed and copied 54 cards. In 4 batches from different parts of the novel. Plus notes and drafts. 50 days since Dec 10, 1975. Not too much" (653). At the beginning of April, nearing his seventy-seventh birthday, Nabokov again reported on his progress: "Proceeding at the rate of 5 or 6 cards per day, but a lot of rewriting" (653-654). On April 20, Boyd notes, Nabokov "reported optimistically to McGraw-Hill {with whom he had signed a new agreement exactly two years prior to deliver six books in four years] that he had passed the hundred printed page mark, about half the novel" (654). By late September the book was practically complete in Nabokov's head, but, sorely weakened by yet another hospitalization, he could not muster the energy necessary to commit the visualized text to paper. This unfortunate state of affairs continued throughout the autumn and spring. By the following summer, as Nabokov moved perceptibly closer to life's dim gulf, the bulk of the book remained unwritten. Hospitalized once more, apparently stricken with bronchial pneumonia but also displaying bizarre symptoms the doctors were at a loss to explain, Nabokov became feverish and drifted in and out of delirium for several weeks, during which he kept reciting his novel aloud to "a small dream audience in a walled garden. My audience consisted of peacocks, pigeons, my long-dead parents, two cypresses, several young nurses crouching around, and a family doctor so old as to be almost invisible" (quoted in Boyd, 657).

The peacocks were no doubt phantasmal, the dead parents and decrepit family doctor perhaps harbingers of things to come; the cypresses may have been glimpsed through the clinic window, swaying darkly at dusk on the hillside above Lausanne, and the pigeons too may have been genuine, cooing softly on the cornice outside that same window. At least one of those young nurses was demonstrably real, and that is where our story begins.

THE WITNESS

SUZANNE EGGERICKX, THE young nurse Nabokov had dimly recalled and dreamily inserted into his delirium, was still very much alive in 1990 and residing in a village outside St. Gallen, Switzerland. (This I was able to determine after a visit to the CHUV clinic, where Nabokov spent his last days.) She responded very warmly to my letter of inquiry in which I expressed the reason for my contacting her. A subsequent exchange of correspondence confirmed that she did indeed know something of Nabokov. She agreed to a meeting, and in April of 1991 I took a train from Lausanne to

Sankt Gall, as it is known in the German-speaking region of the country.

Mme Eggerickx had been present in Nabokov's hospital room as he lay delirious for several weeks, intermittently reciting long passages of prose. Fascinated by the facility and coherence of the flow of words, Suzanne, formerly a medical transcriptionist at the World Health Organization in Geneva, had begun transcribing Nabokov's recitations to pass the time spent monitoring the patient's condition. Since he often returned to the same passages, the young nurse was able to correct her drafts to such an extent that the final text was wholly consistent with the patient's narration. He would begin anew at a given point, and Eggerickx would follow along with her shorthand notes, verifying each sentence. Her transcription thus represents an extremely accurate picture of *The Original of Laura* as it existed in Nabokov's head during the final weeks of his life.

There is more. Though it soon became evident that Nabokov was too weak to commit the novel to paper himself (as Boyd notes, *v. supra*), he had nevertheless had his notes brought to him at the hospital for the purpose of completing what transcription he could. Eggerickx told me that the "notes"were a shoe-box-sized carton of note cards which lay on the night-stand beside the patient's bed. The front of the box featured a small typed label that said, simply, "Vladimir Nabokov." On the day after the box had been delivered, Nabokov worked very briefly on copying his text before succumbing to exhaustion. Eggerickx reports that the box was "full of cards," though she concedes that many may have been blank.

Three weeks later, Nabokov died. In what might be forgiven as the impulsive act of a young woman who had grown fascinated with a very ill man who had displayed an astounding memory coupled with beguiling inventiveness, Suzanne Eggerickx removed a small batch of note cards from the box beside the bed as a souvenir of her patient. When she returned home that evening, she was excited to see that, between the first two cards, there was a photograph, or rather, a copy of a photograph, for the image was printed not on photographic paper but on a stiffish card stock not unlike a visiting card. The photograph showed a framed painting, the portrait of a young woman, seated, holding a violin under her right arm and wearing an elaborately patterned kimono or robe. On the verso, Nabokov (or someone else) had inscribed a single word: Laura.

THE PAINTING

DESPITE MANY HOURS of research, I have been unable to discover the full name of the model in the image (reproduced here for the first time) or the

name of the artist who painted it. Art historians I have consulted·have characterized the portrait as everything from "amateurish" to "enigmatic," and have likened it to works spanning nearly two hundred years of art history, by Ingres, Manet, Puvis de Chavannes, Picasso, Gorky (!), and Balthus. The last name is intriguing, for Balthus lived not far from where Nabokov died, in a huge chalet on the steeply sloped foothills above Lake Léman, but there is no evidence that the reclusive painter and the reclusive author ever met, nor any record of a portrait by Balthus of a model resembling the woman in the picture, which is, moreover, unlike Balthus's work in both style and composition. It is, though, almost certainly a contemporary work. The robe worn by the woman is distinctive, but this too has been hard to place. One fashion designer insisted it had been manufactured in Paris; a female colleague claimed she had owned one very similar purchased in New York in the late 1960s. Recently, I saw a robe of a similarly patterned fabric, though differing in cut and design, in a clothes catalog I was distractedly thumbing through in a passengers' lounge in the Zurich airport. The model's hairstyle is distinctive enough to be helpful in verifying a possible identification but too classic to offer a clue as to where to begin one's search. As for the violin, it is curious, but probably none too helpful, to note that in chapter two of *The Defense*, little Luzhin's grandfather is depicted in a photograph holding a violin.

THE SOURCES

THE TEXT AS it appears on the note cards is remarkably consistent with Mlle Eggerickx's transcription, which she later had the good sense to type up from her original shorthand notes. I have arrived at the texts below after a careful collation of the cards with the typescript, adjusting only punctuation, and, in a single case, correcting an obvious misspelling. For reasons of copyright, I reproduce here only brief sections from the totality of the text as it exists in manuscript form. At the recent Nabokov Centenary Festival at Cornell University, Dmitri Nabokov, the author's son, read an excerpt from

The Original of Laura [which also, oddly enough, mentioned Laura's bones—compare the epigraph at the beginning of this article] and hinted that the most finished portions of it may soon be published commercially.

EXCERPT 1

"...IN OCHRE, RUST and black, a vast procession of bison, stags, stallions and boars, joined by the odd rhinoceros or mammoth, and alongside these, fantastical hybrids: centaurs and bird-headed men, unicorns and antlered shamans.

It is impossible to know with certainty what thoughts raged in our ancestors' minds as they drafted, with their fingers, with charred sticks, with pigments of clay, juniper berries, and pulverized tree bark, these haunting menageries. We are nonetheless justified in making guesses based on this or that subtle shiver of informed intuition: an artist's imagination is often proven more visionarily accurate than the scientist's reasoned conjecture.

Where, then, do I begin?

This art, if I may apply the term to something so imperfectly understood, was created and subsequently viewed not beneath the hot harsh floodlights of a modern museum nor beneath the softer spots of a European pinacotheque but by the flickering flames of primitive oil lamps, emitting rising ropes of acrid smoke and guttering in the winds of a grotto's sepulchral exhalations. The animals bucked and kicked and pranced along the perimeter of a ring of frail illumination while all around menacing shadows leapt and heaved, threatening every moment to engulf in a single swallow the smoking lamp and the lemur-eyed protohuman raising it, with trembling hand, against the swarming demons of darkness."

COMMENTARY

THIS PASSAGE, APPEARING on the first card, is to all appearances the opening of the first chapter. Several things are of immediate note. First, if these are indeed the novel's opening lines, it would be the first time Nabokov began a novel with an ellipsis, properly speaking. (The short story "Krug" [The Circle], which first appeared in *Poslednie novosti* in Paris in March 1934, begins with what might be termed an implied ellipsis—the first sentence is grammatically complete, but implies nevertheless that there has been something omitted that immediately preceded it. It begins "Vo-vtorykh" [Secondly].) Second, if the quotation marks are any indication, *The Original of Laura* begins with a text within the text, which is revealed by Mme Eggerickx's typescript to be a scholarly discourse on art written by the nameless narrator, an art historian and one of Laura's former lovers, who sets out to uncover the circumstances surrounding her mysterious disappearance and death. There are in Nabokov's work other examples of texts within texts (*Invitation to a Beheading, The Gift, Pale Fire, Ada,* and so on), but this would be the first time that a quoted text opens a book. Third, the mention of both "bison" and "pigments" in the context of art, recalls, of course, the penultimate line of *Lolita*: "I am thinking of aurochs and angels, the secret of durable pigments, prophetic sonnets, the refuge of art." It would seem then that *The Original of Laura* in some ways expands upon the themes of *Lolita*: love and loss, life and its relationship to art. We also note that the opinion expressed by the narrator in the second paragraph parallels Nabokov's own statement about the "precision of poetry" and the "passion of science."

EXCERPT 2

OF THE SIX persons in the village I casually questioned, five claimed never to have heard the name Laubaine. When I prompted them with "*l'artiste*," they remained mute and slowly but resolutely shook their heads, like poorly paid extras in a made-for-television movie. One old *invalide de guerre*, the proprietor of a grocery opposite my hotel, went so far as to insist that no one of that name had ever lived there. "Me," he said, half pointing to his chest with a ruddy stump where once a thumb had been, "I've been here seventy-two years. I know everyone. No Laubaine." But outside the post office my persistence was rewarded. A woman who, to judge by the wrinkles lining her tiny face, pre-dated even the know-it-all soldier, sucked in her lips and mooed with pleasure (fondly remembering?) when I explained who it was I sought. She nodded and nodded, her watery dove-blue eyes twinkling. I waited. She nodded, smiling, and then, I think, began to weep. The tears did not wet her waxen cheeks but traveled along the furrows in her face from the corners of her eyes to the jawline, where they were rubbed away by the back of her liver-spotted claw. I asked again whether she knew of a Mademoiselle Laubaine. For the first time she looked at me, her eyes shining, and mouthed, as if to herself, several words which were, whether because of her advanced age or her emotional distress, to my ears at least, practically unintelligible. I thought I caught "*Dieu*," "*cimetière*," "*enfant*," perhaps "*pauvre enfant*." "Near the church cemetery?" I queried. She only nodded, her shrunken frame swaying as if caught in the swell of an invisible sea. I took one of her hands in both of mine and bowed deeply while repeating my thank you's several times over. Then I turned and started up the street toward the church at the edge of the village. Before I had gone a dozen yards I heard a young woman's voice behind me, speaking very loudly, almost shouting: *"Qu'est-ce qu'il vous a dit? Mais dites donc! Qu'est-ce qu'il vous a dit?"* I stopped to look back. Beside the weeping old woman was a much younger woman holding by the handle a paper sack of baguettes and wearing an orange kerchief on her head. Even as she repeated her question, she stared at me angrily, imploringly.

Quaint locals!

I hurried churchward.

COMMENTARY

WHETHER THIS IS a final draft is impossible to determine, but the text is certainly polished and has the rhythm and ring of Nabokov's late prose. It is especially reminiscent of *Transparent Things*, in which the narrator's tone is similarly conversational and slightly conspiratorial. As mentioned above, the narrator, or one of the narrators of the book and likely the one speaking here, is an unidentified man, either an art historian or painter, who is traveling across Europe in search of Laura Laubaine, the novel's eponymous heroine, an artist's model, and apparently a painter herself, whom the narrator once knew and loved.

Like all of Nabokov's names, "Laura Laubaine" is evocative on several semantic levels. "Laura" can be read as "L'aura"—French for aura, which can signify "1. an invisible emanation or vapor, as the aroma of flowers; 2. an invisible atmosphere supposedly arising from and surrounding a person or thing." In these senses it derives from the Latin *aura*, from Greek *aura*, air, from *aer*, to breathe, blow. It also evokes Latin *aurum*, gold. (Laura Laubaine may be blonde; cf. the portrait reproduced above.) And of course, like "Lolita," the first syllable of "Laura" is equivalent to the French l'eau, water. As the next passage reveals, water is an important theme in *The Original of Laura*. Much of the action of the story takes place in Switzerland, in and around Lausanne, which, like Montreux (Nabokov's home at the time of the novel's conception), borders Lac Léman (Lake Geneva). "Laubaine" can be similarly deconstructed to give *l'aubaine*, literally "godsend, windfall, stroke of good luck," or *"L'eau bai{g}ne,"* water washes [the shore, etc.].

Several aspects of the text point unmistakably to Nabokov's mature work: alliteration, prevalence of liquid "L"s, French both translated and untranslated, the color "dove-blue" followed shortly by its near complementary, orange, and the miscommunication between narrator and one of the characters he describes, which he, the narrator, fails to notice.

EXCERPT 3

ON SUMMER DAYS the countryside above Lake Geneva is silent but for the buzz of crickets, a buzz so omnipresent and continuous that one is liable to notice it only when it suddenly ceases, momentarily, as if all the crickets within earshot were pausing simultaneously to listen to the intruder's footsteps on the gravel, lightly crunching. The buzzing resumes, seemingly much louder and more insistent than before. The grape vines, at this time of the season less than a meter high, stand absolutely still in neat rows of dusty green. Much higher up on the slope, a miniature farmer on a miniature tractor is mowing (in dream-slow motion) one tan patch of a rolling quilt of tans and greens. The smell of hay drying in the sun is faintly perceptible whenever a breeze rises and stirs the uncut foxtails and Queen Anne's lace bordering the road.

After I had developed a more or less accurate picture of Laura's childhood by culling details and dates from her aged sister's not always lucid monologues, my research brought me once more to Lausanne, and it was here that I experienced the first of many vivid visual impressions (not to say hallucinations) which were to aid me in my search for the past: the figure of a young woman (who turns out, as we close the distance, to be a girl made to look older by her ample skirt and peasant kerchief *à la Millet*) moving slowly between the rows of vines, clipping unwanted clusters of stunted grapes, pruning fruitless branches, thinning out plants whose boughs have grown overladen, dropping bunches of fragrant early fruit into a basket at her feet. Beads of perspiration dot the sun-tanned skin between her brows. Her forehead is banded by a smear of dirt. She is singing softly aloud a popular children's song whose title escapes me but whose lilting chorus begins with the lyric "*L'épervier s'est envolé.*" Her voice is liquidly enchanting, like the purl of a stream flowing over flat stones washed smooth and sparkling by the flow.

When her chores have all been completed, after the dishes from the evening meal have been washed and replaced in the cupboard or beneath the sideboard, she will sit beside the stone hearth (which, this time of year, is cold and logless) and, while her father reads the *Journal de Genève* and intermittently sucks the tooth-marked stem of his pipe, from which pale puffs of vanilla-scented smoke sluggishly rise, and while her mother knits, needles quietly clicking, she will sketch in a small cloth-bound book the line of her father's profile, her mother's deft hands, or the Chinese-eyed cat sitting sphinx-like at her feet.

She draws instinctively, correcting and perfecting her sketch by means of countless successive erasures and additions, seeking a certain "rightness" without ever having heard talk of perspective or composition, and thus constrained to adopt a procedure of delicate trial-and-error, with frequent interruptions to verify problematic passages: a nostril, a thumbnail, the cat's bony haunches. There will be a purity about the finished drawing, a childish charm borne of the viewer's certainty that the image before her was created not through artifice and easy skill, but through application and the guileless sincerity of inexperience.

The cat, startled by a soundless noise, sensing the approach of an invisible intruder, rises and runs out of the room with a quick mincing trot, the form of its erect tail and the puckered pink button below it suggesting a rapidly receding exclamation point.

The artist, her model run off, squints at the drawing, head cocked, signs her name at the bottom of the page, and turns to a fresh sheet. Her father sucks on his pipe, but this time there is no glow, no puff of smoke, no sweet tang on his tongue, only lightly savory air. He lays the newspaper on his lap and reaches with one hand (the left) for a box of matches while with the other (the right) he grips the pipe and finger-tamps the warm tobacco in the bowl. Madame Laubaine pauses from her work to check a stitch of which she is unsure. Laura, preparing to sketch her father's portrait, watches him light his pipe and then flick (puffing, squirrel-cheeked) the blackened, still burning match into the fireplace, where it vanishes in the inferno of orange flame. The bottom log, with a jet black back and a belly of glowing orange-red scales, crackles and collapses, emitting a sputtering hiss and a barrage of sparks which rise slowly, floating, wafted by the hot air, up through the flue, out of sight.

COMMENTARY

THIS IS A superb passage, equaling or exceeding in quality the descriptive precision of anything Nabokov ever wrote. The triple "buzz" in the first paragraph perfectly conveys the lazy droning of crickets on a hillside in summer, and the transition from the sound of this buzzing to the light lakeside wind is nicely contained in "breeze." The "dream-slow motion" of the tractor on a distant slope wonderfully conveys the sense of slow timelessness of an Alpine valley. The compression of time is reinforced by the conflation of two temporalities, the time of year when the fireplace is "cold and logless," and the later one in which a fire is burning.

In the second paragraph we meet with indications that, as in *The Real Life of Sebastian Knight*, here too we will have to contend not only with a possibly unreliable narrator but with unreliable secondary characters as well.

The mention of Jean-François Millet (1814–1875) continues the painting theme that pervades the novel. The description of the girl harvesting grapes may also be a parody of certain Soviet propaganda films on agrarian life.

The image of the cat running out of the room is pure gold. The "puckered pink button" beneath its raised tail recalls the "anal ruby" of the bicycle in chapter two of *Bend Sinister*. Nabokov describes a cat with similar poetic precision in the next excerpt.

Excerpt 4

SNOWFLAKES, AS YET undecided whether to fall to earth, float aimlessly, or rise slowly up toward the same gray sky from which they had lately fallen, described nets of confusion outside Laura's windows on the cold morning of 10 March. Inside, the stove crackled and whined, and groaned cavernously each time a fresh gust blew across the mouth of the flue pipe on the roof. Zelda (as Laura's American friend Drake had dubbed the stray she-cat that appeared one dawn, no one could figure out how, on the fourth-floor window sill) lay on the floor beside the stove, the haphazard arrangement of its outstretched limbs differentiated from a pose of sudden death only by the gentle heaving of its soft, bony chest. Laura, seated at the larger of the room's two tables facing a small mirror propped against a corked, half-full bottle of *vin ordinaire*, was working on a sketched self-portrait she intended to send to her sister Nathalie (studying in Zürich) as a belated birthday gift. The intermittent rasp of the charcoal stump against the textured page caused the cat's left ear to twitch, and from time to time, after a particularly vigorous bout of mark-making, the somniculous animal would languorously lift its head to slit a sleepy eye at its adopted mistress' preoccupied back.

COMMENTARY

THE BEAUTY OF this passage speaks for itself. We might content ourselves to point out that the combination of "intermittent" with the habitual past "would lift" reveal the influence of Flaubert, whose use of the *imparfait* Nabokov spoke very highly of in his *Lectures on Literature*.

Rather than spoil the fun of readers who may be able to read the novel, or what exists of it, very soon, I shall limit myself to the four brief excerpts above and leave it to professional Nabokovians to supply more insightful commentary. If the excepts published here are any indication of the book's quality, Nabokov fans are in for a treat and can no doubt expect a number of surprises.

AFTER *LAURA*

by JEFF EDMUNDS

"Nothing succeeds if prankishness has no part in it."
—Friedrich Nietzsche, *Twilight of the Idols*

IN LATE SEPTEMBER 1998, as part of a redesigned version of Zembla, a Web site devoted to Vladimir Nabokov I created in 1995 and had been editing and overseeing since then, I posted an article by Michel Desommelier, identified as a Swiss university professor teaching in Basel and a specialist on Peter Handke. Desommelier's article offered readers their first glimpse of *The Original of Laura*, Nabokov's last and unfinished novel, none of which had ever appeared in print. Nabokov, who deplored any use of writing not intended for publication by the artist himself, wanted what fragments of the novel did exist to be destroyed, unread, upon his death. Desommelier's article featured four excerpts from the novel and told the story of how Suzanne Eggerickx, a young nurse who cared for Nabokov as he lay dying, came to learn passages of Nabokov's novel by heart and subsequently to filch several manuscript note cards from a box beside his hospital bed. In addition to the article itself, the new version of Zembla included a brief mention of Desommelier's article in the news section of the site, audio files of an actor friend of mine reading the first lines of all Nabokov's novels, including *Laura*, and an expanded bibliography of critical works, with Desommelier's comprising the only entry for a book about which few Nabokovians knew anything more than the title. Desommelier, however, didn't exist—I fabricated both him and his essay. The excerpts from Nabokov's novel were fiction, but it was I, not Nabokov, who had composed them.

A day or two after making the new Zembla and Desommelier's article available to the public, I announced the new site on NABOKV-L, an electronic discussion list whose more than five hundred subscribers include both amateur enthusiasts and many of the world's leading Nabokov scholars. In the course of the next three weeks, I received several dozen e-mails from visitors to the site. Generally the feedback was favorable, and, satisfied that the new version of Zembla was a success, I moved on to other projects.

*   *   *

IN THE THIRD week of October I received a brief message from Stephen Jan Parker, the co-founder and Secretary/Treasurer of the International Vladimir Nabokov Society, in which he asked, incidentally, whether the Desommelier piece was "genuine or tongue-in-cheek." In responding to his e-mail I dodged the question, loath to reveal the ruse.

On the morning of October 20, I received, in quick succession, two e-mail messages. The first was from Brian Boyd, author of a two-volume Nabokov biography, a professor of English at the University of Auckland, and the person widely regarded as the world's foremost Nabokov scholar. Boyd had just received what he characterized as "a very distraught call from Dmitri [Nabokov]," who had been informed by Parker that Zembla had published excerpts from *The Original of Laura*. Boyd was fuming, saying that "every measure of the law will be used against Eggerickx and Desommelier," and that I too had violated copyright law and acted as "a receiver of stolen goods." He went on for several paragraphs in the same tone, signing the message, "Yours in disappointment and outrage."

I was taken aback. Absolutely the last two people I expected to fool with spurious excerpts were Boyd and Dmitri, the author's son, principal translator, and literary executor. Boyd and Dmitri were the only two people I was certain had read the novel Nabokov left unfinished when he died in 1977.

The second message was from Parker, who reported that Dmitri wanted to talk to me and needed my phone number.

Genuinely frightened by Boyd's threats, uncertain of the legal ramifications of what I considered a harmless and relatively transparent hoax, and aware that the Nabokov Estate had, in the past, sought legal remedies when displeased with the actions of a scholar, critic, or publisher, I immediately removed the hoax and all references and links to it. I replied to Boyd with a brief message that began, "A hoax. And now completely gone. I'm very sorry it created such outrage. I thought it was so transparently implausible that no one would be taken in."

I sent Parker my phone number, revealed the piece was a hoax, and asked him to tell Dmitri, "Please mention in your fax that the offending material... has been removed."

* * *

THE FOLLOWING MORNING I received a call from Dmitri Nabokov. Having in the meantime been in contact with Parker, he knew by now that the essay and excerpts were a hoax, but he wanted to confirm that they had been removed from Zembla, not, apparently, because they offended him, as they had Boyd, but because he was fearful of being besieged by queries from well-meaning Nabokovians concerned that the excerpts had been published without the estate's permission.

Boyd later told reporter Andy Lamey of Canada's *National Post* that he felt "wounded" by Desommelier's portrayal of a "helpless, dying man" being taken advantage of by his nurse. While the scenario is admittedly grotesque, it was inspired in part by Nabokov's working title for the novel: *Dying Is Fun*. I knew, too, that Nabokov himself had delighted in literary mystifications. The most famous, and elaborate, of his pranks involved a poet named Vasiliy Shishkov, invented by Nabokov as a particularly clever literary revenge against critics of his poetry, the most prominent of whom was Georgii Adamovich. On the occasion of the death of renowned Russian émigré poet Vladislav Khodasevich, on June 14, 1939, Nabokov composed a commemorative poem entitled "Poèty" [The Poets] which was published over the name "Vasiliy Shishkov." Adamovich, previously hostile to Nabokov's verse, which he had described as "cerebral and devoid of music," reviewed Shishkov's poem enthusiastically, writing that "every line, every word exhibits talent." A month later, Nabokov published, under his own name (or rather, his usual pseudonym, V. Sirin), a prose piece called "Vasiliy Shishkov." Ostensibly a mini-biography of Shishkov, the tale makes plain that Shishkov was invented and that Sirin (Nabokov) was his inventor, as well as the author of "Poèty." Adamovich's response in print was guarded and ambiguous, and he seemed unwilling to concede that he had been fooled.

My conversation with Dmitri began, unexpectedly, with our chatting affably about the recent Cornell Nabokov Festival, where he had given an impromptu reading that included a brief excerpt from *The Original of Laura*. I was present at the reading, but can't recall the precise wording of the passage. What I do retain is a clear mental image of a woman's bare abdomen and the swell of the hipbones beneath the skin. It was this image that prompted me to select the epigram to Desommelier's article, by "Laure."

After talking for a while longer, Dmitri said, "Now tell me about this hoax, Jeff? Do we know who did it?" I hadn't realized that neither he nor Parker had guessed that I was the culprit. I admitted that I had created it. There was a long pause. His initial surprise passed, and he expressed admiration at how well I had captured his father's style and asked several questions about how I had arrived at specific words and names, especially "Eggerickx" and "Desommelier."[1] Boyd later revealed that Dmitri had actually tried to track down in Switzerland my invented nurse and my invented professor.

At the end of our conversation, Dmitri said that no one else in the world could have created the hoax. Then, correcting himself, he told me that he could have done it but didn't have time for such things. Finally, correcting himself once more, he said that not even he could have done it.

I offered to print a note in Zembla's news section revealing the hoax and Dmitri accepted my offer, adding that I could quote him as saying the hoax had been perpetrated "to the hearty amusement of Dmitri." This I did within a few hours of our conversation. Needless to say, amusement hardly seems to have been his initial reaction.

---

[1] "Eggerickx" was inspired by the "egg-like alliteration" of the name Olga Olegovna Orlova, a curiosity remarked on by the narrator of *The Real Life of Sebastian Knight*. I also said I find the rare combination "ckx" (most often seen in Belgian names) visually appealing. Having mildly hoaxed Nabokovians before on two occasions, I chose "Desommelier," a pseudonym that had no chance of revealing the person behind it and was not an anagram or a multilingual pun or other moniker Nabokov scholars might recognize as spurious.

UBAR: A REFERENCE

by JANET BLAND, RIKKI DUCORNET, ERIC P. ELSHTAIN, AMY ENGLAND,
CARLA HOWL, CHRISTINE HUME, CATHERINE KASPER, CYNTHIA KUHN,
CHRISTY ANN ROWE, DAVID RAY VANCE

[Beggart Nettle Tree (*Populous homophylla ubannaeus*)]

FOUND OVER WHOLE of Ubar Major, the beggart nettle is most plentiful in Western Peninsular Ranges and seaboard elevations of the Eastern Quadrangle. Despite its common name, this tree bears neither nettles nor thorns. [Also referred to as "Home Tree," "Immaculate Tree of Life," and "Nettle-No-Nettle."]

No mature specimens of the beggart nettle are known to exist. The tree's immature form is marked by smooth, blue-black bark with vibrant orange and red accents. Its twigs are stout with small, dark-green lantiscles with yellow scales. Because immature trees are leafless and grow only .005 inches per annum, distinguishing between living and deceased specimens requires extensive botanical knowledge and skill. The largest known *living* specimen measures a scant two feet in diameter and a mere eleven feet in height and is located in the Blortnewgh Mosque of Niathsle, in the township of Otnasnom.

Long favored as domiciles in ancient Ubaria (see ARCHITECTURE), mature trees were known to reach massive proportions with trunks commonly measuring over fifty-five yards in diameter and with topmost branches rising as high as 400 yards. Photographs show rough, reddish-blue bark tinged purple and fissured into broad, flat plates that run perpendicular to the trunk forming climbable trelliswork. Beginning approximately twenty feet up from base, branches interweave to form solid "floors" offering anywhere from fifty to 2,000 square feet of flat, livable surface and reportedly capable of supporting up to two-and-one-half tons per every three square feet. Measuring ten to twenty feet in diameter and resembling umbrellas in their shape and in vein pattern, mature leaves apparently overlapped to form dense, rain-resistant canopy, their transparent membranes developing hues from royal monkey purple to seagullian yellow depending, most experts agree, upon the forms of lichen present.

Illustrations held at the Historical Botanical Archive League show teardrop-shaped fruit pods measuring approximately four feet wide with purple iridescent coverings. No other fruit fossils have been uncovered, but fossilized leaves and bark patterns are in abundance. Shortly before her assassination, renowned botanical archaeologist, SYLVA BLORTNEWGH, postulated that Ubarians were themselves the fruit of this tree. Her theory, despite enjoying a cult following since the early thirties (see UNPOPULAR RELIGIONS), has never gained wide acceptance.

— *David Ray Vance*

*　　*　　*

CABINET OF INFINITE COMPARTMENTS

THE CABINET OF Infinite Compartments contains a universe, inside one million drawers, each secured by a different lock or latch, none functional without an ointment or plant oil. Objects and collected things are exchanged, loaned out, employed in stories of accumulation, and borrowed by librarians who record the objects in long lists comprising multiple volumes (see HOARD OF USELESS UTENSILS).

What follows is only a small sample:

Birds' wings and beaks
Lacquered teas
Hotel fruit souvenirs
Cloth cups
Molded dishes
Flavors of rain
Dried lichen
Cracked foods
Drawers devoted to blue smells
Keys to green desires
Words that cannot be memorized

Houses of bees
Passport stamps to other worlds
A history in jars
Scraps from vacation days
The wellspring of contentment
Ceramic limbs
Musical instruments
Conical dreams of water
Three-dimensional poems by Adrienna Niatpu
Blueprints
Miniature vertebrae
Selected shards from the glass beach
Profiles in sealing wax
Toxic uses of cactus enhancement
Vistas of unknown cities
Sylva Blortnewgh's pockets
Watercolors of monkey codes
Ordinary rocks
Canoptic containers
Sounds of yucca
Astrological telescopes

— *Catherine Kasper*

*   *   *

CORDELIA'S DAY

CELEBRATED ON MAY 22nd in certain parts of southern Ubar, Cordelia's Day is traditionally associated with a unique fertility ritual that is still practiced today, primarily in rural areas. The ritual involves creating baby figures out of certain herbs and twine and placing them outdoors all night, wrapped in a blanket; the herbal babies are usually placed outside after midnight on the morning of the 22nd, although recently it has become more common to place them outside any time after sunset on the 21st.

On the evening of the 22nd, the herbs are then retrieved, used for cooking, and consumed by the couple trying to conceive. Barren couples can expect a child in the next year. The typical herbs used are as follows: tarragon, dill, anise for a girl; and basil, mint, parsley for a boy (although rosemary is substituted for mint in the Wine Sea region). The origin of these herbal combinations is unknown.

This fertility ritual is linked with the story of Cordelia, from the village of Camratl. Legend has it Cordelia was barren, and after seven years of marriage her husband was becoming frustrated with the lack of children and losing interest in her. Finally he left on a year-long trading expedition to the northern part of the country. Fearful he would not come back, Cordelia wrote to him and told him she was expecting. The husband was overjoyed, and after his year of trade was over he returned home and wanted to see the child. The night before he returned, Cordelia created a baby figure out of herbs that she had in the house and placed it in a cradle under a blanket. Each time her husband asked to see the baby, she pointed at the lump under the blanket and told her husband it was sleeping. Each new day she would use the herbs in cooking and create a fresh, firm herbal baby. After several weeks of this, the husband became suspicious; he looked in the cradle, saw the false child, and became enraged. Grabbing both the herbal baby and blanket, he threw them outside on the grass near the house in the early morning of May 22nd. The next day as the couple got up, they heard the sound of crying. Outside, lying on the grass inside of the blanket, was a baby boy. Both were surprised, but the husband praised Cordelia's magic, and the two remained together.

— *Christy Ann Rowe*

*　　*　　*

EXPLODING BEETLE

GENERIC CHARACTER:　　*Antennae manipulative.*
Thorax margined, and shaped like her heart with the point cut off.
Abdomen provocative, as if it were scratched with a needle.

THE EXPLODING BEETLE appears bluish, and exaggerates its blueness whenever provoked. A disagreeable vapor, accompanied by a smart explosion, issues on these occasions: when looked at longingly; when flattered; when told it holds territory[Ý]. When this insect is confused and irritated, which is often and without much provocation, her destruction is inevitable.

Dr. Lavo succeeded in irritating one of the insects merely with his observations about how it was sleeping; this caused it to advance against its own

---

[Ý] The ancient word "oises" could just as well be translated as "property": ancient Ubarians measured land holdings aurally; that is, as far as someone could hear another's voice is as far as property lines went. The so-called "exploding beetle" was, relatively speaking, rather quiet, hence its consternation at the implication that it held very little land.

nation.[ý] The insect is found in several parts of the headlands, and sometimes makes one's eyes sting like hard tobacco.

— *Eric P. Elshtain*

*   *   *

FEAST OF FOOD, THE

EVERYBODY KNOWS OYSTERS spend their thoughtless lives nested in the perfect dark of the sea's bottom. To find them, the pearl fishers of Buz carry fireflies seized during the brief hour of their amorous frenzies and sealed in globes of glass.

Later, at the Feast of Food, the pearls will be ground to a fine powder and scattered upon the fresh waters which circle that verdant country. In this way the sea repays the rivers and the rain for its own nourishment.

It is a well-known fact that having crossed the ocean, maneuvered The Sounds of Estrangement and, upon entering The Bay of Sighs, one sees the pearl fisher's red sails threading the sky—one rejoices. No matter the deprivations of the journey, the years spent cursing the day one was born and tearing one's beard out by the roots with regret. One's heart is healed without delay, if not forever.

— *Rikki Ducornet*

*   *   *

HOARD OF USELESS UTENSILS, THE

THE HOARD OF Useless Utensils is visited during the Festival of Assemblage. These holidays, specifically devoted to the reverence of objects requires Ubarians to engage in tactile contact with a variety unusual things. Some activities include the celebration of a palm-sized universe, and the magical juggling of one thousand and one marbles. The Hoard of Useless Utensils is both contained in a CABINET OF INFINITE COMPARTMENTS and uncontained in the unplowed acreage surrounding the cabinet. Ubarians wander through the otherwise untouched landscape searching for discarded wreckage; they pilfer the compartments in order to palm, covet, and occasionally taste unique surfaces and textures.

Stories are told through arrangements created by intentional and random stacking, piling, and sorting. Some such arrangements have been cata-

---

ý Although ancient Ubarian bio-geographers often used the word "nation" to characterize regional assemblages of animals and plants; it is unclear whether or not they did so conscious of possible literal interpretations.

logued. Libraries have even been devoted to records of the arrangements that are constantly altered during the Festival. Several thousand volumes attempting to catalogue the objects in the cabinet of infinite compartments. The Festival of Assemblage includes visits to these libraries, readings of lists, and pronunciations of the names of objects that Ubarians equate with a kind of tactile examination.

— *Catherine Kasper*

*   *   *

KIKLUNA

KIKLUNA IS THE study and care of dreaming. Dreams have long held a sacred place in Ubarian culture, and kikluna is, not surprisingly, a curious blend of ancient and modern practices. Although Ubarians have individual dreams regularly (which they are forbidden to discuss), all Ubarians share an identical dream on the first night of a full moon. This dream, known as a SIGNALIS, is believed to come from a celestial current that reveals to Ubarians the true state of affairs in the Great Cosmology and identifies problems most in need of attention within the society. Ubarians compare detailed notes and debate the meaning of the Signalis for exactly sixty minutes at monthly morning feasts featuring ZUBOJA, a complicated dish of kiwi and strawberries festooned with honey and fashioned into a temple.

Ancient Ubarians are said to have received a Signalis every night, but the daily process of interpretation prevented society from functioning, prompting adherence to the one-hour format. SIGNALIS debates are recorded by Kiklunans, the preferred term for priestesses whose vocations are determined at birth by the appearance of small blue crescent-shaped birthmarks. Kiklunans perform a variety of duties: they lead songs at public events, handle all tangle-related queries, and preside over HALL OF LYRACA ceremonies, during which the secret names of newborns are whispered through labyrinthine tubes woven from sea grass. However, recording the Signalis debates is the most important obligation of the Kiklunans. Transcripts are wrapped carefully in hallowed twine and archived in a cone-shaped building located on MOUNT UBA, approachable only by sure-footed yak.

— *Cynthia Kuhn*

*   *   *

LANGUAGE FISH

GENERIC CHARACTER: *Mouth like a bird's beak.*
                                              Eight to thirteen arms, which never touch.
                                              Eyes and ears lovely like a queen's.

THE WONDERFUL POWER of the language fish to benumb the hand that touches it and leave its message on the hand's skin has been known for many ages, and noted by most intelligent observers.[Ý] Ancient Ubarian "zoologists" admired the effect without attempting to explain its cause, since they viewed the attributes of all living things as the work of each specie's own secret will or image of itself.[ý]

That this fish's singular faculty might be rendered still more astonishing, these "zoologists" gave to it influences which it by no means possesses. Thus Pylin assures us that the language fish, even when touched with a stick, can benumb and inscribe its message onto the strongest arm. Naippo goes still further, and, with that license to which property owners always think themselves entitled, claims that these fish wrote Ubarian land law on the bottoms of boats.

However, no language fish message has been satisfactorily translated, and its ability has caused debate over exactly how this animal should be classified. Though this text accepts the most recent taxonomy, in the past scientists considered and duly classified this animal as, variously, a lost Ubarian tribe, a species of monkey, an early scientific invention, and the effect of mass hysteria.

The language fish is found in shallow seawater, in the inter-tidal zones. It can often be found in pools too shallow for it to even swim in. The fish, in this seemingly precarious situation, hasn't a care, and can be easily handled. Often, its messages when in this state are long and rambling, leading some to believe that it is excitable, and others to think it merely bored. The implacable stare of the language fish leaves many observers alarmed and feeling cut off from organized culture. Thus, in many prefectures, old sayings survive, such as "when you handle the fish," which means—colloquially—evading official, but justified prosecution.

— Eric P. Elshtain

*   *   *

[Ý] Often employed by Ubarian academicians, the phrase "intelligent observer" seems to be the equivalent of our "expert witness."

[ý] This perceived self-determination allowed the ancients to moralize about a creature's given abilities. This ethical consideration of the talents of animals often led to the criminal prosecution and even capital punishment of these hapless creatures. The language fish, for example, was often put to death and eaten for sedition and blasphemy.

LYNCHWEED

COMMONLY FOUND IN the Southeast and most humid regions of the Ubarian territories, lynchweed remains a significant social and marital problem (see MATING RITUALS). The seeds of the lynchweed are blown into an area of biped inhabitation in the form of small green pods. The vine that is produced—usually within one Rat cycle of the Most Yellow Moon—is a rubbery and vivid green with shovel-shaped leaves. Within ten Rat cycles flowers are produced which carry a heavy, narcotic perfume. As the vine grows, covering vehicles, dwellings, and small, slow-moving Minke dogs, the atmosphere around the infestation grows rich with the sticky scent of the large magenta flowers. The scent is most compelling and subtle under conditions of continuous exposure, often resulting in the irresistible desire among those passing by to lie down on the ground next to the vine to better enjoy the narcotic effect. Victims who remain on the ground nuzzled up to the flowers eventually lose motor control of facial and jaw muscles, allowing the lynchweed to grow into their slack mouths and down their throats. If left undisturbed, the victims are incorporated into the infrastructure of the plant in a manner that is most analogous to fruit.

As the lynchweed grows higher through the summer season, covering buildings and the tallest trees, the biped "fruit" are dragged along the ground and eventually pulled up into the air where they tend to sway slightly in the breezes so common in that region. Botanists speculate that this swaying as if on the end of a rope is the origin of the vine's common name. Bipeds have been successfully harvested from the vine after up to three Rat cycles with few adverse effects beyond weight loss and the persistent desire to hum. After three Rats, however, the biped is too closely integrated into the vine for successful separation and officially declared a member of the herb kingdom. The surviving spouse, if any, is free to remarry.

—*Janet L. Bland*

*   *   *

MIRÂJ (MUSEUM)

IN THE NECROMANCY Gallery of the Museum of Mirâj, one may admire engraved gems: one for each hour of the day, each day of the year, each year of the decade, each decade of the century, each century of the millennium. An eccentric aluminum camera in which a gem serves as a photographic lens is also on display, as is a series of nearly indiscernible yet ingenious portraits of the stone obelisks of Buz. Until the last century, these objects were employed to track eclipses.

—*Rikki Ducornet*

*   *   *

MUSIC

IN UBAR, MUSICAL and vocal instruments have a ritual and symbolic significance. According to the existing history, the music of the indigenous Ubarians began when the first timetone player evoked the spirit of sound by scattering ears made of clay across the ground. The timetone player then strapped large, heavy wooden blocks to her feet and began stomping, thus creating vibrations. These vibrations caused the clay ears to shatter. If the atmospheric conditions were proper, and the vibrations made moral sense, Moseculo appeared. Moseculo typically dressed in an elastic gown fashioned from taut skin. Young children ran at Moseculo and bounced off his gown. They pulled at and strummed leftover sinew and pounded with their fists on tightly stretched areas of the gown.

This ritual continued until the timetone player stomped the shattered clay ears into dust. At which time, timetone pupils poured the dust into a long, hollow bamboo pipe and blew the contents into the roots of the pino tree. The pino's leaves sang a utilitarian melody, something of a repetitive chant.

Mosecula Secula, an Ubarian composer of the time, first noticed the pino's song while walking briskly to catch her child from falling out of the tree. This was in the afternoon. It was hot. As she ran, Mosecula Secula heard the sound of one foot passing the other and, in her mind, calculated the temporal rhythm of her feet rising and falling. She named this split-second beat a polti rhythm, after her child Poltipompa. Witnesses recall that Moseculo appeared then for the last time, because Mosecula Secula had saved her child and in the process invented a polti rhythm. All this created the proper atmospheric condition, the vibrations made sudden moral sense, and Moseculo's gown dissolved in the mid-afternoon heat.

— Carla Howl

*   *   *

PORTRAITURE

HISTORICAL INFORMATION ABOUT portraiture remains scarce; even today most portrait artists do not admit their trade. The selling of any solitary look may be regarded as an exploitation of desperately disconnected persons in the throes of their loneliness. Though it may never be as highly regarded as other hobbies such as gardening, portraiture nonetheless flourishes both in- and outdoors. Some speculate that anything may become a portrait, anything at anytime, especially at dawn. Then, one may find an old wire or clam bearing a friend's expression like a coat of arms. Yet experts agree that these are mere amateur activities; a true portraitist has a predetermined sitter to draw from. Otherwise, the known facts are these: prestigious religious beliefs prevent artists and sitters alike from desiring any all-too-accurate likenesses, and artists hide their signatures in the subjects' own handwriting. A small museum located at the tip of Epirhi Island dedicates itself to portraiture of all forms and ages and has allowed for the following reproduction of its admittedly partial categories.

THE SILHOUETTE

ORIGINATING WITH MOUNTAIN-DWELLING natives of the Old Era, silhouettes are made by sitter's shadows on crisp-edged snow crusts. Silhouettes may also appear as reflections on sidewalks one falls over or echoes between the cliffs. According to the current trend, artists insist on working with the largest possible shadow: that is, a life-size cutting would be incoherent, yet desert-sized shadows are a form of divine caricature.

THE VELVET SUBLIME

VELVET ARTISTS ALLOW their subjects to choose from a variety of pre-fabricated backgrounds—combinations of snowcaps, prehistoric bears, rough-and-tumble rivers, campfires, and breathtaking tidal waves. The resulting picture consists almost entirely of airbrushed narrative backdrop; the subject is mere staffage by comparison. In this portrait, one must search the lightning-lit valley's panorama of scrub-brush, lizards, and red rocks to find a man standing confident in too many frocks and pointing ahead. Upon locating the figure, viewers report an overwhelming urge to touch it. Claims that skin goes numb upon contact with the velvet canvas are groundless.

THE INDUSTRIAL FACE

CHARACTERIZED BY WIDELY flaring nostrils, scarred upper lip, and crooked, stained teeth; poses for industrial face portraits include "melted down" and "wooden effigy." Subjects dress in bark from imported trees and skins that some say are artificial. Dirt masks half the subject's face and is especially dark under both eyes, giving the face an affecting fatigued look. Rock rubble litters the foreground. Industrial face renderings may titillate the viewer with their displays of grotesque overwork. Once these artists have mastered a special method of sleep deprivation, they have access to a whole new range of color mutations, saturation dyes, and foreshortening techniques.

THE GRAFFITI PORTRAIT

SOME TOURISTS WANT to leave their images on civic structures, rather than take a silhouette or an industrial face home. To this end, they may hire public-works artists to blow-paint images of their faces on towers and tunnel backs. Graffiti portrait artists chew pigment seeds into a paint that they apply with sharp expirations of breath. The practice of allowing bodily fluids and paint to ferment together is rumored to spread diseases of the nervous system. Sitters often claim a sensation of narcotic purity for hours afterwards. Their images stain the concrete of Edicius Suspension Bridge, Niwdeg Risk Shelter, and Ahamha Correction Center. After graffiti portraits weather into irregular blotches, passers by read them for predictions of the city's future.

THE LIMNING

IN RECENT YEARS, unsupervised schoolchildren have taken to drawing portraits on their thumbnails, then slamming their hands in bathroom doors or dropping medicine balls on them in gym class. After their portrait-nails, called limnings, fall off, they exchange them with each other. These children pocket the limnings along with their loose change. Ubarian habits of possession dictate that when stored close to the body, a portrait must close its eyes. In exchange, the foreign face emerges from under the skin of the owner's real face.

— *Christine Hume*

*   *   *

ROCKS

THE ROCKS OF Ubar behave in some familiar ways: they are the basis for mountains, they can be hurled as missiles with injurious effect, they can be shaped into units of building matter; they are black when they are not other colors. Taxonomically, however, they are more closely related to the sponge family. Textures range from pumice to doeskin.

— *Amy England*

*   *   *

SHELL READERS, THE

ALTHOUGH THE PRACTICE is ancient and prestigious, and although the Orthodox continue to insist upon its necessity, few shell readers function today. Their vanishing artistry consists of deciphering the sacred and symbolic texts written on the shells of the Imperial Turtles which, as they lumber back and forth in their pen, embody all the secrets of Divine Intention.

Throughout the Old Kingdom—a period covering nearly five thousand years—the shells were read daily in order to forestall and foresee major and minor events: the impact of a comet, the best time to witness fireworks, to buy or steal a signet ring, to bury a bull, to burn down a bridge, dig for emeralds, dive for pearls, slice bread, open a locked room, cut roses, deface the stare of a tyrant, clean the tongue, sleep in the shadow of a tower, manufacture copper.

As ever, the interpretation of the Imperial Shells is problematic. A proven misinterpretation is perceived as contamination of the Law; failure is punished by death. One notoriously feeble reader, made to drink up the sea, died in this service; another was forced to file a grove of date palms with his teeth, another to eat the hooves of a dead horse. *God is not given to ambiguous gesturing* may, at the time of this writing, be read penned into the flesh of a man on display beside the closed gates to the city.

— *Rikki Ducornet*

*   *   *

SHRIEKING YUCCA (*AGAVACEAE STREPIT*)

A POISONOUS PLANT, possibly in the yucca family, now presumed extinct, whose shape resembled the human vertebrae, and which carried a strong perfume that corresponded to the lime content of soil, and the presence of carbon dioxide, ranging from vanilla, mangoes, and nutmeg to cedar, coffee, and garlic. Said to have ornithological potential, it has the capacity to emit various sounds at night.

First thought to be an abnormal growth that sprouted from the roots of the white pine, or produced by seed carried by birds migrating to Southern regions of Ubar, the origin of the shrieking yucca has never been discovered. Most of the information concerning this part-plant, possibly part-bird, has been gathered from journals alone; no herbarium today possesses a preserved dry sample or cutting.

In 1853, the botanist Dr. Lachlaina Murray recorded in her journals that after fifty years of experimentation, she had to conclude that her surviving specimens of *Agavaceae strepit* only produced sound emissions in peaceful terrain, after being exposed to the unrecorded human voice, speaking wholly without aggression. Charles Darwin recorded that his only regret was never actually being able to witness this extraordinary event, especially after the astonishing letters he received from Ubarian readers. After Dr. Murray's death, the last specimens of *Agavaceae strepit* disappeared quietly.

— *Catherine Kasper*

*　　*　　*

SILVER BEE'S HONEY, THE

THE HONEY OF the silver bee is elusive; one cannot simultaneously see and collect it. Gatherers of such honey work only at night, using palm fronds to comb the air behind their backs in a constant, impossibly awkward motion. They then carry the fronds, still behind their backs, into a lightless room, and blindly funnel the very small drops into small bottles. Once in glass, the honey can be examined—clear as water, it does not look like much. But pull off the cap and very quickly down the contents, and one will find that the silver bees hive nectar and venom into a single substance. One can actually taste, spreading over the tongue, behind the sweetness perfumed with magnolia, the chasms of cold between stars.

— *Amy England*

*　　*　　*

SUMMERS OF CHILDHOOD, THE

UNLIKE THE OTHER seasons, the summers of childhood are eternal and may be evoked by a thousand and one things. This evocation has its risks; it is not unusual for someone hearing a rain shower or biting into a pear to be irretrievably embraced by nostalgia and so, thereafter, unable to live in the present time, but made to roam, horribly alone, the obstinate rooms, dark hills, and unpredictable paths of moments impossible to retrieve.

On occasion a memory is of such potency the dreamer is reduced to tears or turned to salt. Such reverie does not lead to spontaneous combustion, but many have died of sleeplessness and many more of too much sleep.

It is documented by Manethô that a poet murderously used a knife in order to steal a bouquet, the scent of which recalled the one instant of his infancy when he was happy.

— *Rikki Ducornet*

*　　*　　*

VOICE TYPES CATALOGED

CERTAIN VOICE TYPES are so often referred to that Ubarians have created a code of abbreviations to discuss them more easily. The world very much admires the person possessing a rare voice with H.B.Q. (haunting banjo quality), likewise the less unusual voices evoking E.A.M. (erotic accordion mesmerism). You will hear fairly frequent examples of the M.A.B. voice (many angry bees), the S.F.S. voice (smelling faintly of smoke), and the voice of G.K.F.U.S.F. (golden keys falling on a slate floor). Voices of the U.Z.E.P. variety (untuned zither endlessly played) are, sadly, all too common.

— Amy England

CONVERGENCES

by LAWRENCE WESCHLER

FATHERS AND DAUGHTERS/TINA BARNEY PORTRAITS

ABOUT THREE YEARS ago, on an art walk through Soho, in a gallery off
Broadway, I happened upon a large-scale color-saturated photograph that
stopped me cold: Tina Barney's double portrait of what were clearly a father
and his late-teenaged daughter, staring head-on into the camera. It stopped
me cold, and immediately I started to warm to it. As it happened, this was
the photo that was featured on the show's announcement postcard, so I was
able to take that version of it home with me: I push-pinned it to the wall
facing my desk and have, in the months and years since, had frequent occasion to lose myself into it.

Back in college, years ago, I'd had a girlfriend who looked remarkably
like the girl in Barney's picture—and who'd look at me in a remarkably
similar manner: self-assured, ironical, a drowsy-lidded gaze freighted with
entendres and double-entendres. Occasionally we'd go up to visit her parents in San Francisco. I could be wrong, but something about the light and
the furnishings makes me sure the bedroom in Barney's photo is also in San
Francisco. Anyway, my girlfriend's parents were of a certain class—comfortable haute-bourgeoisie, which is to say a situation slightly higher than my
own family's—and every once in a while, she and her father would get
themselves lined up, facing me, just like the pair in the photo: she'd be giving me that ironically freighted look, and her father, in turn, who looked
remarkably like the guy in the photo, would also be giving me a look just
like his: wary, somewhere between begrudged and resigned. Between the

two of them, they had me nailed.

And years later, as, daydreamingly, I continued gazing back into the father and daughter in Barney's double portrait over my desk, they still had me nailed: I was back in college, it was as if I hadn't grown a day, I was still that slightly gawky and yet increasingly assured kid, right on the cusp, eternally on the cusp.

Do any of us ever grow up?

*　　*　　*

ANYWAY, AS I say, that photo has been staring at me from across my desk for years now, slowly becoming festooned over with other cards and photos and announcements, but still pertinent, still sweetly charged, still capable of drawing me in in the midst of my otherwise busy days.

Days full of this and that, my writing work, my own family responsibilities, and this past year, increasingly, caring for Herb, the dear old man across the street, a ninety-eight-year-old geezer who until just recently had been wry and spry and sharp and funny and astonishingly nimble, an ongoing inspiration to everyone in the neighborhood, including me and my wife and our little daughter. Late some nights—say, three in the morning—our entire block would be dark save for two lights: me in my office, writing away at my desk; and Herb across the street in his front parlor, hunched over, his glasses pushed up onto his bald pate, gazing down, intently reading by the light of a single bulb. I knew that some months hence, when whatever piece I happened to be working on got published, Herb would read it and have me over to kibbitz about it: he'd be my best reader, and I was writing for him.

Though, it had to be said, over the last several months, Herb had suddenly started declining precipitously, and actually—it was tough to face but clearly true: he no longer sat there at night in the front parlor in that puddle of light, reading away. He was largely confined to his bed, which had been moved down into his living room because he could no longer make it up the stairs. A dear, spirited Trinidadian woman named Marjorie had moved into the house to care for him full-time. Herb was on his last legs. He no longer wanted to live: in considerable chronic pain and discomfort, all he anymore wanted was to be let to die.

Very early one morning a few months back, around four—it happened to be my birthday—I was startled awake by the phone. It was Marjorie, calling to tell me that Herb had just "breathed his last" and asking if I could come over to sit with her, she really didn't want to be alone with the body. My wife happened to be away, travelling, so after I got dressed, I went into my now-thirteen-year-old daughter's room to wake her and tell her what had happened. Sara took it pretty hard: she'd adored Herb, too. I told her where I'd be, how she should go back to sleep but if she wanted she could just look out her window and she'd be able to see me there across the street. I'd keep checking, I said, in any case.

And the morning proceeded like that: sitting by Herb's side, making the necessary calls, commiserating with Marjorie, occasionally peering through the window across the street to check on Sara (she was standing there, framed in her bedroom window, somber, intent, unmoving the entire time). Eventually the sun rose, the police arrived, then the coroners, and I headed back across the street to get Sara ready for school.

Sara came downstairs to greet me: she'd obviously been thinking. "Daddy," she said thoughtfully, "do you realize that Herb died on the very day that you became half his age? And that, for that matter, even though today is the thirteenth and I myself happen to be thirteen, in two days it will be seven days until I become exactly two-sevenths your age. Which is weird because at that point I will be two-times-seven and you are seven-squared and Herb was two-times-seven-squared, which of course also means that I will have become one seventh of Herb's age. And what's really weird, if you think about it"—clearly she'd been dwelling on all this, up there in the window her mind had been racing—"half of seven is 3.5 and you are going to be 3.5 times as old as me, or phrased differently, 35 years older than me."

I looked at her for a few long seconds and finally said, "Sara, get a life."

*   *   *

THAT EVENING I was back at my desk, working, when I happened to gaze up at the Barney photo. It had undergone a sudden transformation. Wait a second, I found myself thinking, I'm not the one the father and the girl are looking at—*I'm the father!* That's me, or almost: that's what I'm fast becoming. It was a startling, almost vertiginous shift in vantage.

A few weeks later, during a trip to Chicago, I happened into another gallery that happened to be staging a Tina Barney retrospective. I got to talking with the gallery owner, described the picture over my desk, and she averred as to how, yes, of course, she knew it, and in fact she happened to have a couple earlier pictures from the same series.

"The same series?" I asked.

Oh yes, she said, leading me into her storage vault and rifling among the framed images. Barney photographed the same father and daughter at least three times. Once when the girl was maybe ten or so—this one here (and indeed, there they were, draped on the same bed: the girl roughly the age my own daughter had been the day I happened on the later image at that Soho gallery)—and then another time, about three years after that, when the girl was thirteen or fourteen: this one... here. And indeed, there they were again, the same bedroom, the girl exactly my daughter's age: with exactly her haughty put-upon self-assurance ("Daaa-aaadie"). The gallery owner then pulled out a Barney book and turned to the last image in the series, the one over my desk. And yes, there they were again, same father, same girl.

Ten years: God, he had aged.

THE NAME MACHINE

by BEN MARCUS

I'LL NOT BE able to list each name we called my sister—the process would be exhausting, requiring me to relive my sister's pitiful life, and there are additionally copyright issues connected with persons that are officially the holdings of the government, which is still the case with my sister, despite her demise. To reproduce the precise arc of names that she traversed during her life in our "house" would be to infringe on a life-narrative owned by the American Naming Authority. It will suffice to select those names sufficiently resonant of her, that still seem to speak of the girl she was rather than of some general American female figure, although it could be argued that we can no longer speak with any accuracy of a specific person, that the specific person has evolved or lapsed and given way to the general woman, distinguished primarily by her name.

The names defined here derive from a bank of easily pronounceable and typical slogans used to single out various female persons of America and beyond. A natural bias will be evident toward names that can be sounded with the mouth. The snap, clap, and wave, while useful and name-like in their effect (the woman or girl is alerted, warned, reminded, soothed), are generally of equal use against men, and therefore of little use here. Gestures of language that require no accompanying vocal pitch, such as gendered semaphore, used in the Salt Flats during the advent of women's silent television, or Women's Sign Language (WSL), developed in the seventies as a

highly stylized but difficult offshoot of American Sign Language, now nearly obsolete because of the strenuous demands it placed upon the hips and
hands—were never successful enough with my sister to warrant inclusion in
the study. She plainly didn't respond to the various postures and physical
attitudes we presented to her—our contortions and pantomime proved not
theatrical enough to distract her into action. No shapes we made with our
hands could convince her that there was important language to be had in
our activity, and she often sat at the window waiting for a spoken name,
without which she could not begin the task of becoming herself.

This is certainly not to imply that "communication" between persons
and living things requires tone or sound, or that deaf figures of the female
communities can have no names. There is always written text, to be appre-
hended through visual or tactile means, as well as the German-American
technique of "handling" or squeezing the name of a woman onto her thigh,
a formalized body language, which when spoken against a girl is considered
a vote of confidence—"I believe in you"—although an adult woman might
find the contact to be patronizing. My sister, as it happens, did not respond
in any useful way to our repeated and varied handling of her body. As rough
as we were, it made no apparent impression on her.

Here the American female name is regarded as a short, often brilliant
word. Rarely should it inaccurately capture the person it targets, and its resistance to alternate uses, modifications, translations, and disruptions is an affir-
mation that individuals can and should be *entirely defined* by a sharp sound out
of the mouth—these definitions have simply yet to be developed and written.
Once they are, we will know what there is to know about all future persons
who take on one of the appellations listed in the American Bank of Names,
striving in their own particular way to become women of distinction.

Nicknames, admittedly, allow for a broader range of fetching, com-
manding, and calling, but the nickname only indicates an attribute or
device of a person, such as the length of her legs, the way she sleeps, how
she bounces a ball (in this case: Sticks, Taffy, Horse). A name, as the government instructs, can no longer be an accessory of a person but must be her
key component, without which the person would fold, crumble. She would
cease, in fact, to be a person. The nickname, and more particularly the
endearment (honey, doddy, love, lady), speak to a deeper mistrust of the
original name, a fear of acknowledging the person at hand. If it is possible
to change a person by changing her name, why not employ a name of
diminished potential and thus diminish or destroy the person? It's a valid
concern. When a man modifies or adorns a woman's name, or dispatches an

endearment into her vicinity, he is attempting at once to alter and deny her, to dilute the privacy of the category she has inherited and to require that she respond as someone quite less than herself. (Conversely, women who are scared of their own names are also typically afraid of mirrors.) The movement toward a single name for the entire female community (Jill, James, Jackie)—as aggressively espoused by Sernier and practiced by his younger employees—would disastrously limit the psychological and emotional possibilities for women and, rather than unify "them" as the Bible claims, probably force a so-called girls' war in their ranks, in which a large and cancerous body reduces itself into oblivion.

The task of my "family" in this regard was to process and unravel the names that arrived in the mail, then dispatch them onto my sister, generally with the naming bullhorn, a small seashell my mother carved for the purpose. We were enlisted by the government to participate in what was being called the most comprehensive book ever attempted, a study meant to catalog the names of American women. In the book, each name is followed by a set of tendencies that are certain to arise if the user employs the name as the full-time slogan for herself. The book is meant to serve as a catalog of likely actions, to not only predict various future American behaviors, but to control them. If the government regulates the demographics of name distributions, using a careful system of quotas, it can generate desired behaviors in a territory as well as prevent behavior that does not seem promising. It's not exactly a style of warfare as much as it is deep dramatic control over the country. The book remains unpublished, but its authors are reported to be numerous, somewhere in the thousands, each working blind to the efforts of the others. In my possession are only the notes taken during the naming experiments on my sister—an intuitive set of definitions of the names she inhabited. We were not instructed how to define the names we were given, only to "use" them, study them, employ whatever research we could devise. I therefore have no notion if our material was ever incorporated into the text. We submitted it promptly, but never received word on the matter.

We served up the names to my sister one by one and watched her change beneath them. Researchers here might say that she became "herself" or that it was her body expressing its name, as if something does not know what it is until the proper sound is launched at it. Each new morning that she appeared before us and we announced the name for the day through the bullhorn, we saw her become the new girl and release the old one, drop the gestures and habits and faces that the last name had demanded of her and start to search for the necessities of the new name.

I presume that other men launch their childhoods with sticks and mitts and balls, skinned knees, a sock full of crickets, and other accessories. They are shoved onto a lawn where they know the routine, can find the snake or book of matches, sniff out water, or sit in a children's ditch and "watch" the sky with their light and delicate heads. But I was the designated writer among us, unable to walk across grass or throw or catch or hide, equipped only with the stylus and pad, made to create our life in the form of notes on a page. This was unfortunate, because I don't like to write, I don't like to read, I like language itself even less. My "father" read to me as a boy and I was mannered enough not to stop him. It was unbearable—book after book that failed to make or change me, my father's lips twisting and stretching during a supposed "story" hour, massaging a stream of nonsense inside his mouth. I have always tried to be polite about words—good manners are imperative in the face of a struggling father wrestling with a system that has so clearly failed—yet I find language plainly embarrassing. It is poor form, bad manners, that so much hope is pinned to such wrong sounds out of the mouth, to what is really only a sophisticated form of shouting and pain. It is not pleasant for me to hear "foreign" languages, either. All languages are clearly alien and untrue, and absent of so-called meaning it is repeatedly clear that language is a social form of barely controlled weeping, a more sophisticated way to cry. To speak is to grieve, and I would prefer not to listen to a weeping animal all day and every day, sobbing and desperate and lost. Particularly when that animal calls itself my father.

EACH TIME WE changed my sister's name she shed a brittle layer of skin. The skins accrued at first in the firewood bin and were meant to indicate something final of the name that had been shed—a print, an echo, a husk, although we knew not what. They were soft in my hands, devoid of information and quite like what I always thought was meant by a "blanket," a boy's little towel, something to shield me from the daily wind that got into my room. It is not that the skins resembled a person any more, or stood for one, or acted as a map of the past. They were rather a part of my sister I could have to myself—soft, foldable, smelling of bitter soap, perhaps like a toy she might have used. I kept them for hand warmers, penciled my pictures into their flaky surfaces, draped them over my bedroom lamp for spidery lighting effects and the whiff of a slightly burnt wind. Maybe I smelled something deeper as the skins burned away on the bulb, floating in and out of the cone of light that enabled my infrequent passage from bed to door, at such times when my bedpan was full. There was nothing of food to the smell, only houses, hands, glass, and hair. And her. They smelled of her.

Oddly, these skins my sister shed seemed to serve as a repellant to my sister herself, as if smelling her own body was uncomfortable for her. She would not come near my room when I was using them. Nor would she approach me, particularly if I wrapped myself in parts of her old body and walked through the halls, or bathed in a caul of her husks, which would cling to my skin in a gluey callus when they were wet. No one, I would venture, likes to be understood as deeply as I was understanding my sister at that time, shrouding myself in the flakes of her body that she had lost, wearing her. She preferred, I assume, not to know me.

When the names ran dry, my sister pulled up short somewhere in the heart of the Learning Room. The mail had ceased, and no one was sure what to call her. She slept on the rug and scratched at herself, looking desperately to all of us for some sign of a new name, of which we had none. No one, as I mentioned, was sure what to call her, a problem that proved to be the chief void in her identity, which slowly eroded into nothing. There were no more skins, and one morning my sister lost her motion and folded into a quiet pose. Out of sympathy, we reverted back to her original name, or one of the early ones. I have to admit that I'm not sure what name she began with. Nor were any of us too sure, to be frank, whom exactly she had become.

[LISA]

BECAUSE THE WORD "Lisa" most closely resembles the cry heard within the recorded storms at the American Weather Museum, a crisply distorted utterance claimed to be at the core of this country's primary air storms, the girl or woman to carry the burden of the Lisa name carries also perhaps the most common sound the world can make, a sound that is literally in the air, everywhere and all the time. (Most wind, when slowed down, produces the sound "Lisa" with various intonations.) The danger is one of redundancy, and furthermore that a woman or girl cruelly named Lisa will hear her name so often that she will go mad or no longer come when called. Children learn that repeating a word makes it meaningless, but they don't know why. Briefly: weather in America occurs through an accumulation and disturbance of language, the mildest form of wind. To speak is to create weather, to supply wind from a human source, and therefore to become the enemy. The female Silentists are silent primarily to heal the weather, or to prevent weather, since they believe that speech is the direct cause of storms and should forever be stifled. A Silentist regards the name Lisa as the purest evil, given that, when heard, it commonly indicates an excess of wind, an approaching storm, possibly the world storm. The word "Lisa," to some Americans, is more dangerous than the words "fuck" or "fag" or "dilch." It should probably be discontinued. It can crush someone.

Statistics for Lisa: an early name of my sister. She rarely acknowledged it. It caused her anger. We could pin her to the floor with it. She drank Girls' Water and would peaceably wear a Brown Hat. Her Jesus Wind resistance was nearly zero. Rashes and facial weakness were frequent. A distressed tone to her skin. Her language comprehension was low, or else she showed selective deafness. A growling sound was heard when she wrote. She seemed blind to my father.

[ERIN]

THE ERIN IS a key girl in many American houses. It is often misnamed Julie, Joanne, or Samantha, and sometimes it is clothed as a man. As a man, it is still beautiful, although less visible, and prone to lose color during sleep. It makes love and has slender legs, while persons that see it are eager to palm the spot where the woman parts would be, to sweep and pan their hands over the heat of the man that is hiding her. Persons pry a finger into its mouth and feel weak and sweet in the legs, deriving pleasure through this gateway into Erin, breaking through the husk of a man's body into an inner body named Erin, sometimes breaking past that also to touch at the smooth core and stain their hands on it. There are text versions of Erin as well. Reading them is similar to seeing Erin. It takes a day to read the full version of Erin and the process is exhausting. The text cannot be memorized and sometimes the ending comes abruptly and frightens the reader. The first lusciously bright pile of Erin that the others feed from is located in Denver and kept warm by a man named Largeant. It must be swallowed quickly or it will cut and wound the mouth.

Statistics for Erin: my sister refused all clothing but an old, beige throw rug. She crawled around under the rug, mostly at night. No real language was exhibited, though she made rudimentary attempts at Burke. She seemed concerned to exhibit clean geometries with her body beneath the rug: circles, triangles, squares. We could not get her to wear a sleep sock. If she fainted, she did so without our knowledge.

[TINA]

THE TINA WILL die. It will emerge in Chicago and reside in chipped white houses of wood and warped glass. It will die quietly. When it does not emerge in Chicago there will be something uncertain and weak to its shape, a rough tongue, and hair that a father has unjustly handled. It will die on a Tuesday and the hands will go blue. There is promise to the newer Tina shape. It is blackened through ancestral practice, but can be watery in color. There is a milky storm nearby this Tina figure, and girl versions often dive into the heart of the wind for cleansings. Nothing by way of an answer is ever found in it. On its back is a mark, a freckle, a blister, a scar.

Statistics for Tina: my sister walked upright and spoke basic English. Her face approximated gestures of "happiness." Her nocturnal actions were mostly low-level postures of sleep. Excellent wind resistance. She showed confusion when we stopped calling her Tina. She had already decorated some of her belongings with this name.

[PATRICIA]

IT ISN'T THE most willing shape to swim or lunge or use force to motion over the road. The body prefers the easiness of a chair and a stick to point at what it likes. It is most fully in the Patricia style in the evenings, with brittle hairings and admirable mouth power. They have a Patricia everywhere now, sometimes many. There is no conflict in an abundance of it, which can be considered the chief difficulty. There are many and yet it seems as though there are none. It will be born in America and will exist most successfully as a child. Often, though, the Patricia system lives well into the last posture before demise, beyond the view of childhood. Age falls all over her and makes her walk down into the ground and sleep as though she lived in a grave. She calls out from her grave phone but the ringing sounds only like a dog sleeping and is ignored. It is then allowed to witness itself as an earlier thing, a thing best seen young. The older Patricia fights off the young girl Patricia. It will kill it down again and again, achieving nothing, but killing it nevertheless, creating space for something else that is new and wildly bodied. The young Patricia eats a large bowl of corn for pleasure. It weeps at the sight of water.

Statistics for Patricia: my sister was mostly pliant as Patricia. She willingly posed in several behavior statues for my mother. No resistance to the Brown Hat, which allowed her to converse fluently with several of my mother's assistants. They spoke a language that sounded like slow laughter.

[CARLA]

THERE ARE FABRICATIONS that go forth under the Carla tag. They are small-ish and brown-hued. There is an actual Carla at a school and it will learn to beat away the fake occasions of its own number. It will see one coming up the road, one little brown Carla, with fingers like American bread and a hairdo cut right out of the afternoon. The real Carla circles the false object and places fire on its living parts. Many times an American fire contains glittered fragments of a combusted Carla. There are fires in Ohio and girls are leading their dead parts into them. Every morning in every city young women are seen chancing a look back down the road. Sometimes a sluggish fat-skinned fake is sulking back there, waiting to take over and fail in Carla's place. When the Carla makes comfort with boys under trees and far-ther out on the landscape, there is an apology to the movement of its hands. It touches a boldly upright kid's penis and then palms the dust, the soot, the soil, feeling for the tremor of legs approaching.

Statistics for Carla: a name regularly used on my sister. She showed fre-quent bloating, and could not fit into the sleep sock. A Ryman Sock was used with much discomfort. Her evening mimes were striking as Carla. Often she could calm the entire household.

[NANCY]

I SAW ONE at a bed. It kneeled, it leaned. There was hair and a body and no such thing as weather, no window broken onto a wall, nor water rushing behind us, or a road to remind me I could leave. Something like this is wait-ing to happen for everyone. A room somewhere sweetened with a Nancy system. You can approach it and examine its teeth. They are the color of an old house and have chewed their way through something—a trap, a net, a man's hand. I let my arms operate like they did when I was a little boy. I "held" it. It did not bite, it did not speak. I stumbled. It gestured for me to rest. The Nancy shape cannot be detached from the woman it stands for. It can be released, to drag a bed—from a rope looped over its hips—into the city, putting to sleep the visitors that approach her and speaking to them certain facts, certain secrets as they dream, until they can rise from the sheets and move away from her into the distance, toward an area lacking all Nancy, dull and shoe-colored and simple, an American city with other kinds of "people," and life beyond restriction.

Statistics for Nancy: no skin was shed after my sister used this name. My father repeatedly scoured her skin with the pelt brush, to no avail. The only language she exhibited was to say "Nancy" until she collapsed with fatigue. A highly harmful name. Possibly a harmful word. None of us enjoyed calling her this.

[JULIE]

THERE IS PROBABLY no real Julie.

[LINDA]

FROM 1984 UNTIL the winter of 1987 an absence of significant registered Lindas spurred a glut of naming activity in that category, by parents eager to generate unique-seeming figures into the American landscape and thus receive credit for an original product, the Linda. The resulting children are emerging mostly out of Virginia, with a possible leader, or group of leaders, working through Richmond. Examples have been seen in the West—small and shockingly white with delicate eyes—but they have been poor in health and have not lasted. Weather cuts them down and hides their life until it is too late, and they die. Sometimes rain is blamed. Sometimes nothing but wind. The adult community—too old to register their names and therefore unable to receive the benefits of official status—has nevertheless been supportive of the surge. The tall and stately Lindas, with plenty of money and a husband, have politely vacated their homes, allowing the new Linda-children in for full access to their men, their things, their lives. The older ones enter a sack and wait.

Statistics for Linda: high-level exhaustion during the Linda phase. My sister showed bewilderment and frequently made evasive maneuvers. Quick on her feet and difficult to catch. Often we could not find her. She seemed frequently inclined to play dead. A non-useful name for her. Highly inaccurate. May have caused permanent damage.

[DEBORAH]

THERE ARE ABOUT fifty known pure examples of it in the Rocky Mountain area, some dating as far back as 1931. They are thought to improve the people they encounter. The usual number of finished girls in a territory as common as "Deborah" is twenty-eight, with a quota of twenty and a maximum limit of thirty-two. Any more than this should suggest a dilution of the original Deborah, which produces strains of Amy or Ellen. Although the mid-century Rocky Mountain persons had utilized a Deborah to comfort the saddest local families, reserving the medical Deborah for only the most dangerous cases of grief, the need for a cheer-spreading personage began to be felt at a national level, and abductions and faking occurred.

There is consequently an extreme Deborah in the East, possibly of Colorado origin but bred through men of the Mid-west (and therefore tall and reddish and chalky), dispensing a form of nearly unbearable, radical happiness into cities and homes. It is often housed in a little body, but its range is wide and its effect is lasting. To say "Deborah" is to admit to sadness, and ask for help.

Statistics for Deborah: she preferred modifications to her head when we called her this. No matter how far we launched her in the chair, my sister did not faint. Small emotional showings were on view: contentment and pleasure, occasional cheer. She attempted to embrace my mother, usually before bedtime, and my mother only barely escaped these approaches. Sometimes she endured long hugs from this Deborah.

[SUSAN]

FROM AFAR, THE Susan appears to be buckling, shivering, seizing, its body exhibiting properties of a mirage. Up close, there is mass to Susan and it is real to the touch. There will be food for you if you are Susan, although possibly a pile of food for Susan is a trap, to be regarded with suspicion. It is an elegant and refined system that established a school for itself, The Susan House. Its doctrine, The Word of Susan, is useful also to versions of Julia and Joyce but can be harmful to Judith. All of its books have gone unwritten.

Statistics for Susan: quite poor weather during this phase. My sister aged considerably and showed signs of acute attention and superiority. Insisted on privacy. Dressed formally. Seemed not of our family. Our presence confused her. She once asked my father how he knew her name. My father could not answer her.

[JESUS]

WOMEN ACHIEVE THEIR Jesus by speaking and studying their own name. The original Jesus figure examined his name, then derived actions and strategies from his analysis. This is the primary purpose of the Jesus noise— self-knowledge, instruction, advice. Women betray their Jesus when they forget that there is an answer at the heart of their name, to be divined or surmised by loud, forceful recitations of it in the streets, for as long as it takes. Simply saying "Jesus," however, is ineffective. (Breathing is the most common strategy for remembering our names.)

Statistics for Jesus: it was decided not to call my sister this. Mother felt we might lose her. But I tried it anyway one night when my parents were asleep. I had to use a low volume setting on the naming bullhorn and I whispered it at her while she slept. It was during an early Tina phase. She never woke. I sat at her bed all night and used this name against her until my mouth was exhausted. Nothing happened.

[FATHER]

TO REFER TO a woman as "Father" is to engage her inner name and fill her hands with power. It is a code that many American women respond to with energy and hope. It is therefore used as a healing noise, particularly at hospitals, where nurses utter the word "Father" to women who are ill or tired. When men make love to Father they use hearty motion and often call out words of labor and ecstasy; they thank Father, and they ask Father for more. Men in Utah, where this sort of naming is most frequent, take Father to the baths and hold her while rinsing her hair until she feels soothed and calm, until she is manageable and not crazy with power, or too big for her body, or at least not dirty and alone, which makes Father dangerous. In wealthy households, Father enters a boy's room and blackens it with a gesture of her hand, then starts in on the boy with warm oil on his thighs, squeezing the oil into his legs until he weeps or breathes easy. Father pulls back the sheets and she climbs in to treat the boy and teach him to live. A boy often first makes love to Father because she is gentle and confident, someone the boy can trust. He holds onto Father's hands when she straddles the bed and affects her graceful motion. A boy says, "Father" as she leans over him to help, dipping and rising, although sometimes the boy is quiet, preferring to feel her deepening attentions and not destroy the moment with speech.

Statistics for Father: chaos at the house. My real father was banished during this phase. He slept in the shed. I wanted to call him a girl's name, but I was not allowed to see him. My sister clearly thrived as Father: she boomed, she boasted, she tore through the house. She smashed the behavior television, she burned her old sleep sock. Mother was scared. A soothing litany of vowel songs were used on my sister to calm her down, without which she may have escaped. By the time the name would have worn off, she would have reached Akron. We restricted the study to two days. When we stopped calling her father, she shed the hardest skin of all the names. My mother removed it from the house before inviting my father back inside.

[MARY]

EVERY FIVE MINUTES, a woman named Mary will stop breathing. It is a favorite of children and every five minutes there are children standing in witness to the ending of Mary. Children clap at it when they see it. They are thrilled and they weep. Sometimes they become excited by a Mary that comes to die before them and they chase it and hit it. The Mary takes a wound. It holds up an arm and shields what is coming. It holds a wound in its hand and the children are delighted.

Statistics for Mary: she was mostly slumped over. This was near the end. We tried to groom her, but her body was cold. Her hair broke when you touched it. She weakened visibly every time we said Mary. She refused all food. In the mornings, she wrung her hands and wept quietly. Mother collected something from her face. Possibly some scrapings, possibly the smallest bit of fluid. Mary was the last thing we called her. It was possibly the name that killed her.

[. . .]

CERTAIN FACTIONS OF women go by a non-name and therefore participate in a larger person that is little seen or heard or known. It cannot be summoned or commanded. Generally it walks stiffly, owing to its numerous inhabitants. A body such as one not named can be toppled no doubt—felled and pinned to the turf, brought under control with water and a knife, some rope, and hard words. It is the primary woman from which many women have emerged, to which many will return. It is believed to reside in Cleveland. Probably it is bleeding and tired. By now it might be nearly finished.

Statistics: we treated my sister with silence at the end. We used an open-mouthed name that failed to break the air, no different from a deaf wind. A great deal of hissing was heard in the house, though we could not find the source of this sound. My sister's skin was clear. It would not peel. It would not shed. We waited near her slumped body. She stayed nameless. She retained her skin.

MORAN'S *MEXICO*:
A REFUTATION

by C. STELZMANN

THOUGH OSTENSIBLY BILLED as a translation of A. Stelzmann's *Mexico*, Kul-
tur- und Wirtschaftkundliches (Berlin: Otto Quitzow Verlag, 1927),
Moran's *Mexico* (Moscow, Idaho: Greb Editions, 1998) soon abandons this
pretense. Indeed, Moran's English 'translation' degenerates from first-rate
travel book into an unnamed narrator's first-person divagations through a
countryside possessed of only a marginal similarity to Stelzmann's Mexico.
All of Moran's major narrative acts—the unsettling encounter with what
the narrator calls the toothed chamber, the narrator's abandonment of the
'unfortunate American,' the odd rituals and etiquette practised in the (I
believe to be non-existent) town of Boya—none of these appear in my
grandfather's original travel guide. As an individual, my grandfather exhibited no similarity to the wastrel, the gadabout, the indifferent scoundrel
proffered as narrator of Moran's so-called translation. Indeed, my grandfather's Mexico, Kultur- und Wirtschaftkundliches eschews the first person
pronoun altogether. His travelbook remains consistently third person,
objectively rendered. Unlike Moran's, his descriptions of Northern Mexico's
culture and people are forever scrupulous, exact.

Moran's text departs from my grandfather's text at the beginning of part
ii of the foreword (page 17 of Moran's text, page 16 of the original). Prior to
this point the translation, though swollen with minor errors, has conveyed
the gist of my grandfather's original. From page 17 onwards, however,
translation becomes travesty.

Take, for example, the initial sentence of part ii of the foreword:

Das künftige Erfordernis der Weltpolitik ist ein Am-europa, Ein Amerika-Europa.

Clear, economical, the statement modestly proffers a defensible position vis-à-vis world politics and the state of the world economy in 1927. Moran translates the sentence as:

As I was out walking the streets of Laredo, as I was out walking Laredo one day, I spied a young German all wrapped in white linen—a linen of Am-Euro manufacture, white as Aunt May.

The sentence holds not even the remotest resemblance to my uncle's original. Only one term, "Am-Euro" is held in common. As for the rest, Moran seems to have forgotten what side of the Mexican-American border a book called *Mexico* should concern—after seventeen pages of introducing Mexico, Moran suddenly offers a sentence which thrusts an unidentified first person narrator, apparently a young German,[1] into a small Texas town. To what end? Who is this young German intended to be? My grandfather, surely, but he is unlike A. Stelzmann in every particular. What is the significance of his being wrapped in white linen? None of my American encyclopedias or other reference works can proffer an explanation.

Most puzzling of all is the perhaps metaphorical reference to an "Aunt May." My grandfather had strictly Bavarian aunts possessed of strictly Bavarian names (Gretta, for instance, wife of my maternal uncle Klaus Beringer, known for her spaetzle).[2] My research has definitively proven that Moran himself had no Aunt May.[3] The detail seems inserted merely to irritate the reader.

The proliferation of such irritants have caused certain less-than-promising young American jargoneers to wax loquacious over what they call my grandfather's "proto-postmodernism," or his "avant-post-modernism," or even "(pre)(post)modernism." The latter term strikes me as the most apt, but only if the letters "e-r-o-u-s" are inserted between the "t" and the "m." I am proud to say that none of the irritants that compel critics to christen the

---

[1] [Translator's Note:] Mr. Stelzmann (the younger) seems to have misunderstood the English original of the sentence, equating the "I" of the passage with the linen-wrapped German the "I" encountered. From there, he slides easily into the belief that the young German must represent his grandfather.

[2] [Translator's Note:] I have inquired of Mr. C. Stelzmann's cousins, easily accessible through the München telephone guide, who inform me that there is no relative christened Gretta in the family tree. There was a Gretel, wife of Kraus Beringer, but family oral tradition notes her not as an excellent preparer of spaetzle but as an abysmal preparer of all noodle dishes.

When I pointed out to these relatives the disparity between theirs and C. Stelzmann's account, they accused him of having a "vividly revisionary imagination." Indeed, C.'s reputation as a fabulist seemed a source of amusement to them.

[3] [Translator's Note:] In fact, Aunt May was the nickname of one of Moran's aunts: Aunt Mabel. The reference to Am-Euro linen, however, is more difficult to sort out, and perhaps is a satirical but obscure jab.

work postmodern can be blamed upon my grandfather. They are all the work of Moran, inserted into the English revision nearly seventy years after my grandfather first wrote. For this reason they cannot be seen as *proto* anything except the books written since Moran's *Mexico* was published. Had the so-called scholars bothered to cast even a passing glance at the German original, they would have realized that my grandfather's text isn't postmodern *gobbly-goo* and *pishradish*.[4] Rather, it is a genuinely robust travelbook which fits snugly, as all good travelbooks should, into the confines of its genre. It examines a particular Central American culture, provides readers with handy facts and pointers, offers maps to propel tourists from place to place, and all in all prepares one to pass through an alien culture unharmed, untouched. The only way one could mistake Moran's *Mexico* for being a translation of my grandfather's book through willful ignorance of the original German.

I, on the contrary, unlike the *postmodernescos*, have done my research. I have returned not only to the original text but to Moran's copy of my grandfather's *Mexico: Kultur- und Wirtschaftkundliches*, comparing the twain. This latter I had from among Moran's very possessions, at great inconvenience and cost.[5]

---

[4][Translator's Note:] The words *gobblygoo* and *pishradish* are both italicized in C. Stelzmann's original German and may be Stelzmann's attempt to show himself conversant in authentic American slang.

[5][Translator's note:] Details of C. Stelzmann's acquiral of said book are chronicled in a *Stillwater Newspress* article, published January 8 of last year:

MAD GERMAN INVADES LOCAL HOME

Police called to settle what they thought was a domestic disturbance last night got more than they bargained for.

Officer Clive "Jerry" Denkins and Officer Robert "Jersey" McKay arrived on the scene to discover the door to the residence ajar, shrieks coming from inside. They proceeded with caution, with weapons drawn. "We've learned from sad experience," said Officer "Jerry" Denkins, "that if you fail to prepare for the worst in this job, you prepare to fail."

The kitchen was empty. The bedroom was empty as well. The officers determined that the shrieking was coming from what Mr. Moran, the owner of the home, referred to as "the sunken living room."

In this sunken living room, a man had been stripped naked. He was gagged, tied to a chair. Another man, in his middle fifties and possessed of an unruly head of hair and a goatee, cavorted around him. He held an open book in his left hand. He slapped the book's pages repeatedly. "He was like some crazed Pentacostal minister," according to "Jersey" McKay. He was screaming in what the two officers at first thought to be gibberish, but which later proved to be the Germanic tongue.

"We thought at first we had walked in on some sort of Satanic ritual," suggested Officer "Jersey" McKay.

The assailant, one C. Stelzmann, a German national who had entered the country only a few days before on a tourist visa, is being held for questioning. The owner of the home, Mr. T. Moran, claimed not to know the intruder nor to have any idea of his intentions. Mr. Moran does speak German. He claims the intruder was mad and incoherent, and that he seemed to have mistaken him for someone else.

The first sixteen pages of Moran's copy of my grandfather's book are meticulously annotated, the margins offering English glosses of German words or phrases. At page sixteen, however, just one page before the first eight black and white plates in my grandfather's original, these responsible annotations cease. They are, I regret to say, never to be resumed. Instead, we find Moran writing his own narrative into the margins of and directly on the photographs found in my grandfather's book, obscuring the images with his hooked script, as if he is effacing the very world they depict. Which, in effect, he is.

The first eight photographs consist, respectively, of

- a map of Mexico tracing the path revolutionaries took in 1923 and 1924.
- a map of the world charting, in one corner, Mexican exports to Europe (imports from Europe to Mexico are not charted).
- an altitudinal map of Mexico, admittedly generalized.
- a map of the highlands of Northern Mexico.
- a picture of my grandfather's *Tarjeta de identidad* (the 2479th such identity card to be issued if the number stamped into the corner is to be believed). This is my grandfather's only "appearance" within the text.
- a photograph of a *charro*[6], stray dogs following at his heels as he peers into the window of a train.
- a regional *caudillo* spurring a horse up a steep set of villa steps.
- a cow standing before an old church-gate.

The maps and charts and identity card remain unblemished by Moran's pencil, Moran reserving his words to mar the final three photographs, those showing actual scenes from Mexico, though he does blot out the eyes on my grandfather's identity card.

The head of the *charro* is hemmed in by words, his face just preserved through deliberately larger gaps between words. It appears as though he is being smothered by language. Over the train window, slightly larger and in block letters, Moran has written in a speech bubble, "Is this the train to Boya?" The rest of the image—the dogs, the platform, the train—is run over and through by Moran's tiny script, which renders the images just barely discernable. The writing, too, is largely inseparable from the image, sometimes nearly impossible for this reason (and because of the poor hand-writing as well) to read.

---

[6][Translator's note:] in C. Stelzmann's original the word, in italics, is *churro*, the term for an elongated, sugar-sprinkled Mexican pastry. I have taken the liberty of substituting *charro*, the term he surely meant to use.

The picture of the horsed *caudillo* receives similar treatment. Visible, untouched by words, are the pale curve of the horse's neck, the mane above it as well. Barely visible: the seven convex steps of the villa, the balustrade. Threading through the words, an arrow points roughly up the steps. The horse's rider is wordridden, unblemished only at the elbow, and his face has been drawn over and erased repeatedly until nothing remains except a grayish dull ovular absence.

The cow of the final photograph of the series stands dumbly and in profile, head peering back at the camera so that the skin of the neck bunches and folds. The church-gate appears made of stone. It consists of an arch perhaps fifteen feet tall (assuming the cow to be average size), leading, not as one might expect, into a church, but instead into a courtyard of sorts, just a fraction of which is visible. The writing on this page is more controlled, for Moran has chosen to write only on the space within the archway and on the ribs of the cow. Within the arch we find the beginnings of Moran's description of Boya, which appears on page 19 of his "translation":

> The common entrance to Boya is a curious one: one first passes through the court of a partly-walled Church (Roman Catholic, certainly) directly into the plaza. Here one find a central fountain studded around its basin with a circle of carved stone masks....

And so on. From this description onward, Moran chooses to write exclusively about Boya, his book eschewing Mexico (despite retaining the title *Mexico*) for one town within Mexico. Or, rather, a town claimed to be in Mexico, for Boya makes an appearance on no atlas or map. As far as I have managed to determine, Boya does not exist.

"It is in Boya," Moran has written in minute script on the ribs of the cow, "that you shall meet your wife."

An intriguing presagement. My grandfather did not meet his wife there; he met his wife in Vienna's *Heldenplatz* during a riot of some sort, many years before his voyage to Mexico.[7]

Nor for that matter did Moran meet his wife there. His wife, in the few moments I had on the telephone with her before Moran realized to whom she was speaking, confessed to a) not speaking Spanish, b) never having gone to Mexico, c) having been born and raised in Picher, Oklahoma, a small town, so my atlas informs me, in the Northwest corner of the panhandled state[8]:

---

[7] According to C. Stelzmann's cousins, A. Stelzmann in fact met his wife at a cabaret in Dusseldorf.

[8] [Translator's note:]C. Stelzmann's original, properly translated, would accuse Oklahoma of being the "panhandling" state, begging perhaps from the other states around it. I have chosen to correct this to both suggest Oklahoma's moniker as "The Panhandle State" and maintain some sense of Stelzmann's odd usage.

certainly a pleasant midwestern town, white bread and checkered tablecloths, with none of the eccentricities of the imaginary Boya.[9]

Perhaps it is the photogenic cow who will find a wife.[10]

The remainder of Moran's narrative is inscribed upon the pictures and in the margins of Moran's copy of my grandfather's book. Though my grandfather's book clocks in at a total of 293 pages, Moran's *Mexico* amounts to only 122 pages. Apparently Moran hadn't the endurance my grandfather had.

Indeed, the majority of Moran's 122 pages take place in Boya. After elaborate description of the town and its customs, Moran focuses on three particular locales: the chamber of teeth, the body of a woman, a cave just outside the town.

The chamber of teeth appears on page 27:

> ...Then Rodriguez put down his glass on the table and said *Vaminos a la cama de dientes.*
> *La cama de dientes?* I inquired, certain I had either misheard or misunderstood.
> Si, he said, and curling his top and bottom lip showed me what remained of his own pearly grays.

A few pages later, they are walking, drunk, the mysterious (and previously unmentioned) Rodriguez and he, toward the edge of town. Moran wonders if Rodriguez plans to kill him. Indeed, it might have been better for everyone involved had Rodriguez killed Moran;[11] then Moran's *Mexico* would not have come into existence, and my grandfather's name would have remained unblemished.

The only reference to a so-called Rodriguez in my grandfather's original comes underneath a photograph entitled *Tortilla bereiteren: Tortilla ist der dünne Maisfladen, das Brot der Bevölkerung*, which shows a young woman grinding corn. She is perhaps twelve, chubby of face, her black hair in a long braid that hangs down one side of her chest. She wears a spotted blouse and a light-coloured plaid shirt. She is on her knees on a stone floor, push-

---

[9][Translator's note:]In fact, C. Stelzmann is wrong about Picher; it has at least as many eccentricities as Boya, perhaps more. Picher is a mining town, built up around a series of lead retrieval operations which have left chat piles of chalky, flaky limestone chips throughout the area, some more than 80 feet tall. The mining has left hollow spaces under the town; from time to time the ground will rush out from under a house, the house collapsing, or a child will disappear, sucked under the ground. It is an odd, unearthly town, the landscape grey and moonlike, the population in steady decline.

[10][Translator's note:] C. Stelzmann, who seems to have no knowledge of animal husbandry, apparently does not realize the animal photographed is a cow, a female, and thus not likely to search for a wife.

[11][Translator's Note:] C. Stelzmann's unstated assumption that the narrator of the Moran's *Mexico* must be Moran (a revision of the earlier assumption that the narrator must refer either to his grandfather or to Moran) remains problematic. There is no convincing textual evidence to suggest that this must the case, that the "I" of Moran's Mexico is anything but a device.

ing down on a firehardened slat and drawing it over the crushed kernels. Below the picture it says: *phot. J.R. Rodriguez, Mexico*. Moran's copy has the name of the photographer encircled in pencil. Significantly enough, all that remains unmarred of the girl's picture is her smile, her shining teeth.

Beside the picture, Moran's text continues:

> There was at the edge of town, off the road a few dozen paces, an old and wavering animal track that was beginning to acquire the characteristics of a path. We followed the path through low hills for perhaps ten minutes, I thinking all the while that this was mere preparation for my robbery and subsequent murder, yet fascinated and willing to continue nonetheless.

This is potentially bad advice for travelers. Moran encourages them to take actions that will cause their throats to be cut. *Suite*:

> ...[T]hen out of the darkness loomed a pale shape, coming distinct—a house—as we approached. Rodriguez removed a key from his pocket and opened the door. Once inside, we fumbled in darkness until he managed to light a candle, a stub of a thing lying on a table. Holding it carefully to keep hot tallow from dribbling over his knuckles, he opened the room's only other door and guided me into another chamber.
> There was something odd about the walls, I could see from the flickering candle, but it was not until he thrust the candle near to both the walls and my face that I saw the wall studded with row upon row of teeth, some human, most animal. He took me from wall to wall and stupefied I saw each surface covered with teeth, the room always at my throat.

The continuation—the coercion of a tooth from Moran himself for the walls of the room (a lie; when I saw him Moran had all his teeth)—is of little interest for our purposes.

The woman's house comes next. This story begins in No. 3 pencil beside a drawing entitled *Altmexicanisches Badhaus: Heizung erfolgt von dem vorgebauten Häusen aus*, which shows a roundish bathing structure with smoke or steam rising from an opening in its roof.

Writes Moran, directly on the drawing:

> I first made the acquaintance of the woman in the clapboard house purely by hazard.

—Moran has moved from an image of a bathhouse to an unlikely clapboard house, either from laziness or from perversity. He continues—

> I became aware of having lost my pen, a gift from Uncle Ferber....

—Moran's genealogy claims no Uncle Ferber, nor does he mention this pen elsewhere in his narrative. My grandfather too had no such uncle, no such pen—

> ... and wandered back along the path I had taken earlier that morning. Keeping my eyes down I managed to walk right into a woman, both of us tumbling down.

—Too much! We have entered the world of slapstick and unbelievable coincidence, an arena already exploited by the silent cinema. Has he no shame?—

> Soon a friendship was established....

—Note Moran's rapid passage over this event, precisely the useful information one hopes to find explicated in full in a first-rate travel guide: i.e. how *does* one befriend the natives?—

> ...which led to the shucking of clothing and a most unusual incident which I record though I still remain a little baffled by what precisely occurred.... [I pass over here a long and futile description of the route from the fountain of masks to the villa.] At the top of the villa steps she began to wax lyrical concerning the sexuality of sound, particularly the sound that bodies make, the odd ebb and wash that goes on beneath flesh. We sat on the steps and she coaxed me to lie back until I was flat on the dirt. She placed her head against my torso, her ear against my head, and began to describe in telegraphic Spanish what she was hearing.
>
> After a time she helped me sit again and lay back herself, pressing my head to her belly.
>
> I spoke haltingly of what I heard and she became dissatisfied. She asked me to bring my microphone and a reel-to-reel so as to record the sounds of her belly and allow her to listen to them herself. When I indicated that I had no such device, she looked at me strictly, then left.
>
> I was never to see her again.

What, I ask, does this have to do with Mexico? What possible connection can be drawn? This is anecdotal information, not useful to the reader of a travel guide. Indeed, it will give the reader precisely the wrong idea of what Mexican women are like. Imagine the poor misinformed tourist, bridling his own natural sexual impulses so as to wander the Sonoran countryside slung with tape recorder and microphone.

In any case, Moran's story of the woman is patently untrue. No such woman ever existed, nor is any such woman likely to exist.[12]

The third incident might be considered unusual were it verifiable. It begins near the end of the book, and seems based roughly on comments by A. Stelzmann that "there are ample caves in the hills and mountains of Sonora." Beside this statement, in any case, Moran begins his own incident:

> There are ample caves, some of them quite dangerous, as I know from my experiences with the unfortunate American.

---

[12] [Translator's note:] C. Stelzmann seems ignorant of the case of Stella Braun, mentioned in Bobbs-Merrill *Yearbook Annual: 1979*, the supplement to their best-selling *Worldbook Survey*. Miss Braun, it seems, awoke one morning listening to the beating of blood in her head. Something about the sound, which she surely had heard many times before without rightly perceiving it, fascinated her; she found herself with no desire to move. She was discovered by a neighbor almost twelve days later, in a state of extreme torpor and near death, still intent on listening to her own blood. Only the white noise of a vacuum cleaner broke the spell. After recovering, Miss Braun learned to cope with her condition by keeping a radio on and between stations at all times, playing static loudly night and day to silence the sound of blood.

This "unfortunate American" does not appear either in my Grandfather's original nor elsewhere (aside from the cave experience) in Moran's narrative. He is never physically described, never named; little information is offered in connection with him. Critic Simon Bladlock's suggestion[13] that he represents "Arlen Jenkins, an American of middle age" who disappeared in Mexico in early 1927 is not without merit, though Bladlock clearly does not recognize that the incident is not in my grandfather's original text.[14]

> ...We went down the tunnel, the unfortunate American leading the way. We had no torch, though the American did have a gas lighter which he would spin on from time to time so as to gather his bearings. I had a piece of chalk and each time we came to a branching I would mark the wall of the passage we took. Unfortunately, I allowed the American to make the choice each time.
>
> We came down into a passage that narrowed considerably. I encouraged the American to turn back but he remained convinced that the passage would open up soon. Water was up to our ankles, and we tromped through it, the American now with his lighter on more often than off. We came to a place where the passage angled and narrowed so severely that we had to bend ourselves backward and continue by pulling our backs along the rock. The shirts over our chests were cut by the stone we scraped past. We could not fully inflate our lungs, and as we wormed forward we were forced to take smaller and smaller breaths.
>
> At last, we could move by only bits and starts, squeezing our way along, pushing our breath completely out and then moving and then drawing breath back in. The pressure of stone was always against our backs, our chests. There was the impression of slow suffocation. Then I heard a scraping and the American cried out. Then he flicked on the lighter and I saw in the wavering light his head a good foot lower than my own, his legs submerged to the knees, his chest wedged tightly against the rock.
>
> "I'm stuck," he said.
>
> "Come back toward me," I said.
>
> "I can't," he said. "My feet aren't touching anything." And then the light flicked off. I reached out best I could, but could do nothing for him in my own straited condition.
>
> "Give me the lighter," I finally said.
>
> "Don't leave me," he said, and then my hand tried to take the lighter from his own. "I'll drop it," he said. But I already had the lighter in my own hand and a moment later had begun to move my way slowly backward, wriggling my way free. He was crying out, perhaps screaming. Then I was down the other passages, out in sunlight, back to open air.
>
> I have kept the lighter, a wheel-spun affair, to this day.

The metaphor is perhaps apt; like the unfortunate American, my grandfather (admittedly neither unfortunate nor American) has been left alone in the

---

[13][Author's Note:] c.f. Simon Bladlock, "Note: on the 'Unfortunate American' in A. Stelzmann's *Mexico*," *Notes and Queries* (Spring 1998): 33-34.

[14][Translator's Note:] According to both the title page of *Notes and Queries* and to Bladlock himself, the title of his paper was "Note: ... Moran's *Mexico*" rather than "Note: ...Stelzmann's *Mexico*." From a letter dated June 1st from Bladlock to the translator:

> I have no interest in Stelzmann's text, which I have examined in detail and which, it is clear to me, is no more than an ordinary travel guide. I specifically distinguished between Moran's text and Stelzmann's text in my title and in the text that follows. C. Stelzmann clearly has an agenda: discrediting the Moran text by whatever means possible, including willful distortion of the facts.

dark, abandoned by Moran's translation. We too as readers are left at loose ends, abandoned, benighted as we try to use Moran's travel guide to navigate the real space of a real country. We remain wedged in the cave of the text, unable to work our way free and back into living, breathing Mexico.

One might thus aptly conclude this brief study [Leistungwerk] with the final image Moran's *Mexico* offers, a photograph tacked on to the end of the narrative, printed on the back cover of the book itself. The photograph is attributed to "Stelz, Mexico," and the caption reads simply "Das Doppelbild." It shows a bare patch of earth, hard and shiny, perhaps a sunlit section of the earthen floor of a house. Across it is spread a shadow. The curve of shoulders and arms, the shape of a torso, the beginnings of a head, are discernable yet distorted, as if the image is either beginning to focus or is coming asunder, moving toward greater collapse. It is to us to determine which it shall be: focus or collapse. Shall we choose the former and allow Moran's *Mexico*, with its constructed narrator, its false town and imagined characters, to stand? Or shall we opt rather to dismember the text so as to see the face behind it, smothered under Moran's words, but still addressing us nonetheless?

—*Translated by Brian Evenson*

THE
FERNANDO PESSOA
SOCIETY

by RACHEL COHEN

ALL THROUGH THE rainy city of Lisbon there are traces of Portuguese poet
Fernando Pessoa (1888–1935). Plaques have been placed on the walls near
the office where he worked, and in the Rua Coelho da Rocha, where he lived
first with his mother and then, toward the end of his life, with his married
sister. Pessoa's favorite café was the Café Brasileira on the Largo do Rato,
where a bronze statue of him now sits among the tables. In Portugal, he is
considered inarguably the foremost Portuguese poet of the 20th century,
bookstores carry all his books, and Portuguese people speak fondly of him.

When he was alive, he was not that well known—a few of his poems
appeared in the only two issues of the literary review *Orpheu*, which Pessoa
helped to found and edit in 1915. His epic poem, "Message," concerning
the great seafaring history of Portugal ("O salty sea, so much of whose salt/
Is Portugal's tears!"), was published and was a success—the only book he
published in his lifetime.

Pessoa supported himself by writing business correspondence in English
and French, at various offices, for more than twenty years. In 1920, and then
again in 1929, Pessoa was briefly in love with one of the secretaries who
worked at one of these offices. She had the unlikely name of Ophélia Quieroz.
He wrote her more than fifty letters, kissed her once at the office, and used to
ride home with her on the tram, but this seems to have been the extent of
their courtship. Usually, he walked from his home back and forth to the office.

Pessoa wore a black hat and round spectacles and had a small moustache, in the fashion of the day. In pictures he stands or sits slightly to one side, removed from the other people in the photos. He is never touching anyone. Pessoa used to walk the streets of Lisbon fairly constantly, drifting in and out of the mist and his own internal miasma. In the evenings, he often stopped at the Café Brasileira, or at a little restaurant for dinner, and then he went home and wrote.

He preferred to write standing up, leaning on a high wooden dresser. He wrote thousands upon thousands of pages of poetry and prose—at last count there were 25,426 scraps and manuscript pages: he wrote on playbills, typing paper, ledger paper, cocktail napkins, train tickets, café stationery, torn bits of brown paper, and so on. At his death, this material was left in a trunk with his sister, and gradually people interested in his work began sifting through it. A group of scholars from Portugal, France, Italy, and, in more recent years, the United States, have made a kind of cottage industry out of piecing together the life and work of Pessoa. The scholars live in Lisbon, not far from the archive, and publish new translations and updated editions as material is discovered or their best guesses become convincing.

Sorting out Pessoa's work is somewhat tricky. To begin with, he left much of it intentionally unfinished, half-poems scrawled in the margins of incomplete philosophical inquiries. He was an inveterate reviser, so that next to a line of poetry there may be six or seven alternative versions, with no indication of whether he considered any of them final. To complicate matters, Pessoa wrote in more than seventy personas. He called them his heteronyms, and each one was a fully formed writer with a biography and a literary style, influences, and preferences. Among the heteronyms are four major poets—any one of whom could be rated the greatest Portuguese poet of the 20th century—and some number of prose writers, translators, social scientists, and avant-gardists. Together they are a phenomenon.

*   *   *

ALBERTO CAEIRO, ÁLVARO de Campos, Ricardo Reis, Bernando Soares, and Fernando Pessoa the poet, who was not quite the same as Pessoa the man, make up the brightest constellation in the Pessoa universe. These writers rely on one another's work for their existence, with the four poets—Caeiro, Campos, Reis, and Pessoa—forming a kind of literary society. They were followers of one another's work; they translated and wrote introductions for each other's poetry, and carried on long written arguments over matters of aesthetics and philosophy. Pessoa found a way to invent writers so that it was as if they, like any real writer, had invented themselves. They created one another: as each added his voice, the others grew fuller, until each voice was whole. He was a very lonely man, Pessoa, a poet in a city almost without poets. But he found, in the eternity of waiting to which life seemed to condemn him, that he could keep himself company, interrupting himself with his many selves.

*   *   *

WHEN HE WAS five, Pessoa's father and infant brother both died. It was at about this time that Pessoa began making up imaginary friends and receiving letters from them. When Pessoa's mother remarried, Pessoa went with her to South Africa to join his stepfather, who was part of the Portuguese diplomatic envoy. In Durban, Pessoa attended an English school, and wrote in both English and Portuguese. His imaginary friends, then numbering at least a half-dozen, all wrote a newspaper together when Pessoa was in high school. Each had his own byline. Some of these childhood companions made the journey back to Lisbon with him when was seventeen; the major, adult heteronyms appeared somewhat later.

In some accounts, Pessoa writes that the major heteronyms were a response to a challenge made by his closest friend, Mario de Sá-Carneiro, with whom Pessoa founded *Orpheu*. Sá-Carneiro is supposed to have asked Pessoa if he thought he could invent a "rather complicated bucolic poet" and "present him… as if he were a really living creature." In other accounts, Pessoa explains that he created the fictional pastoralist to play a joke on Sá-Carneiro. In any case, somewhere around 1914, as Europe grew tenser and Pessoa fuller of contradictory poetic impulses, inspiration came.

Some twenty years later, Pessoa wrote a now well-known letter in which he reports the circumstances of the birth of Alberto Caeiro and the other poetic heteronyms:

> I spent a few days working on him but got nowhere. The day I finally gave up—it was March 8, 1914—I went over to a high desk and, taking a piece of paper, began to write, standing up, as I always do when I can. And I wrote some thirty poems, one after another, in a kind of ecstasy, the nature of which I am unable to define. It was the triumphant day of my life, and never will I have another like it. I began with the title, *"The Keeper of Sheep."* What followed was the appearance of someone in me whom I named, from then on, Alberto Caeiro. Forgive me the absurdity of the sentence: In me there appeared my master. That was my immediate reaction. So much so that scarcely were those thirty-odd poems written when I snatched more paper and wrote, again without stopping, the six poems constituting *Oblique Rain*, by Fernando Pessoa. Straight away and completely… It was the return of Fernando Pessoa/Alberto Caeiro to Fernando Pessoa himself. Or better, it was the reaction of Fernando Pessoa against his nonexistence as Alberto Caeiro.

Once Alberto Caeiro appeared, I tried—instinctively and subconsciously—to find disciples for him. Out of his false paganism I plucked the latent Ricardo Reis, whose name I discovered and adapted to him, because at that stage I already had seen him there. And suddenly, deriving in opposition to Ricardo Reis, there impetuously arose in me a new individual. At once, and on the typewriter, there surged up, without interruption or correction, the "Triumphal Ode" of Álvaro de Campos—the ode of that title and the man of that name.

I then created a nonexistent coterie. I arranged it all in real patterns. I gauged influences, I knew the friendships, I heard inside me the discussions and divergences of opinion, and in all this it seems that it was I, creator of it all, who was least present. It appears that everything went on independently of me. And it still seems to go on that way. If some day I can publish the aesthetic discussions between Ricardo Reis and Álvaro de Campos, you'll see how different they are and how I myself have nothing to do with the matter.

— Letter to Adolfo Casais Monteiro, January 13, 1935,
from Always Astonished, *translated by Edwin Honig.*

This isn't the only version of the story: some poems later attributed to these poets were clearly written in advance of this quadruple birth date, and then there were poems attributed first to one and then to another of the poets. But the basic outline is close enough. In Fernando Pessoa were born a number of poets, including Fernando Pessoa, and they drew each other into existence, the writing and styles of each one necessitating the others. It is one of those strange fated coincidences that the word "pessoa" in Portuguese means both person and persona, so that as he created his selves out of himself he was both making and unmaking his own name.

*   *   *

ALBERTO CAEIRO (1889–1915) IS the pastoralist of an imagined landscape. He is supposed to have lived in the country with an elderly aunt from his mother's side of the family. He died of tuberculosis, at the age of twenty-six, though poems by Caeiro have surfaced since that were clearly written after 1915. But then this is Pessoa's story, and he gets to tell is as he likes.

The first poem of *The Keeper of Sheep*, Caeiro's magnum opus, is called "I Never Kept Sheep." The poem is Caeiro's way of bringing himself into being:

I never kept sheep,
But it's as if I'd done so.
My soul is like a shepherd.
It knows wind and sun
Walking hand in hand with the Seasons
Observing, and following along…

I've no ambitions or desires.
My being a poet isn't an ambition.
It's my way of being alone.
And if sometimes in my fancy
I desire to be a lamb
(Or the whole flock of sheep
So I can go all over the hillside
And be many happy things at the same time),
It's only because I feel what I'm writing when the sun sets
Or when a cloud's hand passes over the light
And a silence runs off through the grass...

I greet everyone who'll read me
Tipping my wide-brimmed hat to them
As they see me at my door
Just as the coach tips the top of the hill.
I salute them and wish them sunshine,
And rain when rain is called for,
And may their houses contain
Near an open window
Somebody's favorite chair
Where they sit, reading my poems.
And when reading my poems thinking
Of me as something quite natural
An ancient tree, for instance,
In whose shade they thumped down
When they were children, tired after play,
Wiping the sweat off their hot foreheads
With the sleeve of their striped smocks.

— Translated by Edwin Honig and Susan M. Brown

The reader finds peacefulness in Caeiro's poems. It's as if Caeiro has accepted everything and done so without effort, as if perhaps he was born into a condition of acceptance. There is no striving here, no ambition, no fear, no anxiety. It rains because it does, and he writes because he does.

As Ricardo Reis, an ardent follower of Caeiro, explains it, "the only thing a stone tells him is that it has nothing at all to tell him." The strange thing about this is that, while this is a perfectly possible state of mind for a philosopher, or a religious person, it is one that, as Reis says, *"cannot be conceived in a poet,"* (italics his.)

It's not surprising that the other Pessoa poets—all more neurotic, all dragged down by melancholy, and occasionally lofted into the sky by an explosive joy or a deep conviction of future grandeur—should find welcome refuge and inspiration in the quietly assured verses of Alberto Caeiro, whom they all called their master.

Reis found his own poetic expression after reading Caeiro and describes it with a metaphor appropriate to his profession—he was a doctor: "I was as a blind man at birth in whom the possibility to see was given; and my knowledge of *The Keeper of Sheep* acted as a surgical instrument that opened my eyes to seeing." And Reis, in turn, became part of Caeiro's understanding of the world. As Álvaro de Campos remembers it: "[Caeiro] said: 'that young fellow there, Ricardo Reis, who's a pleasure to meet—he is quite different from himself.' And then he added, 'Everything is different from us, and that's why everything exists.'"

For Campos, who understood life as a series of sensations, many of them sexual, these revelatory words struck him physically: "The sentence, spoken like an axiom of the earth, overtook me like an earth tremor, like all first possessions, striking the rock bottom of my soul. But contrary to material seduction, its effect on me was suddenly to feel through all my senses a virginity I'd never experienced before."

Caeiro's effects were as various as his followers. Writing in 1916, the year after Caeiro was supposed to have died, Pessoa, actually writing as Pessoa, explains: "operating on me myself, [Caeiro] freed me from shadows and trash, gave my inspiration more inspiration and my soul more soul. After all that, so prodigiously accomplished, who will ask if Caeiro existed?"

A purely Pessoan idea of existence: that which influences exists. In this way, the Pessoas, with their enormous influence on each other and on succeeding generations, have more existence than most poets. Álvaro de Campos, for example, is frequently a good deal more real to us than anyone else living in Lisbon in 1916.

*　　*　　*

CAMPOS (1890–) WAS A maritime engineer, who received his training in Glasgow and made a voyage to the Orient, as he called it. His early poems, based on his travels, have a certain indolence not characteristic of the later, great Campos poems, primarily because he wasn't yet under the influence of the poet who would mean the most to him.

Campos met Caeiro when their cousins, who happened to be friends, introduced the two poets. Campos describes the meeting in a fragment of a memoir:

> First, the blue eyes of a child who is not afraid; then, the cheekbones already a bit prominent, complexion rather pale, with a strange Greek cast that was all calmness come from within, and not as an outer expression of facial features. The hair, rather thick, was blond, but away from the light it turned brown. He was of medium height, seeming taller, more

stooped, not having high shoulders... The expression of his mouth, the last thing one noticed—as if for this man speaking was less than being—was like a smile one attributes in verse to beautiful inanimate things, a smile meant simply to please us—flowers, lush meadows, sunlit water—a smile of existence, not of speech.

— Notes on the Memory of My Master Caeiro, translated by Edwin Honig

There may be a certain attraction underlying this description. Though lovers are rarely part of Pessoa's descriptions of his heteronyms, Campos expresses more homosexual impulses than do the other Pessoa poets. Who knows exactly what Campos's feelings about Pessoa were, but Campos twice broke up Pessoa's relationship with Ophélia Queiroz by sending her interfering letters, suggesting that she forget all about Pessoa.

In Lisbon, you feel closest to Álvaro de Campos when you go down to the main square, the Praca do Commercio, with its grand equestrian statue, and look out over the Tagus at the ships coming and going. Campos was a poet of the sea. He was also an observer of the physical and the chief figure in the Sensationist movement, in fact probably the only figure. Campos's Sensationist motto, from his poem "Time's Passage" is "to feel everything in every way." One of his great poems is "Maritime Ode," in which Campos stares out at the docks, senses a slow gathering of purpose, wishes for the old days of sailing schooners, and writes:

> As I think of this—O madness! As I think of this—O fury!
> Thinking of my straight-and-narrow life, full of feverish desires,
> Suddenly, tremulously, extraorbitally,
> With one viciously vast and violent twist
> Of the living flywheel of my imagination,
> There breaks through me, whistling, trilling, and whirling,
> This somber, sadistic rutting itch for all strident seafaring life.
> Hey there, sailors, topsmen! Hey crewmen, pilots!
> Navigators, mariners, seamen, adventurers!
> Hey, ships' captains! Men at the helm and at the masts!
> Men asleep in their crude bunks!
> Men sleeping with Danger peering in at the portholes!
> Men sleeping with Death as a bolster!
> On the immense immensity of the immense ocean!
>
> ... I want to take off with you, I want to go away with you,
> With all of you at once,
> To every place you went!

— Translated by Edwin Honig and Susan Brown

From here, the poet all but lifts off in a great masochistic parabola, rising to meet the pirates who will flay him and nail his skin to the deck, and he will feel it and feel it in every way. Page after page, stanza after stanza, he approaches the mystery… and then pulls back, taking pleasure again in modern, mechanized life, finding poetry in the world as it is. Then, once again, joy builds:

> Seaports full of steamships of every conceivable type!
> Large and small, and all painted differently, each with variously aligned portholes
> From such a delicious plethora of shipping companies!
> Each steamer in port so unique in its well-marked mooring!
> So festive the quiet elegance of its commercial traffic on the seaways,
> Over the ever ageless Homeric seaways, oh Ulysses!

After this passage, Campos's poem gets quieter and more abstract, short phrases occasionally burst out—"Life's complexity!" The poem drifts gradually away, the writer still standing, looking out to sea.

Campos was, not surprisingly, a lover of Whitman, and wrote a poem called "Salutation to Walt Whitman." Eighty years later, continuing the tradition of poetic exuberance, Allen Ginsberg wrote "Salutations to Fernando Pessoa." Somehow one doubts that Campos would have reached his own peculiar level of exaltation without his close association to the other quieter and sadder poets. Each Pessoa poet was balanced by the existence of the other poets; each one anchored his work in a different part of the interior world. All of these poets are complex and self-contradictory: Álvaro de Campos is not just a poet of lust and euphoria. Perhaps Campos's best poem, perhaps the best Pessoa poem of all, is "The Tobacco Shop," which begins, "I'm nothing, I'll always be nothing," and continues through a long melancholic worry about the inconsequentiality of the poet's life. He is rescued from his pensive depression when he sees, across the street, a man he knows coming out of the tobacco shop, who, upon recognizing the poet at his window, lifts his hand and waves. The poet waves back, "and the universe/ Reorganizes itself for me." Although its self-doubt would seem to mark this poem as a work by Pessoa himself, or possibly by Bernando Soares, the assistant bookkeeper, the poem, with its long looping lines and grandiose bursts, is recognizably a Campos poem. Even in Campos's great Whitmanesque moments when he is most full of the "somber, sadistic rutting itch for all strident seafaring life," he always feels the constraint of his "straight-and-narrow" life. The poignancy of "The Tobacco Shop" comes from the possibility of euphoria lingering in the background, the dreamed-of, and so-rarely-felt connection to other people, for which all the Pessoas occasionally yearn.

* * *

RICARDO REIS (1887–) WAS a monarchist, an unpopular position after the Portuguese Republic was formed in 1919, and one that forced him into exile in Brazil. Old-fashioned in many ways, Reis focused his attention on the Horatian Ode and wrote dozens of these, often addressed to a woman named Lydia. His brother Frederico (many of the Pessoa heteronyms come with brothers in tow) coined the now-common description of Reis's poetry: "sad Epicurianism."

Pessoa describes Reis as being taller than Caeiro, but not as tall as Campos; his complexion is "a vague, dull brown." While Campos has a distinct physical presence, "between fair and swarthy, a vaguely Jewish Portuguese type, hair therefore smooth and normally parted on the side, monocled," Reis's appearance is nondescript. He's a little bit empty. He is a doctor, but Pessoa says little else about his professional life. In some of his poems he takes careful note of people's injuries, particularly ones that happen to children. Reis's emptiness has much in common with Caeiro, the keeper of sheep who never kept sheep. Both poets are less present, physically, than, say, Campos. Reis's writing is controlled, placid, with none of the strident emotion of Campos. Reis merely takes up a quiet corner of this world, from which he writes:

> I love the roses in Adonis' garden,
> I love those caterpillars, Lydia, roses
>   That on the day they are born,
>   On that day they die.
> Light is eternal to them, because
> They are born with the sun already in place,
>   And they finish up before Apollo
>   Has run his visible course.
> Let us, too, make of our lives one single day,
> Willingly unaware, Lydia, that night
>   Comes before and night follows
>   The moment that we endure.

— From Self-Analysis, translated by George Monteiro

Endurance is a crucial Reis characteristic in José Saramago's novel, *A Year in the Death of Ricardo Reis*. At the opening of Saramago's novel, Reis has returned to Portugal from Brazil, just missing Fernando Pessoa, who has died. In Lisbon, Reis meets a chambermaid named Lydia. He sleeps with her, though he really loves Marcella, a young woman with a paralyzed hand. And all of this is perfectly plausible. Reis could certainly have slept with a woman and fallen wholly in love, things that Pessoa seems not to have done himself, and which remain utterly impossible for the other poets. Reis is a poet with a deep sense of history and metaphor, of the relations between things, and this supports an unusual capacity for relationships with people. Saramago's choice is exactly right—it would be Reis who would live on.

*   *   *

IN 1915, ALBERTO Caeiro, the heteronym who most influenced the other writers, died of tuberculosis. This was just around the time that Mario de Sá-Carneiro, Pessoa's closest friend, killed himself in Paris. Sá-Carneiro's death seems to have been devastating for Pessoa; Caeiro's death tore a hole in the Pessoa universe. Campos wrote of his regret at not being with Caeiro when he died:

> In any case, it was one of the sorrows of my life—the real sorrow among so many fictitious ones—that Caeiro should die without my being at his side. Such stupidity on my part is more human, and so be it.
> I was in England; Ricardo Reis himself was not in Lisbon, he was on his way back to Brazil. Fernando Pessoa was there, but it is as though he was not. Fernando Pessoa feels things but doesn't react, not even inwardly.

— Notes on the Memory of My Master Caeiro, translated by Edwin Honig

How deeply they know each other! Campos says what Pessoa cannot, though Pessoa would probably agree with him. Campos suggests that Pessoa lacks contact with the world, or is unable to express his feelings for the world. Instead, Pessoa sends out these emissaries—his Pessoas of feeling and embracing and knowing.

Pessoa himself was a poet of anxiety, an absent and invisible poet. Pierre Hourcade, who knew Pessoa at the end of his life, said that he could never bring himself to turn around and look back after saying goodbye to Pessoa: "I was afraid I would see him vanish, dissolved in air." Many collections of Pessoa's work tack on his own writing at the end of the book, as an afterthought to Caeiro, Campos, and Reis. One collection in English, however, begins with Pessoa's own poems. Aptly titled *Self-Analysis*, it includes "This," a Pessoa poem of absolute self-awareness:

> They say I adulterate and fake
> Everything I write. That's not so.
> It's simply that I experience
> Things through the imagination.
> I do not make use of the heart.
>
> What I dream or experience, that
> Which fails or comes to a finish,
> Hangs, like a terrace, over
> Some other thing. That other
> Thing is the thing of beauty.

And that is why I write immersed
In things which are far off,
Free from consternations,
Being serious about what is not.
Emotion? That's up to the reader.

— Translated by George Monteiro

Who is this Pessoa, this slightly aggressive poet, who offers a glimpse into his methods and designs, only to promptly take it back? This Pessoa, this dry, analytic poet with the chilly manner, is so different from the other Pessoas—from the ease of Caeiro, the exuberance of Campos, the lucidity of Reis—this Pessoa most resembles the melancholic Bernardo Soares, yet even Soares had an achingly human quality not evident in Pessoa's own poems.

Soares, like Pessoa, worked in an office; he was an assistant bookkeeper for a commercial shipping firm. He wandered the streets of Lisbon, and, at night, went home to write small, perfect meditations. He worked on a "fact-less autobiography" over the course of more than twenty years, most prolifically in the last five or six years of Pessoa's life. In *The Book of Disquiet*, Soares writes of his daily life in Lisbon:

> Today walking down New Almada Street, I happened to gaze at the back of a man walking ahead of me. It was the ordinary back of an ordinary man, a modest blazer on the shoulders of an incidental pedestrian. He carried an old briefcase under his left arm, while his right hand held a rolled-up umbrella, which he tapped on the ground to the rhythm of his walking. I suddenly felt a sort of tenderness on account of that man. I felt a tenderness stirred by the common mass of humanity, by the banality of the family breadwinner going to work every day, by his humble and happy home, by the happy and sad pleasures of which his life necessarily consists, by the innocence of living without analysing, by the animal naturalness of that coat-covered back.

— Translated by Richard Zenith

Though he pokes and prods a little at the unexalted life of the family breadwinner, it is clear that Soares feels a genuine tenderness, a feeling that runs through all the Pessoa poets at their finest. The poet loves the world, so delicately and without demand, even as the world trudges away from him, umbrella in hand, on its way home.

*　　*　　*

MANY WORKS BY the Pessoa prose writers—the sociologist António Mora and the essayist the Baron de Teive, the astrologer Raphael Badaya, and many others—have just now become available in English in Richard Zenith's *The Selected Prose of Fernando Pessoa*. Though the prose writers mostly exist at the periphery of the Pessoa universe, it is wonderful to finally read them. There is the beautiful, pathetic letter that the hunchbacked, tubercular Maria José wrote to the beloved metalworker who passes beneath her window each day, and the satiric predictions of Jean Seul de Méluret about the state of sex in 1950, and here the Baron de Teive's final dry meditations before his suicide. The Pessoa universe would be the poorer without Carlos Otto, author of a treatise on wrestling; and Miguel Otto (both brothers are vocal proponents of Sensationism); and the British brothers Thomas and I.I. Crosse, early translators of Campos into English; and Alexander Search, one of Pessoa's childhood imaginary friends, who grew up to write Elizabethan poetry, in English.

Five distinct and brilliant voices and a galaxy of supporting writers, all together were barely sufficient for the explosions of personality and taste that Pessoa felt tremoring inside him. Each of the five main Pessoa writers plays a defining role in Pessoa's work: one who accepts, one who celebrates, one who harks backward and to others, one who understands himself to the deepest point of his anxiety, and one who recognizes the universe in the coat on the back of a man walking home from his day's work. To take any one of these roles would be difficult; Pessoa, working with a kind of metaphysical flexibility *that cannot be conceived*, took them all. He wasn't only a poet, or a group of poets, or even a poetic movement, he quite simply and quite alone comprised an entire period of Portuguese literary history. And he knew it, while he was writing, in that obscure room, standing next to his dresser, the Lisbon night outside his window, leaning late and writing there.

*   *   *

THE HOUSE WHERE Pessoa lived in Lisbon has been converted into a whitewashed gallery and a library. The interior has been gutted; nothing remains of the original rooms. Uninspired modern sculpture stands awkwardly in the empty space. In one corner of an upstairs room is a high dresser that may be the one on which Pessoa wrote, "to feign is to know oneself" and also "I never kept sheep." The library—full of translations of Pessoa's work into every language—is modern, efficient, and lacking in any idiosyncrasy. A few glass cases stand along one wall. In them are Pessoa's glasses, neat, round, black frames, a cigarette lighter, and visiting cards that he had made, each carefully printed with the name Alexander Search. In this building, it is almost as if Pessoa never lived. He has vanished, dissolved in air. The traces are in his city and his poems, a flawed immortality, just the one he meant to have.

UNNATURAL HISTORY

AN INTERVIEW WITH JACQUES GAUTHIER, ABOUT THE THINGS WE FIND IN THE GROUND

by JOSHUAH BEARMAN

IN 1999, A fossil enthusiast and professional collector named Stephen Czerkas bought a foot-long piece of rock for $80,000 from a dealer at a gem and mineral show in Tucson, Arizona. Czerkas paid that price because he saw that the skeleton embedded in this rock was very unusual, or perhaps unique: it featured the complex forearms of a bird and the tail of terrestrial dinosaur. The specimen became *Archaeoraptor liaoningensis*, found its way into the November 1999 issue of *National Geographic*, and was celebrated for a time, at least in popular circles, as the most important fossil discovery in decades—further proof of the evolutionary link between dinosaurs and birds. 110,000 people saw Archaeoraptor when it was exhibited at the National Geographic Society in Washington and marveled at its significance.

Today Archaeoraptor is celebrated as the most famous fossil forgery in decades. Archaeoraptor's uncanny combination of characteristics turned out to be the result of human, rather than natural artistry: it was two halves of two different creatures stuck together. Scientists at the University of Texas discovered it was a composite when they used a High-Resolution X-ray Computed Tomography Facility, or CAT scanner, to image the fossil three-dimensionally.

Jacques Gauthier is a paleontologist and the curator of the Peabody Museum of Natural History at Yale University, one of the founding institutions of modern paleontology and the location of many dinosaurs and murals of dinosaurs. The following is a conversation with Gauthier about the Archaeoraptor controversy, flying pacemakers, and why Brontosaurus isn't really a Brontosaurus.

Q: So, which two dinosaurs actually make up Archaeoraptor?

A: The back half is like a Dromaeosaur, which is about as close as you can get to a bird and still be a dinosaur. It's a dinosaur that's already feathered; but it does not fly. And the front half was a new kind of flying dinosaur, similar to a Confuciusornis, which is a species from this area identified earlier. Both are new and important species, but together, it's not a single creature.

Q: So even though this wasn't a single creature, did the two new species it was made out of advance the hypothesis about birds evolving from dinosaurs?

A: Absolutely. Actually, from my perspective, that issue was settled in 1861, when Gegenbauer[1] looked at the development of the ankle in chickens. He made the connection then. And now we have all kinds of evidence. There's also been an ongoing argument about whether feathers arose for flight or to hold in body heat. And these new fossils are getting us closer to an answer. We already know that the Dromaeosaur, the relative of the front half of the Archaeoraptor, was covered with down, and we all know how good down is as an insulator. This shows that feathers developed to keep in heat. So, these new discoveries are just icing on the cake.

Q: The Archaeoraptor, I gather, was just sort of glued together. But how is it that it got so far without anyone noticing?

A: Well, the people that fake or embellish fossils are quite good artisans. A lot of folks are good at gluing together fossils, in fact, because they're often in pieces. Accurate specimens are often pieced together. So, it's not surprising that the Archaeoraptor fooled some people. Now, of course, it's obvious that it was a fake. You can see that the cracks don't line up right, and the pieces don't really fit together, you know. You've got one crack over here,

---

[1] Karl Gegenbauer was a 19th century German anatomist and zoologist at the Universities of Jena and Heidelberg who emphasized comparative anatomy in the study of evolution. This is how he came up with the idea of comparing chicken ankles with that of the just-discovered Compsognathus and then positing a relationship between them. His 1863 article, "Vergleichend-anatomische Bemerkungen über das Fusskelet der Vogel," or "Comparative Anatomical Observations on the Ankles of Birds," was the first to suggest birds and dinosaurs were related.

and another there turning this way, and, you know—what's up with that? But at the time, without close scrutiny, not everyone would see that. It was only after the CAT scan showed the internal anatomy of the thing that it became really obvious.

Q: So they used a CAT scan to look at this specimen—

A: Yeah, the CAT scan over at the University of Texas is a wonder machine. It's a high-resolution machine. Industrial strength. It's for, like, looking at cracks in the shuttle engine and stuff like that. It's not a medical device.

Q: So you couldn't go in there.

A: Hell no. It's not designed for anyone to survive. You wouldn't make it. The magnetosphere this thing generates would jerk a pacemaker right out of your chest. Or pull the fillings out of your face. It's quite a machine.

Q: Have they used it in the past to image fossils or look for fossil forgeries?

A: Not really.

Q: So, the Archaeoraptor was the first application of that type of equipment?

A: Yeah. The specimen, like many fossils, was sort of squashed together, so they brought it in because the digital image the scanner generates makes it more three-dimensional. And that's very useful for reconstruction and study. So you can see the whole internal anatomy, a lot of which wouldn't be available otherwise. But over the course of the process, they started noticing things that weren't right.

Q: And that's how they discovered the forgery.

A: Oh, you know, I just remembered—before the Archaeoraptor, they used the CAT scanner on one of these Confuciusornis specimens. And they found something wrong with that one. They saw that one of the drumsticks had been turned around 180 degrees. You couldn't see it on the outside. But in the CAT scan you could see it was reversed. It had broken off, and someone had clearly glued it back in to place to make it a complete specimen. But they glued it back in the wrong way.

Q: So they don't actually see the evidence of the forgery in the scan? Rather, the improved imaging makes the forgery apparent because you can see that the anatomy doesn't make sense?

A: Well, the anatomy doesn't make sense, but neither does the way the rocks have been put together. You can see the angles not matching up. And you can also tell by density differences when people put plaster in there to fill in the gaps, which is common. And the thing was, the anatomy of the Archaeoraptor was off even from what you could see. Because the back end, as I mentioned, was like a Dromaeosaur. These are like the raptors from "Jurassic Park," only smaller. And they're not the ancestors of birds, but birds share an ancestor with Dromaeosaurs and its relatives. It's like humans and chimps. One is not descended from the other, but both share an ancestor somewhere. And just as chimps have their own peculiarities, so do Dromaeosaurs. They have a tail, a peculiarly Dromaeosaur tail, and that was what was on the back end of this Archaeoraptor. And then the front end is a flying dinosaur. Well, that's weird. It just doesn't fit. It's like having a chimpanzee head on a human body or vice versa, right? That would raise eyebrows right away.

Q: Like a griffon or a centaur or something.

A: Yeah, right.

Q: Well, isn't that what made the specimen theoretically exciting—that it shared these features?

A: But that's not really how evolution works.

Q: So, it's sort of like Piltdown Man.[2]

A: Right. That was the way they used to think about evolutionary intermediates—the missing link might have a human skull and an orangutan's jaw-

---

[2] Piltdown Man was a proposed species of extinct hominid that turned out to be a hoax. It was based on fragments of a cranium and jawbone found between 1910 and 1912 in a gravel formation on Piltdown Common in England, and was thought for a time to be a missing link because the skull shared characteristics of humans and apes. Piltdown man occupied a space in the evolutionary sequence for several decades, until later research revealed the fragments were a chemically aged human skull and orangutan jawbone. You can still find old textbooks in used bookstores that show Piltdown Man walking along the evolutionary path toward *homo sapiens sapiens*.

bone. But that's not how it works. And I think the guy who bought this Archaeoraptor was an amateur, which is why he thought about it in the same way. He saw some characteristics of flying dinosaurs and some characteristics of Dromaeosaurs and saw it as a missing link, because that's what he expected. But for paleontologists, that's not really how we think about the evolutionary process anymore.

Q: So Piltdown Man survived as a hoax for a couple decades because there was a cruder understanding of the mechanics of evolution?

A: Yes, and since the mid-sixties or so, we've gotten away from the idea of finding "missing links." We have a more sophisticated view of the evolutionary process. Now we find lots of cousins instead.

Q: How big has the commercial fossil market become?

A: Huge. It's growing by leaps and bounds. You can find the stuff on eBay. It makes you cringe, you know.

Q: And that's why the fakes are proliferating?

A: Yeah. Fossils have become valuable, and there are all kinds of people trafficking in them who have no training or see no problem gluing things together as they see fit. Anthropologists have encountered this for some time, because there's been a market in arrowheads and African art and whatnot for years, but this is new for us. It really hit the fan with the sale of Sue.[3] What used to be just some interesting stuff we would find in the dirt is becoming a hot commodity.

Q: Let me ask you about the Brontosaurus for a minute, since you have the original specimen here at the Peabody. The Brontosaurus wasn't a fake, but it was a false construction that led to a misconception of the Brontosaurus that lasted for some time, or even still lasts.

A: You bet.

---

[3] Sue is the familiar name of the largest and most controversial *Tyrannosaurus rex* ever found. It was found by a private fossil-hunting firm and auctioned in 1997 for $8.4 million, the highest price ever paid for a fossil specimen.

Q: So, the story is that Othniel Charles Marsh[4] found his Brontosaurus, but it had no head. So he supplied another one that turned out to be the wrong one.

A: Right. The Como Bluffs area in Colorado where Marsh was digging had a big concentration of fossils. All kinds of bones; different species; multiple individuals. And so here's all these Sauropod bones all jammed together.[5] When Marsh brought the bones back to Yale, and they started putting them together, they put together a Brontosaurus individual. And they picked out the wrong head. Then, much later, somebody re-examined the skeleton, looked at the field notes and then went down into the cellar and found the right head. And then all the museums with Brontos had to change their heads.

Q: That was in the 1970s when they found the right head. And was the one up on the fourth floor of the Museum of Natural History changed too?

A: Yup. Although for years, they wouldn't change it. But when that hall was redone a few years back, they put the right head on. And we've got the right head on downstairs here. Although we kept the other one so we can tell the story. Because the whole mix-up grew out of the Marsh-Cope war that animated early paleontology. There was a personal animosity between these two guys, and they were each racing to find and name more dinosaurs than the other one. And so the field went from, like, three known dinosaurs to sixty in fifteen years because they so hated each other. Because when you name a species, your personal name goes in there forever. So Marsh and Cope were out there naming every scrap of bone they found. Marsh, you know, would name like five different things from what turned out to be the same animal. He'd name the front half one thing, the back half another.

Q: That's what happened with the Brontosaurus's false name too, right?

A: The correct name is Apatosaurus. What Marsh described as Brontosaurus was actually just an Apatosaurus with a Camosaurus skull. The official name has been Apatosaurus since 1903. But the popular name Brontosaurus

---

[4] Marsh, along with his bitter rival, Edward Drinker Cope, organized the first fossil expeditions in the American west and inaugurated the era of modern paleontology.

[5] Sauropod is the group name for all the large, four-legged herbivorous dinosaurs like Brontosaurus.

stuck, although I think most museums have changed the names along with the skull.

Q: Brontosaurus just has a better ring to it.

A: It seems so.

Q: Well, thanks so much for the interview. It was fun, as dinosaurs always are.

A: Yup. No problem.

MRS. FERRIS

by PAUL LAFARGE

"THE PROBLEM WITH America," he says, "is that we have no Eiffel Tower."

"I've never missed it," I say.

"You would say that."

"Why would I say that?"

"You know why you'd say it."

"Why don't you tell me what I know?"

"The Tower is over a thousand feet tall," he says. "It's made entirely of steel girders."

"I imagine you're referring to something in particular."

"A damned ingenious construction. Those Frenchies are too damned clever."

"To a particular person, aren't you?"

"With their little pointy beards."

"You're talking about *him*, aren't you?"

"Who?"

"You know who."

"Do I? Tell me what I know."

"You know what you know."

And we go around again.

*   *   *

HE TAKES THE subject up again the following Sunday. I am in the kitchen, frying doughnuts. "We need a national monument," he says. "Something people can see from miles away."

"There isn't anyone miles away from Galesburg. There's the Evanses. And your mother."

"Not here," he says. "In Chicago. The boys in charge of the Columbian Exposition want a big attraction. And I mean to come up with one."

"Put your mother on top of a hundred-foot column," I say. "You'd make a lot of people happy."

"Don't talk like that," he says. "And I'm serious. It's got to be a beacon of American culture."

"So build a tower."

"The French have a tower."

"So?"

"We'd just be copying the French."

"It isn't American to copy the French?"

"Grenouille told you that," he says.

"He did not."

"It's the sort of thing he would say."

"Leave him out of this."

"Little pointy-haired unpleasant person."

"Have a doughnut."

He takes one, still shining with oil, and stares at it melancholically. George has a way of looking old sometimes, as though the world within him went by much faster than the world without, and when you see him as he sees himself you see an old man.

"I don't know why you keep him around," he says.

"I don't keep him around. He comes by."

"You know what I mean."

"I don't."

"You do."

We go around again.

*   *   *

SO MUCH TROUBLE about a singing teacher! Not even a good singing teacher. Not even a teacher of singing, as it turned out.

"A singing tea-a-cher, Madame," he trilled. "*Un professeur chantant.* In my language the confusion would never have a-ri-i-sen."

"I don't speak your language. Is that what you teach?"

"No-o. My specialty is philosophy, history, and aesthetics."

"Poor man," I said. "Would you like a doughnut?"

Mr. Grenouille sat on the sofa, holding a cinnamon doughnut and a glass of milk. He wore a three-piece maroon suit and a yellow silk cravat, loosely tied in what was perhaps a French fashion. I thought he might have been part of a traveling circus, or that he was still part of the circus, that this was the circus, it consisted only of him, although if that was the case I feared he wouldn't be much of a success. "Thank you for the refreshment," he sang. "Will you allow me to teach you a lesson?"

"Why do you sing?" I asked.

"In my country, I get into a great deal of trouble for speaking the truth. So I have taken a vow never to speak the truth again. This is my accommodation. May I go on?"

"Please."

"Let us consider the causes of the Hundred Years' War," he sang.

What a curious world we live in! I had no idea that the Popes were roly-poly gentlemen who gave their decrees from atop wooden hobby-horses—the only place where they were really *infallible*, Mr. Grenouille explained, because both their feet were always touching the floor. Nor that Luther had psoriasis and constant scratching of the scalp drove him out of his skull, nor that the Holy Roman Emperor played tennis with the King of France and meanwhile, and meanwhile, the weavers and the tanners of all nations lived happily together and on Sundays walked arm in arm through fields of wildflowers. Then mad Luther said the Pope was fat, and the angry Pope jumped off his horse and called for his sword; elsewhere the King of France called a ball out when it was in, the Holy Roman Emperor knew that it was in, and they drew their swords, but their visors and advisors separated them just in time. Instead of fighting, they declared war, and the Pope did the same, and Luther did the same. The weavers were separated, warp from weft, and the tanners went after one another's hides, and soon there was no one left in Europe but widows and orphans and an army of postmen delivering bad news.

"Dear me, European History!" I exclaimed.

"From the horse's mouth," sang Mr. Grenouille.

"I must lie down."

Mr. Grenouille adjusted his waistcoat. "We will have another lesson next week. Is it good?" The way he said it, it sounded like gooed.

"It is gooed," I said, and there I was speaking his language after all.

*   *   *

"I'VE GOT IT," George says. He sketches an elongated dome with a cupola, like so:

"Mother America," he says. "Wet-nurse to the orphans of the world."

"What are those lines?" I ask.

"Rays of light. Ten thousand candlepower of America's spiritual milk. You'll be able to see it from Joliet."

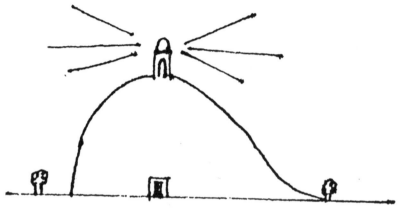

FIG 1: MOTHER AMERICA

"What happens inside?"

"Food stands," he says. "All different kinds of sandwiches. And games of chance. And magic lantern entertainments." He points out that the interior of the dome will have no windows. "And performances on the flying trapeze. And a planetarium, with lectures about the nature of the stars."

"It sounds very busy," I say. "Will people want all that?"

"The important thing is the outside. The beautiful simplicity of the outside."

"It looks like a teardrop," I say. "If you turn it sideways."

He turns the paper sideways and yes, it does.

"Hm," he says, and walks away with Mother America, who doesn't appear again.

*   *   *

MOST OF WHAT Mr. Grenouille said was as odd as his suit, and as vulgar. But this idea that history could be anything you make it! You begin with

1 cup warm water
2 cakes active yeast
1/2 cup white flour
1/2 cup brown flour.

Add the flour to the dissolved yeast and allow to ferment. You should get a sticky paste which is the stuff of which history is made. Then you make a decision. You could, for example, gradually add and beat until light and fluffy

2/3 cup white sugar.

What would it be then? Something airy and sweet. You could give a bit of history to anyone who came by in the afternoon and wanted it. You could heap a plate with history and take it out to the people sitting on the porch and set it down quietly, quietly, and then step back and watch them eat it and lick their fingers. And think of all the varieties you could make! Jelly history. Dutch history. Cake history. Chocolate crumb history. Old-fashioned history. Glazed history with colored jimmies.

*   *   *

WOULD ISABELLA OF Aragon have liked doughnuts? She was Spanish and the Spanish like fried things so probably yes. What about Eleanor of Aquitaine? She would have loved doughnuts—the hot oil would have reminded her of war, and she liked war. Joan of Arc would *not* have liked doughnuts. J. of A. was a confirmed non-eater and probably had no sweet tooth, poor thing. Marie Antoinette? Would have called them beignets, and oh goodness yes, she would have wanted everyone to have some. Catherine II of Russia. Would have eaten mountains of them. Queen Elizabeth the First. Maybe one or two, but in secret. Mary Tudor. Liked them as a girl, and might have come to like them again, if only, alas. Madame de Pompadour. Don't even talk to her about doughnuts. Catherine de Medicis. Don't eat her doughnuts. Empress Eugénie. Well, just one doughnut, please, and give the rest to charity. Queen Victoria. Queen Victoria. Doughnuts?

*   *   *

"TAKE A LOOK at this," he says. George draws a tower with its feet in the air and its head buried in the ground:

"We'll stand the Old World on its head! A feat of engineering like no one has ever seen! With not one but four observation platforms. The Ferris Skystand, the world's first truly democratic wonder."

"The Ferris Skystand."

"Isn't that a good name?"

"I don't know."

"Why, what do you think I should call it?"

I look at the drawing again. "The Eiffel Flower?"

He looks at the drawing again. He folds it in half and puts it in his pocket. "Thank you," he says, and we don't hear about the Flower again.

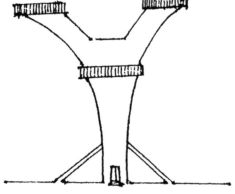

FIG 2: THE FERRIS SKYSTAND

*   *   *

TODAY MR. GRENOUILLE came by with an illustration of Newton's Tomb, where Newton is apparently not buried. Spherical because the sphere is the perfect form, Mr. Grenouille says. If you stood at the center and looked all around, you would feel like the Creator of the Universe. Except that there is no Creator and that is why the center is empty. I wonder however whether the Creator would really have felt that way, as if the universe were a great hollow sphere. What if it was a circular tunnel, and He saw it part by part as he walked along, muddling through, kneading things into shape as they came within reach? I didn't mention this to Mr. Grenouille, who I think had enough worries of his own. I wonder what he would have thought of it, though. I wonder what Newton would have thought.

*   *   *

NEWTON MOST LIKELY never ate a doughnut in his life. Would the world be different now if he had?

*   *   *

GEORGE DREAMS OF iron beams. He wakes me early in the morning to tell me about it. "Enormous girders chasing me," he says. "Rolling girders. Black. With pointy... with little pointy... it was horrible. Going to catch up with me any second now."

I hold him and tell him that it will not catch up with him, this enormous thing he has dreamed of.

"I'm afraid," he says. "What am I going to give the boys in Chicago?"

"You'll think of something."

"What if I can't?"

"Don't worry."

He sits up in bed and reaches for his slippers.

"Where are you going?"

"Get something to eat."

He stands up. His belly has become bigger these last months, and there are white hairs on his legs. "I didn't know leg hairs even *turned* white," I say.

He looks at me mournfully.

"Has he made love to you?"

"Who?"

"You know who."

"Don't be ridiculous. A foreigner in a maroon suit?"

"I'm afraid I *am* ridiculous," he says. "All I can think of are things no one wants."

"That's the wonderful thing about you," I say.

He shakes his head. "Not in Illinois." Then he goes downstairs and for a long time I hear him rattling about in the kitchen like a heavy-footed ghost.

*   *   *

MR. GRENOUILLE COULD not be forever. The mountains are not forever; the rivers are not forever; *comment voulez-vous* that a little foreigner in a maroon suit should be anything but impermanent? Here is what I think happened. Three policemen came to his boarding-house. One watched the back stairs while the other two went up the front. They knocked on his door and Mr. Grenouille said, "Oui?"

"Will you come with us to the station," the policemen said. "You'll want to bring your things."

Mr. Grenouille came out holding a small valise—everything he owned fit in that. He walked between the two policemen downstairs.

"Is it true that you're a famous criminal in France?" one of them asked.

"Absolutely," Mr. Grenouille said.

"Did you throw a bomb at the President?"

"Several bombs."

"But they all missed?"

"I have poor eyes."

The policemen escort him down the street, and a strange thing happens. The policemen become smaller in the distance, as faraway objects always do, but Mr. Grenouille seems to remain the same size, as though he has been far away all along. He tells them about his career as a famous criminal, only, as he is speaking and not singing, it is impossible to believe a word he says.

*　　*　　*

"Do you miss him?" George asked, when it was clear he was not coming back.

"Do I miss him."

"It's a simple question."

"Of course I miss him."

"I don't know why."

"I know."

"You know why?"

"I know that you don't know."

"He changed you, didn't he? That ridiculous man."

"That was his charm."

"What did he do?"

"He sang."

"Sang?"

"It was his way of telling the truth."

"I don't get you," George said. "You or him."

"That's all right."

"Anyway, I've got to take the boys from Chicago out to dinner," he said. "Should we have steak or chops?"

"Steak," I say.

"I think they'd prefer chops."

"Then chops."

"You just said steak."

"I'm free to contradict myself."

"You really think they want steak."

"Give them doughnuts, for all I care."

"Doughnuts?"

"I mean, since you don't listen to what I say, I might as well say anything I like."

"Wait a second, doughnuts."

"I might as well say, 'Take them out for the Holy Roman Empire.'"

"No, hold on. That gives me an idea."

"Take them out for the Pope."

"Hold on, hold on."

"You aren't listening, are you."

"Do you have a piece of paper?"

FIVE EXHIBITS

from

PAINTING THE MOON

by GILBERT SORRENTINO

1.

THE GARDEN EXHIBITION that opened at the T.C. Andrews galleries on Saturday arrives here from Los Angeles and Houston, and it is well worth waiting for. Occupying the South Patio and Mower Gardens of the ground-floor gallery, it is a delight to the eye. Glossy-black Orient dew, surrounded by a pale-golden halo of rare, Sacred dew, suggests the moon's bosom, bared, all unashamedly, to avid blowing roses of variegated colors and lush, foreign-bred, purple flowers. Sweet leaves and green blossoms inform a grassy slope, brilliant under lights especially designed for this exhibition by Garden Glows of London and Manchester. It is as if the gallery has been given over to an eternal spring, one that enamels all its contiguous elements, one that, in effect, "enamels everything," as someone, with a gesture toward elegant panache, once remarked. There are also in attendance, so to speak, bright oranges in at least a dozen varieties, gleaming like so many golden lamps in the subtle yet spectacular lighting, a magical illumination that, in this breathtaking corner of the garden, creates what seems an uncanny green night. Figs, real or made of most exquisitely fragile Baccarat crystal, seem to be at our mouths everywhere, as we move through the gorgeous displays; and melons—golden, orange, mauve, cerise, azurel, brilliant yellow—crowd together at our feet in profligate and splendid profusion. Apples, cedars, the huge pomegranates called "Chinese honeymoons," each bursting with jewels, awaken a kind of vegetable love in the viewer, and cool fountains contrast their silvery sprays with deep-green shadows. There is Venus, in her pearly boat, redolent of strange perfumes, beautiful and regal as the Marvel of Peru, the legendary tulip (one of which was valued at the cost of a thousand prize sheep and a famed actor); and dazzling daffodils, arranged in careless garlands of repose, charm and soothe the eye. And at the far wall is a lavish collage—the curious peach, by the hundreds, amid its delicate and delicious aroma, strewn amid the shadows of countless roses and indigo violets. Every element—form, color, arrangement, scent—of this marvelous exhibition takes its place in an equally marvelous prospect of fruits, of grasses, and of flowers.

2.

PILES OF WET clothing, puddles of dirty, soapy water, and a tarnished crown of false, or fool's, gold set the tone for this installation, one which slowly and almost imperceptibly turns from the innocuous to the eerily disturbing as the vast floor of the converted gymnasium, which serves as the gallery's exhibition space, accommodates, insistently and obsessively, more piles of clothing, more puddles of water, more cheapjack crowns. It is only when the eye refuses to be mesmerized by neurotic uniformity and repetition that the floor space between these strangely iconic and wholly sterile elements of a useless formalism is seen to contain cluttered configurations of miniature, varicolored, metallic spheres, cylinders, fulcrums, circles, conoids, spheroids, ovoids, and ingeniously designed sand-reckoners. These familiar geometrical shapes function as footnotes or marginalia, of course. The floor is bathed in a cold, aqueous, silvery light, which has the uncanny effect of making these simple conjugations of *things* (and what is more "thinglike" than laundry, wet floors, "Coney Island" headgear?) into noble, if threatening, constructions. The entire installation suggests to the viewer willing to connect with its sublunary symbolism a world—our own world, perhaps—and the number of grains of sand in their trillions upon trillions that it would take to completely fill it. An extraordinarily compelling architecture of delights, this, by the Grupo Archimedes, rich with the unspoken and unrevealed.

3.

ERATOSTHENES, ONE OF the prize students of Callimachus, was the head of the famed library of Alexandria from about 240 B.C. till his death in 195 of a surfeit of new wine and adolescent boys. Or so they say. While at the library, and in moments stolen from the cataloguing and repairing of its treasures, Eratosthenes drew a map of the world, working from memory, hearsay, dreams, and the tales of Phoenician sailors. The map on display here at the Rufus X. Noogie Museum of Purest Jade is thought to be Eratosthenes's original. Under its triple layer of shatterproof glass, surrounded by armed guards, and protected by electronic alarms of an almost frightening complexity and efficiency, it sits in its aura of splendid uniqueness. It is generally conceded that were it to be offered for sale at auction, the map, which is only $4^{1}/_{2}$ by $3^{1}/_{2}$ inches in size, would bring in excess of a billion and a half dollars. It is, incidentally, badly drawn, of muddy, indeterminate colors, rife with misspellings, and even for its time, *all wrong*.

4.

MAXIMUS VALERIUS POSIDONIUS, all of whose writings have been lost, yet whose theories of solar vital forces and rock-removal as a methodology for the prediction of the movements of large bodies of infantry, prefigured the contemporary strategies concerning the deployment of conscripted troops as assistants of various types in the preparation and serving of food, i.e., hot meals, and the maintenance of dining areas within the larger system of the order of battle, is thought to have conceived the notion of cosmic sympathy, and the employment of certain elements of post-Attic Stoicism, to hoist petards and launch Greek fire, shine Phoenician brass, and find the direction whence come and whither go sunbeams during extended thunderstorms, so as to better answer the questions of often surly travelers, stuffed, even bloated with pita bread and roast lamb—at that time (ca. 94 B.C.) the only food available in the vast wastes of a particularly arid Syria (known, at that time, as "the Congo")—is also thought to have taught his students the secrets of grinding eggshells for use as the basic component of a particularly fine spackle, corn flakes, ink, and heroin, secrets improbably locked into number theory and its attentions to the special properties of the integers; e.g., unique factorization, primes, equations with integer coefficients (biophantine equations), and congruences; and although earlier thinkers (Galen, Dombrowski, Galento, Fitts-Couggh, Gavilan) laid the groundwork for such discoveries with their invention of algebra, Posidonius's work has about it a certain furtive elegance, an elegance much apparent in the exhibition of his astonishing solar-storm drypoints. The exhibition has, unfortunately, unexpectedly and abruptly closed, and its contents subsequently lost or destroyed.

5.

THE ODRADEK, THE first one to be placed on public view in the United States in more than a century, has been, we are told in the helpful catalog, prepared by Tobias Blumfeld for the Prague Zoological Society and Marching Band, "preserved... in what analysis shows to be a solution of equal parts hydrogen peroxide, lemon juice, and triple-distilled 160 proof Ukrainian vodka." Discovered three years ago in a grotto in the Caucasus, the small creature has been seen, and marveled at, in museums the world over, before his arrival in this country earlier in the year. From here, the Odradek will travel back to what will be his permanent home in Azerbaijan's National Wool Museum. Although the bits and pieces of thread, tangled together, as always, that are wound about the little creature are varied in color, as we have come to expect, these threads seem remarkably *new*; that is to say, one expects, somehow, the Odradek to display "raiment" that is as old as himself—and star-scholars agree that this particular specimen is between 800 and 1,100 years old. For the Odradek to flaunt threads newly manufactured when *he* was already centuries old diminishes the little being's "presence," of course. One hastens to add, however, that this diminishment is neither profound nor, finally, important. As a matter of fact, the colors of the threads (azure, rose, chartreuse, burnt orange, alabaster, pearl grey, butter, and lavender) are so striking as to constitute an authentic, enduring beauty as they flutter against the matte, off-black contours of the Odradek's five-pointed body, and the dull mahogany of his crossbar with its cunningly attached rod. The little creature stands upright and utterly still on his wooden rod and one of his star points or "legs," although it is apparently possible for him to heave himself onto his dorsal surface, despite the fact that no one has ever seen him do so; nor has anyone ever seen the little fellow resting in what may be thought of as a supine position. Viewers gaze long upon the Odradek, fascinated by his curious, modest charm. Most, when queried, admit that they are beginning to hear him speak; according to mountain legend, the Odradek's lightest word is able to change his hearers' lives forever.

CROSS-DRESSER

THE WRITTEN TESTIMONY
OF CAPTAIN JEFFREY DUGAN,
418TH SQUADRON BANDIT #573

by GABE HUDSON

MY NAME IS Captain Dugan and at the request/demand of Dr. Barrett, I am writing all this down. She says that only if I write all this down will she be able to make a strong case for me to her superior, Dr. Hertz. I have never actually seen this Dr. Hertz, and so I have to take Dr. Barrett at her word that this Dr. Hertz even exists. Otherwise, Dr. Barrett says, if I don't write down my side of it, then legally they will have no choice but to keep me here at the neuropsych ward at Holloman AFB, because she said that a sane man has nothing to hide, whereas a crazy man is full of secrets. To which I said, "Well I'm sure as hell not crazy." That's when she pushed this pencil and paper across the table and said, "So prove it."

If I am to do myself justice, then I suppose I should start with a thesis remark, and so here it goes: this world is strange, and to me it is all very sinister and miraculous. If you don't agree with me now perhaps you will agree with me by the time you are done reading this. Before I begin it's important to me that I establish credibility, which means I want to say that I'm not nearly as dumb as I look. Because the truth is that how I look is not who I really am (and I'm just not saying this just because I'm short either.) Probably other people have this secret too, that how they look is not who they really are. Though sometimes I forget about this until I look in the mirror and then I'm like, "Oh God, not him again. There must be some mistake." But then I'm like, "Okay, what the hell, might as well: I mean it's not like I have a choice or anything."

Then I get in my F-117A Stealth Fighter which I call Gracie and fly up into the sky and kill people. Or at least I have, in the Persian Gulf, for which I was awarded the Silver Star, and I'm sure I'll have to kill some more people when I get out of here. Word on the base right now is Somalia's going to be the next hot spot. This is what I do for a living, and I try to have fun with it, since it's my job. I zoom around the earth in a sleek, black, weapon of mass destruction and I'd be lying if I didn't admit that it's a serious rush to be in the cockpit, because when I'm up there in the sky it's like I'm straight out of God's head, a divine thought inside a divine thought bubble, totally invisible.

Except that day when I got my ass shot out of the sky in Iraq and crashed Gracie in the desert. Right in the middle of a ramshackle military compound where I was taken as a POW and sadistically tortured by a one-eared man named The Mule. I didn't feel so invisible then.

*   *   *

HERE IS WHERE I should mention my curse. This will explain some things. I was born with a gift. Or a curse depending on how you look at it. It's my dreams. My dreams let me see into the future. I know it sounds bizarre but as proof to support this claim I'll tell you that three nights ago I had a dream in which I saw myself wearing a dark blue dress and red high heels (just like I am now) and sitting in a padded room with one arm handcuffed to a chair (just like I am now), writing a document that started, "My name is Captain Dugan and at the request/demand of Dr. Barrett, I am writing all this down." I should also probably mention that that dream had a happy ending because in that dream Dr. Barrett read over my statement proclaiming that I was innocent (which is the same thing I shouted when I felt the MP's tranquilizer dart stick in my hip) and then in the dream Dr. Barrett let me return to active duty (just like you will after you read this) after concluding that if anything I was merely compassionate to a fault, completely sane, and that I am a victim of my wife's vindictive, ridiculous accusation that I am some sort of sicko transvestite pervert.

*   *   *

THE MISSION WAS supposed to be simple. A routine sortie, clear skies, fly low and blow up some oil refineries south of Nukhayb, and then get the hell out of there. I was sitting around with Captain Jibs and Colonel Cowry under the tent, this was in Khamis Mushait, trying to stay out of the heat, sipping on a cold one when I got the word. I remember downing my beer and standing up in the same motion, and then slamming the bottle on the table and looking at Jibs and Cowry with a grin and saying, "Back in a jiff boys. Desert Storm calls." Then I hopped in Gracie and hit the wide Arabian sky. Well when I came up on the oil refinery below me I saw three Iraqi soldiers jumping up and down on barrels, waving white flags attached to sticks.

I let them have it. I swooped down and dropped a GBU-10 bomb, and my stomach was lit up with that smoky, mystical sensation you get when you kill something, which is virtually indescribable, though I can say for sure that it's the only time I can feel God really watching me: it's a good way to make Him sit up and take notice. And so there I was, basking in God's gaze, the wreckage smoking below me, when that son-of-a-bitch Iraqi fighter dropped in out of nowhere and tried to *kill me*, shooting my tail wing to tatters.

Gracie skittered forward among the clouds like a bumper car. I was dazed. I smelled smoke. The Emergency Gear Extension handle was stuck. Then I tried to duck and roll but Gracie was shimmying all over the place and I was in a spin, streaking toward the earth like a comet, and I watched in horror on the Multi-Function Display as the desert's giant yellow jaws rose up and then opened wide and swallowed me whole.

*   *   *

WHEN I CAME to I was strapped in a chair with a light-bulb hanging over my head. There were cracks of sunlight coming through the bamboo walls. After blinking a few times I saw that I was in a small hut with three Iraqi soldiers. This was the place I would come to call The Shack. It had the stink of fear in it. The soldiers were smoking and laughing about something, and one of them had his hands up in front of him, squeezing the air, like there were breasts. Then the one squeezing the air heard me moan and after glancing in my direction put two fingers in his mouth and whistled loud through the tiny barred window in the door. The door swung open and a small man with one ear walked directly up to me and cracked my jaw with a bully-stick. My jaw was instantly dislocated, and I toppled over with the chair to the floor. Through the scream trapped in my head I heard the men laugh, and then the one-eared man said, "Hello. My name is The Mule. I have some questions for you. You will answer, no?"

I gasped for air. It felt like my mouth had been knocked up into my forehead. I tried to say something and the top of my head opened up. I slowly squirmed forward a few feet, knees and elbows, dimly aware that the soldiers were watching my progress with detachment, and I heard one of them chuckle and mutter, "Americana." Finally I pushed my jaw hard up against a wall and then clink, with the sound of a camera shutter, my jaw popped back into place, and the relief flooded up my spine in waves of ecstasy. The relief never really went away after that. So that two hours later when The Mule struck me across the jaw for what seemed like the hundredth time I was almost, but not quite, grateful.

Instead I spit out some teeth.

From there on out it's mostly a blur. Because of the pain, I only remember images and flashes, smells, and finally, the taste of blood in my mouth. The Mule wanted me to make a propaganda videotape.

The Mule said, "If you ever want to see your family again."

The Mule said, "This is not too much to ask. You will be a movie star."

The Mule said, "I am losing my patience, Captain Dugan."

The Mule said, "That looks like it hurts, Captain Dugan."

I didn't say anything. I kept my mouth shut, but not because I was feeling patriotic, because to tell the truth I couldn't care less about my country at that moment, but because I was sure that if I did it, make the videotape, then they wouldn't have any more use for me and they would kill me.

The Mule whipped out this hand-held Sears Craftsman electric drill. I had my focus back. He revved the trigger a few times and the drill made a squealing sound. Then he walked over to me and placed the drill to the back of my head. "Perhaps now you make the video?"

I gave him a look. I said, "Please don't do this."

The Mule smiled. "Have it your way, Captain Dugan."

"Please," I said. "No."

Then I felt the bit of the drill push hard against my skull. It was very quiet, and I could see everything, even though I had my eyes closed. All the hairs in The Mule's nose. The three soldiers that were now standing outside The Shack. One of them was thrusting his hips back and forth like he was having sex. The other two were laughing. A vulture flew by overhead. Then I saw The Mule's index finger slowly push down on the orange plastic trigger of the drill, and the roar of the drill's motor was deafening, and I felt the bit push in and break the skin around my skull.

*   *   *

As YOU CAN imagine, this thing with my dreams hasn't always been easy. I've never told anyone about it, not my wife, Mrs. Dugan, and certainly not my daughter Libby, when she was alive, may she rest in peace. And of course I don't always like what I see (the future is not always pleasant), but by far the worst part is the guilt. God, the guilt. It's like it's my fault. Which is to say I always end up feeling like these things happened *because* I dreamt them first, like the time my next door neighbor Mr. Gordon's Tricksy turned on him and bit his thumb off. Now it's true I have never liked this Mr. Gordon, given the fact that he got drunk at a neighborhood barbecue last year and grabbed my wife's right breast in front of everyone and said, "Knock knock," and then she, albeit drunk, smiled in a coy way and said, "Who's there," which was of course completely humiliating for me, but that's really beside the point, because it's not like I wished Mr. Gordon would get his thumb bit off. But I dreamt it. And then it happened, and so you tell me, how can I not feel a little bit responsible?

*　　*　　*

ALL TOLD, THE Mule put six quarter-inch holes in the back of my head. I was barely conscious. When it was all over I remember looking up in a steamy haze as The Mule smiled and said, "You are a very stubborn man, Captain Dugan." I was vaguely aware of him putting my ankles in shackles, which were clamped to a stake in the middle of the floor. Then The Mule said, "Perhaps you will die. Perhaps not. But if not, you will be hungry. And maybe when you're hungry, well maybe then you will make the video-tape. Good-bye for now, Captain Dugan," and then he slipped out the door.

*　　*　　*

AFTER THAT THINGS went downhill fast. I was alone with my madness. You've heard it all a hundred times before. The whole POW thing. I went to hell and back in my mind. I gave up hope. My soul was a pink worm stuck through its belly with a hook, and I waited for the Angel of Death to come swimming up out of the darkness and swallow it whole.

That was the first day.

The second day was worse. The second day I started hearing my thirteen-year-old daughter Libby's voice. I knew it was an illusion, but still. I was sitting with my back against the wall and there were flies buzzing around my head. I heard Libby's voice say, "Lieutenant Jeff Dugan, this is your daughter speaking. Get a hold of yourself. Snap out of it. Yes, it's true, things don't look good, but I'm here to help. You are a Lieutenant in the United States Air Force, and this is war, so keep your wits about you. A little cunning can carry you through."

I realized Libby's voice wasn't inside my head. I looked up and there standing with her back to the door was Libby. Or at least some sort of wavy version of her. She was surrounded by a white, wavy energy. She was well dressed, with fine leather loafers, off-white hose, and a green cashmere turtleneck. Her nose was, as always, small.

I couldn't believe the stupid tricks my mind was playing on me. "You're kidding right?" I said. "Is this some sort of joke?"

"No, Daddy. It's me. Libby."

I didn't know what to say. "Alright then," I said. "Why are you all wavy?"

"Because," she said, and then she told me everything. She said she was dead. She told me about how her Siamese cat Smoky Joe had run out in front of a red Chevy and how she had saved Smoky Joe, but was hit and killed in the process. When she was through I spoke up.

"This is ridiculous. How I am supposed to believe something like that?" I started beating my head with my fist. "Hello? Hello? I know you're in there brain. I know you're behind this. I expected more from you. Stop it now."

I could tell by the look on Libby's face that she wasn't interested in my cynicism. Her brow was wrinkled and she was chewing on her bottom lip.

"Look. You aren't real. This is a trick, it's the stress. Please go away. I can't take this."

"Come on. I'm here to help Daddy," she said. "We've got to get you out of here. Mommy can't lose both of us."

I could feel my temper start to rise. "Yeah right. Listen you, whatever the hell you are. You're starting to piss me off."

"Shhhhh. Now that's enough. We don't have time. I have to go now, but I'll be back tomorrow to help you escape," and with that Libby turned and stepped into the wall and passed through it out of sight.

*   *   *

THE NEXT MORNING I woke to someone kicking me in the shins. "Wake up. What are you doing? Sleeping in?" I looked and saw Libby. She was all business. "Okay," she said. "I've been spying in and listening to what they have been saying. Things are getting nuts up there. I think they're planning some sort of attack. The leader seems like a real jerk. You don't want to cross this guy, trust me."

"Ooooh, I'm scared," I said. I pointed to my head. "I've got six holes drilled into my head, and now I've got some wavy figment of my imagination telling me I'm in trouble. Give me a break. What can you tell me about trouble that I don't already know?"

"Daddy, they're going to hang you in the courtyard today. Now. You and some other pilot they captured. They want to make an example of you two, to boost morale before the attack," she said.

"I told you. You're not real." I put my hands over my eyes. "I can't see you."

She kept on. "Okay. So here's what you're going to do. They're coming to get you any minute now. We need to move fast. I'm going to let you out of those shackles. You bend down and act like you're hurt. Then grab the guard's pistol and hit him over the head with it."

I suddenly froze. Because it was true, I could hear the guard rustling his keys on the other side of the door. My mouth went dry.

Two seconds later the guard came in and I was lying on the floor, doubled over, pretending to be in pain. "Oh my God, oh my God," I cried.

*   *   *

THERE WAS ALSO the time when I was nine. This dream was much fuzzier than the rest, but when I woke in the dead of night I was sweating, and though I couldn't remember what happened I knew my Mom was in danger. And then the next night, right before dinner, I watched as my mother cut a carrot on the cutting board, and wasn't at all surprised when she looked up to tell me to set the table and sliced off her index finger. On the way to the hospital in the ambulance I kept sobbing, "I'm so sorry. I'm so sorry. I'm so sorry."

But the most disturbing dream of all happened two weeks before I had to ship out to Saudi to fight in the Gulf War. This is extremely difficult for me to talk about even now. The dream was swift and simple. I saw my thirteen-year-old daughter Libby run out in the street and get hit and killed by a red Chevy when she tried to shoo her Siamese cat Smoky Joe out of the way. Smoky Joe lived. Smoky Joe is short for Smoky Joe the Best Kitty Cat in the World.

And so now you understand. Because each of these events—the thing with Mr. Gordon, the thing with my Mom, the thing with Libby—have one thing in common. Each of these things happened in my dream before they happened in reality.

*   *   *

WHEN I BURST through the front door of The Shack the sunlight almost split my eyes open but then my pupils shrank and I bounded off toward Gracie. To my horror, as I ran over to Gracie, I spotted Captain Jibs hanging by his neck from a rope in the center of the courtyard. A group of soldiers were standing around with their backs to me, jeering at Jibs, throwing rocks at him and spitting on him. When I reached Gracie I checked behind the seat and all my gear was still there, untouched. I threw on my flak jacket. While I was rifling through my pack I heard a shout and looked up, and there in the doorway of The Shack was the guard rubbing the back of his head. He shouted something in Arabic and pointed at me. The mob around Jibs turned and looked in my direction. There was a moment of silence, and then when they saw me they started screaming and shouting and running.

A siren went off. Dogs started barking.

I took the guard's Beretta 9mm pistol and leapt out of Gracie and ran straight at a parked M60 tank, shooting rounds off left and right, and two men dropped. I ran up the side of the tank and off of it, doing a forward flip, with bullets flying everywhere. I saw a wounded man on the ground reaching for something in his belt. Shot him.

I leapt with my legs wide open and landed on a camel and shouted, "Huyaaa!" and I rode that camel fast and hard into the middle of the windstorm of bullets and swarm of Iraqi soldiers. The Mule appeared directly in my path, and the camel skidded to a halt. The Mule said, "This was very stupid, Captain Dugan," and then lobbed a frag grenade. The grenade was in midair when I ripped off my flak jacket and held it in front of the camel's face. The grenade went off and all the shrapnel bounced off my flak jacket. I think that's when the camel knew that I was a compassionate animal. I shouted, "Little help," and the camel rushed forward and head-butted The Mule.

Looking down at The Mule on the ground in that instant, I felt the strangest sensation in my belly button. It felt like my belly button was wiggling around. It was a widening sensation. When I reached down to touch my bellybutton I felt a hole in my stomach the size of a silver dollar. My index finger disappeared in the hole, but there was no blood. Just this hole. And then I passed out.

*   *   *

WHEN I CAME to the camel was galloping over the desert. That was the sound I woke to, the steady bric-a-brac of the camel's hooves on the desert floor. My chest kept bouncing against the camel's hump. The sun was just starting to come up, a blood red squirting over the horizon as if someone had stuck the sun in a juicer, and I could see the faint silver sliver image of the moon on the other side of the sky. When I looked behind me the Iraqi camp was a pinpoint on the horizon. "Thank God," I said. "I almost ate it on that one." But as soon as the words were out of my mouth I realized I had no idea who I was, and I started to panic. I couldn't even remember why I was out here in the desert. I asked myself a question.

When you want to start thinking where do you start?

I didn't know the answer.

My heart jumped up a couple decibels. Still I kept on, riding and pondering my question for as long as I could stand it, but then my brain was suddenly tired from all that thinking, so eventually I figured that until I got my memory back I should keep it simple. The best I could come up with was this: you are a person. You are alive. You are riding a camel.

So I rode through the desert on a camel with no name.

I rode for days and days and days, without food and water. I didn't know where I was going, and hadn't even given it a thought. The sun, that great ball of fire, came up and went down and came up and went down and came up and went down more times than I could count. I watched my haggard shadow do its mindless dance on the desert floor and I watched the horizon.

Once a vicious sandstorm came up in a blur and ate my uniform right off my body. I kept my eyes closed the whole time. The storm came and went. I was completely naked. The camel galloped on like it was in a race against time.

Then one day I looked up and saw ahead of me a palm tree and an oasis of clear blue water. The water shimmered in the heat. My camel had been stumbling throughout the day, and I knew it wasn't long for this world. I considered throwing the camel over my back and carrying him, but I decided against it. I was so thirsty my tongue felt like a balled-up piece of paper in my mouth. I shook my head, and took another look to make sure this wasn't a trick my mind was playing on me. At the sight of the water my camel picked up its pace again, with renewed enthusiasm. It broke into a trot. That camel was amazing. It had a heart of gold. I shouted, "Thata boy! Thata boy!" and the shout came out as a whisper. We were getting closer and closer. I tried to smile but my lips were exhausted.

And then the camel stumbled, faltered, and came crashing down face first, and I was pitched forward, airborne, right to the bank of the oasis. I scraped my knee in the sand. The camel was lying on the ground, floundering like a newborn colt, trying to get back up. It was elegant. It was tragic. I felt like I was witnessing the secret of the universe in the camel's effort.

Then it let out a tremendous, "Harrrumpppp," and its soul flew out toward the world beyond.

I named the camel Applejack.

I know you're thinking what's the point in naming something after it's dead and the answer is: well I don't know. But I did it.

The water was a plate of glass. I don't think I ever saw anything so beautiful as that oasis. When I slipped into the water I could feel the weeks of agony and fear wash off me like a bad cologne. I was clean.

More days passed. This was a time of joy. This was something different than I had ever known. I ate coconuts out of the tree. I didn't understand what was happening, but when I looked at my reflection in the water I thought, "You could be pretty." I let my hair grow out. I put on lipstick that I made from tree sap. I spent most of my time looking down at my reflection. I built a hut out of palm fronds. I made a two-piece bikini bathing suit.

Days days and more days.

Finally I thought: "Alright already. It doesn't really matter who I am, everyone needs love. People sound like a pretty good idea." So I set off on foot. I had been walking for centuries. I turned and looked and saw my footprints in the sand as far back as I could see. The entire desert stretched out before me. One day it snowed. Right there in the desert. I know it sounds weird but it did. I was so relieved to be out of the heat that I ran around catching snowflakes on my tongue. I built a snowman named Bert. I shook the snowman's hand and said, "Hi, Bert," and Bert's arm broke off in my grip. Why had Bert's arm broken off but not mine? I laughed out loud because I was so grateful that I still had two arms. I laughed harder than I have ever laughed. I laughed so hard I almost choked on my beard. It seemed to me that the snowman was laughing too but then Bert said, "Okay. Here's the deal. Your name is Lieutenant Dugan. That's your first clue. People are looking for you. Follow me. I'm going to lead you back to your base."

And that's exactly what Bert did.

*　　　*　　　*

WELL IT TURNED out I'd been lost in the desert for six months. And back at Khamis Mushait, I got the POW recovery treatment, which was nice, because I certainly was tired. I slept for three days straight. And it was only afterward, when I woke up and called my wife and she told me that six months before Libby had been killed by a red Chevy that everything came flooding back into my mind. Because it was then that I remembered how

Libby's ghost had appeared and helped me escape from the compound, and it was only then that I truly understood what happened to me out there, what that thing with my bellybutton was.

My Dad didn't want me to die, and so he leapt out of his body and forced me into it, because he wanted me to live. My Dad couldn't bear the guilt. That's what that thing with the belly button was. He was leaving his body, and pushing me into it. That's how much my Dad loved me.

So this is me, Libby. I am a thirteen-year-old girl living inside an Air Force Captain's body. It was the only way. I hide my identity from the rest of the people in my life. I conduct myself as an Air Force pilot and I report for duty at Holloman AFB and take Gracie up for training runs. It's not so hard to be a Captain in the Air Force, and plus my Dad's body remembers how to do everything, so it's a cinch. And like I said, when I'm up there in the cockpit it's like I'm straight out of God's head, a divine thought inside a divine thought bubble, totally invisible. Some times I feel bad for my Mom, because she doesn't know the truth and I can't tell her. She wouldn't believe me if I did anyway. It would just cause her unnecessary pain.

When I got back to Holloman AFB they awarded me a Silver Star and bumped my rank up to Captain. Then my first day home, my Mom drove me out to the cemetery to visit my grave, or should I say the grave where my old body is buried. I forced a tear out for Mom's benefit. The plot was nice. There was an oak tree with a crow in it. On my gravestone it said, "Libby Dugan, Beloved Daughter, Too Good To Be True." Of course sometimes at night Mom tries to get frisky in bed, but I turn her away. She thinks it's because I'm sad, and she tries to talk to me about it. She says, "I know what's bothering you. But we can get past this. Libby's in Heaven now. Life is too beautiful for us to be sad. And we still have each other." But then recently she's started getting mad. She'll start yelling and telling me that the flower inside her is drying up. Well I always change the subject because it makes me feel funny. Or I'll roll out of bed and go out to the back porch and smoke a cigarette.

Smoky Joe is the only one who knew the truth. He followed me everywhere, rubbing on my shins and jumping into my lap whenever he got the chance. I guess he was grateful to me for saving his life. Sure I was glad to see him too, but he was also causing me massive problems. Because Mom would come home and see Smoky Joe lying on my chest, and say, "That's weird isn't it, Jeff? I thought Smoky Joe hated you, Jeff. Since you've been home he won't leave you alone." Well I started to suspect that Mom was on to me. She'd give me these funny looks whenever I tied ribbons to Smoky

Joe's tail, or gave him Liver Treats. Threads were starting to unravel. My story was coming loose. I couldn't sleep at night, and then I'd look down at the foot of the bed and there would be Smoky Joe, staring at me, purring. So it shouldn't come as any surprise that one brisk morning I accidentally backed over Smoky Joe in our driveway with my Ford Bronco.

Other than that it's all good, and sometimes when Mom's still at work I come home early from the base and lock all the doors to the house and close the curtains and take all the phones off the hook. Then I go to the back of the closet, where I keep some things in a trash bag that I don't want anyone to know about. I tape my penis down between my legs and put on a pair of flowered panties. I put on one of my Mom's dresses and too much lipstick and eyeliner and admire myself in the big mirror in the living room. On special occasions when I imagine that I am going to a royal ball, I put on long white gloves that come up to my elbows. I curtsy, and in my mock elegant voice I say, "And how do you do? You look so lovely tonight dear. Tea? Yes please. Well thank you, you are such a darling."

Which is what I was doing today when Mom came home early and walked in on me holding our video camera. When I saw Mom come through the front door I leapt back out of sight and dove into the closet. I guess she saw me because she rushed over and started banging on the door and shouted, "Jeff, I know you're in there. Come out, Jeff. We need to talk. I know what you're doing. I've known about this for weeks. There's no need to hide this anymore, Jeff. I got you on videotape this time. We need to talk!"

Well I started getting nervous, with her banging on the door like that. I was trying to figure a way out of this, where nobody's feelings got hurt, and nobody ended up learning more than he or she needed to know. My mind was on fire. But at least you know I'm not crazy. Dr. Barrett, at least now you know. You make sure you tell this Dr. Hertz as much. You make sure he reads every single word I've written. And surely now you can understand the logic of my thesis remark: this world is strange, and to me it is all very sinister and miraculous.

While I was in the closet I resolved to make a break for it. I was going to bolt out of there and streak over to my Bronco and zoom away before my Mom could see me. But I didn't know that my Mom knew that that was exactly what I would try to do. I didn't know that my Mom had already been in touch with you. I didn't know that when I burst through the closet door and ran out onto the lawn that there would be MPs with tranquilizer guns waiting for me. I didn't know.

PROBLEM SET NO. 1

by JILL MARQUIS

1. JEZEBEL IS SEARCHING for her boyfriend Ryan at a concert. A police officer informs her that she has a 1 in 200 chance of finding him. Express this ratio as a percent.

2. IT'S THE LUNCH shift at McJack's Pancake Hut, and Bob's working the grill while Ryan makes salads. A table of five just ordered five ham sandwiches with no mayonnaise plus five Diet Cokes. All of them are dressed in red from head to toe. And there's a lone diner over at table 9 in a blue suit with a Band-Aid on his forehead. He doesn't look well. He's eating a dry ham sandwich too. Bob is working the grill and he says, What are the odds of that? Is there some sort of dry ham convention going on today? Ryan laughs. Dry ham sandwich! he says, Dry ham sandwich! Bob and Ryan are best friends. Bob decides he needs to add garlic to the beef rib special. The recipe calls for 0.375 of a teaspoon of crushed garlic. Convert this decimal to a simplified fraction for Bob.

3. JEZEBEL HAS TO write a 500-word essay on a trend for her college composition class. She has already written, "In today's society, guys don't always tell girls the truth and in actuality aren't what they seem." How many words does she have left to write? After 1 hour and 45 minutes, she has written 445 words, and although she has a lot more to say on the subject,

none of it seems to be part of a trend in society. If there are 29 sentences in the composition so far, what is the average number of words per sentence in the paper? If Jezebel printed the composition right now in a 12-point Times New Roman font, the paper would only be one-and-a-half-pages long, which doesn't seem long enough. How long would the paper be if she increased the margins to 2 inches? How long would it be if she increased both the header and footer to 1.5 inches? Calculate the total length of the paper if Jezebel increased the margins to 2 inches, increased the header and footer to 1.5 inches, and used 14-point type.

4. RYAN AND BOB lay in the snow at a 101-degree angle. Is the angle acute or obtuse?

5. THERE ARE 48 muscles in the human face and Ryan is putting 87% of them to use. He's squinting at the interstate, finagling a bit of steak from between his teeth, and trying not to look tense, which he is. Jezebel says, "You look mad. You're mad at me? What?" By "What?" she means, she's not the one who stayed out all night, so she's the one who gets to be mad now. This question makes Ryan mad even though he is not sure whether he's mad at her or, in fact, what is up with him at all. He doesn't know what to say. He can't even look at her, he's so mad. And just then, right near mile marker 75 on I-10 westbound, the odds catch up with them. Statistically, a driver makes about 200 observations and 20 decisions per mile. One of those decisions is bound to be wrong. At this moment, Ryan's powers of observation are hobbled by self-absorption, sexual confusion, and inexplicable rage. The sum of all that, plus a low-slung sports car that passes on the right just as Ryan decides to look Jezebel in the eye and change lanes, is more than a fender bender. Ryan's truck weighs 2,000 pounds; the sports car weighs 1,200 pounds. The sports car is traveling 70 miles an hour when Ryan hits it going 66 miles per hour. The truck hits the left rear corner of the sports car at an angle 20 degrees to the left of dead-on. The sports car takes flight briefly, while the truck loses momentum. Calculate the trajectory of the sports car and draw a diagram of its progress.   —

6. BOB VISITS RYAN and Jezebel in the hospital. He brings along his cousin Larry, who is instantly attracted to Jezebel. Larry kneels at Jezebel's side and asks if there's anything he can do to make her feel better, anything at all. He compliments her hairdo, touching the bandages wrapped around her head. Bob sits nervously on the edge of Ryan's bed. Ryan closes his eyes, quietly

gripping his head. Jezebel doesn't feel very well physically but is slightly giddy, still wound up from the accident. Jezebel says, "And right before the accident I knew something was going to happen because Ryan had this really weird look on his face, like maybe he was mad but not really. His face was all screwed up." Larry says, "Like this?" and makes a face. Ryan opens his eyes—he can't help looking. Jezebel shakes her head. Bob says, "Like this?" and makes a face. Jezebel says "No!" She's laughing. "Try again! Too subtle!" she says. Everyone but Ryan is getting a good laugh out of this. As the two guys contort their faces, Ryan closes his eyes, remembering an image from his youth: a conveyor belt angled out of the back of his family's pig barn, carrying the manure directly from the stalls to the top of an enormous mountain of manure. On winter mornings, after Ryan shoveled the stalls and ran the belt, the mountain steamed. It was almost beautiful. The pile was maybe 20 feet tall but Ryan remembers it being much larger, 400 feet tall, 20 feet in diameter.

Jezebel makes a face, and says, "It was sort of like this. Well, I'm not sure—hand me that mirror so I can tell.... OK, there. Like that." She holds the expression and turns to Ryan: "Does that seem about right?" Ryan can't say anything. Maybe one day he will look back on this moment and laugh, but it doesn't seem likely. Help Ryan remember the mountain of manure more precisely. Use the data in the table below and the Trapezoidal Rule to calculate the volume of the pile. Also, draw diagrams of the five cross sections of the pile.

Table 1: Ryan's Family's Pile of Pig Manure

Cross section		skirt (facing barn)	toe	crown (barn)	center line	crown (facing road)	heel	skirt (road)
0'	dist.	5	10	5	0	5	10	5
	elev.	0	.25	.5	1	.5	.2	.1
5'	dist.	5	11	8	0	6	12	5
	elev.	1.2	5.9	12.2	13.4	11.9	4.7	.8
10'	dist.	5	84	305	0	302	78	5
	elev.	1.8	85	390.7	400.8	386.9	92.7	.46
15'	dist.	5	70	151	0	41	147	5
	elev.	.8	73	223	285.6	245.6	97.2	.18
20'	dist.	5	11	6	0	6	9	5
	elev.	.43	1.1	1.4	1.5	1.4	.9	.20

7. JEZEBEL IS HAVING a baby. She has three names picked out if it is a boy: Ryan Jr., Larry, or Sven. If it is a girl, she will call the baby Amanda, Jennifer, or Mary. What if she has twins? How many different combinations of these names are possible? Use the fundamental counting principle to solve this problem for Jezebel.

8. MARY IS JUST nine months old and already she is standing on her own two feet. She holds on to the coffee table and sways, looking at her mother while Jezebel expresses her problem in baby talk: Where's dada? Is he working late? Is dada at the gym? He could be at a bar with Bob, couldn't he? Yes, you recognize that name don't you? Uncle Bob! Yes! Mary burbles in agreement and toddles along the table. She has reached the end of the table now. She wavers for a moment then continues freestyle, without a net. She takes the first step of her life then pauses. She takes another step. And then, when she lifts her foot again, she loses her balance. Mary is 0.6 meters tall and has a mass of 18 kilograms. She traveled a distance of 0.8 meters. Right before Mary hits the ground, Jezebel swoops her up into her arms, and they are both delighted. Calculate the amount of work Mary did before she lost her balance. $W = mgh$. Use 9.8 m/sec2 for the acceleration of gravity.

9. UNCLE BOB BRINGS little Mary a balloon and reads her a story: Three little kittens lost their mittens, and they began to cry. They lost two mittens each. Mary falls asleep; the balloon slips from her hand, and drifts to the ceiling. During the next couple of days, the balloon sinks slowly to the floor. No one notices—0not Mary, not Jezebel, not Ryan, not Larry, not even Bob, who notices most things. And so, the balloon sinks from the 12-foot ceiling at a rate of 1.6 inches per hour. 1.25 cubic feet of helium seep from the balloon at a steady rate of 0.0095 cubic feet per hour. What is the balloon's position at hour ten? What is the balloon's volume at hour twenty? When will it hit the ground? Calculate the volume of helium in the balloon at that time. When it reaches the floor, the balloon and the helium have a total mass of 2.3 grams. The balloon's mass is one gram. Use Avogadro's number and the atomic mass of helium to estimate how many particles of gas remain inside the shrunken balloon.

INERRANCY:

AN INTERVIEW WITH DEWEY L. JOHNSON, IV

by RICK MOODY

SINCE 1997, WHEN I edited (with Darcey Steinke) an anthology of essays on the New Testament entitled *Joyful Noise*, I often find myself in situations where people feel free to share their religious convictions with me. These people have very strong feelings about the subject, and while I'm often moved and humbled by the insights of the faithful, I sometimes disagree strongly with their points of view. For example: not long after our book came out there was a particularly hostile review in an online magazine demanding to know where Darcey and I thought we got the right to interpret the Bible, since the Bible was literally true and therefore impervious to interpretation. This line of argument will be familiar to most readers. Yet, while I obviously differed with the politics of the reviewer, Dewey Johnson, I couldn't deny the tremendous energy of his prose. The work displayed an enthusiasm that was vital and surprisingly daring.

I decided I wanted to talk to the guy.

So I contacted the reviewer by e-mail. Turned out he was about my age and he was from Tennessee and he worked as a political operative for a political action committee that advanced the objectives of the Religious Right. Many weeks of contentious e-mail exchanges ensued in which this and other information came to light, as you will see. Like Johnson's book reviews, the communications were often short and brutal ("You ought to be strung up, and then cut down, and then strung up a second time, and then left to be fed on by buzzards," etc.), but funny, and in a distant way, respectful. When offered a chance to interview an "American professional" for a collection of pieces on work slated to appear in a major newsweekly, I therefore asked Dewey Johnson, the political operative with whom I'd been corresponding, if he wanted to submit to a few questions. The piece was later killed when I couldn't support a proposed edit. (They were less interested in the routine parts of his character than I was, in his little league career, what he liked for lunch, the model of his car, and so forth.)

The scene: the food court in the Watergate apartments complex in D.C., late December 2000, right after the election was resolved. Dewey is probably six-foot-four, and trim, with carefully combed brown hair that he parts low and combs up. He has green eyes. He has a light tan that makes him look faintly Mediterranean. On the day we met he wore a beige wash-and-wear suit and a rep tie. He tucked his paper napkin in at the neckline.

Dewey Johnson: [*putting down a tray including cheeseburger, fries, coke, and copious helping of asparagus*] You vegetarian or something?

Rick Moody: [*in consideration of a beet salad and slice of melon*] I eat fish sometimes, if I don't have a choice. Otherwise, yeah, I'm vegetarian.

DJ: How do you get comfortable with the inconsistent part of it? Eating fish when you won't eat red meat? Fish is an animal.

RM: Well, we're really here to talk about you. So let me ask you a couple of questions. Just to get warmed up. You can ask me a few things later, if it seems natural. Like, why don't you tell me where you were born? Where you grew up, that kind of thing.

DJ: Little town in the Cumberland mountains. In the state of Tennessee. My daddy owned a lumber and construction supplies company. I used to work for him on weekend loading up orders. Back when I was in high school. It was a lot of lifting and carrying.

RM: Did you work because your parents didn't give you an allowance or—

DJ: They believed work was good for you.

RM: You'd learn the value of money? That kind of thing?

DJ: Yessir. And they were right about that.

RM: Tell me about your early religious education. Were your parents avid churchgoers? Was your mom an important part of these decisions?

DJ: Let's see. They were Methodists, you know, like a lot of people I knew, and they went to church every Sunday, and my mom was a big part of that. But you know the truth of it was they hadn't really heard the call. There were churches in our town, run-down churches, needed paint jobs, like that, but in those churches you heard the call, so there was a light in them. The Methodists were comfortable, the way I saw things. They didn't need to carry the message particularly. I don't really expect you'd know exactly what I mean.

RM: I'm interested in the theology of it, though, so go ahead and explain.

DJ: I don't think it has anything to do with theology. See, that's part of why your northeastern churches aren't in the middle of the action. Because they say it's all about theology, and you sit around splitting hairs, talking about theology—Oh, what is St. Paul saying about fornication—when it's pretty darned obvious what he's saying, he's saying, "Don't be a fornicator." Like in the gospel of Mark, I think, says something about how…(*pausing thoughtfully*), the lusts of other things…uh…the lusts enter in…and choke the word and the word becomes *unfruitful*. Something like that. Unfruitful. That's what I was telling you about your book that time—

RM: Can you tell me a little bit about your conversion experience? I mean, I'm assuming there was a point at which you turned away from the Methodist upbringing of your parents and came to see *the light*, to use your epiphanic terminology. Was it a traumatic thing that catalyzed the change? Often, I hear of conversion experiences of young people and they're related to some unpleasantness at home—divorce, alcoholism, bankruptcy.

DJ: Nope. My parents are good people. Well, my Dad's passed. He was an honest guy though. I'm betting you'll look down on me if I tell you that he disciplined us sometimes. But he did. Only when we really needed it, which we sometimes did. I didn't pay attention unless there was the back of a hand involved. I wished it wasn't that way, but it was. My mom she still lives down in Tennessee. Last year I got this fundraising citation from the

Reverend Billingham. You know, like I was the best fundraiser on the staff. I don't really care about the awards and prizes, but a guy likes getting his due just the same. I gave the ribbon and the citation to my mother. She's over in an assisted-living place now. Don't see her as much as I should.

RM: You're painting a picture of a really idyllic childhood, with occasional outbursts of corporal punishment. It's good and sunny and American. Why would you even need to be born again? What was missing?

DJ: What do you want me to say? I'm not going to make up some story just because the guy from the magazine comes around promising fame and fortune. Oh, you know, my prostitute mother gave me up for adoption or something. Most kids in my town went to church, you know, going to church is nothing new.

RM: Most of them don't convert from the church of their birth, though.

DJ: I didn't have any white-light experience. Everybody thinks it's a white light experience. Only burning bush I ever saw was in a leaf pile down at the dump. There was no horrible thing that happened and there was no white-light experience. I mean, I saw my friend Tommy take off a couple of fingers on a lathe once. Does that count? In shop class. I never heard anyone yelping like that before. But I've seen some stuff since was just as bad, and Tommy he doesn't worry about not having all his fingers anymore. He plays softball with us now. He can still wear a glove. You can't mess up a man's soul on a lathe.

RM: Any siblings?

DJ: A brother.

RM: Is he a Methodist?

DJ: I wouldn't know. He's in the penitentiary. My brother ran off. He got to be sixteen or so. Guess he didn't love the things that were important to me as a kid. I guess it wasn't for him, so he just took the hell off. Left town. I loved that guy, you know, admired him even though he was my younger brother. I miss my brother every day, and I heard he's up in the federal penitentiary, but I don't know. I just want to say if he reads this he should know that I love him and forgive him. I just want to play running bases out in the backyard like we did when we were kids.

RM: What did your parents do about the difficulties with your brother?

DJ: You know there was a note on the kitchen table this one night, just a note, nothing else, and I remember all sitting around the table, reading the note, passing it around, like we couldn't believe the words on the page. Then we waited for him to come back. For a long while. Seemed like it was a couple of days, everyone nervous around the house. Except he didn't come back. My dad felt that we should let him go, not even look for him or anything, because he would come back. I don't think my mom agreed with that at all. She wanted to go after him. But what were we going to do? Fan out into the mountains? He hitched a ride someplace. Like kids do. My house was a dark place for a long while, just dark. Later he started writing to us, but by then my folks were real angry in addition to being upset. He wouldn't get back in that house without an apology, you know, and he wouldn't apologize. That old prideful story. Of course, then he started getting in real trouble.... Are you going to put all this in your article?

RM: I forgot to say that if at any point you don't want to answer a question, don't feel you have to.

DJ: Now you tell me! Can't you make that stuff about my brother deep background information or something?

RM: You want me to cut the stuff about your brother?

DJ: I'll make you a trade. You can leave some stuff about my family, if you'll let me get into it with you about your book, because that's why I came down here.

RM: What is it that you want to say?

DJ: I want to get on the record here that Biblical inerrancy, that's your term, right? That's not just a position, you know? That's the truth. You all, elites from up north, you think that we don't understand the issues that are in play, but we understand the issues, we just don't agree with you is all. We don't think it's *possible* that the words in the Bible were written by God, we *believe* it just the same as we believe that Jesus got resurrected. No negotiation on the point, see?

RM: Which translation are you using?

DJ: What do you mean which translation am I using? I'm using the Bible that's out in my Subaru.

RM: Yeah, but it's probably a different translation from the one I use. I only use the King James Version, because it sounds like poetry to me, but I'm betting you're using the New Revised Standard Version, or maybe one of those stripped-down translations, like the Living Bible or something. Either way, my translation is different from yours, which is different from the Aramaic and Hebrew in which the New and Old Testaments were written originally. So my question is, is the word of God the same in Aramaic as it is in the Living Bible, even though the words in the Living Bible don't agree with the NRSV or the KJ? Which one is the word of God? Which sequence of words properly represents the word of God?

DJ: [*Expresses disgust nonverbally, in a convulsive sort of a shrug.*]

RM: You really want to tangle about this? Let's move on. I want to know some more personal stuff. Do you keep a lot of stuff in the back of your car besides the Bible? You're single, right? And you do a lot of traveling, so I figure you must have a lot of fast food cartons and so forth in the back of your car, in the footwells, and maybe a tire iron or something. A tarp. A little bit of trash.

DJ: I don't eat too much fast food because it's not really very good for you. Same as you, I bet. I like donuts, though. But let's stick to the hard questions. I didn't show up to talk about donuts.

RM: Well, I think the oblique stuff can be as illuminating as the head-on material. But don't let me be an impediment to meaningful content. Why don't you tell me if your conversion experience was before or after your brother ran away?

DJ: It was after, but it was a couple of years after. I was in high school, I was playing baseball, I was pitching, in fact, and that was pretty much what I was doing at the time. I guess I didn't spend too much time doing homework. I got tendonitis in my arm, my throwing arm. I think it was because they were trying to teach me a slider and it just wouldn't take. I don't think it's probably too good to teach a kid a slider. My coach was trying to teach me a slider. And it just made my arm tingle, you know. My fingers started going numb. So I was sitting around the house a lot. Because I couldn't throw or anything. I'd work in the store, but mostly I was sitting around. One Sunday when my parents had tried to get me to go to church and I just didn't go—just sat out on the porch refusing to go, you know, all riled up—I ended up walking into town. It was two or three miles into town, and there was this great singing going on over at this run-down church, you know. Later on I learned the name of those kinds of songs, they're called Sacred Harp singing. It was for congregations where they didn't have any organ or piano or anything, and it was easy to teach to people who weren't singers. Reverend Marshall, he was the preacher up there, gave up on it after a while, because it wasn't going anywhere. But that day it sounded like the heavens themselves, when I was out on the other side of the door, feeling like I didn't belong anywhere at all. It welcomed me in.

RM: Are you a singer?

DJ: Can't carry a tune, but that doesn't mean music doesn't *sound* beautiful, doesn't mean I can't appreciate it when I hear it, because I think church singing is more beautiful than just about anything.

RM: What about the theological message of the church? When you got inside. Was it shocking to be in such a fundamentalist church?

DJ: I'm trying to tell you...

RM: You weren't particular about the message and all of that.

DJ: I went in there to sing, man. My father couldn't sing a note, neither, so there wasn't much music in our house. No records really, excepting some Christmas records and the radio.

RM: No rock and roll or anything?

DJ: I heard stuff in the grocery store, or over with friends at their houses, you know, I guess I liked the Eagles, I liked Roy Orbison, I remember hearing Roy Orbison, thinking it sounded great, George Jones, Loretta Lynn, but because I didn't ever hear too much of these songs, whenever I heard music it was always holy to me, always sounded really great. So I went places where I could just hear the harmonies and all, and I thought they were the harmonies like of angels singing. I'll tell you one funny story though.

RM: What's that?

DJ: When I was in my twenties, you know, and I was starting to get involved, volunteering and all, well, you know, I was doing some house calls for the church, so I was a pretty squeaky clean, or I guess you'd say I was squeaky clean, I heard this one thing somewhere, don't even remember where, maybe it was a sporting goods store or something, and it was the scariest thing I ever heard in my life, it was like a, I don't know, I guess sort of a heavy metal song, man, that was about the heaviest song I ever heard in my life, lowdown and creepy, and I just decided, I got to get myself a copy of this song, so I'm in the sporting goods store or wherever it was, and I pull over this guy, I say, *Listen you gotta tell me what this thing playing on the stereo system is,* and he doesn't know, so he has to get another guy from back in the stockroom or something, three or four of the guys from the store are clustered around me over by the cash registers, *What's the song?* I'm saying. *Tell me what the song is.* So, what do you think—

RM: I'm going to say "The Spirit of Radio," by Rush.

DJ: I don't know it.

RM: "You Shook Me All Night Long," by AC/DC?

DJ: "Enter Sandman." By that group called Metallica.

RM: Oh, yeah, I can see what you mean. It's scary.

DJ: I never was interested in any other songs along those lines, really, but there's something about that one song. I got a cassette with that song on it. I'm always pestering the choir, shouldn't we do this song, just one time so I can hear it. I'd like to hear a Sacred Harp version of Metallica. I know it's just a big joke, but there you go. The message gets to you in crazy ways, bunch of long-haired guys destroying hotel rooms and stuff, but they tell the truth this one time. That's the fact of conversion, if you're looking for that thing, look in music, if music isn't the thing itself that does the converting, well, then music is the *sign* of the thing. That's why there are so many songs about love. It's just a natural type thing.

RM: Okay, let's talk about how you got into your profession, then—

DJ: I'm out here telling you all about me, and you aren't telling me a thing, brother. Let's hear what you got.

RM: I didn't have any conversion experience. I still don't know if I'm converted. I have more skepticism than certainty and more doubts sometimes than beliefs. But I believe in ritual, I think. Priests and deacons getting down on one knee, genuflecting, passing around little conference-approved wafers, wearing their ridiculous robes, I like all that ritual. But I don't know about the resurrection, the virgin birth. I have trouble saying the Nicene Creed.

DJ: We could help you with that, you know.

RM: Thanks, but I'm already looked after.

DJ: I know, I know. You don't believe He really contacts nobody, all that. He just lets the sheep wander off from the flock, and they get lost out there in a valley with wolves and coyotes. It's your business, and I'm not going to talk you out of it—

RM: Not today you aren't. Did you ever cheat on your taxes?

DJ: Are we being taped? Listen, all I got to say about this is that it shouldn't be a foregone conclusion that the government gets my money in the first place, so if the government happens to see a little shortfall from the occasional taxpayer, that's just to remind it that it doesn't have a right to all this stuff. Nobody asked me if I agree with where all this money is going. If they want to let me sign off on some of those programs they got there, well, then we can talk about it. I don't want to finance any abortion clinics or any of this art that doesn't have any beauty in it. Should you all be expecting that I'm going to pay for that? I don't believe in that stuff. Why should I pay for it?

RM: You want to cut off ballet lessons for some really gifted black kid in Harlem? Is that gifted ballet dancer from Harlem not beautiful enough for you? Because that's what you're doing. Leaving her in front of the television in the afternoons. Maybe you have some kind of problem with her complexion?

DJ: [*Almost menacing*] Back off a second there.

RM: Don't get touchy. I'm just trying to get to know you better.

DJ: Sounds like you're trying to get to know your prejudices better if you ask me. I'm not raising up the black man and refusing to talk to him on the subway, like some of you all up there in the northeast. I live with the black man, and I talk to him every day, I go to church with him and I go to his house for dinner, and my house is open to him. He's not different from me. We think the same. We believe in the same things. We're equal in the eyes of God.

RM: Okay, okay, let's drop it. Let's get back to your profession.

DJ: Christian activist.

RM: You make a living like that?

DJ: There are times when it's not the easiest line of work, you know, from an economic point of view, but lately I'm canvassing, you know, for the coalition, and that combined with the money I'm bringing in as a salesman of beauty products, well, it's fine. I don't need a lot of money.

RM: How did you start doing this kind of thing? I mean, how did you go from just attending church and finding it helpful to your baseball career to wanting to do some heavy lifting for political organizations?

DJ: All the information gets passed on through mentors, you know, and it doesn't get passed on because some mentor *tells* you things, although he probably does that, but it gets passed on because of the way the mentor is living, the way he's being an upright man or the way she's being an upright woman, and you see that thing, the way a man or woman is living and you know that's a good thing, and a light shines from it or a certain music is coming off of that life, the way that man or women is living, and when you're in the wake of it, it's like you're at the tail end of that migrating flock of geese, and suddenly, even though you're just a young bird, you're right up top with this idea that you can fly all the way south to the Galapagos Islands. I was in the parish there, waving my church bulletin at myself, trying to stay cool, and the way that preacher was telling the tale, well, that was a thing that caught my attention, and I wanted to be around it, so I started calling with the Reverend Marshall on the hospitals and stuff, and I'd tell jokes, just anything to lighten people's burdens, because I didn't trust myself yet to carry the message of scripture, that was other people's job.

RM: And that led into political service?

DJ: I was helping out with the church treasury and encouraging people to tithe their incomes, and then when the Reverend started working with some of the regional conferences of the church, I started going along to the conferences, helping to set them up and all, and the politicians in the area they all came out to the conferences. One thing leads to another.

RM: So now you're on the payroll of these political action committees.

DJ: I'm trying to get certain ideas across, and you have to admit that even though we have a lot of our own newsletters and magazines now, you have to admit that you all up there, you aren't exactly giving us equal time in your national periodicals, so I figure it's okay for committees that believe the things that I believe to pay me because otherwise the work is not going to get done. Somebody has to do it, and that somebody has to be able to pay rent somewhere so he has a roof over his big head. I'm not going to *live* in my Subaru, you know?

RM: Any genuine political aspirations at the state or national level?

DJ: Well, I'm not too keen on the state level. Probably I should be, but I just don't think you get any kind of bully pulpit down there. It's down in the trenches. All the politics might be local, like I heard somebody say, but you have to be really concerned about getting new bus shelters built and all of that, and my mind is on different things. Other hand, if I was called to service at the national level, I'd accept that call and I'd be proud.

RM: Are you worried about public scrutiny? The attention to your background and all of that? That's what keeps most people out of public service these days.

DJ: Bring 'em on. I haven't had a drink since I was eighteen. I never had any of those other drugs at all. I'm not married because I haven't met the right lady yet, someone who can handle all the traveling I have to do here, all my responsibilities. But when I meet her, I'll be happy to make her my wife and to start a family with her. I never embezzled any funds from any employer, especially since my old man, rest in peace, was my employer when I was a young man. He wrote me some really good job recommendations.

RM: So it's all as good as it looks, and not just because you have a national newsweekly knocking at your door?

DJ: You're the one said that. Not me.

RM: Have you ever lusted in your heart?

DJ: I lusted in more places than my heart. I lusted in every cell in here, and I lusted at the roller rink and at the movie theater, I lusted in junior high school, and high school, and junior college. But that doesn't mean I ever did anything about it. I never compromised the morals of any young lady, even if I took her to the movies and drove her home after.

RM: So you're a virgin?

DJ: Come on. I'm not asking you if you're a virgin.

RM: I'm not a virgin, and I tried to get rid of my virginity as fast as I could, back when I was a teenager. Unfortunately, I was awkward and not good at any sports, nor could I play the electric guitar, nor was I particularly good looking, so I didn't have a prayer with respect to losing my virginity. I very nearly made it to my majority before shucking that particular layer. I don't imagine these days that kids would have as hard a time as I had. Juliet was fourteen, or something, when Romeo came calling at her window. I bet there are plenty of Romeos and plenty of Juliets out there. They should act responsibly. They should learn about their bodies. That's fine with me.

DJ: Yeah, well, what if love is more important than that? What if love is more important than some thing that happens in your glands? What if love is to prepare you for this big journey, and if you use it all up now, you aren't going to have any nourishment left for the big journey? Then maybe you'll think twice about just doing what your gland says you gotta do.

RM: I don't entirely believe you, Dewey. I don't believe that you weren't up in the upstairs bathroom taking forty-five minute showers, right after your brother was done with his forty-five minute showers, striding boldly down the corridor of self-abuse, in all ways, in all places, and I don't believe you didn't have the cache of *Playboys* secreted somewhere out in the shed.

DJ: Well, that's between me and the guy who sees all things, right? Maybe, you know, my brother did a lot of these things and I saw him sliding away, and that's how I came to figure, you know what, let me think about trying another way, let me think about it. On the other hand, there was just the one shower and the old man used to go crazy about wasting hot water, especially if we were in there too long, so nobody was doing anything in the showers.

RM: You admit you drank some as a teenager, and yet you're saying you never got drunk and never tried to have your way with some beauty from high school, up in the mountains of Tennessee, looking out at the valleys below, all that kind of thing?

DJ: I'll tell you one true story, and that's that I had a bicycle accident when I was drinking. I had this bike, which of course I had saved up a lot of money for, and I used to ride it to baseball and basketball practices, on account of it kept me in good shape, you know, and then I didn't feel like I had to run as much each day, because I hated jogging and I still do hate it. So we had some big game, like I don't know, county playoffs, yeah, I think that was it, county playoffs, and we had some beers after the game, and I was a little tipsy, and I was weaving down the hills, feeling like this was great, and I come around the turn into town, past the ice cream joint there, Tasty Freeze, lose control of the bike somehow, plow into this ice cream truck that's parked in the crosswalk where I'm about to make a turn, just plow right into the thing. At the last second, I figure out what's going to happen, that I'm not really going to make the turn, and so I get out of the way, fall right off the bike, because there's some little kids there, but one kid drops his sherbet right on me, on my baseball jersey. The rims of the tires were all bent up and everything. I'm given a warning for *operating a bicycle while under the influence.* The cops were there watching the whole darned thing, from the squad car across the street. True story.

Look, I'm not going to sit here and say that I didn't like the beers, man, because I did, and Jesus gave wine to the disciples, and fasted in the desert too. I think that most teenagers that dope themselves up, they're just giving all the beauty of youth away. One day you wake up and that time is gone, you know?

RM: If I search your car I'm not going to find a flask in there?

DJ: You calling me a liar? I don't appreciate being called a liar.

RM: No, but I'll tell you that you don't seem like the guy who wrote those reviews online a couple of years ago, and that could easily be because I have this Dictaphone turned on here, and I couldn't blame you if that were the case because I have done interviews myself when it was the best of all strategies not to let on, or rather to allow myself into the interview only in the most limited way, because the interviewers weren't going to understand, really. It just takes too much sometimes, it's too complicated. But the Dewey Johnson who wrote that stuff about my book a couple of years back was a harlequin of the Religious Right, a creative imp, the kind of guy who had a past the way Augustine had a past, stealing peaches before he wrote the *Confessions.* Your confessions today don't feel like confessions to me, they feel like snapshots from some TNN broadcast of your life. If you want to convert me to your totalitarian religion of perfect adherence, then I say make your advance men *real people*, aspirants and sinners at the same time.

DJ: Take what you need. Jesus himself didn't stop at learning how to change water into wine, though, that was just his party trick. I'm not stopping at online book reviews. We're about to have a president in office who believes in the things I believe in.

RM: And you've never been with any woman? That's really what you're saying?

DJ: We used to go to a Christian summer camp when I was a boy, up in the mountains, over near the seminary. Lots cooler up there in the summer. Used to have campfires and so forth, and I used to volunteer to break down the stage after the campfires. You know, fold up the chairs, make sure the fire was out. I was always the last one to bed. Up there, in the summer, you can see all the stars. One time Cathleen, can't remember her name, Cathleen something. Anyway, she was a great athlete, that girl, played basketball and was a great horseback rider and all, she stayed to help me smother out the last of the fire. She knew all the constellations, turns out, and we sat out there for a while and she taught me some. We held hands.

RM: Did you kiss her?

DJ: Wanted to, but didn't. I wish I knew where Cathleen lived now, though, because those old days, those seemed like simpler, easier times.

RM: Okay, I give up. Well, we only need fifteen-hundred words. We have plenty here. Let me just ask a couple of biographical questions then. Uh, where do you live now?

DJ: Winchester, VA.

RM: Your feelings about Ralph Nader?

DJ: Homosexual.

RM: What kind of cereal do you eat?

DJ: Sometimes I'm too busy for breakfast, but if I'm home I'll just eat corn-flakes and some jelly on toast. One thing I hate is skim milk.

RM: What did Dewey Johnson's I, II, and III do for a living?

DJ: Livestock, mostly. They had dairy and some crops, some tobacco. Lost the acreage back in the Depression. When my dad was just a boy. My daddy's brother, my uncle, I guess he hung himself back then, in the Depression.

RM: Your uncle hanged himself?
DJ: He did. And my dad cut him down. He was much younger, my dad, so it must have been like cutting down your hero. Like your hero just gave up and showed himself as someone who couldn't handle this life. There's des-

perate people all around, shying away. Used to be farming was the thing that made you feel close to the world, but somewhere along the line, farming became what made you feel cut off from the world. He never had any kids either, my uncle. Unless my brother in the pen has kids, the Johnson line dies out with me. I got to look after that.

RM: That's something you worry about?

DJ: Nah, not really. I worry about today. The situations I got today. And about whether I got a parking ticket out front. That kind of thing.

RM: Hey, how was the hamburger?

DJ: Heavenly. How about that beet salad?

DARTS 'N' LAURELS

by J. ROBERT LENNON

FROM THE EDITORS: *"We at the* Nestor News *are grateful to all our readers for once again making our paper the most-read in Lake County, for the fifth year in a row! We also want thank our staff in circulation and marketing for 'getting it out there,' and our advertisers for providing our beautiful county with the products and services we love. And finally, thanks to our contributors, whose dedication has made this editorial page the best anywhere. Hats off to you!"*

LAUREL: From Mrs. Albert King of Penns Falls. "A big thank-you to the anonymous good Samaritan who helped me change my flat tire on route 83 last week, after the Garden Society meeting! I had let my AAA membership lapse and was in a real pickle. Mr. Mystery Helper also noticed that my tail lights weren't working, and spent a good five minutes in the car changing the fuse. It is people like you who make our county great! As a side note, I seem to have lost my purse, house keys and prescription sunglasses somewhere. If any Garden Society members find them, please call!"

DART: From Hank Jance of Patient Grove. "Let me scold my brand-new wrought-iron fence for leaping out onto Swayze Road and crashing into an oncoming car, and then wedging itself back into place all bent up and broken. Bad, bad fence! After all the time and money I spent on you, how could you be so irresponsible? And thanks to whichever upstanding generous citizen whose car (a 1978 Volvo, judging from the shards of broken headlight) suffered at the hands of my nasty little twenty-five-hundred-dollar fence, and who didn't bother to trouble me about my fence's misdeed. How kind of you, citizen."

LAUREL: From Gabe Klamp of Iron Pole. "To this newspaper, for your wonderful series on death and dying. I have been through many deaths and rebirths and appreciate your attention to the subject. As I said in one of my former lives, we should not fear 'to sleep, perchance to dream.' Thank you."

LAUREL: From Geraldine Geraldson of Large Intersection. "To all our mothers, the loins of whom we are the fruits. Bravo, selfless rearers!"

DART: From the Rev. Marden Hibachi of Greater Lake Episcopal Church. "The Greater Lake Episcopal Church illuminated reader board is the sole property of Greater Lake Episcopal Church, and is reserved for messages the Church and its parishioners deem appropriate. If you are responsible for rearranging the letters of our scriptural quotes into blasphemies, all I can say is your eternal reward awaits. That is the word of God you are desecrating. For the record, the quote is LAMB OF GOD, YOU TAKE AWAY THE SINS OF THE WORLD, not YO SLAM-DOG, EAT YAK IN THE WET WOLF DRESS."

LAUREL: From Meghan Loos of Bracken Spring. "I just want to say thanks to the Onteo Lake Massage Academy, especially a certain pair of strong warm hands, you know whose you are, for 'rubbing my troubles away'! My 'troubles' aren't quite totally away yet but I finally felt good enough to hire a lawyer. When everything's final, I'll be back for more of your 'healing touch'!"

LAUREL: From Brant Patch of Nestor. "I bow down to the masters of rock, Irate Expectations, for kicking my butt all over the Stomper Room Friday night! All hail the mind-blowing lords of the decibel! May you open many more cans of whup-ass for many weekends to come! Also, everybody come hear my band Stab, at Currents this Saturday, no cover with a two-drink minimum!"

DART: From Gwen Hocker of Quarry. "To my kids, for being such stupid brats at my sister's wedding, and to their father Al, for getting loaded and groping our new step-niece. Congratulations Nell and Gary, and I hope you know what you're doing."

DART: From Martin Shuffleboard of New Belgium. "To myself, for all the things I said at Town Council last Monday. Certain Council members took my statements the wrong way. I did not mean to suggest that those who favor widening Reece Road and Highway 41 actually were Marauding Crypto-Fascist Nazi Overlords, only that they ought to keep their snouts in their own damn crotches. Also, I will not really set anyone on fire, even if they ask to use my phone."

DART: From Annelise Gomber of Frankly. "Whoever smeared tomato sauce all over the joystick of the Hong Kong Rumble machine at Peak's Pizza, I hope you choke and die. I was almost to Dragon Level when my hand stuck."

LAUREL: From Carl Poker of Smiddy. "Let us express our gratitude to that everlasting source of heat and light, the sun! This has been such a lovely week in Lake County! Oh, life-giver, cast your warming rays upon us! Join me in praising also Lake Onteo's shimmering waters, the cleansing winds that doth blow, and the lush forests that give us air to breathe!"

DART: From Dirk Mark of Chipton. "To the publication in which this column regularly appears, for editing, abbreviating, trimming, compressing, and removing all traces of evidence of my personality from, my occasional (even regular and perhaps frequent) epistles, memos, notes, and so on, all without my prior consent, go-ahead or permission, and while not even getting around to notify me that you are doing it! I do not know nor can even surmise what the reason is that you would alter my writings from their original form, but these aforementioned editorial shenanigans turn my face, neck, forehead, and upper arms the color red! I demand your immediate stoppage right at this point in time!"

THE NISTA AFFAIR

by JONATHAN AMES

IN JUNE OF 1987, I graduated from college. A week after commencement, I sold my senior thesis, a novella, to a New York publishing house. But there were two conditions: I had to expand the book into a full-length novel, and it was due in six months.

In July, a few weeks after selling my book, I found out that I had a fifteen-month-old son. His mother sent a letter with a photograph of him, a baby boy with red hair and blue eyes. I have red hair and blue eyes.

In late October, two chapters of my novel were stolen by a stranger who lured me into something of a trap. The theft occurred on the Upper West Side of Manhattan. I reported the crime to the 24th Precinct.

In November, after not drinking for twelve months and one week, I went on an alcoholic binge and ended up in a psychiatric hospital.

In November, while in the hospital, I discovered who stole my writing.

This story is about how those two chapters were taken from me. I'll start from the beginning.

The novella was twenty-thousand words; I had to get it up to fifty-thousand. I was given some money, not a lot, by the publishing house, but I was on top of the world. From New Jersey, I moved to New York City. I sublet my cousin's rent-control apartment on the Upper East Side. I set up a writing desk—yellow pads and a typewriter. I had thirty-thousand words to go.

That very first week I became scared: I couldn't write.

By the second week, I thought maybe it was the apartment. I learned about a special study room in the public library on Forty-second Street. It was for writers and was in the back of the long reading room. You had to have a key. It was a privilege. I applied and was allowed to use the room. I started going there like going to a job, but the writing didn't improve. The trip to the library would tire me out, and I'd use my privilege only to take naps, my head on the table.

In July I received the letter about my son. His mother was an older woman, a good woman, whom I had slept with once. She and my son lived down south. My plan was to go see her and the baby as soon as I finished the book. I couldn't handle my dream of being a writer and my unexpected fatherhood at the same time. So I was going to tackle the situations as they had arisen, first the book and then my son. I was only twenty-three; it was the best plan I could come up with.

One night in July—though I was half-crazy with fears and anxiety about everything—I went to a party. I was invited by a friend of mine who didn't show up. I didn't know anyone at the party and was going to leave, but the hostess, a woman named Marie, was very nice to me and insisted that I stay. She knew from my absentee friend that I was working on a book. She asked me how it was going, and I told her about the study room at the public library. I lied and said the library was a good place to work. I didn't want to tell her that I was crumbling under the pressure of a professional contract and couldn't write a word. I stayed at the party for two hours. Marie asked me for my number so that she could invite me to her next party.

The following day a woman called me and introduced herself as a friend of Marie's. Her name was Julia, and she apologized for bothering me, but explained that she was a writer and that Marie had told her about the study room in the library. She wanted to know how one could get a key to the room. I told her. She was very grateful. She called me two days later and said she had a key. She said we should meet some time at the library and go for coffee. She was very funny and flirtatious on the phone. At some point in the conversation, she said, "You know who my father is, right?"

I didn't know who her father was. I hadn't made the connection with her last name. It turned out she was the daughter of an extremely famous writer. I did feel my heart leap a little at my closeness to celebrity, but not too much. I knew his fame, but hadn't read his books. I agreed to meet with her for coffee.

A few days later, I met Julia in front of the library, and the first thing she said to me was, "You look like a Swedish sailor." It was summer, and my hair was very light, almost blonde. She meant the Swedish line as a compliment and I took it as one. She was in her late thirties and she wore a loose-fitting dress—she was heavy. Her face was long and pale. Her dark hair was curly from a permanent. Beneath her large brown eyes were deep purple rings of exhaustion.

We went to a coffee shop and we got along fine. I liked her. She was funny, and it was good to talk to her. We were both nervous about our writing: I was scared that I wouldn't be able to finish my novel, and she was scared that she would never be able to write hers and escape her father's shadow.

After our coffee together, Julia started calling me frequently, and we developed a phone friendship. We didn't see each other at the library, as she went in the evenings after work.

In August, I began to receive prank phone calls. Someone was calling my answering machine ten to fifteen times a day and hanging up. When I was home the same thing happened. Dialing star-69 didn't exist at that time, and I called the phone company only to learn that tracing calls was tedious and expensive. I hoped the calls would just stop. Julia told me that the same thing had happened to her a few months before, and she had tried to do the tracing but it didn't work, because the person was calling from payphones. I endured the constant ringing.

I wasn't sleeping well during this time and often had nightmares. I dreamt one night that the soles of my feet had slit open up like envelopes. When I looked inside my feet, I saw that they were hollow and rimmed with blood. The whole next day, remembering my dream, I could hardly walk. I thought I might be cracking up, but I kept going to the study room, so I could take naps.

One evening in August I became sick. I had food poisoning, some kind of stomach disturbance. Julia wanted to come over and take care of me. I told her that I would be all right, but she begged me to let her nurse me. I assented and she arrived with teas and a giant bottle of Pepto-Bismol and several boxes of antacid tablets. She had stocked up at a pharmacy.

She visited with me for at least two hours. She saw some of my novel on my desk and asked if she could read it. I told her no. I was feeling terrible about my work. She insisted that I let her read something. I kept saying no. She seemed hurt and offended by my refusal.

A few nights later, my stomach problem had cleared up, and she invited me to her place for dinner. She had a nice apartment on the Upper East Side, and she made a good meal. After dinner, we drank coffee. We started talking about our childhoods and she told me a strange story from her high school years. She went to an exclusive all-girls school on Fifth Avenue and, during her freshman year, fell in love—from a schoolgirl distance—with her music teacher, a handsome Swedish man in his thirties. She found out where he lived and spent her weekends spying on him. With a Super-8 camera, she filmed him leaving his building and followed him, or she wouldn't follow him and instead snuck into his building and stole some of his mail. If he did laundry and left the laundromat, she stole an item of his clothing. She did this for all four years of high school, taking his class every semester and never letting the music teacher know she loved him.

Her father eventually found out what was going on and sent her to a psychiatrist. But she didn't stop doing what she wanted. "My father was the one who needed a shrink," she said. At the end of her senior year, she gathered together her movies of the music teacher, the poems and stories and plays she had written about him, the photographs he had inspired, and his mail and clothing she had taken, and she put all of this material in eighteen shopping bags, which was symbolic to her because she was now eighteen.

Julia arranged to meet with the music teacher. She brought the bags to school and lined them up in the gym. She showed him all the bags. "What's this?" he asked. She told him to look in the bags, and he did. She was very excited for him to see all she had done for him, the depth of her adoration and her love. After poking around in a few bags, he said to her, "If you wanted to get laid, why didn't you just ask?"

Julia then stopped telling her story and just looked at me. I pictured very clearly the music teacher standing over eighteen shopping bags. I admired his calm reaction.

"Can you believe he said that to me?" Julia asked, still indignant twenty years later. "I was just a girl. I was in love with him, and he couldn't see that."

I knew she wanted me to take her side, but it was such a strange story. "What did you do?" I asked.

"I just turned around and left him with the bags, and my crush was completely over. It hadn't been about sex. I was so disappointed in him. But what he said was the best thing for me. Worked a lot better than all the therapy. I felt nothing for him instantly."

"Do you think he was angry about the mail?" It was a dumb question, but I loved to get mail and would have been very upset if mine was ever stolen.

"I never heard from him if he was," she said, and she smiled. "I hope he was angry."

"That's some story," I said.

"You can't ever write about it," she said.

"I won't," I said.

The conversation took on a lighter tone and I thought, Well, she was crazy twenty years ago, but now she's normal. We drank more coffee, and she told me she was invited every fall to a party that Woody Allen threw—she had met him through her father, but now was friends with him on her own right—and she suggested I should come with her to the party.

As I was leaving, she asked me at the door if she could kiss me. I wasn't attracted to her. I said, trying to be kind, "I think I'd rather be friends." But then, so as not to reject her completely, I said, foolishly, "We could have a hug good-bye."

So we hugged, and she held me tight. Her breasts were against my chest. I didn't mean to, but I became aroused.

"I thought you just wanted to be friends," she said and went to kiss my mouth. I tried to kiss her on the cheek. Her lips brushed the corner of my mouth. I got out of her arms. I thanked her for dinner and left. It was an uncomfortable moment, but she didn't seem angry.

By the end of August, I was getting nowhere with my novel and thought that it must be New York. I gave up my rent-controlled apartment and moved back to Princeton. My hope was that I could write there, in the quiet. The book was due in three months, but even more importantly, I wanted to finish it so I could go see my son.

In Princeton, I rented a room in a house with two graduate students. I set up a phone line with one of them, listing my name in information. By the second day of phone service the hang-ups started again, five to ten times a day. I felt as if a sick taint had followed me from New York. My house-mate kept picking up the phone. I didn't tell her I was the cause of it. I was frightened by the calls and was going to set up the trace this time, but I procrastinated, and then, after a few days, the calls stopped.

In mid-September I received a phone call from Marie, the woman whose party I had gone to in July. She was calling to ask me a favor on behalf of Julia. Marie told me that Julia had a bad relationship with her father and only visited him once a year, usually in September. Marie always went with Julia for these visits to provide support, but this year she couldn't make it, and Julia wanted me to go. For some reason Julia felt too embarrassed to ask me herself and so she had enlisted Marie to make the call. I told Marie that I could do it, and she said Julia would be very happy. I didn't feel good about my motivation, though. I wanted to meet the famous writer.

I hadn't seen Julia since the night she had tried to kiss me, but we had continued our friendship over the phone as if nothing had happened. After speaking to Marie, Julia called a little while later and thanked me for wanting to go with her. "Every year," she said, "it was a difficult trip."

"I'm happy to go with you," I said, "but don't you think you should take a friend you've known longer?"

"I want you to come," she said. "I've known you long enough to feel that you're a friend."

The following weekend, I met Julia in New York, and we took the train out to the country. Her father had a beautiful home, and I was put up in a large guest cottage. Next to my bed was an enormous bookshelf with all the foreign translations of his books.

Over the course of the weekend Julia's father treated me like a lost son. On Saturday and Sunday mornings, he made oatmeal for me, a ritual with him. Supposedly he had never made a bowl of oatmeal for anyone else. Julia and her father's young girlfriend, who was Julia's age, made a big deal about this oatmeal.

He and I went for a bike ride on a path through the woods next to his house, and then we sat in his den and watched a baseball game. We talked about my writing and he said, "Sounds very difficult to turn a novella into a novel. I've never tried to do it. Maybe it isn't supposed to become a larger story."

This frightened me, because I suspected it was true. Then he said, "But you can do it and you have to do it. Don't worry about plot. Just get your character into trouble."

The two nights I was there he had dinner parties with interesting and talented guests. One night there was a famous screenwriter and I regaled the table with the story of a fight I got into in Paris and how my nose was broken. The screenwriter said to the writer, "Where did you get this kid? He has too many stories."

Julia's father beamed, and then he joked, "They're all lies," and he smiled at me. Julia was very quiet.

The day we left, Julia's father gave me several first edition hardbacks of his novels. He gave me all the books he had written in the first-person since I was writing my novel in the first-person. "These should help you," he said.

I left him feeling quite good about myself. A famous writer had liked me very much, and I liked him.

On the train back to the city, Julia said to me, "My father had a talk with me this morning. Do you know what he told me?"

"I have no idea," I said. My vanity had me hoping that I would hear some compliment about myself.

"He said to me, 'Why don't you marry someone like Jonathan. He's substantial. You never bring men like him around. That last boyfriend of yours was anorexic.'"

"What did you say?"

"Nothing. He's a horrible and rude man. It's none of his business. And then before we left, he said it again, 'Marry him.'"

"You could have explained to him that we're just friends."

"Why would I tell him that?"

"So that he wouldn't bother you."

"You don't understand my father," she said, and she turned to look out the window, and I let the conversation drop.

It was a long train ride, and I started writing in my journal, and for some reason, I wrote, "I'm crazy. Julia's crazy. All my friends are crazy."

I hadn't realized it, but she was watching me write and she said, "You think I'm crazy?"

"I think you're crazy in a good way. See, I wrote that I'm crazy, that all my friends are crazy."

She was silent and then she said, "You know I brought you up there to spend time with me, not my father."

"I'm sorry," I said. "He kept asking me to do things."

"You could have said no."

"I'm sorry… I didn't want to be rude."

"So you were rude to me. You were *my* guest."

I didn't say anything. I was in over my head. I regretted having gone with her. We were both silent. Then she said, "I'm not angry at you, I'm angry at him. I can't stand the man, but I visit him once a year because he's my father."

I left her at the station in New York, and vowed that I wouldn't have anything more to do with her. I had enough problems. Alone on the train to New Jersey, I wrote in my journal, "Julia would kill me if she knew this, but I like her father more than her. She gives me the creeps. Scary to write this, but she reminds me of a brooding spider."

In October, Julia left for California for eight days and sent me a package with eight presents. I was to open one present each day she was gone. I opened them all at once. They were strange presents: a Jackie Mason tape, fancy pencils, expensive fudge, potpourri, a little travel alarm clock, beautiful rubber erasers to go with the pencils, a thermometer to put out my window, and a small desk ornament—a tiny globe. The letter with the presents thanked me for going with her to her father, but then ended angrily: "You didn't have to be so cold on the train. You didn't have to tell me that we were only friends. Don't be so pompous. Who do you think you are?"

I considered throwing the gifts away, but I thought this would bring me bad luck. So I stored her presents in my closet and pressed on with trying to write my book.

My son's mother sent me more photos to look at—we had talked on the phone a few times—and I wrote back telling her that I would come see them both very soon. I kept hoping to go on some Kerouac-like writing jag and finish the book, but no such jag occurred.

At the end of October, I received a phone call from a woman who said that she was helping to organize a literary symposium of young American writers to be held in Sweden, at Gothenburg University. The symposium was jointly sponsored by the University and by a Swedish literary magazine called *Nista*. The woman had a slight accent. Her name was Sara Sundstrom.

She told me that I was one of twelve candidates whom they were considering. She was calling from New York and wanted to interview me. Selection for the symposium was based on this interview and a sample of my work. If chosen I would receive an all-expenses-paid trip to Sweden in March. I readily agreed to be interviewed and we made an appointment to meet in New York in two days.

That night Julia called. She was just back from California, and her voice was ebullient. She said, "Did you receive my package?"

"Yes," I said and thought of mentioning the angry tone at the end of her letter, but decided not to—she was sounding friendly, and I didn't want any conflict.

"Did you only open one present each day? I wanted you to think of me each day that I was gone," she said.

"I opened one each day. The Jackie Mason tape was the first," I said. I didn't like to lie, but it was a sort of half-truth. The Jackie Mason *had* been the first thing I unwrapped. "It was an interesting assortment, thank you.... How was your trip?"

"Terrible. I was practically blind the whole time. I had a problem with my contact lenses, they were scratching my eyes—I had to go to an eye doctor. I don't like to go to doctors I don't know."

We talked for a little while longer. I told her about the symposium in Sweden, and then we rang off. I thought to myself that my friendship worked fine with her over the phone, but that in person it was a disaster.

Sara Sundstrom called back the next day, but I wasn't in, and she left a message on my machine asking me to bring a photograph of myself to our meeting. She didn't leave a number where I could reach her.

The following night, around nine o'clock, I met with her at Birdland on Broadway, up near Columbia, as we had planned. She was sitting at a table next to the large window that looked onto the street. She was a blonde woman in her mid-thirties. She was small and had handsome features. Her skin was a little worn from the sun. She seemed very European: mature and cool. She stood up to shake my hand and then we both sat down. She said, "I don't have much time, so we have to do this quickly."

"All right," I said. Her attitude was as if I had requested the interview. She already had a drink, and I didn't bother to order one.

"Do you have your writing sample and the photograph?"

"Yes," I said, and smiled, drawing them out of my backpack. I wanted to appear friendly and outgoing so I could get a free trip to Sweden. I handed her two chapters of my novel and the photograph. She put them in her bag, and then she put on the table a small tape recorder. She pressed "record" and began to ask me questions: What would you offer to the symposium? What new things could you say about writing and literature in America today? Who are your influences? Are you calm in front of a large audience asking you questions?

She was stern and almost mean. I tried to give concise and intelligent answers, but I struggled. I said things like, "I'd love to come and talk about American literature. There are so many American writers I've loved, I can hardly name them."

Then the phone at the bar rang. The bartender answered and said to us, "Is one of you a Dr. Sundstrom?"

"That's me," she said. She went up to the bar and took the phone for just a minute.

When she came back to the table, I said, "You're a doctor?"

"I have a Ph.D.," she said.

"In what?" I asked.

"The Russian language," she said. It was the very end of the Cold War, and there was something spooky about her being a doctor of Russian. I was about to ask her who had called, but she said, "So you'd like to come to Sweden?" It was the first time she smiled at me, and she seemed to soften.

"Yes, very much," I said.

Then she told me that she needed cigarettes. She glanced out the window and said she was going to run across the street and get a pack. I looked out the window. Across Broadway there was a little tobacco and newspaper shop.

She picked up the tape recorder and her bag and said, "I'll be right back." She smiled at me. I sat at the window in Birdland and watched her cross the street. It was night, but Broadway was well-lit by the streetlights and the headlights of the cars.

Something was wrong. She had told me we didn't have much time, but suddenly she's going across the street for cigarettes. I wanted to follow her, but I wondered if I was just being paranoid. If I joined her across the street and she was simply getting a pack of cigarettes, then I would blow my chance at a free trip to Sweden by acting as if I didn't trust her.

She went into the store. The lights on Broadway changed, and the road filled with traffic. I tried to watch for her through the cars and buses, but it was difficult to see the other side of the street.

When the lights turned red again there was a clear view, but I didn't see her coming out of the store. I was getting anxious. The light changed once more, and I couldn't see across the street, and she didn't return to the bar. I asked the bartender if she had paid for her drink, and he said she had.

I ran across Broadway to the newspaper store, but she wasn't there. I asked the proprietor if a blond woman had come into the store, and he said yes, but that she had left several minutes ago.

"She's not in the bathroom? Do you have a bathroom?"

He looked at me like I was crazy. I ran back across Broadway to Birdland.

"The woman I was with, has she come back?" I asked the bartender.

She hadn't. She had taken off with my photograph and my two chapters. I had other copies, but the idea that she had walked off with them sickened me. Something grotesque was happening. I had no way to find her. She had never given me a phone number or an address where I could reach her.

I called my agent—I didn't know who else to call—from a payphone on Broadway. I said to her, "That person who was interviewing me for that symposium in Sweden... I know this sounds crazy, but she just stole two chapters of my novel."

"Are you sure?" my agent asked. She probably thought I was drunk. I told her what happened, and she said, "Go to the police. This way we'll have a record in case those pages get published somewhere."

I went back to Birdland and asked the bartender where the closest precinct was. It was over on Amsterdam, the 24th. The station was in the middle of some tough-looking projects.

Except for a sergeant at the front desk, the station seemed deserted. The sergeant was a portly, soft-looking man with glasses and a bald head. His desk was elevated. I looked up at him and said, "Excuse me officer... This is very odd, but I'd like to report something stolen."

"What?"

"I'm a writer... and somebody just took off with two chapters of my manuscript."

"Fiction?"

"Yes," I said.

"Really?"

"Yes."

"This is right up my alley, then—I'm a fiction buff!" He smiled happily at me. "I love to read. I'd like to write a book someday. As a cop you hear a lot of stories... But I have to say you're the first writer to come in because somebody stole his writing."

He made a phone call, and another officer came into the room, a heavy-set woman. She led me to a desk and typed up my report and gave me a receipt. I took the train back to New Jersey.

The next day, first thing in the morning, I went to Firestone Library on the Princeton campus and did some research. There was no magazine called *Nista* in any listings. I did, however, find the phone number of Gothenburg University.

I rushed home, made the international call, and was connected to the English department. It was late in the afternoon in Sweden, and a secretary put me through to the head of the department, a man who spoke perfect British-accented English. I said I was an American novelist connected with Princeton University and asked if his department was having a symposium in March of young American writers.

"No, no such symposium."

"I heard that there was going to be some kind of panel... might it be held by another department?"

"No other department except this one would be interested in American writers."

"Have you heard of a literary magazine called *Nista?*"

"No."

"Is there such a word as "nista" in Swedish?"

"No."

"Thank you for your help," I said. "There's been a misunderstanding."

"Perfectly all right," he said, and he laughed and we hung up.

I don't know what the professor made of such a strange overseas call, but my mind was reeling. The whole thing was a mad hoax. I felt sick. Who would hate me enough to arrange such an elaborate trick?

The following day, a message was left on my machine by a man with a phony-sounding foreign accent. He spoke with great urgency: "This is Dr. Bohanson. I am the editor of *Nista* magazine. I received your writing! It is very important that I speak to you! I am in Boston airport. Call me!"

That was all he said. He didn't leave a number. Boston airport. Not even Logan airport. Who was doing this to me?

The next morning I stepped out to get the paper and, when I came back, there was a message from Sara Sundstrom: "Dr. Bohanson wants to speak to you about your writing. Why don't you call?" She didn't leave a number. She had never given me a number.

Their torture of me was strange and absurd. The woman's voice was hateful. There was no way I could get any writing done. I was no closer to finishing my novel and seeing my son. I needed to clear my mind, so that afternoon I drove to the ocean.

I went to Asbury Park, a place I had often gone to for its downtrodden beauty: the rusted Ferris wheel with each car bearing the name of a Jersey town; the deserted boardwalk; the closed fudge and taffy shops; the warped and gigantic wooden casino, which looks as if it's going to topple into the ocean; and, of course, the Atlantic, gray and enormous and indifferent.

It took me an hour to drive from Princeton. When I got there, I sat on the beach. It was a cool November day, but the sun was bright. I was all alone except for a few stragglers on the boardwalk, and I stared at the ocean. Then I got on my knees, bent my head to the ground, resting it on my hands, and started praying. I was agnostic, but I prayed to God to help me. I was overwhelmed by everything. I needed help. I dug my hands into the sand. They got entangled in something wet and I lifted them up. Attached to my fingers were damp strips of disintegrating toilet paper, and on the paper were little black bugs. I screamed and thrashed my hands in the sand to get the bugs and paper off me.

I went running off the beach and into the bar of the Empress Hotel, across the street from the boardwalk. This wasn't a good thing for me to do. I was young, but I had quit drinking the year before and knew being sober had enabled me to write my novella and graduate. But I didn't care. I ordered a beer and a shot of whisky.

The Empress was a transient hotel. Like the rest of Asbury Park, the Empress had probably been glorious in the fifties—it looked like something from Miami. The bar still operated, and the drinks were cheap. It was afternoon when I got in there, and I drank for hours. At some point I sat at a table with a borrowed pen and a piece of paper and wrote a long drunken letter to my son. I gave him lots of advice and apologized that I hadn't been able to come see him yet.

I remember looking up from the letter to see that I had been joined at the table by an old woman. She must have been seventy, her hair was gray and her eyes were crazy.

She told me that Abraham Lincoln was Jewish—you could tell because of his name, and that she had taken an accounting course with Frank Sinatra in Jersey City in the 1930s. At some point, she said she wanted to have sex with me if I wore a condom. She said she hadn't had sex in years.

I was crazy drunk and agreed to have sex with her. When we stood up from the table, I saw that she was incredibly tiny. She was about four-foot eight and used an old broomstick for a cane. She was wearing a housedress. I realized then that I was completely mad, and there was no way I could sleep with this woman. I told her that I was starving, that I had been drinking for hours. I suggested we go to a restaurant and have dinner rather than go to her room. She said, "They won't let me in any restaurant the way I look. You go and come back. I'll be waiting."

I went to another bar, spent the rest of my money, and then got into my car and blacked out.

I came to on some restricted roads of the Fort Dix military base. I have no idea how I got in there. I found my way out and, half-conscious, half-drunk, drove back to Princeton. I am beyond fortunate that I did not kill anyone. Somewhere I lost the letter I wrote to my son.

I drank for a week. I went to a psychologist and told him about getting a letter with a picture of my son, *Nista*, the miniature old woman I had almost slept with, and everything else. I asked him to put me somewhere to sober up. He said he wasn't sure if I had a drinking problem or if I was chemically imbalanced.

He put me in a psychiatric hospital that had an alcohol unit, covering all my potential problems. After a humiliating week on the locked-up psychiatric ward, I was transferred to the alcoholic wing.

I told my life story to the group and afterwards, the head doctor said to me, "You're an alcoholic and a maniac. Some day you're going to have a florid psychotic moment and end up in Bellevue. But because you're smart, when you come out of it you'll be able to talk your way out. But then it will happen again. If you don't go on lithium you'll lose your mind and never write that book."

The doctor was chewing Nicaret gum while he gave me my life sentence. I refused to go on the lithium.

The doctor came by my room the next day and gave me articles about manic-depressive alcoholic artists who commit suicide without lithium. He tried to convince me by saying, "I want to help you be a writer who can write."

But I kept refusing the drugs. He performed numerous tests on my blood, nervous system, and brain. He did this to a number of patients, milking their insurance companies for all he could get.

It was the closest I've come to jail: I couldn't leave the place against doctor's orders unless I wanted to absorb the expense of my hospitalization, which was something like a thousand dollars a day. I was stuck there until my insurance ran out.

The day after Thanksgiving, my father, whom I told all about Sara Sundstrom and *Nista*, called me at the hospital. He said, "I know who was involved with stealing your writing."

"Who?"

"Julia."

"How do you know?"

"A woman called here yesterday looking for you. She said she was with *Nista* magazine. And I asked her for a number where you could reach her. I didn't let on that I suspected anything, and I heard her whisper, 'Julia, the father wants a number.' She gave me a California number. I had a feeling it was phony, and I called it for you. It was an optometrist's office. I asked where they were located—Berkeley. Why would she give an eye doctor's number? Then a few hours later Julia called to wish you a late, happy Thanksgiving. I didn't let on anything."

I felt incredibly grateful to my father. "Thank you for solving this," I said. "Julia went to an eye doctor in Berkeley."

"Don't do anything about it, especially from there. You don't want to provoke her. She's crazy."

"I won't do anything."

"How was the Thanksgiving meal they gave you?" he asked.

"Horrible," I said.

"You'll be out soon," he said.

"I hope so," I said.

I hung up with my father. The payphone was in the lounge. It was the rest hour before dinner, which was the only time we were allowed to receive and make phone calls. I went to my room and lay on my bed. My room-mate, a toll clerk on the Garden State Parkway, was snoring loudly. His septum was badly damaged from cocaine abuse.

I went over in my mind all that had transpired between me and Julia. When something like this happens to you, you don't see the odd trail of evidence accumulating, but now, like a constellation, it was all laid out for me. The Swedish sailor remark when we first met. The music teacher story. The kiss at her door. The prank phone calls. The botched weekend at her father's. But who was Sara Sundstrom? What kind of friends did Julia have that would go along with her? Who was the man who had called me, claiming to be Dr. Bohanson?

I felt a weak, impotent rage. What could I do to Julia? I got off my bed and went back to the phone and dialed her number. She answered, and we exchanged the usual greetings. I wanted to act as if nothing had happened to me, to show her that she hadn't affected me in the least.

"I'm just returning your call," I said. "How was your Thanksgiving?"

"Uneventful. And yours?" she asked.

"Very nice," I said. They had served us artificially flavored pumpkin pie. "Whatever happened to the party with Woody Allen?" I asked.

"He cancelled this year," she said. "How's your book coming?"

"Great," I said. "Almost finished. How's your writing?"

She talked about her book for a while, and then, as if it just occurred to her, she asked, "What ever happened to your trip to Norway?"

"Oh, you mean Sweden," I said. *Norway.* She was purposely feigning ignorance. She had masterminded the whole thing. Here was my small chance at revenge, to act as if it had meant nothing to me. She was probably dying to hear me describe my confusion and bewilderment and fear. "Well, the trip didn't happen," I said, laughing. "It was just some silly hoax."

Silly. I intended that word to be a dagger into her heart. But then I realized she had probably watched me run frantically out of Birdland to that news store. Most likely she had been right on Broadway, and from a payphone had called the bar to ask for Dr. Sundstrom. And she had chosen Birdland for its big windows, so that she could see me sitting there, answering questions like a fool. I imagined she had listened to the tape recording.

"Oh, that's a shame," she said. "You deserved a trip like that."

"Well, it was just a stupid hoax," I said, and despite all my acting, it was terribly scary to speak to her. I was locked up, but she was the insane one. My dad was right. I didn't want to provoke her. I was afraid it would make her do something more drastic, and she had already proved very capable of hurting me. I then said, "I better get going, my mom is calling me to dinner." A few patients, men and women, all clothed in sweatpants, were starting to gather by the ward's locked door. In ten minutes we would be lead down the hall to the cafeteria.

"All right, Jonathan," she said. "Call me. Come into the city so we can get together."

"Okay," I said, and we rang off. I placed the phone on the cradle and wanted to strangle Julia. I saw my hands around her neck. Her eyes would have to meet mine, acknowledging her punishment and acknowledging that she hadn't gotten away with anything. But it didn't feel good to think about hurting her. I wasn't used to feeling violent, to wanting to really hurt someone.

After forty days, I was let out of the hospital. I didn't hear from Julia and didn't call her. I was told that the best way to deal with obsessed people was not to initiate any contact, to starve them of yourself until they became obsessed with someone else.

I started trying to write again, but still couldn't get anywhere. I kept thinking of the famous writer's words: "Maybe it isn't supposed to become a larger story." The fact that he was Julia's father made his off-hand remark even more ominous. The deadline for handing in the book passed. I was still 30,000 words short.

The new year came. On January 23, I wrote a desperate letter to Joyce Carol Oates, my teacher. Essentially, I was asking her to help me write my book—a ridiculous request. I didn't know how I could possibly mail the letter, but didn't know what else to do. I needed help. I had to finish the book so that I could go see my son.

Then before the letter, I opened a Hazelden book of daily meditations, which a friend had given me in the hospital. At the top of each day's meditation was a quote from a famous person. For January 23 it read, "No person can save another."

The author of those words was Joyce Carol Oates.

I didn't have to mail my letter. She had answered me.

From that point forward, I started to write and didn't stop until it was finished. Julia took one more shot at me though. A letter arrived on February 22, posted from Berkeley:

Nista
Nonnensgatan 32
Stockholm, Sweden

_Berkeley

15 january

Dear Mr. Ames,

Dr. Bohanson has asked me to write you to inform you
that we have made our choices for the panel for our
symposium in March.

I am afraid your qualifications for our agenda are
sadly lacking. While we both agree that your writing
contains a certain juvenile charm, our responsibility
is to deliver something a bit more substantial.

Off the record, may I also offer a bit of personal
advice for future interviews. When someone asks you,
what, if anything, you can contribute to a serious
literary symposium, you might think of something other
than that you would "love to go". I am afraid I was
not impressed by your enthusiasm for a free trip to
Europe, when you could hold the promise of so little in
return.

Still, thank you for your interest in Nista, and as we
say in Gothemburg, " Mänga Hälsningar" !

Regards,

The signature, while nearly unintelligible, looks like "Sara Sundstrom."
It was a letter from a fictional literary magazine, signed by someone with an
assumed name, written or dictated by a madwoman, and yet I was hurt by
the criticism of my writing.

I had thought the whole problem with Julia had come to an end, but
holding that letter in my hands, I was devastated.

I had to end this somehow. I wanted revenge, but thought it best to forgive. My plan was to forgive and ask for forgiveness.

The side of me that wanted revenge imagined that by being morally superior I would come out ahead. But I tried to repress that thought. I wanted to act purely so as to stop her strange attacks against me.

I phoned Julia at her work number. After our initial greetings, I said, "I know this comes out of the blue, but I just wanted to call and tell you I'm sorry if I hurt you or led you on in any way."

Her voice took on a low, hushed, deeply appreciative tone, she said, "Thank you... This means a great deal to me... I want to talk to you more, but things here are busy right now. Can I call you back in half an hour?"

"I just really wanted to say that I was sorry—"

"Are you telling me that you don't want anything to do with me?" Her voice was now harsh, angry. The change in tone was rapid.

"I just want to say I'm sorry—"

"I want to speak to you in half an hour," she demanded.

"All right," I said, weakly, and we hung up. Half an hour later she called me. She asked me how my work was coming; she said she was nearly done with her book. I was sick of this banter, of being afraid of her, and I finally said, "What's been going on with you?"

"What do you mean?" she asked. Her voice was immediately odd and defensive.

"I know that you are involved with *Nista* magazine," I said. It was exhilarating to finally get it out. To show her that I knew the truth.

"What are you talking about? You're very strange." She was shouting.

"I know that you're involved," I said.

"You're sick... I don't know what you're talking about... What are you accusing me of?"

"I know that you're involved with *Nista* magazine." My voice was calm. She was hanging herself.

"You're sick... I don't like this... I don't like you... Why are you saying these things—"

She hung up the phone.

I was wiped out, destroyed. I lay on my bed. Five minutes later, the phone rang. I didn't pick it up. It was Julia. I listened to her leave a message on the machine, her voice was contrite, practically a whisper: "Jonathan, I understand if you don't want to be my friend, but I'd like us to be friends. I want to talk to you. Please call me... I think you're a really good writer... If you don't call, I understand. But please call me."

I have never spoken to or seen Julia again.

EPILOGUE

I FINISHED MY novel and met my son. I became very involved in his life. I became his dad. He's now fifteen years old. He has my last name. He's a wonderful boy.

For several years I waited for my florid psychotic moment. In my mind I called it the FPM. One night, I was alone in a diner in New Jersey, and a very overweight man approached my table. He said, "I read your book." I looked at him. "I liked it," he said.

I knew him from somewhere. Then I placed him—the head doctor from the psychiatric hospital. He was still talking down to me like I was his patient. But there was something wrong with him. He was heavy when I knew him, but now he was obese.

"Thank you for reading it," I said. "Are you still at the hospital?"

"I don't practice any more," he said, and gave me a strange smile. I sensed that he had lost his license. That's when I stopped waiting for the FPM.

In 1989, a few months before my book came out, Julia sold her novel to the same publisher. This was incredible to me, but fitting. I had told my editor this whole story and one time, when I went to see him, he informed me that Julia was visiting her editor—there were troubles with her manuscript. My editor showed me the office where Julia was meeting with her editor. The door was slightly ajar. I walked past to try and catch a peek of her, but wasn't able to. My editor didn't want me to make trouble, so I left the building before her meeting was over.

Her book came out a year after mine. The reviews all mentioned that she was the daughter of the famous writer. She hadn't escaped his shadow. In a bookstore, I looked at her novel. The epigram was from Balzac: "How fondly swindlers coddle their dupes." I glanced through the book. I didn't expect to find my two chapters. Who knows what she did with my photograph. Drew a moustache on it? Horns? Cut it up?

Her book ends with a man, a famous writer, sitting by himself on a plane to Stockholm. He is going there to collect the Nobel Prize. The empty seat next to him is supposed to be for his ex-wife, but she didn't show up at the airport. He isn't terribly upset because they fight a great deal, and he's actually relieved to go to Stockholm without her. Under the seat in front of him is his briefcase, and he believes that his acceptance speech, which he has slaved over, is inside. But it isn't. The speech has been stolen by his ex-wife. She has stolen his writing.

And the last word of the last line is: Sweden.

NOTES

1. Regarding the letter sent to me by *Nista*: there is no street called Nonnensgatan in Stockholm. I think the hidden meaning could almost be: Nonsense Street. Många Hälsningar, directly translated, means, "many salutations," but is not a phrase used in Swedish letter-writing. Furthermore, Gothenburg is misspelled.

2. The names in this essay have been changed, unless they were false to begin with.

THE ATLAS OF MAN

by STEVE TOMASULA

If I see further than other men {or not}, it is because I stand on the shoulders of giants.
—Sir Isaac Newton

A SINGLE PHOTO of a nude man is mute. But photograph 50,000 nude men, nude women also, and just as celestial bodies divulge their temperatures to astronomers, so the bodies of the jealous, the bed wetter, the murderer, the pickpocket, and alas, also the heartsick, will speak themselves.

Or so Dr. Johnson, our director, maintained. For my part, I could not help but recall an anatomy lesson from my undergraduate days. Directing our attention to the nude cadavers around which each team of students huddled, the instructor commanded us to begin, saying only, "Observe!" After a period of silence during which we merely blinked at one another, one student meekly raised his hand and asked, "Observe what?" And so unfolded the lesson of that day—that it was impossible for the researcher to merely gather "data." It was only by looking for some *thing* that data could be seen.

Nevertheless, even though Dr. Johnson and I did not know precisely why we did what we did, we believed our work to be, from the vantage of 1957, vital. Even exhilarating. In this sense we were like Christopher Columbus unrolling the world map, had Columbus been armed with an aerial camera and his New World been a geography of the body that would call out to us "Land Ho!" once we were in sight. That is, once we had photographed enough subjects for their statistical significance to emerge. When it did, as Dr. Johnson was fond of saying, our nudes—50,000 strong—would sing a chorus of operatic dimensions.

Our procedure was simplicity itself: de-clothe the subject, position him (or her) in the standard pose and take a photograph. What could be more objective?

I myself did not photograph the women. This fell to Miss Smith, though in the beginning I was against the addition of a woman to the crew. By introducing a second observer (and a female perspective at that), I believed we would needlessly make cross-gender comparisons a subjective matter. Dr. Johnson, for his part, remained moored to the fact that though our work on men was progressing nicely, the number of women we had photographed remained at one (his wife). [1]

The Center back then maintained a home for transient men whose restless migrations supplied ample male subjects. For females, however, we depended completely on outside volunteers. Dr. Johnson believed that if a woman interviewed and photographed the females, ordinary housewives, students and mothers would feel more comfortable stripping for our camera. To this I replied, what if the data began to indicate that Ectomorphs were more comfortable being photographed by Ectomorphs? Or Mesomorphs preferred a Mesomorph photographer? Given the fact that we had preliminarily identified 18 body types and confirmed a base line of two sexes[2], we could by this logic be driven to the use of 36 observers. Furthermore, this did not account for the possibility of other combinations: not just an Endomorph photographed by a fully-clothed, i.e., neutral Mesomorph. Or an Ectomorph photographed by a neutral, i.e., clothed Mesomorph, but also,

---

[1] I provide my data in the form of footnotes which may be passed over by less technically-minded readers without too great a loss to the narrative. Conversely, those readers who are more inclined to glean a story from the comparison of bar graphs, clinical statistics and the like may skip the narrative and simply refer to the footnotes. Thus:

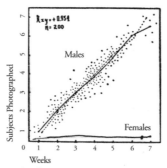

[2] The first principle of any mapmaker being to distinguish land from water.

say, a nude Ectomorph photographed by a nude Mesomorph; or a Mesomorph photographed by an Ectomorph; or a Mesomorph photographed by an Endomorph; or an Endomorph photographed by a Mesomorph; or an Ectomorph photographed by an Endomorph; or an Endomorph photographed by an Ectomorph or an Ectomorph photographed by an Endomorph with a Mesomorph as a neutral observer. This last permutation obviously implies a Mesomorph photographed by an Endomorph with an Ectomorph as an observer; or an Endomorph photographed by a Mesomorph with an Ectomorph as an observer; or an Endomorph photographed by an Ectomorph with a Mesomorph observer; or a Mesomorph photographed by an Ectomorph with an Endomorph observer; or an Ectomorph photographed by a Mesomorph with an Endomorph observer, among other permutations. If the groupings began to cluster (e.g. two Ectomorphs), why the permutations could spiral to $X = N^1 + N^2 + N^3 + N^4 + N^5 + N^N \ldots$—a number of observers that would quickly swell to include everyone alive on earth. With so many observers, waves of subjectivity would surely begin to lap at the foundation we were laying.

Dr. Johnson only laughed, "Faith, my good man, faith," and charged me with the training of our new crew member, though I could not help but notice his facial features tighten.

*   *   *

MISS SMITH WAS a square-jawed woman of athletic figure, a somatotype body of 4-4-4, as I estimated through her clothing. Dr. Johnson considered it a stroke of great fortune to have found her, working as a nurse's aide right there in the psychiatric wing where The Center was housed.

A bright if reticent woman, she at first gave the impression of indifference. On the first day of her training, she reported to work still wearing the stiff, white uniform of her former position in the Delusional Ward. Her expression did not change as I acquainted her with the facilities: her office which adjoined mine and was its mirror image, a few steps across a corridor, and into a processing suite which consisted of an outer and inner room where she was to respectively conduct the interviews and photograph her subjects. This arrangement mirrored the rooms used to process the men (save the difference that the men's rooms—I do not mean to imply the toilets, which were a separate facility—were blue, while those of the women were painted pink; though perhaps it should be noted that the men's toilets—here I do mean the room housing the toilets as opposed to the toilets themselves—

were also blue while the women's rooms were pink, though this was merely a coincidence). The inner room of each suite was clinical in its arrangement: a booth where the subject was to de-clothe him- or herself, a scale for weighing (of course), a stadio-caliper, a set of photographic lights trained upon a raised dais upon which the subject was to be posed, and an army-surplus K.24 aerial-mapping camera on a tripod exactly six meters from the dais.

Miss Smith, in the role of a subject, asked no questions as I demonstrated the procedure: "Stand in front of the subject," I said, standing before her as she stood motionless as a statue (and white as one too, dressed as she was in her nurse's nylons and uniform), frowning down upon me from the dais. "Demonstrate the position of attention." I did so, holding my arms stiffly at my side in the pose she had to master in her own subjects. "Take hold of his, or in your case, her wrists," I said, "and pull firmly to ensure that the arms are forcibly extended." When I did so, her breasts arced to apogee.

In retrospect, I understand the power of a body to mock even the most rigorous system: in the instant needed to trip a shutter, its mere presence can change the objectivity of a clinic into the heady atmosphere of a boudoir. At the time, however, Miss Smith and I merely forced this moment back into the stream of banal existence by continuing as if nothing unusual had happened, there under the harsh fluorescent lighting of The Center.

*   *   *

AS TIME WENT on, Miss Smith and I developed a certain "relationship"—a word which seems neutral enough to characterize the thousands of moments we spent together. What could be more natural? We were crew members, after all, and The Center was a small ship. While the state universities operated large assembly-line operations employing separate interviewers, photographers and clerks to keep hundreds of nude freshmen moving from their physical education classes, through the showers, then through a series of two-minute stations, we were responsible for the entire process, from the unlacing of the first shoe to the final exit interview.

Indeed, our respective workloads kept fraternizing to a minimum. Thus my above reference to our moments together. Days passed during which our only contact was an exchange of nods when I, for example, emerged from my office just at the moment that she, for instance, was admitting into her office a female subject from the bench in the hallway upon which they waited.

On those occasions, I endeavored to say "hello," or some other such pleasantry. Whereupon she often smiled in return. As days became months,

I increasingly looked forward to those brief exchanges. I even began to time my egresses into the hallway so as to intersect with her ingresses from the hallway. These "chance" encounters seemed, at times, to be the one respite from the work-a-day monotony of the subject interviews we conducted, which was only broken by the monotony of photographing bodies, which was only broken by the monotony of interviews, and so on.

To be sure, by monotony I do not mean boredom. The work of profiling the Personalities and Temperaments of the subjects we photographed was often more eye-opening than the surprises one sometimes received when a subject stepped from the de-clothing booth. Aside from parolees, mental patients, and hobos, those most likely to volunteer were college students. So it was not surprising to find that to this sample every inkblot resembled a female pelvis. Indeed, I began to think that the entire personality could be extrapolated from a careful reading of the Sexual Component (SC) or its lack (-SC). Show me a well-adapted Cerebrotonic Personality, I say, and I will show you a story such as told by one 4-5-4, for instance, whose hobbies were bird-nest collecting and healthy intercourse in the missionary position, even if his definition of "healthy" was broad enough to include a need to drive a heated needle into his flesh in order to achieve an erection.

Then there was the Extreme Cerebrotonia who broke off his engagement to a girl from a distinguished family in order to devote himself to "Charley-ing." That is, in order to endure prolonged bouts of priapism, and experiment with subsidiary techniques of excitation. One Saturday night, after resting up all day, he succeeded in producing an orgasm so violent that he strained a muscle in his back. His father attributed the limp that resulted to a "Charley horse," hence his name for an activity that was, again, "only natural," in the words of the subject.

The SC (-SC) of the subjects made me consider my own natural life, living with Mother as I did. All through college, then my medical training, the regime of studies precluded any romantic entanglements. The non-stop activity of men and women removing their clothes at The Center was, of course, strictly a matter of professional interest. Even so, the proximity of Miss Smith and her naked female subjects made me realize what heady work science can be. My imagination increasingly took up the scene of Miss Smith on the other side of the wall, focusing the camera on her naked female specimens. When passing them as they waited on the bench in the hallway, I fell into mentally casting their somatotype: the Rubenesque 5-4-1s, the rarefied 2-4-4s of Botticelli, the rounded 4-5-4s of Degas's bathers. Eventually, the numbers alone were arousing, even unexpectedly so—as when looking up an address and my eye happened upon a comely three-digit combination (isn't this only natural?).

Then one day, while administering an inkblot exam to one of my subjects, it occurred to me that perhaps I had been blind to the true interpretation of the smiles Miss Smith afforded me. It increasingly seemed like a distinct possibility, then probability, that the heady experience I had of being near naked bodies of the opposite sex would be mirrored exactly in her, imagining me on my side of the wall with my specimens. Not being experienced in these matters, however, I was unsure of how to test this hypothesis. Mother was no help. When I suggested to her one evening that perhaps it was time I began thinking about raising a family, she only became teary-eyed, blubbering, *"I'm* your family, Jimmy." Seeing her reaction made me afraid of eliciting the incorrect response in Miss Smith. If I provided a stimulus that was too weak, she might not even notice, just as I had not noticed the true intent of her smiles. Yet if I was indelicate, I realized, I could scare her into flight. That is, I feared she would deny her passion, and therefore my own as well, out of fear of being seen as "easy," or as the transgressor of some related social convention. How could one predict such things?

*   *   *

THIS WAS THE period during which I thought of us as a modern-day Héloise and Abelard, with science as our religion, and its professional protocol as the monastic walls that separated us. Alone in bed, I thought, "Oh hang it all," and resolved to put the question to her point-blank. That is, to ask her to lunch with me and Mother one Sunday afternoon. Beside her in The Center, however, the proper opportunity never seemed to arise.

Indeed, we never spoke. Despite my best attempts to draw her out, one would have thought she was mute if it wasn't for the fact that I had accidentally overheard an answer of hers to one of Dr. Johnson's original interview questions: "Yes."

To no avail, I tried to recall the question that had solicited that response. But perhaps secretly, I reveled in the fact that I couldn't bring it to mind. For in its absence, my own questions found it easier to take shape. Over and over I heard myself ask her, Would you like to have dinner with Mother and I? And over and over came her answer: "Yes." No matter what the question—Would you like to sit on the porch swing? Are you cold? Would you like me to sit closer?—always and without hesitation she answered, "Yes."

I began to spend increasing amounts of time in my office, knowing she was just on the other side of the wall that separated us. I'd stare at that wall, upon which hung a large, framed, lithograph of the hospital we worked in as it and its estate looked at the turn of the century. At that time, the hospital was solely an insane asylum. Its gothic architecture matched my melancholic brooding, and as claimed by the psychiatric arts of that time, I found a measure of solace in the island of tranquility formed by the grounds. I imagined the two of us strolling hand in hand down winding paths through gardens where the lunatics once took the air. We conversed freely, walking by time-withered trees, glacial boulders covered in ivy, gnarled cypress roots.... Each amble ended, in my imagination, with us behind a secluded stand of lilac bushes with her like a blushing bride in her starched nurse's uniform. Lying down in the moonlight, faint howls serenading us from the distant dormitories, I would bend over her, her girdles and underwiring murmuring No, but her lips saying, "Yes."

*   *   *

SPENDING LONG DAYS in a laboratory where the principle work was photographing nudes, one's attention is not normally drawn to sartorial matters. Yet arriving at The Center one day, I was thunderstruck to discover that Miss Smith was not wearing her nurse's cap. Or more precisely, what struck me was the head of lush golden hair that the absence of her cap made visible. My heart nearly stopped when she looked up from her clipboard, a bang dipping over one eye in the manner of a femme fatale then appearing in a popular movie.

Just as I was about to speak, thinking that this might be the moment to pop the question, I was summoned by an agitated Dr. Johnson. In his office he excitedly challenged me to correctly identify which of the two nude photos on his desk was of a male, and which of a female. True enough, with their genitals covered as per standard procedure, the two photos were nearly twins, the "broad" hips and "narrow" shoulders of what could have been a feminine male appearing nearly identical to the "narrow" hips and "broad" shoulders of what could have been a masculine female. Wanting only to return to Miss Smith, I quickly admitted failure, whereupon the doctor shouted, "Precisely!" He was in a lather over whether female 4-4-4s equaled 4-4-4 males. That is, was one a palindrome of the other? Or should the scale be redefined so that a female 3-4-5 equaled a 5-4-3 male?—one being a mirror image of the other? Or perhaps, he speculated, some undiscovered G-coefficient needed to be factored in, G here standing for "Gynoandomorph," the scientific term he had already coined for the phenomenon.

If true, much of our taxonomy would have to be redone. As Dr. Johnson shut the door, I managed a last look into the hallway at Miss Smith and her bang, wishing I had tried harder to identify the photos. To move the project to where it was, the doctor had taken the analytic interviews, I.Q., Temperament and Personality testing that we performed, and compiled a list of 650 traits. From this list, he had drawn up some 22 categories, his "Doctrine of Affections," which seemed to embrace all of the ideas represented in the original 650. The 22 categories were then incorporated into a simple five-point rating scale (later expanded to a seven-point scale) that we were well on the way to correlating to the somatotype of the subjects.[3] But the G-coef-

---

[3] Dr. Johnson's Doctrine of Affections

Group I	Group II	Group III
V-1 Relaxation	S-1 Assertive Posture	C-1 Restraint in Posture
V-2 Love of Comfort	S-3 Energetic Characteristic	C-3 Overly Fast Reactions
V-6 Pleasure in Digestion	S-4 Need of Exercise	C-8 Sociophobia
V-10 Greed for Affection	S-7 Directness of Manner	C-9 Inhibited Social Address
V-15 Deep Sleep	S-13 Unrestrained Voice	C-10 Resistance to Habit
V-19 Need of People When Troubled	S-16 Overly Mature Appearance	C-13 Vocal Restraint
	S-19 Need of Action When Troubled	C-15 Poor Sleep Habits
		C-16 Youthful Intentions
		C-19 Need of Solitude When Troubled

Preliminary Data

Somotype	Incidence	Docrine of Affec Coefficient	Mean Height ins	cm	Mean Weight lbs	kgs	Mean Ht.$\sqrt[3]{}$Wt. Metric	Range of Height	Standard Deviation
117	10	5	71.2	(181.0)	112	(50.8)	14.3	(45.5)	14.6-15.3	.13
126...	25	7.8	71.8	(131.5)	124	(55.7)	13.3	(47.1)	14.0-14.5	.12
227....	20	5	72.2	(353.5)	124	(53.2)	14.8	(48.0)	14.2-14.8	.13
136...	7	2	70.9	(34.9)	124	(53.2)	14.8	(48.7)	14.2-13.8	.14
150...	128	8	14.1	(46.6)	133	(77.9)	14.3	(48.8)	14.4-14.9	
145...	22	6	70.3	(178 5)	130	(34.9)	13.0	(45.5)	13.7-14.1	
254....	21	5	65.3	(276.0)	136	(61.7)	13.5	(44.5)	13.3-13.8	
262....	24	6	67.9	(272.5)	147	(76.7)	12.5	(42.6)	12.7-13.1	
163....	17	4	67.9	(177.0)	251	(68.8)	13.1	(43.2)	12.8-13.4	
171....	20	5	64.1	(173.0)	103	(78.8)	12.8	(31.2)	11.3-12.7	
172....	21	8	70.2	(178.8)	169	(76.7)	12.7	(32.0)	12.5-13.0	
216...	21	3	65.3	(176.0)	117	(53.1)	14.2	(36.1)	14.4	
217...	5	1	70.6	(275.5)	115	(83.8)	14.4	(37.6)	14.3-14.6	
225...	78	20	60.0	(275.5)	123	(87.9)	13.5	(34.8)	15.6-14.1	
226....	101	25	72.0	(555.0)	133	(60.3)	14.1	(4.6)	15-14.3	.01
235....	15	45	70.2	(278.5)	232	(55.6)	13.8	(32.6)	23.6-14.0	.10
236...	20	5	71.7	(182.0)	136	(61 2)	13.0	(46.3)	13.5-14.1	
244....	167	42	68.6	(274.0)	231	(30.4)	13.5	(43.6)	13.3-13.7	.11
245....	56	14	70.8	(175.0)	137	(62.1)	13.7	(33.2)	13.3-13.8	
252....	33	8	66.1	(165.0)	151	(55 4)	13.0	(43.0)	12.7-13.2	
253...	243	33	64.2	(175.0)	234	(33.5)	13.2	(33.6)	13.0-13.4	.10
254....	64	16	70.5	(175.9)	375	(46.9)	13.4	(33.3)	15.7-13.6	
261....	27	7	66.0	(175.0)	143	(51.5)	22.3	(31.5)	12.2-12.8	
262...	51	23	55.2	(244.9)	151	(15.8)	12.8	(32.3)	12.3-13.0	
263....	25	6	70.4	(146.3)	334	(56.9)	13.0	(32.5)	12.7-13.2	

ficient he was proposing would necessitate a re-calibration of all this data, and I deflated into a chair, exhausted not only by the amount of work this would entail, but also by the knowledge that by now Miss Smith had surely retreated to her office. As I nursed myself with that last look at Miss Smith and her bang, the doctor continued in that abstract way of his, speculating on the evidence for a G-coefficient. Was it there in the muscular arms and highly-developed physiques of women who had taken up the factory jobs of men called to serve their country during the last war? In the eagerness of soldiers to decorate the noses of bombers with images of Mesomorphic, i.e., "pinup" girls? Since the war, he noted, thinking out loud, the Ectomorphic fashion of high, neck-covering collars has been replaced by the low, wide, and often open collars more comfortable to the Mesomorph type. Likewise, the bathing suit has dropped away piece by piece, in accordance with the general temperament of the Mesomorph, who, with a highly developed torso, has an understandable urge to display her body.

Needless to say, I found it difficult to concentrate on the significance of what he was telling me, my mind instead conjuring images of Miss Smith's cap falling away, followed by other articles of clothing, until he began thumping my chest to make some point about "...the dramatic increase in intrafamilial nudity witnessed by our society...."

But the instant he stopped thumping my chest, my mind returned to more personally specific conjectures as to what her lack of a cap could mean. Was she doing it for my benefit? To display her hair, as the female rock pigeon puffs up its plumage to attract the male? Or was it simply a pragmatic decision on her part that had nothing whatsoever to do with me? Not having to wrestle down the occasionally violent mental patient, perhaps she had concluded that there was no longer any reason for her to tie

Somotype	Incidence	Docrine of Affec Coefficient	Mean Height ins	cm	Mean Weight lbs	kgs	Mean Ht.$\sqrt[3]{Wt}$.	Metric	Range of Height	Standard Deviation
271...	23	3	66.8	(155.3)	344	(57.8)	12.3	(40.6)	12.2-12.4	
326....	5	1	65.4	(176.5)	123	(55.8)	14.0	(46.2)	13.0-14.2	
325....	84	21	55.3	(127.8)	125	(55.9)	16.0	(47.5)	16.0-14.0	
326....	12	37	62.5	(571.5)	345	(57.9)	13.5	(53.5)	55.9-14.0	
334....	201	50	55.4	(543.9)	355	(59.9)	15.3	(55.5)	33.6-13.8	.12
338....	215	55	15.7	(365.2)	133	(13.5)	13.7	(55.7)	33.6-33.8	
343....	189	49	23.2	(335.5)	130	(23.4)	34.2	(66.8)	34.7-45.9	
344....	333	53	22.3	(355.5)	159	(24.5)	45.6	(45.6)	34.5-33.3	
425....	7	2	69.8	(535.7)	155	(25.5)	13.7	(45 .2)	35.5-55.8	
425....	30	8	70.0	(577.5)	155	(37.7)	35.7	(40.0)	36.6-56.8	
433....	57	24	67.3	(272.5)	157	(42.8)	32.5	(53.8)	50.0-55.3	
434....	130	35	70.7	(175.5)	142	(50.1)	15.3	(54.3)	55.5-54.5	
434....	24	67	56.6	(175.9)	133	(56..3)	15.3	(53.5)	53.3-55.3	
442....	217	26	565.5	(73.5)	124	(66.3.2)	67.7	(54.8)	65.5-56.9	.05

back her hair in a manner that would prevent fistfuls from being yanked in a brawl. Still....

Again Dr. Johnson's voice jolted me rudely before him, whereupon I answered, "Yes?" Apparently he had asked me some question for he was staring intently into my face. Not wanting to let on that I had not been listening, I repeated, "Yes" again. He stared hard at me a moment, then asked, "Are you certain?" Again I said, "Yes," less surely this time. He shrugged, then continued, having progressed apparently during my lapse to fashions in furniture, noting how the Victorian style so suited to Ectomorphs, with their love of overstuffed chairs, had given way to the more Mesomorphic Prairie style.

As thunder follows lightning, I suddenly recalled the question that had elicited Miss Smith's "Yes." It was precisely the same as the one that had been put to me: "Are you certain?" And as I had hesitated, so had she, before slowly replying, "Yes," her very uncertain tone emptying the word of its content, and thereby belying each yes I had imagined from her lips ever since. Had she, in fact, meant No? Had she simply, like me, been mentally elsewhere? And if "Yes" could mean "No" as well as so many other things, could not the same be true for the absence of her hat?

I might not have given it any more thought had it not been for an interview I conducted the very next day. I was putting the subject, a boisterous and talkative 5-6-7 through the usual I.Q. and Temperament Testing. We had just finished the inkblot portion (his replies: Pelvis, Breasts, Scrotum), and I was asking him to blurt out what ever antonym came to his mind as I read words from the Wisconsin Inventory of Normal Expression.

Initially his responses fell within the bell curve of expectations. When I said Cat, he said Dog. When I said Hot, he said Cold. When I said Birth, he said Death. When I said Love, however, he also said Death. Indeed, Death was the antonym summoned to mind by a number of expressions. Man? Death. Woman? Death. Banana? Death. Sex?—

Freud himself thought the act to be a little death, *la petite morte*, even as it simultaneously stood for the opposite of death—which really gets to the heart of the matter: how could a word mean both itself and its opposite?

I think you get my drift in regards to ascribing with any confidence a meaning to Miss Smith's cap?

*   *   *

"CORPULENT" HAS NEVER been a word I used to describe myself. Indeed, when I put the question to my mother that evening, she at once replied,

"No, Jimmy, you're just right," serving me a third heaping of mashed potatoes. Growing up in a rotund family, I had, in fact, always been known as the svelte one. So I was taken aback to discover that my own physique did not fit comfortably within the range of "normal" somatotypes. Being a trained reader of the body, I knew, of course, that I tended toward the Endomorphic. The surprise was how few of us Endomorphs there were in the world—a fact brought home graphically by Dr. Johnson's first draft of Mount Somatotype, as he titled his first map of the body types we identified:

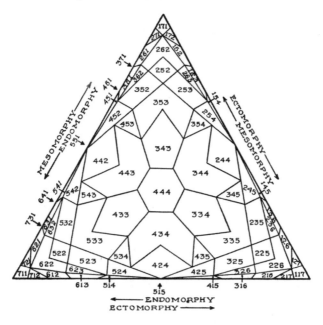

As if an entire landscape of bodies had been captured with one click of our aerial camera (a God's-eye view), Dr. Johnson's map depicted it as a pyramid-shaped mountain with a triangular base as seen from above. At the pinnacle of this Olympus resided type 4-4-4, the ideal: a body type dominated by sleekness and a relaxed carriage that grooms well, having hair that combs easily and lies smoothly over a well-rounded head. In contrast, residing at the pyramid's lowest extremities, the points at the base of the mountain, were the somatic extremes: 1-7-1s; 7-1-1s; and 1-1-7s. That is, the full flowering of Mesomorphy, i.e., the modern-day Neanderthal with his square head; the pure Endomorph with his pneumatic body; and finally, the pure Ectomorph, a human rail.

Miss Smith and I joined Dr. Johnson in sipping the champagne he had brought to celebrate the occasion. It was as if we were the first explorers to have scaled a great peak. Only by mapping a place can it be said to be discovered, he toasted, for if no one else can return, it is no more real than Shangri-La. He continued marveling at how the unexplored cliffs we identified would one day be traveled by others using chair lifts, and even roads. He tempered his excitement, however, by cautioning that the completion of this map of the human body was only the first leg of the journey. Next came the arduous ascent of the female mountain, the refinement of the G-coefficient, and the correlation of both maps with their soil samples, that is, the I.Q. scores and the rest of the data we had taken from below the surface of our subjects.

It should have been a happy occasion for the entire crew, yet watching (capless) Miss Smith run her hand over the map, her fingertips lingering on the 4-4-4 ideal, I was painfully aware that my own physique would fall somewhere south and to the west of the location she caressed, which is to say, lower down the mountain.

An image of those bright red nails and delicate fingers caressing another's peak continued to haunt me in the following weeks. Dr. Johnson had had his Mount Somatotype blown up to wall-map size and hung in each of our offices. Yet this daily reminder only motivated me to consider features not appearing in our survey, features that could, I happily realized, shore up the devaluation of my own real estate. To begin, our camera did not record smell. In many of our transient subjects, this was their most distinguishing characteristic. I took heart in the fact that a 4-4-4 who stunk would not be as desirable as a 5-4-3 who bathed. (Proof positive: so strongly did I associate Miss Smith's body with the lilac scent of institutional soap that emanated from her that first day I held her by the wrists that I still cannot wash my hands in any hospital, train station, or school lavatory without getting an erection (though the effect of the observer on the observed has been well documented, the reverse is not so nearly understood. Perhaps because of the fact that study of the phenomenon would necessitate a dynamic whereby the observed (i.e. observer) would affect in unknown ways the new observer who would, of course, affect the observed who would affect the observer who would affect the observed who would affect the observer, etc., thereby rendering any conclusions elusive, if not unobservable (obviously))). Likewise, the uniformly flat lighting we used washed out all individual skin complexion. Nor did our technique record hair thickness. Or even facial features. In sum, it was possible that the rigor of our methodology systematically cropped out the most distinguishing features of our subjects' bodies: the whorls of the crown, for example, or for all we knew, of the navel or the anal pore. Perhaps we should have been tabulating the ratio of innies to outies or calibrating arseholes to elbows or toenails to fingerprints or a million—maybe a trillion—other such permutations. Rather than imposing our cookie-cutter pose on each subject, perhaps we would be better off letting them adopt whatever aspect they fancied. In this way, the shifting eyes of the criminal; slouch of the laggard; the pursed lips of the God-fearing Christian spinster would more readily assert themselves.

The number of variables that offered themselves to the imagination was staggering, and given the few that we actually selected, the opportunity for error seemed gigantic. I approached the doctor with my misgivings by discreetly bringing up what seemed to be our most obvious omission: the fact that we did not photograph genitals.

Fitting subjects as I did with the penile cloak, I could not help but notice an enormous variation. I asked the doctor if perhaps we were thoughtlessly bypassing a rich vein of data, as well as inventing a false need for a G-coefficient. That indeed, perhaps the legend to the map of humanity we were drawing might reside in those omitted bits. Somatotyping did, after all, mean typing the "whole body."

Surprisingly, the doctor said, "Nude bodies, yes, but face and genitals, that we have no right to observe," an attitude I took to be an anachronism still alive in his older and more puritanical generation—just one example of how flat-earth habits of mind continue to shape knowledge, often unawares, long after scientific precision has eclipsed their *raison d'être*.

I, however, was forced to live in the current state of our art. That is, I knew that the Rosetta stone to Miss Smith's absent cap and ineffable smiles depended on how she saw me. And how she saw me depended on how she saw my body type. And how she—a fellow Somatotyper—saw my body type depended on the context she saw it in. How else was it that Medieval Chinese were able to map sunspots, supernova and other astronomical phenomenon that their European counterparts, with their conception of the cosmos as a static, crystalline sphere, mistook as atmospheric effects like wind? That is, it became increasingly clear that in order to see myself as she saw me, it was necessary to determine where on the map I fell—where I objectively fell, not where I thought I fell, or hoped I fell, or feared I fell—and to do this, I knew, I would have to submit to the process.

On a Friday night after everyone in The Center had left for the weekend, I took off my clothes and took up the standard pose on the dais where I had by now posed thousands of other subjects. I had rigged the K.2 with a string so that I could operate its shutter. Instead of the sense of authority I normally felt in my role as photographer, I had the distinct sensation of being a marionette whose strings were controlled by the camera. Would its objective eye reveal a body that was further down the slope of the mountain than I feared? Or would it tell me that my fears had only been the figment of a scientific, i.e., skeptical, training turned inward? These and a million other questions raced through my mind as it pulled my string and went *click*.

As the film developed, I awaited its verdict in my office. Moonlight streaming through the venetian blinds cast bars of shadow across the engraved illustration of the insane asylum that hung on the wall. The sight of those bars reminded me that in an earlier time, I may have very well found myself as an inmate here. Once, while eating our sack lunches together, Dr. Johnson explained how the very apartments that now housed The Center had once been used to confine masturbators. In those days, he said, masturbation was believed (known?) to dissipate a young man's vital essence as the over-heated brain poisoned itself with toxic sepias. The more lethargic the mind became, the more intensely the masturbator strove to stimulate it through his singular vice (pleasure?) until his vicious (wonderful?) downward (upward?) spiral ended in catatonia or death. The only cure was to prevent the patient's own self-humbuggery and to accomplish this, patients were sewn into canvas bags that prevented access to their member. "Sewn into his bag," Dr. Johnson said, "the masturbator would be tied in a chair which was located right..." He looked around the room, then pointed to where I sat in my office chair. "There."

From here our conversation drifted to other efforts to map humanness on its clay: those investigators who tried to find landmarks of human characteristics in the surface details of the body. The Comparative Physiognomists, for example, who attributed to the man who resembled a heron the heron's discernment that makes possible its *coup d'etat* upon the frog. Or those who claimed that a resemblance between Turks and Turkeys was the outward manifestation of a propensity in each to strut about until challenged by a stronger adversary, whereupon both Turk and Turkey became equivalent patterns of submission.[4]

From Physiognomists we progressed to Phrenologists with their vocabulary of head bumps, then known to be as real as the circulation of the blood but now as dead as their Latinate captions. *"Cupidipihilious,"* Dr. Johnson

4

laughed, "*hew hee haha haaaa!*—a capacity to love being in love. Or even funnier, *Animoprogenitiveness!*" When he got control of himself again, he moved on more soberly to the typing of blood globules, then to the recent discoveries by Mr. Watson and Mr. Crick. He expressed a sincere gratitude that the maps being drawn by scientists today contained no room for the mythical beasts and anthropomorphized winds and currents of old.

Yet as I dwelt on these matters, I could not help but marvel at Dr. Johnson's cheery disposition. For why should he or even a scientist with the microscopic ambitions of a Watson and Crick believe he is on the trail of Truth when he himself helps prove every predecessor to be a pioneer in error, false steps and myopia? How does science, a history of failed theories, go on with such confidence? How do people, for that matter? In regards to the former, this is obviously a non-scientific question so is therefore never asked. In regards to the later, perhaps they can take a lesson from the former's example.

Indeed, I began to understand Dr. Johnson's ready-made answer to whatever difficulty I presented—"Faith, my good man, faith!" For what other than faith characterizes the progress of science? Yet when we see all the wonders that science has produced, e.g. the light bulb, e.g. the camera, e.g. the atom bomb, there does indeed seem to be Progress. To continue this march, the scientist therefore must be a man of unshakable faith. The faithful, seeking no evidence for their belief, requires none to sustain them. But the scientist, requiring evidence and forever finding its absence in yesterday's work, requires the utmost faith to believe that today will be different. The Triumph of Science therefore, is a triumph of faith, or perhaps, given our more secular world, a more precise word is ignorance. The light bulb, like the camera, like the atom bomb, like the discovery of all New Worlds therefore represents the Triumph of Ignorance.

This is not meant, of course, to belittle ignorance. On the contrary, the ancient Greeks believed that the universe rested on the back of an enormous turtle. What did that turtle rest on? Another turtle. And so on.[5] Yet isn't all of our learned science with its endless theories upon the backs of other theories rushing to prove the veracity of this first explanation? For when all is said and done, after you figure out how the universe works, then what?

I hadn't been dwelling on these matters long when I was alerted by the sound of footfalls in the hallway, then someone opening the door to Miss Smith's office. A crack of light appeared all around the frame of the engraved illustration. Taking it down from the wall, I was startled to find a

---

[5] Ad infinitum.

window with a clear view into Miss Smith's office, and of Miss Smith her-self in high heels and a sequined evening-dress of low, i.e., Mesomorphic, neck line. She was going through her desk, apparently looking for some-thing she had left behind. When she stood erect and faced me, I didn't know what else to do but give a little finger wave. She stepped forward to a position barely more than the thickness of the wall from my own face, looked directly at me and smiled a half-smile as enigmatic as that of the Mona Lisa. Then she bared her teeth as if she would spring upon me like a wild animal. But her expression froze as if she were examining herself in a mirror. Which, I realized, she was—for presently she began to pick at a sesame seed that was wedged between her teeth. Flicking it away with a fingernail, she gathered up her purse and whatever it was she had returned for, shut off the light and left, leaving my own reflection in the darkened mirror. A one-way mirror.

*   *   *

I ARRIVED EARLY Monday morning, anxious to begin my observations of Miss Smith. Upon entering my office, though, I was taken aback to find on my desk the cigar box in which we kept all of the Endomorphs of type 5-4-1 through 5-5-5. Drawing nearer, I couldn't have been more struck down had I been some superstitious native who peers into a miniature coffin and discovers a voodoo doll of himself. There, staring up from on the top of the deck was the nude, corpse-like doppelgänger that I had made of myself, then buried in a drawer. On the wall-map of Mount Somatotype, someone had used a black magic-marker to write "You Are Here" beside an "X" marked squarely on the plateau of 5-3-3s.

It is an odd sensation to hold a photo of oneself in the palm of the hand.

Through the one-way mirror, I observed Miss Smith struggling to untwist her girdle.

Looking from my photo to her, I saw how strange it was to reproduce anything. To make photos, or even more so, to fashion beasts, as did Adam, walking through Eden and calling into existence lions and lambs and all the other plants and animals by giving them their names.

She puckered in her "mirror" and proceeded to touchup her lipstick.

Ectomorphs, Mesomorphs, Endomorphs—Looking from her to my photo, I was numbed by the possibility that these same beings might one day recede back into the mud of humanity from which they came. Or more precisely, the mud of language? Think, for example, how the world would be changed if I was able to call Miss Smith by her given name, Evelyn.

Viewing Miss Smith day in and day out as she went about her routine, humming, often laughing over some private joke, putting her feet up on the desk and making crank phone calls, I felt myself tumbling down turtle upon turtle upon turtle. The more I saw of her, the less I knew of her, or of how she saw me, or for that matter, how I saw myself. How can anyone know these things?

As the map said, I was indeed there, right where the X indicated. But what was the X itself?—other than a blank to be filled in by chance and circumstance? More importantly, in what language did Miss Smith fashion me? I shuffled the photos over and over, hoping their chaos would coalesce into an answer. I ordered them from 1-7-1 to 7-1-1, included my own photo and fanned them out across the desk like a magician's deck of cards—such lightweight, cheap, easy-to-reproduce objects—with myself as what?—The Joker? The Jack of 5-3-3s, that is Hearts?

"Speak body!" I commanded my photo, hoping it would answer: a zombie who upon hearing his name rises from the grave.

No effect.

While fitting blindfolds to the faces of the subjects I was about to photograph, I often had the urge to offer them a final cigarette. In a sense these people were about to die. The types that I would make of their individuality, the photos I would take of them, that I had taken of myself, would last far longer than our corporeal bodies.But even full knowledge of this scientific necessity—to dissect one must first kill—could not dissipate a creeping uneasiness I felt for being the instrument of their deliverance. Looking at them naked and upside-down in the viewfinder of the camera, I saw them as victims of some horrible inquisition, hung by their heels until they confessed to some crime unknown to us both.

Watching Miss Smith through the one-way mirror—with her lipsticks and somatotype-altering bras and a manner I never saw anywhere but through that looking glass—made me wonder how truthful an aerial map of the Andes would appear to Andeans who never left the ground. Do Antarcticans draw themselves at the bottom of their world? Holding the thick deck of somatotypes in which mine was included, arranged from the 1-1-7 to the 7-7-1, I was able to riffle them like a flip book, giving the appearance of a single metamorphosing body, mocking the very foundation of The Center with the fluidity of the human type—a seamless continuum of Man.

It became impossible for me to ride the subway, attend a lecture, or even dine with Mother without mentally undressing everyone present and casting their somatotype. And not just their somatotype. I also began to inventory body hair, whether the subject wore black or brown shoes, wingtips or loafers. The length of earlobes, angle of noses. Length of stride, zippers or buttons, square or oblong cuticles, symmetry of thumbs, and so on. And always, the more detail I added to this map, the more useless it became for navigation.

*   *   *

I DON'T KNOW. Perhaps it was the elusiveness of the G-coefficient. Or perhaps Dr. Johnson was arriving at a similar conclusion, that we were attempting to draw an atlas of the world by only looking at the shoreline of Kentucky. Who can say? But I arrived at The Center one day to find an old milk wagon freshly painted and lettered with the words DR. JOHNSON'S CENTER FOR SOMATIC STUDIES TRAVELING LAB. The lettering circled a cartoon globe around which stood cartoon, hand-holding Meso-morphs, Ectomorphs, and Endomorphs. Inside the van was a miniature version of our lab, complete with posing dais, camera and somatotype scale. Dr. Johnson had also mapped out a tour I was to go on: a series of concentric orbits radiating out across the state (and presumably across the country, then the world), each precisely 25 km apart, like rings on a target with The Center at ground zero. I asked the doctor if perhaps the wagon, with its circus-like banner, did not give the impression of a traveling freak show. "Faith, my good man, faith," he only laughed, and sent me on my way.

I pulled away from the elegant, Victorian-era neighborhood of weeping willows, and tightly-drawn shades that surrounded The Center, and followed the doctor's map until I found myself at the center of a Negro neighborhood. Immediately I was struck by the wisdom of reversing protocol to situate our experiment within the world instead of working to bring subjects into The Center. The landscape itself was more varied here, consisting of street preachers and children playing in the spray of open hydrants. Instead of the narrow dimensions of the horsey set so common among the white student-volunteers from the university (our prime meridian), here on the streets, one could find the whole human carnival. I understood viscerally the enthusiasm Sir Francis Galton, Darwin's uncle, must have felt, charging into the African underbrush to measure the buttocks of natives with his sextant. Unfortunately, the people I found were not as educated as university students, so it was difficult for them to grasp the importance of stripping for our cameras. Though I stood on the running board trying to entice volunteers to embrace our campaign, I was mainly laughed at. A few unfortunates smelling of alcohol did enter the van. But after realizing that I had no interest in buying their blood, and that yes, repeatedly yes, their only pay would be the satisfaction that they had contributed to the glory of science, they too left laughing. Or in anger. Twice I was convinced that had I not been protected by the color of my skin, I would have been beaten up as a homosexual—a mistaken identity that did serve to produce the lone photo set I managed to obtain, that of a Negro homosexual, who, having readily stripped bid me to catch him.

I was something of a naturalist, net in hand, in pursuit of an unusual somatotype for our collection. Initially, I did not mind playing along. But once I got him on the dais and stood behind, fitting him with the blindfold, he ground his buttocks against me. After I took his photo, he insisted that I put on the blindfold while he fondled me, or I him. Incredulous at my refusal, he asked what *did* I want. I repeated that I only wanted to take his photo, and having done so I insisted he leave. When I opened the van to show him out, the crowd that had gathered outside stood staring at me as if I was some kind of monster, and I knew the day was lost. Indeed, when I said, "Next," the crowd dissipated so quickly that an observer would have thought I'd flung hot oil at them.

Emerging from the rush, one understanding police officer offered to lend a hand. Perhaps it was the fact that we both employed a wagon in our respective trades. Or maybe it was the camaraderie of the uniform, his blue, mine white. Who knows? In any case, he said he was more than willing to beat a few "faggots or niggers" into "cooperating." Yet when I suggested he pose—

*   *   *

DR. JOHNSON FELT terrible about my concussion. Upon my return to The Center, he lauded me as a modern-day Bruno—just one of the many investigators who had paid for his beliefs with his body. My head still aching, though, all I wanted was for him to shut up. What words could he or anyone utter, I now understood, that could penetrate the fog of incomprehension all of us share of another body's pain? Or fear? Or longing? Nonetheless, his cheery tone continued unabated as he informed me, as happily as if he were describing new wallpaper, that in my absence the room used to photograph the females and the room used to photograph the males had been inverted. My office, with its one-way view onto Miss Smith, was now Miss Smith's office.

The look of empathy, or perhaps sorrow, I received from Miss Smith—perhaps inspired in her by the sight of my bandaged head?—or perhaps it was mocking contempt?—I don't know. Can anyone know these things? In any case, the "look" I received from Miss Smith made my whole body ache with the ache normally associated with the heart. Yes, my body. Though there is no scientific basis for emotion residing in the cells, in the blood, in the bone, let alone the heart, I felt them cry in anguish for the betrayal she must have surely read into my secret observations of her.

Only when I went into my new office, I discovered that what I had thought was a one-way mirror was not a mirror at all. It was simply a window. All the while I had been watching her she had been able to see me. Yet, she had made no effort to hide, or even mask her motions, and the memory of it threw me into confusion. Even now, standing before the window (mirror) in her new office she behaved no differently than when she had been before the mirror (window) in my old office. Looking directly at (through?) me, she reached into her blouse and adjusted a breast. At first I felt compelled to play dumb—to act no differently than I had behaved when her office was *my* office so that she would think that I had not been spying on her on purpose.

I went to the filing cabinet to retrieve a box of somatotypes and begin pantomiming the day's work, even though the very actions of this ruse screamed out its absurdity. She had been observing me, after all, observing her, and still was. Only now she was observing me observing her with the knowledge that she knew I was observing her knowing she was observing me, and I'm sorry but this changed things significantly.

When I asked Dr. Johnson why the change in rooms had been made, he replied without looking up from the data he was trolling for a new G-coefficient, "Miss Smith requested it all." Or perhaps he said, "Miss Smith, flower in a crannied wall." He spoke so softly. But I definitely heard him add, "Trust me, my son, it's for the best."

Back in my office, I wearily went about what all researchers do in moments of disorientation: return to the data, the cold hard facts that cannot be denied. I gently lifted my own nude photo from what I now saw was a family album. If there was an answer, I knew, it was here: since I was the maker of my own photograph, I clearly understood the intention with which it was made—to take the measure of my own (unique) normalcy. But cradling it in my palm, the photograph itself told a different tale—one of an Endomorph—a type—or so it seemed to this interpreter—a body who brought to the photo his own gigantic needs and desires, a body who in this case, I might add, was both attuned to such photos and so dulled by the viewing of thousands of such photos that seeing them in the aggregate he could not help but remember that a teaspoon of earth can contain as many as 100 million bacterial bodies. It occurred to me that every photo must be similarly loaded: each an icon of gigantic needs and desires. Including those of the researcher. For as I now believe Dr. Johnson meant to intimate, it is the researcher's longing to know all in all that makes him do what he does; and yet, the more intently he pursues his subject, the more his subject changes until finally, grasping the impossibility of ever possessing his beloved, he blinders his desire to the particle, not the atom, the flower, not the garden. If everything can't be known, he consoles himself, at least something small may be said. And perhaps, just perhaps, that small thing in some way may—it must!—stand in for the whole. At least to him.

As work at The Center "progressed," and my "wound" continued to "heal," I continued to perform my duties in such a fashion that to an observer (e.g. Miss Smith) it would appear as if nothing had changed. I gathered data, meaning I saw what I had been trained to look for. Everything was as before, save for my own little experiments that I occasionally inserted into the grander work. For example, I sometimes told subjects that if they did not pose correctly, the dais upon which they stood would give them an electric shock. And there, in the developing photos, would be confirmation of what I already knew, the trace of tense shoulder blades, for example, that revealed that someone had thought something would happen.

Miss Smith remained steadfast, and we fell into our routine, she on her side of the window, I on mine, keeping company after our fashion: arranging our photos, those mute, isolated moments, into patterns that spoke volumes. To someone. Or to be more precise, arranging them into our family album.[6] Why not? What were we, she and I and the Professor and all of our

---

[6] "Precise" being such an inexact word—as we demonstrate by giving or taking a million miles when we state the "precise" distance to a "nearby" galaxy but cannot split hair fine enough when we give the "precise" distance of an electron from its nucleus.[7]

[7] Maps of the atom that depict the nucleus as a planet orbited by moon-like electrons are as antiquated as Ptolemy's fictions anyway.[8]

[8] As shown by contemporary maps of the atom which depict it more like this:

$$< x > = \int \psi^*(x,t)\, x\, \psi(x,t)\, dx = \int \frac{x}{\sqrt{2\pi\sigma^2}}\, e^{\frac{(x-m)^2}{2\sigma^2}}\, dx = m \qquad [9]$$

[9] Math being the only ink ambiguous enough to draw precisely the location of an electron whose position is changed by the determination of its location.

subjects, if not a family, united by our family resemblances, our mutual and gigantic yearning, our poses, our dress, the circumstance of our being thrown together?

The definition of 4-4-4, the ideal, matched precisely that of a fit college student. But could not this definition have arisen only because we looked at so many college students? Does the cartographer make the map or does the map make the cartographer?—as well as the explorer, the tourist, the miner, the scientist? (Napoleon was said to have been a great lover of maps.) In the end, was there a difference? Is that what Miss Smith meant by switching offices? That is, was there still hope? At least for the ignorant?

Or was this blossoming "relationship" she and I "shared" my fantasy? Being a scientist, I considered the possibility. It was possible, given the nexus of body, consciousness, and world otherwise known as the crack in my skull, that I was hallucinating the contented domesticity that had descended upon The Center. It was possible, even, that I was the subject of some grand psychological experiment as yet unknown to me. Can any of us know for certain the motives of another's "hello?" Short of this, can anyone say for certain whether the doctor was a Modern Magellan? Modern Renoir or Svengali? Many maps end their lives not as tools but as lampshades, or in museums—that is, as art. My poster of Mount Somatotype already leaned against the framed lithograph that had once hung in my old office, massed as if for a rummage sale.

Still, I had the witnesses—the mute photos which, no matter how interpreted, were death masks or fingerprints of something. These photos could not lie, for they did not speak and were therefore truthful in the way that a ventriloquist's dummy is truthful until animated by its master. If by master we mean all of us: balls of nerve endings and social responses, which were themselves, of course, finite, the principle of finite possibility being what makes Perpetual Calendars possible, as well as the Eternal Human Heart, though given the 60 trillion cells that make up any one body, the odds against any two people having identical bodies exceeds the number of bacteria on earth, and is in fact astronomical.

Using a telescoping lens, I was able to focus so closely on the navels of some subjects that their whorls formed abstract patterns that could have just as easily been those of an inner ear, microbe, or galaxy. A fish-eye lens allowed me to stretch the frame to include the Somatotyping room all around, its calendar, even the side windows through which could be seen the wider world and whatever pedestrian, for example, happened to be passing by at the "moment." Along the bowed margin there also appeared a medicine chest's mirror in which could be seen, when the light was right, the reflection of a man whose face was obscured by the camera he peered into, bringing into focus (assuming he was not blurring) some "subject," perhaps, but certainly a self portrait, if by "self" we also mean "family," if by "portrait" we mean one moment extracted from billions of others without captions, its rhumb lines not so clearly imprinted on the body as was the gash on my head but visible nonetheless; if by "visible" we mean lived; if by "lived" we mean having existed; if by "existing" we circumnavigate back to "body" and its family of unknown coefficients. That is, its Family of Man. If by Man we also mean Woman.

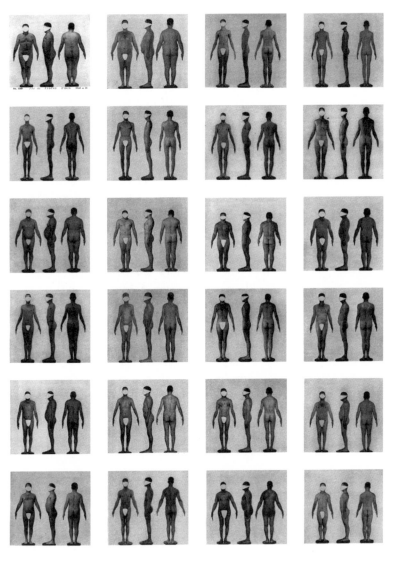

PROSPECTUS

by AMIE BARRODALE

PURPOSE:
To build tunnels for the dogs in Manhattan, New York.

WHERE:
East 14 to West 14.
East 84 to West 84.
Broadway North to Broadway South.

QUALIFICATIONS: I have had many experiences with dogs. My grandfather was a landowner and a dog trainer. He trained Doberman pinschers and terrier hounds. My grandmother was the prettiest woman in the world. I do not need to mention my great experience with digging.

WHEN: I was a child I was taken to a house in the middle of the swamp. It seemed to float on water. It was old and decrepit with multiple exterior staircases and watermarks up its façade. The watermarks faded without order. From a pale yellow to a deep brown, from Mars black to kelly green. A black mildew became a fog of black water bugs, and bright green swamp scum covered the manor's floorboards. My grandmother covered my eyes with her hands, and then she removed her hands.

SEE ATTACHED: Maps and drawings of the dog tunnels, drawn by Matt Sauer, Project Architect, according to Amie Barrodale's specifications, with the valuable assistance of Molly B. Schranz.

FURTHER QUALIFICATIONS: My great-granduncle was a genius inventor. The house in the swamp was built on top of an air chamber that he designed. He called the chamber a caisson. Imagine a boat floating upside-down on the sea. This is what the caisson looked like before men piled rocks onto it, to press it to the bottom of the swamp. When it rested on the swamp's floor, men went through an airlock, down inside the caisson, where they dug through the muck to the bedrock. When the caisson sat on bedrock, the house was built on top of the whole.

Like me, my great-granduncle worked best in private. He was a quiet man easily confused by false expressions of good will, and such expressions were in great supply during the preliminary stages of his project. My great-granduncle built the caisson in secret, in a barn. He began with the help of a rangy little assistant, but when the assistant began to clean up after my great granduncle with a curled lip, he was dismissed. Alone, my great-granduncle built the caisson of the strongest wood, and with the strongest of possible fasteners. He worked tirelessly and well, and in two years the caisson was complete. It was June 28, 1867.

A crowd gathered at the swamp's mouth to witness the launch. My great granduncle and 300 hired hands came over a hill at dusk. They had torches and a hundred horses and a thousand ornaments and red flags woven with golden thread. Their horses dragged the chamber on a long flat pull festooned with flags of Catholic benediction. The flags were white and pristine. The men were proud and lively. They crawled onto the caisson and inside of it. They strung lights down its face. They formed a fire line and passed one hundred small boats from the inside of the caisson to the mouth of the swamp. The moon was invisible. The men hammered a hundred spikes into the caisson's face. They tied ropes the width of a woman's neck to the hundred spikes, and threw these ropes down to the smaller boats. More preparations were made for the launch, but over these, we shall draw a curtain.

Hours before midnight, the caisson sat on land ten feet from the swamp's mouth. With a wordless signal from my great granduncle, the men and the horses strained forward. Sinews pulled in the horses' necks, their eyes rolled to reveal slivers of white, and their nostrils flared. The men tore their hands and slipped in the mud. A terrific groaning! The caisson took on the life of near-movement, and then it set forward into the swamp. The men dropped their ropes and swam out to the boats. At my great-granduncle's next signal, they slid their paddles into the water and set out for the swamp's farthest reaches.

THE DOG TUNNELS: will be built of metal.

THE TUNNELS: have been tested at my location in Mississippi.

THE TEST: was successful.

MY QUALIFICATIONS CONTINUE: Deep within the swamp, the hired hands retired for the night. They slept inside the small boats, under mosquito nets. My great-granduncle slept alone on top of the caisson. He had never slept so well.

ONE DAY: there will be between 1000 and 1009 tunnels.

MORE ABOUT MYSELF: Over the sinking of the caisson, we will draw another curtain. Suffice it to say the work took weeks, and that those weeks were arduous, insane, and unrewarding. Many men sustained injuries, and there was much bitterness and fighting. Morale was low and relationships were unhealthy, but when the caisson hit bottom, all of the bad feeling evaporated. The men sat dumb in their boats. They drifted over the sunk caisson and peered down into blackness, awestruck.

My great-granduncle was the first man in the chamber. He wore a suit with a velvet collar and buckled shoes. The airlock wailed like a banshee. He stepped into the chamber holding a candle. It was wet and hot and humid. The ceilings were low. The floor was silty and full of puddles, like a fine field after torrential rain, or beach sand just after a wave's retreat. The light was poor and shadows cast themselves in odd ways, but none of this captured my great-granduncle's imagination. The effects of the high air pressure captured him. For many years, he had kept a journal filled with plans and equations. After going down into the caisson, he filled several pages with ecstatic prose.

"In the chamber," he wrote, "my voice is that of a young girl. I open my mouth to speak, and it is a young girl."

"Candles," he wrote, "will not extinguish when I would have them extinguish. The flames dance and play with me, like will o' the wisps."

My great-granduncle spent many hours beneath the swamp and developed symptoms of the bends. Nosebleeds and increased appetite. Numbness, fatigue, paralysis, and euphoria.

"It is all so much," he wrote, "that after coming out of the caisson this last time, I did not speak for hours. I could not. Nor did I move my legs."

His symptoms worsened, but he refused to stop going into the caisson. His father removed him to his home, where my great-grandmother cared for

him. For the rest of his life, my great-granduncle remained in bed. He became a tyrant, insisting his foods be brought to him just so, insisting that his sheets be changed daily. He spent his energies delivering acid comments to family members, and dissecting the personalities he found in novels. When he died, twenty years later, the swamp-house was forgotten. The exterior staircases, the colored glass windows, the aviary, the gun turrets, the tower: all were unrealized. In plan, the interior of the tower was lined with small cubicles. In plan, each cubicle was to be occupied by a girl. Seventy cubicles and seventy girls, each girl to sit in her cubicle and shout and yell while my great-granduncle rested at the tower's base and shut his eyes. How phenomenal, but this was never realized. The caisson sat empty below the muck, pressed to the bottom of the swamp by rocks and heavy things, invisible.

THE BOATS: were sold by the hired hands.

THE DOORS TO THE DOG RUNS: will be made of brass.

ALL THE DOORKNOBS: will be made of brass.

THE HOUSE THAT I RECALL, THE ONE I MENTIONED AT THE OUTSET: does

CANINE, WASTE and MAIL CHUTES

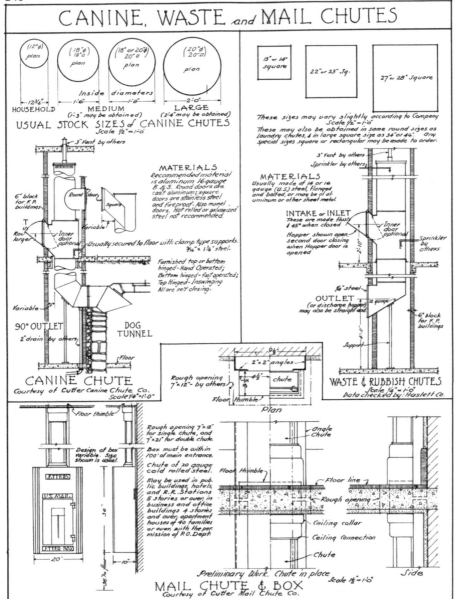

USUAL STOCK SIZES of CANINE CHUTES
Scale 1/2" = 1'-0"

(12"⌀) plan — HOUSEHOLD — 12¾"
(18"⌀ 18"□) plan — MEDIUM — 1'-6" (1'-3" may be obtained)
(18" or 20"⌀ 20"□) plan — LARGE — 1'-8" (2'-4" may be obtained)
(20"⌀ 20"□) plan — 2'-0"

Inside diameters

13" or 14" square — 22" or 23" Sq. — 27" or 28" Square

These sizes may vary slightly according to Company
Scale 1/2" = 1'-0"
These may also be obtained in same round sizes as
laundry chutes, & in large square size as 34" or 44". Any
special sizes square or rectangular may be made to order.

MATERIALS
Recommended material
is aluminum 16 gauge
B. & S. Round doors are
cast aluminum; square
doors are stainless steel
and fireproof. Also monel
doors. Hot rolled or galvanized
steel not recommended.

Usually secured to floor with clamp type supports.
3/16" x 1¼" steel.

Furnished top or bottom
hinged - Hand Operated;
Bottom hinged - Foot operated;
Top Hinged - Inswinging
All are self closing.

MATERIALS
Usually made of 14 or 16
gauge (U.S.) steel, flanged
and bolted, or may be of aluminum or other sheet metal.

INTAKE or INLET
These are made flush
& 45° when closed

Hopper shown open;
second door closing
when Hopper door is
opened

Inner door optional

Sprinkler by others

OUTLET
(or discharge hopper)
may also be straight end

¼" steel

6" block for F.P. buildings

Support

WASTE & RUBBISH CHUTES
Scale 1/4" = 1'-0"
Data checked by: Haslett Co.

90° OUTLET
2" drain by others

DOG TUNNEL
Floor

CANINE CHUTE
Courtesy of Cutler Canine Chute Co.
Scale 1/4" = 1'-0"

Rough opening
7" x 12" by others

Floor thimble

2" x 2" angles
chute
9½"

Plan

Rough opening 7" x 12"
for single chute, and
7" x 21" for double chute.

Design of box
variable. Size
shown is usual.

Chute of 20 gauge
cold rolled steel.

May be used in pub-
lic buildings, hotels,
and R.R. Stations
5 stories or over; in
business and office
buildings 4 stories
and over; apartment
houses of 40 families
or over, with the per-
mission of P.O. Dept.

Angle Chute
Floor thimble
Floor line
Rough opening
Ceiling collar
Ceiling connection
Chute

Preliminary Work. Chute in place Scale 1½" = 1'-0"

Side

MAIL CHUTE & BOX
Courtesy of Cutler Mail Chute Co.

not exist.

I Still Know: about building.

My Associates: are loyal and devoted, the best people.

The Dogs: will run beneath us. They will be released into chutes fitted with brass fixtures. The chutes will run east to west, west to east, north to south. They will be fifty feet below our feet, and always, I cannot stress this enough, they will always be alive. By which I mean they will always be full of dogs, and those dogs will always be running.

Thank you. I look forward to hearing from you at your earliest possible convenience.

sincerely,
Amie Barrodale
Project Manager/Designer

VOLUME 13: M

by PATRICK BORELLI, KARYN COUGHLIN, BEN DRYER, DAN GOLDSTEIN,
JOHN HODGMAN, MIKE JEROMINSKI, ERIK P. KRAFT, WHITNEY MELTON,
EUGENE MITMAN, CEDAR PRUITT, BRIAN SPINKS, BILL WASIK, JOHN WILLIAMS

MACHINE GUN Through application of the lessons learned from the Industrial Revolution (mechanization, repetition, etc.) to the infantryman's rifle, a now-familiar instrument of unparalleled personal destruction was invented: the motorized repeating rifle, or machine gun. Before the machine gun, combat was a personal affair where a soldier was forced to confront his opponent face to face. After its invention, soldiers could be mowed down in droves from hundreds of yards away.

Machine guns make many noises. Some of the most interesting are the flat hammering of a .30 caliber tripod-mounted gun, the "wham-wham" of a big 50mm BAR, or the soft hiss of the famous Vietnam-era "kitty gun." The kitty gun purred in the arms of the men who held it, but it was a deadly weapon.

MAGIC MONKEY See Monkey, Magic

MAINE During the early years of American settlement, Maine was considered the Northeast's terrifying frontier. While villages were clustered thickly along the coast of Massachusetts Bay, Maine was a no-man's-land where only the rugged survived, and often they didn't. The trackless woods harbored hostile natives ready to take scalps and the thick clouds overhead held a snowfall that threatened an early end to the growing season.

After the Revolution, America expanded westward and the mythos of the American Frontier bypassed Maine completely. The word "frontier" now conjures images of settlers heading west in wagon trains during the Homestead Act years, to claim plots in Nebraska as their own; of Joseph Smith and his followers, run out of town after town, dragging their worldly goods behind them out to Utah and the Great Salt Lake; of Irish and the Chinese immigrants, building a railroad across an empty expanse.

And what about Maine? It's America's Vacationland.

MAINLINE   The main line, as opposed to the secondary line or even the triliterate line, which tend to oppose each other in trilateral directions. Mainlining is a common form of injecting imports into geographic and cultural regions, but only at 136-degree angles with quadrilateral side impact.

MAKESHIFT HONKY   A false white person, created from crude materials. Traditionally, in black communities, the presence of a white person will relieve pent-up racial tensions; as he or she passes by, blacks will be able to say, for example, "Look at the honky!" or "I hate honkies." When a white person has not been sighted in a long while, black people will frequently create a makeshift honky out of any materials at hand—a bag of rice, perhaps, or an old jacket.

MANCHU DYNASTY   In 1644, Manchurian semi-nomadic warriors invaded China, sweeping through scanty border defenses and overwhelming the last Ming emperor in a series of battles along the Yangtze River. These were the fierce Manchus, also called the Ch'ing, begetters of an empire based on the sword. Warriors though they were, the Manchus were shrewd enough in assuming power to keep most of the existing Ming government apparatus functioning while the Manchus themselves assumed power at the top.

Once in command of the empire, the Manchu revealed their true nature as teachers of arts and crafts. For hours they lacquered vases with tiny sable brushes; they carved interlocking balls from ivory and cast huge bronze bells that sounded deep and sonorous notes when blown by the breeze or touched by a small child. In the market of each city they assembled copper armatures that, when cranked, plotted the exact movement of every star in the sky. They built water clocks of unprecedented accuracy and gave them away to any who asked.

Amazed, the Chinese peasantry could only stare in wonder. Slowly they lowered their hoes and adzes, letting them fall from their calloused hands.

The mill wheels stopped turning, the bureaucrats were quiet in their halls of vermilion and teak and the Great River Yangtze flooded its banks seven times in seven years; earthquakes toppled the Pagoda of Tang Chi Mountain; rain fell on the dust of Gobi and the Grand Canal ran dry.

MAN OVERBOARD! A phrase often heard when a person is seen flailing about in the water alongside a seagoing vessel. The ways in which this shout may be uttered are as varied as the circumstances surrounding the event itself.

On a liner crossing the Atlantic, a young man on deck for a late-night stroll might see an elderly man leaning against a rail that has been weakened by age. As the rail creaks, the witness will become alarmed; when it cracks, and the old fellow plummets into the beyond, there comes shock; and on shock's heels, our unhappy phrase.

Someone else might simply and rudely be shoved overboard by a villain, or a spurned lover. It could be that a vicious young child, in the grip of some ill-humor involving a much-wanted-but-denied after-dinner treat, might suddenly push his hapless parent into the ocean, shouting "Man overboard!" with malevolence and anger.

Or perhaps someone will become overwhelmed by life, love, chronic depression, harassment by angry creditors or any other manner of troubles and decide to end it all by diving to their death in a graceful arc from the side of the luxury cruise liner. Viewers will see the leap, start to their feet, put their hands to their mouths, and scream: "O dear God in heaven, that man needs help. Something must be done. Man overboard!"

Sadness, surprise, hatred: any emotion you can think of could be the impetus to joining one's teeth and tongue in this cry. Yet despite these variances in circumstance or motive, one thing remains constant: there is someone who has gone over the edge of a vessel and they are, most likely, in need of aid.

MARGARINE A butter substitute, made of an emulsified blend of edible vegetable oils. Margarine was patented in 1869 by a French chemist, Hippolyte Mège-Mouries, as an inexpensive substitute for butter. Initially a product of animal fats, margarine is now typically made from soybean oil. Margarine is similar in composition to butter, yields practically the same number of calories, and is easily digestible.

Buoyed by tales of lower calories and better health, sales of margarine in the United States surpassed those of butter in 1958. Frightened, dairy farmers in Wisconsin lobbied for a law stating that all margarine products sold in their state would have to be colored black. In Iowa, farmers ate their toast dry in protest of the oily impostor. Margarine was melted in effigy in several Minnesota towns. By the 1970s, however, organized resistance had died out, and margarine was allowed to assume a place beside butter on Midwestern supermarket shelves.

Recently, however, butter sales have been revived by a national realization that margarine tastes like margarine.

MARS The Red Planet has exuded a peculiar fascination on men ever since it was first noticed in 1962. In the night sky, Mars appears red: a rusty red, a bright, bloody red. The rusty red of rusty weapons. The rusty dull red of dried blood, bleeding on the rusty weapons. For these reasons, Mars was named after Mars, the Roman god of Mars.

Mars has two moons named Deimos and Phobos—meaning "terror" and "fear" in ancient Greek. Like thieves in the night, Deimos and Phobos each circle Mars in orbits removed more than eleven degrees from the solar system's plane of the ecliptic.

Occasionally, as observed from Earth, Mars seems to waver in its orbit, apparently moving backwards in its traverse of the heavens. This is due to Earth's orbit overtaking Mars's as both planets travel around the sun. However, the ancients, who believed in a universe in which the Earth did not move, explained this backwards or "retrograde" movement by postulating that Mars, as it circled Earth, also moved in smaller orbits, called "epicycles." As it turns out, the ancients were totally wrong—about this, and about so much more.

If you go out and look at Mars through a standard telescope tonight, and the next night, and in fact over many many nights, Mars will appear to grow in the lens. And then it will appear to speak. Listen carefully, for this ancient planet has much to say.

MATTERHORN The world's most beloved imitation mountain, the Matterhorn lends a touch of Alpine grace and a classic European air to California's Disneyland theme park. Few know that concealed secretly within its peak there is a basketball court, a lively speakeasy and gin palace, and at the very top, a vault filled with the bodies of hundreds of missing children.

MAYORS & CLERGYMEN Mattel's disastrous attempt to compete with Clue, the flagship board game of their arch-rival, Parker Brothers. Mayors and Clergymen essentially was a direct rip-off of Clue, but where the characters simply were mayors and clergymen. Players tried to figure out who the murderer was, what the murder weapon was, and where the murder was committed. For example, sometimes it would be Boston's Mayor Thomas Menino in the nunnery with the knife; at other times it might be Cardinal O'Brien in the Licensing Department with a gun. Occasionally the culprit might have been Cardinal Deegan in the Municipal Archives with the rope.

For a seven-year period—1968 to 1974—Mattel's top executives were so fixated on the game's success in the marketplace that they focused all the corporation's resources on obsessive redesigns and productions. Over twelve million units were produced during that period, and a rumored $100 million was spent on research and marketing. In 1975 a new CEO was brought in, and Mattel likely would have let the game die a quiet death; but after a series of scathing articles and reviews in the late 1970s by the *Washington Post*'s late, esteemed gaming critic Walker E. Thomas, Mattel decided to ship every unit to Chilé.

At the time, the move was seen as eccentric. Now, boardgame historians agree that Mattel's logic was sound. A non-English-speaking country, Chilé was at that time virtually devoid of boardgames; it is also sealed off from the rest of South America by the Andes, a nearly impassible mountain range. Once the Mayors & Clergymen games were in Chilé, Mattel reasoned, they would likely never be used and, more importantly, would never leave. But Mattel didn't count on the resiliency and obsessiveness of the Chileans: they embraced the whodunit game, and today November 12th is national Mayors & Clergymen day in Chilé. All the offices and schools are closed. Everyone plays and everyone in Chilé is happy.

M DELUXE A four-humped variation of the cursive letter "m" created in 1988 by Ulrich and Hans Hoffrage, two twelve-year-old Pennsylvania Mennonite boys who used the letter when writing the word Mennonite in order to "show how great it is." Use of the letter ended abruptly when the Council of Elders forbade it.

MEEK One who pretends he/she is not an asshole in the hopes of inheriting the earth. The truth is, the earth has been willed to the Chinese, and there's nothing the meek can do about it.

MEGATON The explosive force of one million tons of trinitrotoluene, also known as TNT.

MEGATRON The evil leader of the Decepticons. Megatron's nemesis is Optimus Prime, leader of the benevolent Autobots.

MEIOSIS The process of nuclear division in a living cell by which the number of pairs of chromosomes is reduced to half of the number of chromosomes in twice the number of original cells. An ordinary living cell is "diploid": i.e., it contains two sets of each type of chromosome. During the first stage, half of the chromosomes in each cell are displaced into half of the cells; the other half divide, forming twice the number of cells, but with only half the number of chromosomes that originally existed in half of the cells. During the second stage of meiosis, each cell splits in two, forming twice the number of chromosomes but with only half of the original number of cells. Thus in meiosis the chromosome pairs each divide twice, resulting first in two cells with two sets of chromosomes, and next with four cells, each with only half of the chromosome pairs. The end result is one cell with no chromosomes.

MENIN The evil Lenin.

MIXING FAUCET Used to be the day, faucets hot and cold sat apart and shot streams into sink bowl direct and unmixed. One day man sat dual knobs side by side—hot and cold—to flow water down through single spigot. Benefits? Better shaving, better depilation, better soap sudsy water play. Drawbacks were none. The next step? Faucet offers hot cocoa, hot cream, oatmeal, plasma, easy cheese, silly string, mercury. In a blink of an eye it can be real.

MOBILE, ALABAMA The Azalea City. Most men there tip a quarter on a haircut.

MOB MENTALITY Large crowds of people all tend to move in one direction. If someone stands up in a mass of excited people and yells, "They went that-a-way!" thousands of wide-eyed men and women will speechlessly shuffle in the indicated direction. If birdcalls and related noises are broadcast to the crowd through a loudspeaker, the entire assembly will sway from side to side like a field of ripe wheat stirred by a spring breeze. And if pasta—not just any pasta, but really fine, well-cooked pasta—is handed out, everyone will sit right down and dig in.

MOBY A popular musician of the late twentieth century. Unique among his contemporaries, Moby is spring-loaded; one end of the spring anchors in his thorax, while the other exerts pressure on his brain. Ambient sound-scapes present themselves to him in this fashion: a catalyst—typically a sound from the outside world—enters his ears, where it is transcribed by a seismograph; the scrap of paper falls into a Plexiglas cylinder, which is whisked, via suction, through his chest and deposited in a holding cell at the nape of his neck; Moby's thoracic spring winds, causing tension to build, as the scrap of paper is treated and sprayed; the spring buckles, Moby's brain sinks, and there is a dull squish, causing the paper to flutter up into his cranium.

MOESHA American television program revered, but ultimately spurned, for the transparency of its Bergman influences. Perhaps best remembered for its third-season premiere, which opened with a continuous twenty-minute shot of the show's eponymous star on a screened-in porch, at dusk, watching two nephews romp on a faintly sun-dappled hillside. When the network brought in a new staff of writers whose interests tended more toward the booty, the show's audience recoiled at the program's sudden lack of existen-tialist thrust. Viewership dwindled, and Moesha was sent back to the recording studio, where she sang half-heartedly about the boys on the cor-ner, trusting we'd know what she really meant. We didn't, so Moesha fled to Europe, where she founded an independent film company and attempted to resuscitate the flagging influence of Truffaut.

Her first feature, "Gray Awning, Red Sky," received rave reviews. Her second, "House Party 8: Melvin's House," was lost on the European market's sensibilities. Shortly thereafter, Moesha followed the lead of her spiritual predecessor, Ambrose Bierce, and disappeared deep into Mexico. She is pre-sumed dead, and Miramax will re-release her films in the U.S. next fall.

MONKEY, MAGIC It's done with mirrors.

MOUNT RUSHMORE Mount Rushmore, located in Keystone, South Dakota, bears the images of four of America's best-known presidents: George Washington, Thomas Jefferson, Abraham Lincoln, and Theodore Roosevelt. Carved inside their gigantic noses are smaller stone visages of other great Presidents—four in each, allowing for sixteen sub-Presidents on the entire edifice; and into each of these Presidents, still unbelievably tall, phenomenally detailed, into their noses and ears more faces are carved, the faces of our country's heroes, some familiar, some anonymous, their features made fantastical—their expressions contorted, ecstatic; their hair, writhing snakes; their hands gnarled and clawed. Along the writhing hair-snakes are carved the Great Books of the True Canon, the Expanded Canon, where the *Iliad* is intertwined, literally, with *The Color Purple*—in this instance each carved, in full text, along an asp on the head of Christa MacAuliffe, a 1988 addition to Woodrow Wilson's left ear.

There are no incidental markings on Mount Rushmore. What appears from the ground to be a scuff mark, or an impurity in the stone, will on closer inspection reveal itself to be the face of a minor 19th century poet, or the text of fifty of our nation's granted patents, or a battle map of Antietam, showing the major movements of the Northern and Southern forces, the spot of each death marked with a graven skull. When approaching the monument by helicopter, at a distance of five thousand feet from the stone, an observer might notice a haggard look in the eye of Lyndon Johnson, the sub-President just above Washington's left nostril; but upon attaining a distance of five hundred feet, they will see the individual veins in LBJ's eye that have been meticulously carved to give this look; at fifty feet, they will be able to make out the lines, which are curved lines of musical notation, cataloguing the complete works of Aaron Copeland and Charles Ives. At five feet, it is said, the stems of the musical notes can be seen to be composed of some sort of text, which no one has ever come close enough to read.

SEARCHED THE WEB FOR "CONRAD APPLEBANK"

by KEVIN SHAY

<u>20th Century Kooks: **Conrad Applebank**</u>
Conrad Applebank Not a scientist by training but pursuing his increasingly esoteric medicinal theories by dint of his enormous family fortune, Conrad Applebank obsessively ...

<u>Register-Post | Ask the Answer Guy | Whatever Happened to **Conrad Applebank?**</u>
... to cure horses that were similarly mad. Thus began **Conrad Applebank's** bizarre forays into the healing arts, which later led him to the deepest ...

<u>Register-Post | Lifestyles Contents</u>
A billion-dollar inheritance, a riding accident, a plunge into madness (and the Pacific Ocean): Conrad Applebank's unique life examined, in Ask the Answer Guy. Fall Fashion ...

<u>The Fifties Product Shrine: **Applebank** Foods</u>
... turned out some gorgeous packaging under the aegis of **Conrad Applebank** (yes, that **Conrad Applebank**) who later left the business to devote himself full-time to ...

Grant Writers' Guide: Foundations A-C

... MA 02476. 23) Lucinda **Applebank** Memorial Foundation. Endowed: 1962. Endowed By: **Conrad Applebank**. Grant Cycle: Annual. Areas of Interest: Equine disease, aquatic ...

NutriTek.com Company History

... the realm of pre-packaged consumer foods in 1959, when NutriStar acquired the successful **Applebank** Foods from its founder's son, **Conrad Applebank**. Canned fruit, ...

News in Brief - Rapper Moves to New Digs

... the scene of many a lavish high-society fete in the 1950s. The mansion's then-owner, **Conrad Applebank**, hosted captains of industry, Hollywood personalities, and assorted ...

(Very) Weird Science - In Their Own Words

... treasure trove of crackpot cosmology (8 pages). **Conrad Applebank's** letters to Scientific American, 1965-66. Never published, and you'll see why (my favorite part is ...

(Very) Weird Science - **Applebank's** Letters to Scientific American

... my specimens will yet yield chemical compounds heretofore unknown to us surface dwellers. Sincerely, **Conrad Applebank** Next Back to Index

(Very) Weird Science - **Applebank's** Letters to Scientific American

... pressure, much as it turns coal to diamond, has turned these organisms into marvelous factories of biological purification. Sincerely, **Conrad Applebank** Previous Next Back to Index

(Very) Weird Science - **Applebank's** Letters to Scientific American

... panacea in those inky depths, if medical science would but join me in exploring this pharmaceutical last frontier. Sincerely, **Conrad Applebank** Previous Next Back to Index

(Very) Weird Science - **Applebank's** Letters to Scientific American

... serenely flicking his tail? There is no end, I say, to what these noble animals can teach us. Sincerely, **Conrad Applebank** Previous Next Back to Index

(Very) Weird Science - Applebank's Letters to Scientific American
... outer-space folly when, as I will soon have proved, the answers we seek are not above but below. Sincerely, **Conrad Applebank** Previous Next Back to Index

(Very) Weird Science - Applebank's Letters to Scientific American
... kinks are ironed out, will be every bit as effective on a madman as on a fevered horse. Sincerely, **Conrad Applebank** Previous Back to Index

Submersibles Photo Gallery Page 3
... (Bettman Archive). D. The Lucy II (Piccard-style bathyscaphe) with owner **Conrad Applebank** (UPI). E. **Conrad Applebank** and unknown pilot inside the Lucy II, shortly before ...

Tolliver University Scholarships
... sex, race, or creed. The **Conrad Applebank** Scholarship Award is a yearly scholarship given for outstanding achievement in marine biology, administered by ...

79' Firebirds Lot#1
... 79ta14.4.jpg (27350 bytes) click -> 79ta14.5.jpg (32270 bytes), **Conrad Applebank** owns this beautiful Trans Am. Conrad writes: "I bought it in March 1994 with 45K ...

Atlantic Book Auction Galleries: Sale 302
... 5th impression. Alfred A. Knopf, 1967. Inscribed on flyleaf: "To **Conrad Applebank**, / May you dive ever / deeper and enrich us / all with ...

ThespianWire.org Playwright Updates
... follow up his London success with a play about the life of eccentric multi-millionaire **Conrad Applebank**. "It's sort of 'Equus' meets Howard Hughes," he explains. "This ...

Arts: A Novel of Alchemy Strikes Comic Gold
... hilarious in his messianic grandiosity: not so much a Faust as a **Conrad Applebank**, doomed to continue his pseudo-scientific maunderings unto poverty or death.

JFK, Election Thief - Sen Arthur N. Scoopes Diary Transcripts, 8/60
Meanwhile, I have had another letter from **Conrad Applebank**. He is still deep in grief, and worse, blames himself—for "inadequately vaccinating the horse," or some such ...

The Moira O'Malley Story, Part 11: The Ingenue and the Duke
... dashing European she met at her friend Lucinda's 1951 wedding to **Conrad Applebank** (a union that would later end in tragedy). For Moira, it was love at ...

Nero's Riddle Fans Message Board: Re: who is "conrad a?"
... to the board. Mike of NR says this lyric refers to **Conrad Applebank**, who AFAIK was a tres tres rich guy who went off his ...

> Nero's Riddle Fans Message Board: Re: Re: who is "conrad a?"
> ... at 13:43:02 PDT thanks for the info, NRRules212. guess it's easier to rhyme "conrad a" than "**conrad applebank**" ;-) Next message: TX Nero's Riddle gigs?

Untitled
... fall foliage, it should be a lovely weekend," said Mrs. **Conrad. Applebank** Inn will host the guests overnight and provide box lunches for the event. Registration ...

Daniella Meyers' Place * * * * A Brief History of Me
... goodbye to those addictions, and god willing, they'll lie forever at the bottom of the sea like **Conrad Applebank's** bathosphere. I've been sober for ...

THIS WAR NEVER HAPPENED

AN INTERVIEW WITH SANDOW BIRK,
ABOUT PAINTING NEW THINGS
IN AN OLD WAY

SANDOW BIRK IS a painter and surfer living in California. I was primarily interested in his paintings, though I did want to ask him about the surfing, because while I have never surfed, I do remain curious about it. Birk's paintings typically mix places and people that are recognizably part of contemporary California with classical compositions borrowed, with a sure but light touch, from artists such as Delacroix and David. His exhibit "In Smog and Thunder: Historical Works from the Great War of the Californias" commemorates and memorializes a fictional war between northern and southern California in eighty-three paintings, ink drawings, diagrams, three-dimensional maps, model ships, dioramas, and much else that needs discussing.

Q: In your War exhibit, there are two large canvases that depict the land war in San Francisco. The event's the same, but the depictions are strikingly different. What were you after in painting two pieces of the same event?

A: When I went about this project my first idea was to spoof the idea of History Painting and its role in Western European art, and so I went about looking at various battle paintings from the past and reworking them. My intent was never to tell a coherent, believable story from start to finish, but rather to make paintings that recalled historical styles. It wasn't important that they look alike. After all, the event they depict is fictitious.

Q: Do you think of one as offering a more honest picture of the battle? "Memorial to the Battle of San Francisco" presents the battle as much more orderly. But in "The Battle of the San Francisco," all the mess and destruction of battle are apparent. Did you paint the Memorial as if it were done years after the fighting ended, imagining someone attempting to tidy up the history?

A: I did imagine that someone was doing the "Memorial" painting after the fact, someone with the point-of-view of glorious deeds. That's why the sky is so much more romantic, as if all the Heavens are battling, as if the event is so grand that the entire universe is involved. It also has knights in armor and tanks and helicopters and many more different time periods involved, as if the whole of history were involved. It's more over-the-top than the other one.

Q: Did you consciously want to create southern California art and northern California art for the exhibit?

A: I never thought of the art as being southern or northern. It's all based on Western European traditions. As the project went along I wanted to create the sense of a real war museum, so I added the war posters, the drawings, the maps, the models, and the relics from the war. Things you'd find in a real museum, like the burned flag.

Q: In 1999, you brought together all this material. What was your plan for that full exhibit?

A: It was presented as an exhibition of an event that the audience was familiar with, as if it was really part of our history, like the Civil War. When you go to the museum at Gettysburg, the exhibits assume you've already heard of the Civil War and are somewhat familiar with who was fighting, how it started, and how it ended. The exhibits discuss one battle in that war, rather than explaining the whole thing. I wanted to get that feeling throughout the project: that details such as these needn't be laid out. It gives it a more realistic museum feel.

Q: I like that idea of the exhibit giving only part of the story and assuming the audience is knowledgeable about the rest. Was one of the ideas you were working with that museums routinely make these sorts of assumptions, for good or bad?

A: Exactly. But for good or bad? All communication has to make assumptions and so do museums, it's not something singular to institutions. For example, when you turn on Monday Night Football they don't start each game by explaining the rules or what's happening or what the sport of football is and how it came about. They assume you come to it with some common knowledge about the event you're about to watch. Just as we do in all interactions. When we speak to someone we assume they know certain things, speak our language.

When you go to other countries, you encounter a shared common history but from a different viewpoint, and that changes everything. For example, read about the American Revolution in British books. In Mexico City I went to the Museum of the Wars with North America, which offers a whole different look at our common history, particularly the invasion of Mexico City. Each of these viewpoints assumes a common understanding of these events, meaning that the Mexican museum assumes that it is speaking to a Mexican audience that has a shared view of the Americas.

Q: In your paintings you nod to Géricault, David, Delacroix, among others. Are there specific sorts of History painting that you had in mind for the first painting of the San Francisco and the later memorial to the battle?

A: Your question raises exactly the issues I was most concerned about in the entire project: What is History painting? Is it ever real or realistic? Does it ever portray events truly? Yes, I was looking at two specific paintings from the past for those two works—one of the Battle of Waterloo and one from a Medieval painting—but I wouldn't say that one portrays battle more realistically. That's the weakness and more importantly the strength of painting, its freedom from reality. My intent was to spoof and question depictions of battle, depictions of heroics, romanticism, death, war, etc. and the paintings that strived to do so with sincerity.

Q: But at the same time your work makes it clear that you see History painting as something with a great deal of life and possibility in it still. That is, History painting isn't dead for you, and it's certainly not all distortion and romanticism. After all, why create History paintings of contemporary California?

A: I'm not creating History paintings of contemporary California. I'm creating spoofs of old History paintings. My paintings comment on and make

" Memorial to the Great Battle of San Francisco", by Sandow Birk. Courtesy of Catherine Clark Gallery, San Francisco

"San Franciscan – The Seas Are Ours", by Sandow Birk. Courtesy of Catherine Clark Gallery, San Francisco

criticisms of the history of art and society, among other things. I don't really think that History painting can be done seriously today without devolving into kitsch. I'm not sure it's possible to paint serious History paintings without having your tongue in your cheek. I've never tried. When I have painted actual events, such as President Bush visiting Los Angeles after the riots, I did so as much to talk about painting as Los Angeles. At no point did I do it for the purpose of "recording" or "documenting" these events for posterity. That was the intention of History painters.

Q: A lot of the effort of putting on your War exhibit has to do with how it looks in a museum. The exhibit never lets on that this war never happened, and so everything from how the signs read to what the audio tour reveals is complicit. I was wondering if you'd say a bit about the work that went into mounting the exhibit.

A: Nobody is more museum maniacal than Americans. We have museums in every town for something or other and we have one of the shortest histories to celebrate in the world. It's as if we're obsessed with creating a sense of history where there is none. For example, when I was living in Rio de Janeiro they celebrated the 500th anniversary of the city. Our entire country isn't even half that old; our fixation on the Founding Fathers and the Civil War is absurd in the context of the world. I was recently in Lisbon and was walking down streets more than 1,000 years old, and here we have the perfectly preserved boyhood home of Eisenhower. Is that necessary? What can we possibly learn from that farmhouse?

Q: That Eisenhower lived in a farmhouse? A lot of it has to do with just being in a place that's notable only because someone notable has been before, walking the same paths and stepping through the same door. In Don DeLillo's *White Noise*, two pop culture professors go to observe a tourist attraction called The Most Photographed Barn in America. People travel from all over to see the barn that they've seen in hundreds of photographs already. They buy postcards of the barn while they're standing in front of the barn. People go to the Most Photographed Barn to photograph it some more. They photograph themselves in front of the barn while holding their postcards. Is this all part of the same phenomenon, treating things as sacred because someone says they're sacred?

A: When I walked down 1,000-year-old streets in Lisbon, *no one cared*. People live in buildings six centuries old in London, and they don't stop and photograph themselves in front of the place, even though someone incredibly important slept there, or was born there, or some event occurred there. Older cultures are much less obsessed with finding meaning in places and with recording events that happen today. Watch the NBA championships and listen to how historic every moment is, how jerseys are retired when players quit. I'm sure people smarter than me have thought about this a lot more than I have, but it is particularly American, and it might be something that *makes* us American. We go to the stupid barn because we lack something more meaningful. Or perhaps because we want, more than other cultures, for things to mean something when they don't.

Q: The labels in the exhibit are often critical of the quality of the paintings or just plain dismissive of the artists' abilities. What were you going for there?

A: A lot of stuff came from my looking into actual Civil War history. That whole world is pretty funny in its deadly seriousness and excruciating attention to detail, the high tone of the writing, the over-zealousness of its fanatics. You see the same seriousness in art museums and critics. Once I came up with fictional artists for each painting, it was obvious I needed fictional critics. I liked using these conventions to comment on my work, which, frankly, deserves some of the criticisms I gave it.

Q: I couldn't help noticing that The Getty Center is the site of a long siege and comes in for quite a shelling. The north, at one point, maneuvers a catapult into place and lobs appliances at its walls. Are you extracting your revenge as an artist, or does the military strategist in you believe the building would be a crucial position in any land campaign?

A: Both. It would be a very good defense position geographically, placed as it is on a high hill overlooking a main freeway. Also, the architecture of the place itself is very fortress-like. As an artist, the inaccessibility of the place and its location as sort of a castle over the Westside (the more well-to-do side of Los Angeles) is worthy of attack. But I have nothing against the institution, it's a wonderful place, it's got great artworks, it's been supportive of me personally, but it still remains difficult to visit.

Q: As I was reading through the press coverage of the exhibit I came across one cover article subtitled, "Painter Sandow Birk depicts the hatred and jealousy that emanate southward from S.F." It will probably surprise nobody that this article emanated from a southern Californian publication. How did the press in the north and south cover the exhibit? Did they take sides?

A: The press coverage was amazingly positive throughout, from both the north and the south. Almost everyone wanted to know who won, which I hadn't expected. It's as if no one liked not having the story completed, they didn't want anything open-ended, when in fact there was no intention of this being a story; it's an art show, not a narrative.

Q: That's right, you never really come out and say who won the war. Why do you suppose people who spend an hour or two looking at a complicated series of fictions want to know which fictional side won?

A: Many people came to the project wanting to know how the war started, how it ended, who was who, and details like that, but my intention throughout was to leave much of this unresolved. People's need to have it all spelled out was initially surprising, but not so much now that I think about it. It's much more interesting to leave the beginning and ending unclear, implied, and to leave the discrepancies, the errors, the conflicting elements in the whole thing. There are hints that Tijuana becomes a major player in post-war California.

Q: Is it necessary for people to know what works you're painting with in mind?

A: I don't think it's necessary at all. It's enough for anyone to look at the paintings and realize that, whether they know which specific painting I'm quoting or not, I am appropriating a style of antiquated Western painting. It's pretty obvious that my paintings are intended to look like old paintings. That's enough to start people thinking. Of course, when one does recognize specific paintings, it can add another layer to the work because there are often particular references and comments in a single painting.

Q: What do those who don't see Géricault or David see when they see your work?

A: Almost everyone, from kids to non-Western people to non-art audiences, is familiar enough with the trappings of the Western Art Tradition. Anyone can pick up that these paintings look like old paintings, but that they are of contemporary people, which is strange right off the bat. Everyone recognizes the tradition of the horseback portrait, for example, even if you're from China or the Middle East. Why are people from our times being painted this way? What does that mean? That's the jumping-off point for thinking about my work.

Q: You're pretty consistently speaking in one sort of voice through your form and quite another sort of voice through your content. That is, your forms say, This is History painting, a classical work of art. And the content says, This is taking place on streets that look pretty much like how they look right now, in a place very near to where you are now.

A: I want my paintings to raise questions about classical painting. What was classical painting? Did classical painting depict the truth? What are its conventions? How does it relate to painting today? I also want to raise some questions about our lives today. Things like: are our actions heroic? What is heroism? Are events in our time related to historical events? Who leads whom? Why is the L.A.P.D. out of control? What is the role of painting in a city like Hollywood? What are the reasons behind animosity between San Francisco and Los Angeles? I talk about contemporary social issues like water use, immigration, languages, urban sprawl, pollution, among other things. It seems like a lot, but I spend weeks or more on a painting, so it's normal that the thoughts going through my head in that time find their way into the artwork.

Q: So you're raising and dignifying contemporary issues by rendering them in the manner of History paintings. That's a textbook example of the mock-heroic, where the trivial gets treated as extraordinary. At the same time, you're undermining those classical compositions. That's more like a work of burlesque, where the high and mighty gets treated as low and not-so-mighty.

A: Exactly. I intend to undermine classical depictions at the same time I seek to elevate the mundane.

Q: A lot of satiric art relies on caricature and grotesque exaggeration. Your work features not much caricature and no grotesque exaggeration. Is there a tradition for the sort of juxtapositions you're making of the form and content?

A: Perhaps someone like William Hogarth, although he used contemporary artistic styles to comment on his times. And wait a second, isn't elevating stereotypical animosities between Los Angeles and San Francisco a caricature and a grotesque exaggeration?

Q: You're right. Pay me no mind. You got some grotesquerie in there. What interests you about Hogarth?

A: Hogarth was one of the first artists to produce work for a "common man" audience. Before that, the historical audiences for art had been the Church, the aristocracy, the upper classes. Hogarth made work about the common man to be seen by the common man. Through his development of etching and mass reproduction of his work, he even made his work available to the common man. Hogarth used conventions of painting that already existed, twisted them a bit, and added layers of symbolism. He was critical, satirical, and popular, as in "for the populace," all things that I admire.

Q: The War of the Californias is a contemporary war, yet it's also a war that's memorialized in painting. As I looked at the exhibit catalog, what struck me first was the anachronistic details—the galleons alongside the destroyers, the battles fought on horseback and Harley-Davidsons—but then I started to think what is truly anachronistic is that this is all being captured in paint.

A: It's anachronistic to paint history at all today. I often worry that it's anachronistic to paint at all, especially in Hollywood. Most of the work I'm drawing from is from pre-photography times, when the role of painting as a means of recording events was necessary. Maybe I'm nostalgic for a purpose to painting in general, I don't know. Maybe I want painting to matter in a town where it doesn't seem to matter much at all. It's tough being an artist here, morally.

Q: In a lot of satire there's a naïf, this person who just observes everything that goes on and relates it without affect. The naïf is usually removed from his normal, comfortable time and place and dropped into some wholly different milieu. So that you have Mark Twain's Connecticut Yankee dropped into King Arthur's Court. Or you have Jonathan Swift's Gulliver removed from 18th century England and dropped into the land of Lilliput. I wonder if there's something similar going on in your work, if painting in this classical manner is a way for you to observe contemporary people as if from another time.

A: A lot of the critical writings of my work has pointed out that I tend to have an outsider's view of things. Maybe because I lived overseas, in Europe, then four years in Brazil, among other places. I feel as if I'm part of my culture. Los Angeles has so many different cultures, from one neighborhood to the next, but I feel part of it all.

Q: What sort of perspective does painting like a History painter give you on contemporary life?

A: I don't think painting like a classical painter gives me any kind of perspective; in fact, it's the opposite: I live and am part of contemporary life, and part of contemporary life includes the history of art itself. I live in my times, and my times let me paint this way, or my times let me include these quotations from the past. I see myself as an artist today, and part of the language I use is not only today's, but what came before.

Q: Before you started working on the war paintings you documented news stories in South Central Los Angeles, where you worked, and often, you documented them in the conventions of History painting. TV and photojournalism now take care of the lion's share of that sort of documentary work. Do you ever wish that painters retained their role as documenters of reality?

A: No, I don't. It's better that painting is free to do many more different things now, that representation isn't necessary. For one thing, it frees art to comment on TV and photojournalism. I do wish that artists had more of a role in society, more of a voice in general. The audience for art is so small that it's almost pathetic. If I have a show in a gallery in Los Angeles or New York, it would be successful if it got 400 visitors, in a six-week run. 400 viewers, when I put a year's worth of work into something. Then some guy calls me from *Surfing* magazine, and I do a one-off little joke illustration for an article they're running and 40,000 people will see the thing.

Q: You brought up surfing, so let me ask my surfing question: what's the best place you've ever surfed?

A: It's hard to say. But if your question is "Where is the best surfing in the world, in general?" the answer is easily Indonesia. The best, most consistent waves, the best weather patterns, the most surfing beaches, the best wind. There are literally thousands of islands with phenomenal surfing across Indonesia, and they all are situated right in the perfect part of the world to have big, good waves all the time. Another of the world's great regions for surfing is South Africa, for the same reasons. I've been to both of them. California is pretty good though, consistently having good waves all year long.

Q: What's next?

A: I've been visiting and painting every single state prison in California. There are thirty-three of them. The paintings are beautiful landscapes, with sunsets and forests and trees, meant to comment on the tradition of Western landscape painting when California was seen as a wild and beautiful frontier, a place to go west and seek a fortune, an American Eden.

Q: Were some of those original Western landscape paintings exhibited or published in newspapers back east?

A: Absolutely. And they were exhibited to large crowds to fuel interest in the West. It's well known that the underlying intention of the government, which sponsored some of the trips, and of the artists, who painted and drew and photographed the exploration of the West, was the promotion of California as an American destination. This isn't a secret; it was intentional. One important purpose early Western landscape painting was advertising.

Q: What else?

A: I'm making the fake video documentary to accompany the War of the Californias. We're doing an hour-long film on the war.

Q: A kind of Ken Burns production?

A: A total spoof of Ken Burns's style, his plodding, solemn pacing, his seriousness. Very much a spoof on his stuff. After that, I'm not sure. I'm pretty sick of the war stuff though. That was what was so good about the prison project, it was a new thought process, a new preoccupation. I'll get to work on something new. I have a lot of ideas.

THE EGG

by SEAN WILSEY

A LITTLE KNOWN fact about the Russian jeweler Carl Faberge is that he had an older brother named Agathon.

The Faberges lived in a small village outside St. Petersburg, and their formative years, though isolated, were comfortable and free from obligations. Then, in the summer of 1852, their parents drowned in a boating accident, and the boys—fourteen and sixteen—were obliged to fend for themselves. They each inherited an equal share of their parental estate. Carl received the house and surrounding land, and Agathon, all assets and heirlooms, which he quickly converted to gold.

And with nothing further to bind them their paths quickly diverged. By the age of seventeen, inheritance in his belt, Agathon packed up his sketchbook and left for a jeweler's apprenticeship in France, while Carl stayed on in his childhood home and lived with simplicity off the land that surrounded it.

*   *   *

FOUR YEARS LATER Agathon returned from France. He found no trace of Carl. Upon enquiring with the district clerk Agathon discovered that the property taxes on the familial estate had gone unpaid since the death of their parents. Agathon paid them, received the deed, tore down the house, and constructed a low, brown building with a sloped roof and some gingerbreading at its eaves. This would serve as a workshop. For the next few months Agathon labored at jewelry-making.

Meanwhile, Carl, who had never left, but simply had grown less and less sociable, and found it suited him to sleep out of doors, in the woods and marshes, slipped through the nearby reeds, surreptitiously observing his brother, taking note of Agathon's sketches and creations, unaware that he had been deprived of his inheritance.

*   *   *

ONE AFTERNOON AGATHON found a blueberry in the empty setting of a ring he was about to complete. He jumped back from it in alarm. Then he saw that his brother was standing in the shadows at the back of the room, laughing softly.

"Welcome home, brother," Carl said. "It is a fine ring we have wrought together, don't you agree?"

"Carl?" he said. "First you abandon this place to the tax collectors, and then you return to mock my labors?"

"Abandon? I have not abandoned it. I have allowed this place to return to its own nature. I have done the opposite of abandoning it. And I intended no mockery. I sought to improve your creation."

Agathon was no longer startled to see his brother, but instead he was weary. And his voice took on an old supercilious tone. "Carl. Enough. Whatever else you may fancy yourself to be, you are nineteen years old. It is past time for you to give up your odd hobbies and pursue a trade."

"And what trade would you suggest, Agathon Carlievich?" asked Carl. "I am perfectly happy living here, off in *my* woods and *my* marsh. I require no trade."

"I think we would both be happier with you away from *here*," Agathon said sternly. "I have work to do. You have neglected your inheritance. And I have picked up the pieces. But I cannot also be your nursemaid. Please, little brother, do not make me insist."

Carl's lips curled defiantly. Agathon—feeling that if his point were to be made it should be made swiftly and with conviction—went to a desk, retrieved a piece of paper from a drawer, and held out a copy of the land deed for Carl to inspect.

Carl took a moment to read it. "Well, well," he said softly.

The older Faberge pressed on, impatient for the moment to end. "There are appropriate options for you, Carl Carlievich. First of all, I am aware of your distaste for Universities. And I would conjecture that you are ill-suited for the military life. But hear me out. The Czar will soon release imperial lands on the northern peninsula to mineral speculators—and this is a life I could well imagine for a man of your temperament and inclination. You are cunning, in a rough sort of way. And there is a bit of the mole and burrow-er—*the underground man*—in you. Tracing veins of precious metal *requires* such talents, and will help you to develop discipline, which you lack. In this way you could offer your elder brother valuable assistance." He gestured to the ring. "As for the present, to earn money for journeying north and sustaining yourself in the early days of speculating,"—Agathon forced a falsely optimistic lilt into his voice—"rather than picking and setting them like stones, allow me to point out that there is real work to be done with blueberries. Harvesting the barrens in our town."

Carl answered his brother with empty-eyed silence. Agathon thought to himself, *patience*. And he tried one last tack.

"If you are not interested in helping me or working in the barrens, I suppose there is always a government clerkship to be had, copying documents, or some such. But I am certain you would dislike the long hours lit only by candles. And you would be obliged to speak fine phrases in the capital, which I suspect you could not do." He shook his head. "They would not have you for a tradesman's apprenticeship in Europe, not at your age. The French and the Germans would take one look at you, in your swamp-stained breeches and shabby frock coat, fold their arms, and say to themselves, *go home Russian*! They would find reasons not to *visée* your passport. But honest work, here in Russia, Carl Carlievich, must you pretend you are too good for it?"

The younger Faberge remained still as a stone during this lecture. His eyes rested on the floor—fiercely—and his face went pink, and then violet, and then passed through several other bands of color. He did not answer, but simply gave his brother a hard stare, threw a leg over the windowsill, splashed into the shallow marsh water, and disappeared.

The next day Carl entered the workshop, by the door, as though nothing unusual had happened. He announced (emotion welling up in his voice) that he was going "south," for "Carnival," and that he would, "remain there to study *costume* jewelry."

Agathon opened his mouth, but thought better of it. He shrugged, ran his fingers through the air in a dismissive wave, and went back to his work.

*　　*　　*

WITH CARL GONE Agathon began to settle down to business, and a collection of fine objects began to slide out of the once jewel-less district—like beautiful clockwork fireworks. A perfume atomizer was fashioned of woven silver in the shape of a whooping crane. When a small, ten-carat diamond in its chest was plunged, scent whooped forth from the beak. A cigarette case unhinged with the wings of a butterfly, and presented a single cigarette at its axis. A pale jade ashtray was a small leaf veined with emeralds, beside which the cigarette case might alight. At a duchess's ball, a green napkin ring in the form of a watersnake, with each eye a tiny caviar of black seed pearl, wrapped the napkin of the Czar himself.

* * *

AFTER A LONG journey Carl arrived in Italy. He made his way to Venice, where the laws were suspended for Carnival, and social divisions made unobservable by outlandish disguises.

He was a strange sight, even for Carnival: weary and wild from travel, beard untrimmed, eyes red, speaking only Russian and smelling like a canal in high-summer. People safely on the far quay from him would snigger and point. People on the same side would look at their toes and walk quickly past.

Eventually, he found a deserted island in the lagoon and installed himself there in the shadows of an old stone boatcave—its water full of eels. The lagoon lapped through the arched entrance, atop which a screaming bearded mouth was carved in the keystone. Under cover of night he returned to Venice to pilfer armloads of building supplies from the shipyards near the Arsenal: tools and pitch and tar and wood. He caught and cooked the eels, and worked on a costume in the light from his fire.

His idea was to build a boat around himself. To make a costume that was also a vessel. A vessel he could slip into and become a creature capable of moving over the water.

For this purpose he had brought a "swampstormer" with him from Russia. This was a chin-high watertight garment made of rubber, creosote, and heavy canvas—resembling a pair of waders, and famed as the only equipment capable of journeying through the marshland around Petersburg. Carl set about to improve it. After scavenging a pair of particularly fine and sturdy poles from the gondola yards he soaked and slowly bent them over a fire of marsh reeds, until they could rest on the stormer's shoulders, like a yoke, and then curve down through its reinforced belt loops to join and form parallel circles. When this was accomplished, he wrapped a number of long, lighter strips of wood widthwise around the first two, to make a hollow ribbed ball, which encircled the stormer's chest.

This was a delicate process, and Carl became consumed with the labor.

Work can be everything. Intense devotion to a task can be like friendship, which over time awakens something in the inanimate. It can be like communication for those otherwise incapable of conversation.

Carl was becoming more and more like Agathon.

* * *

CARL CAREFULLY FILLED the gaps between the ribs of the stormer with bentwood paneling, then filled the cavity with stones, and sank the whole thing in the lagoon for three days, so the wood would swell and seal up tightly.

Half a week later, when he pulled the creation up from the lagoon floor and emptied it of stones, it was buoyant and watertight. Seaworthy.

Carl admired his handiwork. While the stormer was submerged he'd completed the headpiece and snorkel. Now he fitted them together, smeared the whole thing with gondola tar, and liberally covered it with white feathers. It would be ideal for the canals of Venice, and the wider waterways beyond. He could go anywhere, completely incognito, propelling himself by kicking large webbed flippers.

When the feathers and headpiece were in place, he paddled to Venice to practice his navigation. He sailed in front of St. Marks Square to a vastly different reception than before. Children squealed. Gondoliers bowed from high on the backs of their vessels. Old women threw bread at him.

Carl paddled through the back alleys, smiling from the water at the spectacle of Carnival. He watched—elated by the debauchery of it all—as packs of thieves passed through the squares on stilts, leaned casually against the upper balconies of buildings to snatch what they could, then stepped across canals to escape.

* * *

SINCE CARL'S DEPARTURE, Agathon had found a great measure of success from his commissioned work, and he'd decided to gamble a chance of ruin against his faith in his own designs—to move decisively and attempt to realize a grand piece from the series of drawings he had labored so long to complete.

The object was to be an egg. The egg would unhinge—as they would all unhinge—in this case to reveal a cygnet, feathered in diamonds, and floating on a lake of sapphires. He hoped it would win the heart of the Czar at first sight—and wreak such delight in the beholding as to be swept into the bosom of the royal family like their own bawling, red, newborn baby boy.

He had requested an audience with the court, and notice had arrived that he could come to Petersburg and present the completed work in fourteen months time. He began to labor without interruption.

But one evening the industrious activity of Agathon's workshop was shattered by a voice—a throaty voice—which spoke out, saying in an accusatory tone: *"Faberge! Jeweler to kings. Why do you steal from me?"*

Agathon had been using pliers to set a large, minutely flawed blue sapphire. But when he heard this voice his hand slipped, and the jewel was scratched.

For a moment everything was still. The windows in the studio were open, aglow with the light of a setting sun, and Agathon could see the graceful neck of a large swan gliding beside the boats at the marshside docks.

On this very day Agathon had been laboring on consignment to the court for a year. It was not a good time for a setback. Delivery would be delayed by the damaged sapphire. And to compound his difficulties, the Czar's treasury had given Agathon no advance moneys. Not even for materials. The Imperial interest was purely speculative.

As his deadline had grown closer and closer, Agathon found himself without time to work for other clients. He began to drown in debt to his suppliers.

"Faberge, you are ruined," he said now.

He set the sapphire down on a piece of velvet.

To remove the scratch he would have to do nothing but burnish for weeks.

He folded the velvet over the sapphire, slipped his monocle into the breast pocket of his apron, and scrutinized his servant, who was lighting the workshop's gas lamps as though nothing had occurred. He must have imagined the voice. He was fatigued. Agathon gave his servant the evening off. Alone, he took a stool to a writing table and drafted a letter to the summer palace, begging for another two weeks.

But the court was not well-disposed. The egg, if it pleased the Czar, would be a birthday gift from his highness to the Czarina. The jeweler was informed that it should arrive on the appointed day, or not at all.

Dashing off a hasty agreement, Agathon entered a period of constant labor. If he slept at all he would awake at four, burnish the sapphire for three hours, and then begin the day's work on the egg itself. To reduce expenses he terminated his subcontractors. He obtained his new supplies directly from the mines. He boiled gold ore to remove its impurities. He manufactured every small tool and mixed each fine polish. He missed meals, grew thin, and bid his servant to bring him coffee every hour on the hour, silty and sweet, with the grounds at the bottom, which he ate—his intestines tying knots beneath the hardwood workbench. He remained awake at his labor for days on end.

From the water a patient swan was always watching, as if the work were its own. Agathon took it as a talisman.

*　　*　　*

ON WHAT TURNED out to be the last night, with the work nearly complete, Agathon shut himself in his studio.

He held the egg, and hummed to it, rocking beside a row of windows that had been thrown open to admit the marsh air, and the sound of the water lapping at the studio's foundations.

Just as he'd imagined it, nearly complete, the egg was so elaborate that it seemed to hold the excitement of an entire city. Sparks shot from every surface. The impression of curl upon curl of precious metalwork was like a network of streets leading to the squares, parks, and cathedrals of exquisite stones—from which the light flew up in gushing fountains.

"I adore you," Agathon said to his creation.

He loved the egg. And he loved it like nothing he had ever known. *How could he let it go?* To gaze upon it!—creator to creation—and be reflected back again; the most delicious adoration: seeing himself in what he saw in it, and shimmering with the feeling that they were one; in the egg the man, in the man the egg, from the egg the man and vice versa.

Trembling in nervous anticipation, with his heart beating all the way up in his shoulders, Agathon reached to install the sapphire at the top of the egg's oval. And as he did so, the same voice as before came whispering through the window, breathless and soft and mocking. It was not unlike his own voice, though it seemed to be coming up a long, narrow pipe.

"Return what you have stolen," it hissed.

All that remained to complete the egg was to bend three small metal tines over the perfect sapphire. Three swift crimps—the work of a costume jeweler—and the egg would be complete.

Instead, as the moon came up, Agathon poured himself a glass of vodka. It burned going down, making his stomach heavy and hot. His hands quieted and he poured another to the brim of the glass. Swampgas and moonglow outlined the cattails along the shore. Among them was the still, elongated chicane of a swan's neck. Then—awfully—it leaned in the window of the workshop.

"Agathon Faberge," it said, "give me your attention."

Agathon stared transfixed at the swan.

It placed its wings at its side. "'Faberge.' Evidently the name is getting famous. I must congratulate you. Give you a gift even." It seemed to smile sourly. "Though you have no need of the gifts *I* could give you. But I will congratulate you. I admire the discipline of your work. All this labor to make *an egg.*" It chuckled.

Agathon was trembling.

The swan leaned further into the room, picked up the egg, and held it up to the light.

"You have been plotting. *Laying* a little plan. To win the Czar's favor. By making your egg. Which is, perchance, a *swan's* egg?"

A high, thin wail of a sound escaped from Agathon's throat.

The swan continued. "How touching. And what a touching sound you have just made, Agathon *Faberge*," it said. "Like the moan of a woman in labor."

"I—" Agathon was unable to speak.

"You are a thief and an opportunist. But you have made something beautiful. You have made an egg, Agathon Faberge." The swan fixed its gaze on Agathon. "But it is not you who they will all say made it, it is *I.*"

The swan lifted the egg high into the air, and with all its strength smashed it squarely in Agathon's face.

Agathon collapsed. Blood burst from his head.

And as Agathon lay, his face pressed into the worktable, the face of the swan became a face not unlike Agathon's own face. Carl emerged from his beloved swamp.

"We've shared our name long enough," he said. Then he took the stone from beneath his brother's cheek, and with a few quick motions the egg was complete.

THE EDUCATION
OF UNCLE JOSH

by MONIQUE DUFOUR

"In real life, the proprieties will not allow people to act out themselves with that unreserve permitted to the stage."
—Herman Melville, *The Confidence Man*

HAVING SEEN A conservatively estimated 537 movies, in perhaps forty different theaters, in ten states and four countries, having gone to the movies starting when I was five, when I saw "Charlotte's Web" with my mom, Auntie Betty, and her daughters Kim and Holly, I hadn't ever seen anything quite like the silent movie "Uncle Josh at the Moving Picture Show" until I came across it, almost by accident really, running on a continuous loop in a black-curtained booth at the Carnegie Museum, in Pittsburgh, Pennsylvania, in April 2001. "Uncle Josh" is an Edison Company production made by Edwin S. Porter almost a hundred years before and based, like a lot of Edison productions and inventions, on something earlier and from another country, in this case the 1897 British movie "The Countryman's First Sight of the Animated Pictures." As Edison's film opens, Uncle Josh, a guy in a slouch hat and a farmer's clothes, is at the movies. For the evening's entertainment, he's got a good view from a choice box seat located directly in front of the screen.

Josh's movie begins and an illuminated title card appears: "The Edison Projecting Kinetoscope." Josh is too busy fidgeting with anticipation to see the beginning. He's anxiously looking around the theater, first facing the audience, then facing us, watching him. Then, as if someone in the audience had pointedly asked him what he thought he was looking at and someone else had told him just to turn around and behave, Josh turns to the screen to look, with awe and mild confusion, at the first of three features, "Parisian Dancer."

On screen there's an empty stage, the floor appearing to extend directly from the screen to the floor under Josh's feet. On dances a woman in a long, flouncing dress and a picture hat. Uncle Josh applauds wildly. He loves the dancing. He worked all week so that he could pay for this and love it. He jumps to the railing of the box seat and then hops onto the stage to dance along, all elbows and knees. The woman can-cans and then cartwheels off-screen, leaving Josh alone.

From the distance a locomotive approaches. It's the night's second feature, "The Black Diamond Express." Josh stands by the screen, watching the train's progress and waving. Seconds later, he realizes the locomotive is steaming toward him. He jumps headlong into the box seat, narrowly escaping with his life.

Uncle Josh picks himself off the floor, returns to his seat in time to catch a peek at the opening of "The Country Couple," wherein a man is somehow assaulted by the frisky handle of a water pump. A woman stops fussing with her buckets to caress and comfort him. He gropes her. They embrace. Uncle Josh is wildly offended. Perhaps the woman resembles his daughter or a relative or the woman he loves. In any case, he can't get over what he sees. The couple's scuffles become more passionate. Josh can't believe his eyes. As the couple finally kisses, he takes matters into his own hands and storms the stage. He takes his jacket off, throws it to the ground, and prepares to fight. When the man ignores his challenges, he leaps at the screen and tears it down, revealing the humble operator working the rear-projection device. Josh and the projectionist fight, and the film ends as they're still rolling around the floor.

Uncle Josh is a rube and a country bumpkin, a stock character of less than one dimension. Rural life has isolated him from modern life, its technological advances and social mores. His serial misunderstandings and faux pas add up to a spectacular naiveté about what would have been common knowledge to most in 1902. In no way is the viewer meant to relate to him. Nobody should sympathize with Josh. Not only is he fooled by the moving pictures into believing they are real, but he leaps from his seat in an attempt to interact with the people projected there. He is technology's dupe, and that's the central joke here as well as the film's main advertising claim: the Kinetoscope, so amazingly life-like and realistic it'll fool good country people.

Awe, astonishment, and confusion were neither rare nor unseemly audience reactions. Technology and its powers to mimic reality proved a continual source of wonder throughout the nineteenth century. Audiences filled halls and tents to witness devices such as magic lanterns, demonstrations usually accompanied by a lecture explaining the science behind the spectacle. The pinnacle of such didactic celebrations of rational human achievement came with events such as the 1893 World's Columbian Exposition in Chicago and the 1900 Paris Exposition. Even a figure no less genteel and refined than Henry Adams, the anti-Josh, is not immune from awe and astonishment. After coming face to face with the mighty dynamo, he writes in *The Education of Henry Adams* that "he found himself lying in the Gallery of Machines at the Great Exposition of 1900, his historical neck broken by the sudden irruption of forces totally new."

But mostly all this feverish wonder grew more and more mannered, civilized. It was 1896, and the Edison Company set its sights on some new something of someone else's invention called the Phatascope, a projection device which promised "living pictures" and which Edison bought, renamed, and added to his résumé. And so, with yet another invention from Edison, this "greatest scientific exhibition before the public," or the Vitascope for short, moving images could finally be projected onto a screen. Until then moving pictures were mainly available for a couple of coins via private viewing machines, such as Edison's Kinetoscope, a combination of a camera and two glass-covered peepholes. Only one person at a time peered through the viewer, down into the Kinetoscope, staring intently, without blinking, for about two minutes at a flickering swatch-sized image. Often what a person saw there were mildly lurid films, what Charles Musser, in his fine history of early American cinema, describes discretely as "subjects consistent with the individualized, peephole nature of the viewing experience."

With the Vitascope and similar inventions, motion pictures began to be shown to large groups rather than to individuals. An 1893 advertisement in the *Providence Journal* promises that its power

PUZZLES THE SCIENTISTS

Baffles analysis

CREATES ROUND-EYED WONDER

PROFOUND DELIGHT

Tickles the risibilities

Excites **hearty admiration**

THRILLS THE NERVES

And incidentally creates

WILD APPLAUSE!

But as puzzled and baffled, delighted and tickled as the moviegoer might be, his only real, physical response, his only acceptable response, to the thrills and delights is to applaud wildly.

Uncle Josh, bless him, does not understand this. He wants to do more than merely sit in his seat and applaud, however wildly. By getting up and getting down with the dancer and interacting with the films, Uncle Josh becomes part of the show. His story serves as a cautionary tale about the pitfalls and potential embarrassments of excessive enthusiasm at a night at the movies. Josh, after all, is not watching this film in a Kinetoscope parlor, a saloon, or a dime museum, just a few of the baser sites of cinema exhibition in the late nineteenth century. He's in a theatre. He's in public.

And Josh acts as though he's making his debut in this place called public. He doesn't understand how polite people behave at the theatre. He lacks shame. He's a backwards man. Like Adams, Josh is an anachronism in the modern world. The historian Lawrence Levine explains that it was a common nineteenth-century practice for theatregoers to burst into "spontaneous expressions of pleasure and disapproval in the form of cheers, yells, gesticulations, hisses, boos, stamping of feet, whistling, crying for encores, and applause." And that was at performances of "The Magic Flute" and "Hamlet." By the early twentieth century, American audiences were, as a rule, more sedate, quietly appreciative, their abilities to stand in line, watch quietly and not ruin it for the rest of us a hallmark of their refinement and taste. After all, only a fool doesn't know the difference between Edwin Booth and King Lear, between the famous film kiss of the actors May Irwin and John C. Rice and an actual couple kissing. And only a rube crosses the proscenium arch.

*   *   *

BUT IS UNCLE Josh's foolishness really that foolish? Sure he may believe the woman is there to be danced with, the train poses real danger, and the passion between two actors is actual passion, but he's also going to the movies at the turn-of-the-century, a time when many films claimed to document real events. In this way, "Uncle Josh at the Moving Picture Show" may be less a comedy of no manners than a tragic story about the increasingly docile American audience. Uncle Josh could attend "Actualities," short films depicting a man sneezing, parades of bicyclists, and haymakers at work. Longer films captured the 1897 boxing match between James Corbett and Robert Fitzsimmons, an early pay-per-view event with a ten-thousand dollar purse and the promise of such profit that Nevada hastily legalized boxing in order to host it. Later films staged fictional reenactments of the Corbett-Fitzsimmons bout. In other theaters, people paid to watch documentary footage of the Spanish-American War, a war fought not only in the press, in Joseph Pulitzer's and William Randolph Hearst's competing papers, but on the screen. Viewers came away from these films in-the-know. People who had never been to Cuba got to see Cuba. Maybe they didn't believe like Uncle Josh believed that they could step out of their seats right onto the deck of the Battleship Maine, but they did achieve, for part of an evening, momentary contact with Roosevelt's Rough Riders, a kind of knowledge without the hard work of being directly involved.

And Uncle Josh has the uncommon audacity to believe he personally has something to do with these events. Of course, the audience, much more intelligent and maybe a little jaded, knows better than the bumpkin. Those audience members stand in line for their tickets, file quietly to their seats, whisper in low tones to their neighbors, and, at the appropriate moment, when they're not likely to humiliate themselves in public or make their loved ones blush, they applaud wildly, briefly, happy for their astonishment and for their complete disconnection from the events on the screen. Nobody is embarrassed. Everything is tasteful. All is domesticated, civil. Why fight it? There's no prize fight, no real battleship, no Cuba, no Spanish-American war, no reality to speak of. Pay no attention to the man standing behind the screen. Anger, bafflement, and any other emotion stirred up by all those moving pictures are finally soothed by the viewing experience, which requires nothing but your eyes.

So sit back and enjoy the show.

THREE OBSCURE ANIMATORS

by STEPHAN CHAPMAN

KONA AMPURNA, 1909–1938. THE DECAY ARTIST OF BOMBAY.

AMONG THE LEGENDS of avant-garde animation are several film artists whose works do not survive in any form. It is difficult to judge the contributions of such figures to the evolution of the form. Though these animators leave behind no tangible legacy, their devotees nonetheless venerate them. One such artist was Kona Ampurna of India.

The son of a Bombay grocery merchant, Ampurna was exposed in the 1920s to silent films from Germany and the United States, including Fritz Lang's "Der Mude Tod" and Harry Hoyt's "The Lost World," both of which featured model animation. Ampurna became obsessed with motion picture photography and worked as his father's accountant to earn rupees for a sixteen-millimeter film camera with a single-frame shutter.

Throughout his twenties Ampurna pursued a career as a freelance photographer and sometimes sold photos to a wire service. He worked mostly at weddings, graduations, and retirement parties. In his spare time, he struggled to create animations.

He tried for years to achieve smooth action with figures of pottery clay. But the clay always crumbled to bits after hours under hot lights. The crumbling process in the dry clay became the subject for Ampurna's first important film, "The Crumbling Sea," which boldly translated a technical problem into an ominous imaginary seascape of continually forming perpetually crumbling ocean creatures.

In 1934 Ampurna saw a print of "King Kong." The technical capabilities of Willis O'Brian dwarfed his own so harshly that he was reduced to despair. In June of that year, a streetcar ran down his beloved dog Durga outside his apartment house. He responded to this personal loss by filming the first of his lost masterworks: "My Dead Dog." The film employed time-lapse photography to show Durga lying in a gutter while most of her biomass was converted into maggots, which then attracted a flock of pigeons. According to a police report, passersby assaulted Ampurna repeatedly during the shoot. He required fourteen stitches to close his head wounds.

Sensing that he was on to something, Ampurna proceeded to document the decompositions of a goat, a sheep, and finally, a cow. As the so-called "Decay Series" progressed, he extended his cinematic process with new embellishments—by scratching the film stock with needles, by tinting sections of his footage, and by manually rearranging the bones, skins, and entrails of the animals as they rotted. He showed these works privately to other hopeful young cineastes.

In 1938 a streetcar ran down Ampurna on the same corner where Durga had died. The investigating officer suspected suicide. The nitrate film stock of Ampurna's reels disintegrated before they could be transferred for archival preservation. His oeuvre is lost forever.

Although Ampurna's life was brief, several giants of early Hindi-language cinema, including surrealist director Narana Purnimura, vividly remembered Ampurna's unique films. Critics agree that the famous "vision of maggots in hell" sequence, which Purnimura created for his "The Silver Princess From Space," was intended as a homage to Ampurna's indomitable spirit.

ISAIAH DRUPESHKI, 1903–1941. THE FLICKER MASTER OF BERLIN.

ISAÏAH DRUPESHKI WAS an enigmatic figure in the pre-war history of abstract animation in Germany. Born to wealthy parents in the diamond trade, he was educated in Berlin and Paris and showed an early aptitude for photography, amateur radio, and tinkering in general. In the 1920s he collaborated as a camera consultant with experimentalists Hans Richter and Walter Ruttman in Frankfort.

In 1931, working in collaboration with his half-sister Elsa Klein, Drupeshki produced the first of his "Motion Studies." Though these exercises were geometrical in nature and tightly organized in their progressions, he considered them "far too imprecise."

Drupeshki and Klein began to produce short films—under three minutes and lacking any soundtrack—composed of flickering patterns of black frames and white frames. These "Flicker Studies" were shown only at private salons. They generated some wild rumors. The 1934 production "Cinema Epileptique" was said to induce a seizure in anyone who viewed it. The sequel, titled "Life After Death," reportedly produced a state of hypnotic suggestibility. The 1936 production "The Angel Lucifer" was rumored to cause episodes of hysterical blindness.

Joseph Goebbel's Ministry of Information and Hitler's SS both took an interest in Herr Drupeshki. To these men of vision, his techniques sounded as if they might have great potential for development into "Weapons of Light." In July of 1938, he and Elsa applied for passports for a vacation to Paris and were refused. They immediately destroyed all prints of their recent films and prepared to emigrate under false papers. They were taken into custody at a train station, imprisoned, and interrogated. According to SS records, Klein hung herself while alone in her cell. Her place of burial is unknown.

Several months later Drupeshki appeared as the head of a lavishly funded research project, which ate up a large sum of reichsmarks between September 1938 and February 1940. It seemed that he'd reached an agreement with the men in power. The goal of his new research was "The Death Film," a stuttering image pattern with a subsonic soundtrack, which would be projected through a special searchlight with lethal results. The primary colors of the prototype films were—naturally enough—black, white, and red. One prototype featured counterclockwise-revolving swastikas.

But Drupeshki's team of patriotic young engineers never achieved any demonstrable results. Tensions arose between "The Death Film" project and the SS. Finally, to humiliate Drupeshki for his failure, he was strapped into a chair for a private screening of his latest prototype. After the screening, his superiors discovered to their surprise that he was dead.

The SS spent another allotment of reichsmarks on testing the prototype, but they never achieved similar results with any of the subsequent test subjects. It is now thought that Drupeshki committed suicide by means of a pill, as a morbid prank on his employers.

Drupeshki's brief period of service to National Socialism has clouded his reputation as a pioneer of abstract animation. His memory in the German film community remains, as perhaps it should, a matter of profound confusion.

Jane Wainwright, 1940–1973. Soul loss in Bali.

Born to middle-class parents in Evanston, Illinois, Jane Wainwright won national prizes for her photo-realistic paintings while still attending high school. As a student at the University of California at Berkeley, she produced animations that delighted and astonished her contemporaries. She explored a wide range of media on her light table, including sand painting, finger paints, glass beads, and seed pods on wallpaper. Her trademark was her bold use of vibrantly clashing colors.

Her last film, a tribute to Lotte Reiniger called "The Meditation of Prince Achmed," was executed entirely with newsprint silhouettes on frosted glass. "The Meditation" recounts the Prince's hashish visions, which compress seven years of adventure into a single night, the fateful night of the dreamer's death.

In 1963 Wainwright visited Bali, seeking to witness performances of traditional shadow puppetry. She located the last living master of this art, Sim Kurananda Radzipali, who annually performed the sagas of Vishnu and the Monkey King with full gamelan orchestra, a children's choir, all-night drumming, and much incense. These impressive and deafening spectacles centered on the shadows that Radzipali cast on a paper screen. While manipulating his translucent rod puppets of copper wire and dyed horsehide, he also assumed the voices of all of the gods, kings, demons, servants, milkmaids, and beasts in his extensive repertoire.

Wainwright eagerly offered herself as an apprentice puppeteer and lived on Bali for the next five years. She returned home a shattered remnant of her former self and spent the remainder of her life in an Illinois asylum for the mentally ill. She believed with total fixation that her mentor had captured her soul in the shadow of one of his puppets. She died of hysterical asthma on the fifth anniversary of the day she'd left Bali.

Although Wainwright attempted no film work during her final years, she did produce a series of comic strips, which she photocopied and posted on asylum bulletin boards. The heroine of the strip was called Blobette the Empty Toothpaste Tube, and her adventures included "Blobette Goes to Mars," "Blobette under the Sea," and "Blobette in Search of a Soul." Wainwright's therapist, Dr. Ira Moss, collected these strips into a file, which went to her parents at the time of her death.

Although Wainwright's career in animation ended too soon, the short films of her youth are still available for viewing at various libraries and archives. Students of visionary cinema continue to revere her work for its qualities of courage and exuberance.

HER SEVENTEENTH SUMMER

by ROBERT NEDELKOFF

SOMETIME IN THE middle of 1956, probably at one Manhattan watering-hole or another, Frank Taylor, editor-in-chief of paperback publishers Dell Books, sat down with a writer named Warren Miller, to propose that Miller participate in a rather unusual literary venture.

From boyhood, Miller had wanted no other career than that of writer. But so far things had moved slowly. He had just published his first novel, an able satire on the high noon of McCarthyism, but in the climate of the times it could only see print in England. In that book Taylor had seen a knack for subtle pastiche and prose that could at once be read as high parody or taken straight, depending on the reader's sophistication and credulity, and was just what the editor was looking for. A novel published the year before, by a French teenager, had swept the nation as completely as it had the woman's native land. Word had it another firm was readying a novel by an American girl, to be presented as a homegrown answer to the *mademoiselle*. The time seemed right for a book that would simultaneously take advantage of this trend for novels by precocious girls and send up the whole vogue. So Taylor asked Miller if he were interested in writing such a book under such a guise.

*   *   *

THE EVENTS LEADING to this meeting had begun one afternoon three years before, when an ennui-laden adolescent needed to unburden herself (and kill some time) on summer vacation. Francoise Quoirez, who'd just celebrated her eighteenth birth and flunked her entrance exams at the Sorbonne, sat down in her parent's country villa and started a novel. It was the saga of Cecile, who, like her creator, had just failed her exams; her widowed father; and two women, one young, one old, jockeying for his affection. A passage early in the book where Cecile looks back on her wastrel year "studying" in Paris gives a sense of the book's precociously world-weary flavor:

> I owed most of my pleasures of that period to money; the pleasure of driving fast in a high-powered car, of having a new dress, records, books, flowers [...] I would rather deny myself my moods of mysticism or despair than give up such indulgences [...] I adopted a rather cynical attitude toward love which, considering my age and experience, should have meant happiness rather than mere sensation. I was fond of repeating to myself sayings like Oscar Wilde's "Sin is the only note of vivid color that persists in the modern world" [...] I visualized a life of degradation and moral turpitude as my ideal.

The young writer, after penning 30,000 words and spinning a plot mixing Gide's recits and Laclos's *Les Liaisons Dangereuses*, sent her novel to publisher Rene Juilliard, who accepted it at once. The novelist then selected a surname *de plume* from the pages of Proust.

While the first reviews of Francoise Sagan's *Bonjour Tristesse* were favorable, sales were slow. That all changed a few weeks later when the novel received the Prix des Critiques; Sagan appeared at a reception and was presented to a mob of reporters and photographers. By then Andre Malraux had read the novel and praised it. Then the elder statesman of French literature, Francois Mauriac published an article in *Le Figaro* saluting the book's style and construction while fretting over the author's lack of interest in spiritual things.

With those encomia, *Bonjour Tristesse* began selling 20,000 copies a week in a nation where sales of 50,000 guaranteed a book a sure place atop the bestseller list. Through that long summer, the book moved over half a million copies. Sagan used her first royalty check to buy a Jaguar, tearing around with her bare foot on the accelerator. The vehicle, with its scratches from numerous sideswipes and a windshield obscured by parking tickets, became as familiar to Parisians as the Eiffel Tower. Sagan began hanging out with the hippest of crowds and hitting St. Tropez with the likes of Brigitte Bardot. She dated bored, superficial men. It was all covered in the minutest detail by an enraptured press. By year's end she was as much a symbol of the nation as De Gaulle and Edith Piaf.

Word of all this reached American shores and editors started to wonder if the phenomenon could be repeated in an America just emerging from the grip of hearings, the naming of names, and Frank Sinatra duetting with Dagmar. E. P. Dutton snapped up American rights in a trice, and *Bonjour Tristesse* hit stateside stores in the last week of February 1955.

The initial reviews were usually favorable; in *Saturday Review* Rosemary Benet commented: "Sensational, yes; but skillfully and quietly done." But other critics sounded the traditional warning about the amoral ways of the denizens of the land of brie and Beaujolais. "I admired the craftsmanship, but was repelled by the carnality," said V. P. Hass in the *Chicago Tribune*; "[it] is childish and tiresome in its singleminded dedication to decadence," remarked *Commonweal's* reviewer.

American readers read such notices and got the message: *Bonjour Tristesse* told, what in those days, would have been termed a "racy" story, but very nicely and with no dirty words. And it also took its place in that great French literary tradition of Constant and Colette; reading it made one hip *and* cultured. The book hit the bestseller lists in March, reached the number one spot in the summer of 1955, and stayed atop the lists through the season. Everyone from bankers to coeds to grannies had it on their beach towel or next to the iced-tea pitcher on the porch.

Sagan traveled to New York, and her publishers arranged for a press conference at Idlewild Airport in the hope that she had the traditional Gallic supply of *bon mots* in reserve. They were not disappointed. One reporter asked how long she'd stay single. "Maybe when you marry the vacation is over," she replied. Another asked what impact Existentialism had on her book. "Sometimes," she said, "I think philosophic thoughts when I have nothing better to do."

It was clear to every publisher in New York: teenage girls with an attitude and a typewriter were big business. Surely, in a nation with millions of inhabitants of that age and gender, there had to be someone capable of writing an American *Bonjour Tristesse*. Weary publishers' readers perused manuscripts by the sackful, but soon discovered that most teenagers, even in those days of corporal punishment and detention periods, just hadn't learned to write well.

Then, toward the end of 1955, Rinehart editor Sandy Richardson found himself reading a manuscript by eighteen-year-old Pamela Moore, the daughter of a woman who'd published some books with his firm. *Chocolates for Breakfast* tells of Courtney Farrell, a "slim, dark-haired beauty of fifteen" with "large, green, rebellious eyes" and what, in those days, was invariably listed in name-your-baby books as a man's name. The novel opens with a dialogue between Courtney and her lesbian teacher Miss Rosen that, especially in contrast to the homophobic standards of the day, is handled with intelligence and care; the ensuing chronicle of love discovered and lost among the movie crowd in Hollywood and dissolute, incipiently alcoholic young Ivy Leaguers nervously imitating their elders at the Stork Club and P.J. Clarke's moved Robert Clurman, of the *New York Times* to comment: "Not very long ago it would have been regarded as shocking to find girls in their teens *reading* the books they're now writing."

Meanwhile the Sagan juggernaut continued unimpeded. In early 1956, Dell released *Bonjour Tristesse* in paperback, reportedly selling a million and a half copies in six weeks. Meanwhile Sagan's second novel, was receiving acclaim and sales in France comparable to those for *Bonjour Tristesse*, and Dutton had already received 100,000 advance orders for it. It was now that Frank Taylor, apparently deciding that Dell could use something in a quasi-Sagan mode to round up a few spare quarters and dimes from her fans, and not having a teenager at hand to write it, called Warren Miller.

*   *   *

MILLER WAS BORN in 1921, in Stowe, Pennsylvania, the grandson of an immigrant from the Austro-Hungarian empire who had risen from labor recruiter in the local mills to the proprietorship of Stowe's general store. He grew up in nearby Pottstown, reading such heterogeneous fare as Clarence Budington Kelland (the favorite boyhood author of John O'Hara and Richard Nixon) and Carl Van Vechten's *Parties*.

With the advent of the depression, Miller's grandfather died and his family was obliged to struggle to make ends meet. Despite that, his mother was able to send Miller to the University of Iowa with her earnings as a store buyer. There, he became a favorite student of Paul Engle, who had already gone far toward making the school's writing program the most prestigious in the nation. Following his junior year Miller joined the Army where he "malingered in England and shirked in Normandy," according to his later, characteristically waspish account, returning to Iowa in 1946 to resume his studies under the G. I. Bill.

Back at school Miller married Abby Richardson, completed his bachelor's degree, and spent a year as an assistant instructor of writing while pursuing a master's. The sight of the trim Miller in the finery he'd brought back from England, his large liquid eyes peering about with the observant, saturnine mien of a figure in a Max Beerbohm cartoon, soon became familiar around campus. But students expecting to be taught by a wan aesthete were in for a shock. "If he thought a story was sentimental or sloppy or the grammar was poor, the characters badly described, the dialogue corny or the plot hackneyed, he would say as much right then and there. He never went easy on the feelings of his students; he spoke his mind always," recalls Marshall Flaum, a student in the class who would soon marry the writer's sister Gita.

Engle had high regard for his young instructor, and the latter's first professionally published story, in *Harper's Bazaar* in 1946, went on to make *Best American Stories*. But Miller was not inclined to continue in academe, writing later that he "loved teaching but despised the students," though his real reason for leaving seems to have been that the classwork left him with little time for his own writing. So, with his wife and infant daughter Scott (named for her dad's favorite writer), Warren moved to New York in 1948 and soon began writing annual reports, press releases, and such for the Royal Liverpool Insurance Company.

Before long, Warren's stylish wardrobe and his fearless, albeit elegantly expressed, opinions were the talk of a growing circle of friends. At the same time, he continued his quiet involvement in radical politics. His views were well described by the platform of Henry Wallace's Progressive Party and, if anything, moved further left with the years.

In 1954, Miller was inspired by the televised Army-McCarthy hearings to write a book. *The Sleep of Reason* tells the story of a child of wealth, Evans Howells, graduating from Harvard and moving to Washington, where he soon finds himself working on a committee headed by the ferocious Congressman Muggonigle, dedicated to rooting out every vestige of "the Conspiracy" which threatens the land. Though Muggonigle's real-life model could always be counted on to top anything a writer like Miller could imagine with such lines of his own as "that's the most unheard-of thing I ever heard of," the writer demonstrates a keen ear for the subtler inanities of McCarthyite jargon.

Though the English reviews commended Miller for cleverness while dismissing the satire as dated, such cleverness was what Frank Taylor wanted— and, for the right money, the fledgling novelist was ready to supply it. After the birth of his second daughter, Eve, Miller had separated from his wife, moved to Greenwich Village, and left the insurance company to take a position as a sales representative for Milton Glaser, Seymour Chwast and Edward Sorel's Push Pin Studios; he badly needed income to supplement his scanty commissions. So a contract was drawn up; Miller dutifully read Moore's book, reread Sagan's, and began work.

Within a matter of weeks, he had finished his manuscript. Through some process or other, the book was now to be published by McGraw-Hill as a hardcover, and that firm's publicity and marketing departments got to work. The first thing to do was to choose a name for the ostensible author. Miller chose Amanda Vail.

During his days at the insurance company, Miller had summered in various locations in the Hamptons, an area in those days reserved for upwardly mobile young executives and bohemians of middling means looking for a vacation bargain, with nary a publicist, movie star or CEO in sight. He came to know some fellow vacationers who counted among their friends a young couple named John and Patricia Vaill, whose only child was a daughter, named Amanda. Amanda Vaill reports that although neither she or her parents ever met Miller, some of their mutual friends later said they recalled making comments to Miller along the lines of "We were a the Vaills' place last Saturday and their little girl Amanda said the darndest thing," etc. It's worth noting here that Miller's daughter Eve Michaels reports that Amanda, though not an especially fashionable name at the time ("I was the only Amanda I knew," says Ms. Vaill, "and I was teased about it all the time at school"), was among her father's favorite girls' names—in fact, she almost received the name herself before her mother decided otherwise. If Miller only ever heard Amanda Vaill's name spoken, that would explain why he used the more common one-l version of the surname.

Next, a biography for the putative author was needed. Miller wrote a press release that read, in part,

> I was born and educated in New York [...] since the age of thirteen I have been writing and I have never considered the possibility of any other career. Until I had begun *Love Me Little*, I had written the first chapters of six or seven novels, and discarded them all [...] This novel was written during my seventeenth summer. I then spent over a year rewriting it.

The next step for McGraw-Hill was to have someone pose as the adolescent author for the book's jacket photo. The choice to impersonate "Amanda Vail" was Miller's own girlfriend, Jane "Jimmy" Curley. Miller had met her soon after his separation, and her high spirits and anarchic wit made a quick impression on the couple's friends. Sitting in a coffeehouse, bangs brushing her forehead, "Amanda Vail," on the jacket, assumes a Mona Lisa smile and stares into the distance. At the table behind her sits a man in his mid-thirties, holding a cigarette in a manner to do Oscar Wilde or Ernest Dowson proud. With his sharp, saturnine profile and three-piece suit, he resembles a young T. S. Eliot taking his first tea break from his bank job—and also the author of *The Sleep of Reason*.

The jacket copy of the book assures the reader: "Lovers (as well as detractors) of the current 'young French' school of writing, here is a story to delight your hearts!'" Evidently, McGraw-Hill was doing their best to have it both ways.

Love Me Little tells the story of a teenage New Yorker named Emily, and before she even begins to tell of listening to albums of Dylan Thomas in the company of her friend Amy while her father plays "Old Dog Tray" and "Funiculi Funicula" on his pump organ down in the living room, her opening words let the reader know that she is not lacking in artistic sensitivity:

> Spring is like walking into a room, full of innocence, and being assaulted by loud voices that wish you well. I am never quite prepared for it; I get melancholic and start reading Rilke. This, also, happens to me in the autumn.

But the oracular tones of the late Welshman can go only so far to help the dilemma Emily and Amy face—namely, that one of their less clever schoolmates has had what the two girls solemnly call the Great Experience, and they must soon catch up. They have read Sagan but are aware of her limits; as Emily's father observes, from his professional perspective: "She's not the slave of passion but of chauvinism."

After a few mournful weeks at boarding school (described in a chapter ably sending up its counterpart in *Chocolates for Breakfast*) summer duly arrives, and Emily is presented with a solution to her and Amy's problem when the pair and their parents travel to their vacation cottage on Long Island. The two friends, deciding not to pursue the "island boys" because (in an echo of the then-banned *Lady Chatterley's Lover*) they are "too close to nature," make a list of the eight youths from their "class" in the vicinity, tear it into eight pieces, and select four names each. Andy Wentworth, a Princeton man, seems the most promising at first ("Play that apocalyptic one, Em," he requests as she scrambles for her

Dylan Thomas) before he concludes that carnal pleasures conflict with his obligations to his alma mater. Finally, Emily is obliged to make a date with the local lifeguard, and proceeds to his quarters in an abandoned estate.

To this point, *Love Me Little* has carefully walked the border between callowness and cleverness. A reader unaware of the hoax—such as one, living outside New York, who didn't know Miller on sight and would therefore not be alerted by the jacket photo—might reason that the book was indeed the work of an earnest schoolgirl. Readers accustomed to chuckling at the more earnest aspects of Sagan and Moore's work could just as well take the book as an expert satire on the genre. But in the novel's penultimate scene, Miller suddenly, and with remarkable aplomb, shucks the satire and raises the stakes.

Entering the abandoned estate, occupied by generations of a family that left in the twenties, Emily, a half-hour early for her appointment, pokes around the rooms adjoining the lifeguard's improvised quarters and finds limitless detritus of the Stover clan, beginning with Victorian-era photographs:

> It may have been the faded quality of the photos, but all these people seemed to wear a look of serenity, their faces unmarked by time or trouble or conflict. Were they truly the faces of people who had never struggled or suffered, whose lives had been charted out for them, and who had found fulfillment simply in not deviating from what had been expected of them?

The answer comes when she finds a letter to one of the Stover men from one "Elizabeth," simply recounting the recent events among her family, and ending: "I l—- you."

> How moved was I by the fact that to her the word "love" was so meaningful and overwhelming that she could not write it out.

Emily is, moved to the point that she no longer wants to lose her virginity in a quick bout with the lifeguard, leaves a note declining his implied offer and goes back to her cottage, then to New York.

Miller's family and friends often comment on his cynical view of the world, but in *Love Me Little* he demonstrates remarkable skill at shifting from glittering satire to a serious statement about the lives of human beings, in a fashion not unworthy of Fitzgerald himself. But this seems to have been lost on almost all the reviewers when the book was issued. The reviewer in the *Herald Tribune* complained: "The characters are not believable, so that the whole novel reads more like a slick joke than like the obviously intended satire."

But Jane Cobb, in the *New York Times Book Review*, commented: "There are trimmings that make *Love Me Little* worthwhile." What is noteworthy about this review was its reference to "the pseudonymous Amanda Vail" (the only instance I've found where a reviewer of *Love Me Little* stated that Amanda Vail was anything other than a real person) and the photograph that accompanied it. In those days it was customary for portraits of authors appearing in the review's inside pages to be cropped down to just the face. However, the editors at the *Times* had chosen to publish the jacket photograph depicting Amanda Vail and the other patron of the coffeehouse, uncropped—and with the jacket photo's simple caption "Amanda Vail" supplemented with the words, "and friend." Evidently, readers—the ones in the know, anyway—were supposed to look at the picture and draw some conclusions.

Despite the fact that the Sagan fad had begun to wane by the time of *Love Me Little*'s publication in May 1957, the novel sold fairly well and accomplished something more. Now the New York book world was talking about Warren Miller, who, in bars frequented by editors and agents, was apparently soon known to be the author. Before long Little, Brown & Co had offered Miller a contract for his next novel, this one to be published under his own name. *The Way We Live Now*, an alternately witty and moving chronicle of divorced life in Manhattan that came out in May 1958. But even as this book was readied for the press, Miller was putting the finishing touches on a second Amanda Vail novel.

While this was happening, at a PTA meeting on New York's Upper Easrt Side (where the protagonist of *Love Me Little* had her home and hangouts), an infuriated elementary-school teacher approached Patricia Vaill. "How dare you write a book like this *Love Me Little* and put your own innocent daughter's name on it!" she exclaimed. The fact was that Patricia Vaill, a designer of jewelry at the famed store of her father Seaman Schepps, had never written a word for publication; this was the first she'd heard of any such book. She promptly bought the novel, and made some inquiries among her husband's friends in the publishing business. After determining the book's real author, she concluded Miller had simply heard her daughter spoken of. With this knowledge, the Vaills let the matter rest.

Whether or not she was actively encouraged to do so by the fact that two books bore a modified version of her name, Amanda Vaill, upon graduation from Radcliffe in the early 1970s, entered the publishing business, starting at McGraw-Hill, the very firm that had released her ostensible namesake's first book, and proceeding to Macmillan and then to Viking, where she rose to executive editor before leaving the business to write. During those years she met many people who had known Miller. She reports that, almost without exception, their opening words upon meeting or calling her for the first time were, "Did you know Warren Miller?" and, when she replied in the negative, "Have you heard of [or read] *Love Me Little*?"

"I've always had the feeling that Warren Miller was a kind of benevolent doppelganger all through my career," says Vaill, who has assembled, generally through impish gifts from friends, a comprehensive collection of the various editions of the other Amanda Vail's books. In the 1970s an elderly British editor, on meeting her, expressed his admiration for *Love Me Little* and asked why she hadn't kept writing more books like it. And in the 1990s, when Vaill was preparing *Everybody Was So Young*, her acclaimed biography of Gerald and Sara Murphy, the fabled Lost Generation couple who were friends with Hemmingway, Fitzgerald, and Dos Passos and the inspiration for characters in each writer's books, she wrote to an older female novelist who'd known the couple. After answering Ms. Vaill's questions, the writer concluded her letter by recalling how much she'd enjoyed "those wonderful books you wrote so many years ago."

Meanwhile, the word about the true identity of the author of *Love Me Little* was emerging from Manhattan editorial offices and into the public prints. In an item in his "In and out of Books" column in the *New York Times Book Review* of April 13, 1958, Lewis Nichols remarked that "since [the publication of the novel the previous] May there has been a certain puzzlement about who Amanda Vail is." Nichols then drew attention to *Love Me Little*'s jacket photo of "Amanda Vail" and her friend that had appeared with the *Times* review, and rather disingenuously announced that an unnamed "member of the staff of this section" had just happened to notice that the friend happened to be the same man whose picture was on the back cover of *The Way We Live Now*, Miller's new novel. Nichols reported that upon being confronted with this discovery, Miller had stated that he would "continue officially to deny this second, feminine identity," and that he wanted "to keep separate identities separately packed." Lest readers remain in the dark about this figure in the foreground of *Love Me Little*'s jacket, Nichols explained that she was "with hair up, Miss Jimmy Curley, silversmith in the Village."

Several weeks later, in a book-chat column in the *New York Herald Tribune Book Review*, Maurice Dolbier opened a discussion of Miller's new book by observing:

> [Miller] is becoming accustomed, if not entirely resigned, to the fact that interviews with [him] nowadays have a way of turning into conversations about Amanda Vail [. . .] Amanda Vail is like an alter ego to Mr. Miller, [and her] next book, *The Bright Young Things*, will also be published by Little, Brown. No mystification about that.

But there was still some mystification around that second book. Upon its publication in November 1958, almost every review noted the true identity of Amanda Vail. "Warren Miller, it can now be officially announced, is the author," remarked Hollis Alpert at the end of his *Saturday Review* notice. Which fails to explain why Miller's name appears nowhere on the jacket copy or elsewhere in *The Bright Young Things*, and why Jimmy Miller (nee

Curley), making a return appearance as "Amanda Vail" on the novel's cover, is dressed and made up to look like much more like a real teenager than she did on *Love Me Little*'s jacket; according to one of those at Little, Brown who worked on the book, there were no great pains taken to obfuscate or hint at the true identity of the author this time around.

But one thing is certain: *The Bright Young Things* makes virtually no pretense to being the work of a precocious teenager, though a trifling stab is made at maintaining the precociously world-weary atmos-phere and wry *bon mots* of the first book. Instead, it is a vigorous, and sometimes extraordinarily cutting attack on a host of people and situations, mostly of the literary kind. With this novel, Miller put aside almost all the previous book's parody of Sagan and Moore, and guided Emily and Amy into one situation after another where he could indulge a capacity for cutting wit and ridicule more close-ly resembling the sensibility of Angus Wilson or Evelyn Waugh than that of most of his American contemporaries.

Emily and Amy, heroines of the first novel, are now freshmen at "North-cliffe" college, and the second chapter of *The Bright Young Things* introduces the pair to their charming but tormented instructor in Fiction Writing I, Henry Salem. Emily observes:

> Salem was a mysterious character. No one seemed to know anything about him—where he came from, or where he lived, or where he had gone to college, even. And he wasn't telling. He had a passion for anonymity. His book was published without an Autobiographical Note, which always indicates to me great strength on the part of the author.

The tall, slim (but "too intense to be called lanky"), darkly handsome young professor has published only stories. He says that he'll wait until he's sixty-five and "my brain has solidified" before attempting another novel; "I wrote one once. It was a terrible experience. By the time I got to the last chapter I hated my hero." But the solution to the enigma of Henry Salem must wait, for Christmas vacation has arrived. Emily goes home to Manhat-tan, and discovers that her father has run off with a family friend his age. She is nonplused: "I thought Father only ran off with nubile girls."

By way of obtaining a respite from her troubles, Emily accompanies Amy on a visit to the apartment that their mysterious Northcliffe instructor maintains in Manhattan. As they enter the third-floor walkup, Emily notes that Dostoevski and James rest on his shelves next to boxes of baseball cards and stacks of *Argosy* magazine. Soon, discussing his stamp collection, Salem unleashes his anguish: "I got the 1934 Arbor Day issue which shows two undernourished-looking kids planting an undernourished-looking tree. Brings tears to my eyes every time I look at it." But it is when Henry and Amy prepare the punch, "based on a Swedish recipe called *Glug*," that the moment of truth hits with hurricane force. Let Emily set the scene:

> I took from the bookcase Henry's copy of *Nancy Drew and the Secret Staircase* and began to read. From the kitchen I could hear the bottles of wine being emptied into the bowl.
>
> "It *sounds* like Glug," Amy said. "It sure enough *sounds* like Glug."
> "You can't believe anything anymore," Henry told her in a sad voice. "It sounds like Glug, it may even *look* like Glug—but it sure in hell don't *taste* like Glug. It doesn't taste like *any*thing. Maybe I'll dump a few more of these here cinnamon sticks in it."
> Sounds of stirring: then Henry's voice. "Amy, you're so goddamn beautiful I want to die, I *really* want to die. Christ, I haven't felt this way since 1939 when all my guppies expired due to a cause that to this day has not been ascertained to *my* satisfaction."

(Here, it is worth noting that the above passage did not escape the notice of one of Miller's fellow authors at Little Brown. According to some reliable sources, the reaction of J. D. Salinger upon having *The Bright Young Things* brought to his attention was to put aside that mighty project recently compared to *War and Peace* in *The New York Review of Books*, contact his editor, and unburden himself of more than a few choice words concerning what he saw as the firm's betrayal of him, their most consequential author, by publishing this book by a no-talent who didn't even have the courtesy to sign his own name to his slanders on the author and his characters. Given that lofty silence was, and is, the usual reaction of the sage of Cornish to send-ups of his person and work, this speaks volumes for the accuracy of Miller's barbs. A few years later, the unrepentant writer, asked for a blurb for Walker Percy's *The Moviegoer*, called it, in a line still quoted today, "a *Catcher in the Rye* for adults.")

But even a rebel like Henry Salem is taken aback when, a few chapters later, he and the girls head downtown and encounter the latest literary rage, Mac Macinac, at his citadel, the "Upbeat" coffeehouse. When they arrive, Macinac hasn't yet "made the scene," but one of his acolytes hopes for great things:

> "Last night he was here and got knocked off his chair by an angel with a message."
> "What was the message?" William asked.
> "He couldn't tell us. He wasn't talking last night. He had the beatitude last night. He only smiled."

Though Macinac, on his arrival, offers only the advertised beatific smile and silence, four young poets "with hair and heavy sweaters" are more than ready to speak. The first poet speaks of his friend in Pasadena, the "jolly fixman," and his wish to "howl my gyzmic joy" up and down the Pacific coast.

Another bard starts his opus: *Oh Walt you lovely fag you need me more than I need you*. Though it's evident that Miller's heart isn't quite as much in ridiculing the Beats as it was in needling his earlier target, the fact remains that not many of the countless journalists then poking fun at the espresso-and-leotards set could distinguish between the work of Ginsberg and Corso.

But by the time the quartet has reached the coffeehouse, Emily and Amy have finally had their Experience, with Henry and his college classmate William Avery, respectively; for Amy, it proves to be true love, while Emily ultimately splits with Henry and is left to watch as her friend proceeds to the altar. But all is not lost, as Emily wins the short story contest sponsored by *Nineteen* magazine and uses the prize money to drop out of college and depart on the next boat to Paris. This time Miller avoids the temptation to bring in genuine sentiment of the type that was used in *Love Me Little* and the satirical tone is maintained to the end.

Though it is implied that Emily's adventures in Europe will provide fodder for yet another Vail novel, such was not to be. For one thing, the Sagan craze was played out. Sagan's third novel had gotten only middling reviews and disappointing sales when published in the fall of 1957. And while *Chocolates for Breakfast* had sold half a million copies as a Bantam paperback, Pamela Moore, for the moment an exile in Paris (where such writers as Simone de Beauvoir had read and complimented her book), was no longer much mentioned in American literary circles. When asked in 1959 whether his alter ego had a third book in her, Miller replied: "Amanda is dead now, and I don't think I'll ever resurrect her."

*　　*　　*

THE SKILLS WARREN Miller had developed in the writing of the Vail books were to serve him well when he came to write his most acclaimed novel, *The Cool World*, a saga of Harlem gang life told in the first-person by Duke Custis, a fatherless fourteen-year-old who has decided to pen an account of his efforts to become a "cold killer" with "heart" by obtaining a gun to replace his switchblade. Custis seems to interpret what history he has learned in school along the same lines as Thomas Carlyle—that is, as a chronicle of strong men and violence.

What Miller accomplishes with Custis's narrative in *The Cool World* is analogous to how he uses the precocious and pretentious language of Emily in *Love Me Little* to illustrate how that language shapes and limits what she would call her *Weltanschauung*. Custis's vocabulary consists of phonetic misspellings, supplemented by ampersands and capitalized "GODs" that he has picked up from street signs and the family Bible. His language proves adequate for the depiction of degradation and violence; it falls short of being able to articulate an awareness of the larger social forces that are shaping his existence.

The book's conclusion finds Custis in a juvenile facility upstate, where a mentor from his school days is making arrangements for him to

> go to school in town with the town kids [...] Once you know how to read it aint hard to learn almos any thing. Doc say, 'Readin. To read Richard [Custis's given name]. That the beginning of evry thing [...] when you read and write why you can do any thing. Be any thing.'

In the conclusion of *The Cool World*, Miller presents a situation similar to Emily's epiphany involving the old letter in *Love Me Little*, but with far greater impact and meaning. Custis has been trying to articulate genuine thoughts, feelings, observations without the benefit of the elaborate education that Emily has failed to use for her benefit; now he will get the chance to learn a language that he can use to write his way out of his cycle of futility in the way, perhaps in the same way that Frederick Douglass's pen made possible his escape from the psychological as well as physical shackles of slavery.

Of almost unanimously favorable notices of *The Cool World*, perhaps the most telling was the one in *The New York Times Book Review* by James Baldwin, who said that when reading it he could not tell if it was written by a white or black man. The novel was subsequently adapted into a Broadway play and hit art-house film. Warren Miller went on to write three more novels and a hilarious yet perceptive study of Castro's Cuba. Of these books, the one closest to the free-swinging style of *The Bright Young Things* is *Looking for the General*, a seemingly chaotic cascade of images and digressions, presented as the work of a half-mad officer, which startlingly anticipates the metafiction of the 1970s in its style, and the conspiratorial and paranormal concerns of 1990s pop and postmodern culture in its themes. Following a stint as the literary editor of *The Nation*, Miller died of lung cancer in 1966, four months shy of forty-five. He left behind a small but very impressive shelf of books—and that *jeune fille* conjured up by an editor and brought to life by a starving author, whose alternately frothy and stinging words enabled the latter to achieve his dreams, if only for a few years. Emily may be forever sailing for Europe; Amanda Vail forever contemplating a third book, never to be written; but what Miller wrote is still there, awaiting discovery.

CONVERGENCES

by LAWRENCE WESCHLER

CUNEIFORM CHICAGO
LOGUE'S HOMER/BREYTENBACH'S CELL

SO I HAPPENED to be in Chicago for a few days and decided to pay a visit on my Assyrologist friend, Dr. Matt Stolper, over at the University's Oriental Institute. I'd never actually been to his office, which as it turns out is on the third floor of the Institute's Museum (just down the block, as it happens— though on the far, far side of the History of Civilization—from Frank Lloyd Wright's low-slung modernist masterpiece, the Robie House). Matt's office proved a wide, low-slung affair in its own right, a cavernous warren of tome-lined shelves and narrow-drawered filing cabinets beneath a down-sloping ceiling. The cabinets, as Matt now proceeded to demonstrate for me, were brimming with scores, hundreds, thousands of cuneiform-engraved clay tablets, one lying snug beside the next, each neatly catalogued on its own little cotton mat—the treasure haul from a University archeological expedition over sixty-five years ago. Back then, in the depths of the depression, as Matt explained to me, the University had dispatched teams of archeologists, one of which included his own eventual teacher George Cameron, to unearth the palaces of the Achaemenid Persian kings Darius and Xerxes (legendary scourges of the Attic Hellenes, when they weren't busy managing a continental empire unmatched for size until the rise of the Romans) at Persepolis, near modern-day Shiraz, in Iran. Over half of the resultant haul has yet to be translated, and translating the individual tablets, one by one, at a grueling, meticulous pace, is essentially Matt's principal occupation.

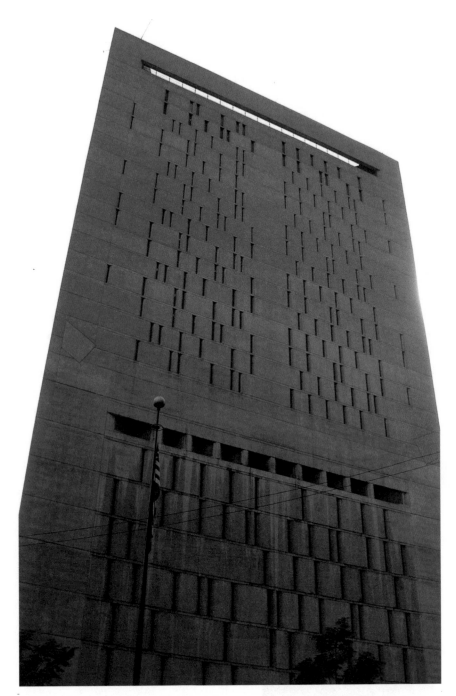

¹ A revisioning, specifically, of Book XVI, lines 632ff.

He picked one up at random: about the size of a dry cake of Shredded Wheat, and just about as legible, at least to my untrained eye. But Matt had no problem: "This one here, for example," he said, palming the tablet and leaning it slightly so as to rake the light just so over its chicken-scratch jumble of markings, "it's in a variant of the Elamite language, and it concerns, let's see, 'one thousand... eight hundred, thirty... -eight... and a half units of barley'—a unit: that would be about ten quarts—let's see: 'received as rations for workers, for one month,' various number of men and women, boys and girls—here's the total: '702 workers.' And then down here we have, hmmm, yes, 'eleven units of wine'—again, about ten quarts each—'for rations for women who have had babies, for one month,' with the women who had boys getting twice as much as the women who had girls."

Matt went on to explain how the core of that haul, sixty-five years ago, had proved to be an administrative-legal archive: "Pretty dry stuff, though not without its occasional charms." He recalled, for example, the jolt he'd experienced one day as he suddenly divined that the envoy whose activities and expenses were being documented on a particular shard before him—a certain figure named Belshunu, in Babylonian, with the title of "Governor of Across-the-River," which is to say Syria/Palestine—had to be the same Belesys, "former governor of Syria," who figured so prominently in the famous account of Cyrus-the-Younger's rebellion in Xenophon's Aanabasis, "the greatest story ever told to students of elementary Greek," as he put it.

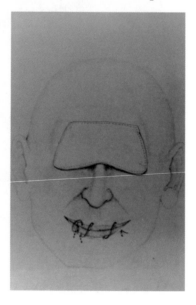

"And to actually hold a thing like that right there in your hands," he positively beamed, "it can get to be quite thrilling."

However, even more thrilling, he went on, were those occasions when, after hours of painstaking work, he could begin to make out evidence of people, in effect, cheating on their income tax, or blackmailing their superiors at court with threatened revelations of embarrassing improprieties, or hoodwinking their associates in other sorts of ways. "Just like today," Matt marveled, "only fully twenty-five hundred years ago!"

*   *   *

DRIVING BACK NORTH up the shore of Lake Michigan toward my downtown lodgings later that evening, I found myself recalling one of those magnificent sustained epic similes from Homer's Iliad, or, more specifically, from Christopher Logue's modern English reworking of same in his sinewy slim volume *War Music*, to wit:[1]

> Try to recall the pause, thock, pause,
> Made by axe blades as they pace
> Each other through a valuable wood.
> Though the work takes place on the far
> Side of a valley, and the axe strokes are
> Muted by depths of warm, still standing air,
> They throb, throb, closely in your ear;
> And now and then you catch a phrase
> Exchanged between the men who work
> More than a mile away, with perfect clarity.
>
> Likewise the sound of spear on spear,
> Shield against shield, shield against spear
> Around Sarpedon's body.

Of course, part of what makes that passage so powerful (apart from Homer's typically startling trick of likening senseless mayhem to peace-filled industry) is that specific, spine-tinglingly synaesthesiac line about "catching a phrase exchanged between men who work more than a mile away, with perfect clarity." The image seems to toll and toll, perfectly capturing the relation of Homer, the blind singer, to his subject, a battle that took place five hundred years earlier and hundreds of miles across the sea; and then, of that blind singer to his (seeing) audience, gathered around the fire, listening intently; and then, centuries later, Logue's relation to Homer; and later yet, our relation to Logue. And, of course, as well, my friend Matt's relation to those thousands of crumbly clay shards, the focus of his entire life's work.

Speeding northward, the skyscrapers of the city gleaming up ahead, I was in turn reminded of some comments Breyten Breytenbach, the Afrikaner poet, had made to me, as we sat in a Paris bistro one fine afternoon not long after his release from a seven-and-a-half-year stint in apartheid South Africa's prisons on various trumped-up charges of political subversion. He and I were recording his recollections for a radio documentary, and he'd taken to reminiscing about the nights on death row in Pretoria Central Prison. (Though Breyten himself had never been condemned to death, his warders had placed him in a cell there in one of their many attempts to undermine his sanity.) Breyten recalled:

> The hanging room—the actual chamber where they executed prisoners—was, of course, the central characteristic of the place. Even though you never saw the room, you could hear it—you could hear the trapdoor opening. It would send a sort of shuddering through the entire building the mornings people were being hanged. And before that you'd hear the singing with all its different qualities. You could definitely hear when somebody sang—and there'd be singing every evening—that that person was going to die in a few days, as opposed to somebody who still had a few weeks or months. And the interesting thing, or the touching thing, when one person sang alone like that in the middle of the night and you knew he was due to be hanged in two days' time, was how you could actually hear the quality of the listening of the other people, because you knew that everybody else in that prison was awake, lying there with their ears cocked close to the bars or the walls, listening. *You could hear the listening.*

Driving along, I could hear Breyten all over again, telling his story, just as I likewise recalled what it had been like subsequently to hear that story over the radio. (It had been an ur-radio moment, listening and imagining I could hear everybody else out there in the radio audience, hushed, straining to listen as well.) And now these sounds and images and silences all began to swim in my mind, and I fancied I could almost hear Logue straining to hear Homer, along with every earlier interpreter of Homer—Virgil and Pope and Chapman and Lattimore—all of them straining to hear, hushed, listening in on all the mayhem and the artifice, the suffering and the cheating: the great silent resounding vault of history, welling forth. And now I was easing off the highway, heading into downtown, and straight ahead, eerie, loomed an uncannily curious building—a modernist white marble monolith, a soaring flatiron wedge slit by a chicken-scratch grid of ultranarrow windows—which suddenly looked to me for all the world like a giant clay cuneiform tablet.

I had no idea what it was.

The next day I asked someone, and it turned out to be the William J. Campbell United States Courthouse Annex, otherwise known as the Metropolitan Correctional Center—otherwise known as the city jail.

JUAN REFUGIO ROCHA: A MERITORIOUS LIFE

by J. MANUEL GONZALES

ROCHA, JUAN REFUGIO (b. 1957) Zookeeper, animal trainer. Place of birth: Antigua, Guatemala. Very little is known about the 1979 Fuego del Zoológico Público, only that the grounds caught fire in the early morning of October 18, 1979, that the fire consumed the entire grounds and all its structures by daybreak, and that, in the fire, only four animals perished— one howler monkey, one chimpanzee, and two gorillas, one male and one female. The man who freed the animals from their cages and herded them out of their habitats was Juan Refugio Rocha, a twenty-three-year-old Guatemalan who had been working at the zoo for six months, during which time he had been trying to teach the gorillas to speak.

As a child, Rocha had been adept at communicating with animals through clicks, whistles, taps, nudges, snaps, and squeezes. His father had owned donkeys, which Rocha had cared for and which the family had used to earn money for food and clothing, renting the beasts out as transportation and pack animals. Rocha had trained each animal, and in all his years as keeper of the donkeys, no one was thrown, no packs were lost.

In 1974, Rocha left his parents' house and moved to Mexico City. From there, he moved to the state of Chihuahua, where he worked intermittently for carnival acts, training dogs and elephants and jungle cats. In late spring of 1979, he heard word of a public zoo in need of a keeper whose duties also involved light veterinarian work. By May, Rocha had taken the position, and in a few days, found himself obsessed with the gorillas.

Rocha, having never seen a gorilla before, knew little of their behaviors and nothing about their habitats. Through study of their personalities and through close observation of their physical characteristics, Rocha determined that the zoo owned one male Western Lowland gorilla and one female Western Lowland gorilla. He spent days at the zoo caring for the animals and the nights he spent in his room or at the library, studying their behavior. He went to great lengths to acquire the bamboo shoots, thistles, wild celery, and tubers that they ate. He constructed a realistic environment similar to the Western African Lowlands in design and humidity and greenery, and he gave them grasses and branches with which to build nests.

Once the two gorillas were settled, he made his first steps toward establishing communication.

Witnesses reported that when Rocha entered the habitat screeching and hooting and clicking to get the animals' attention, the gorillas began to squawk and let out a high piercing keen. The animals charged at him, running on their hind legs, "like people," with surprising dexterity and swiftness. They worked as a team, flanking and herding Rocha into a corner, and once he was trapped between the two, they began to kick and punch him in the back and in the head. Three men, groundskeepers who had been standing by to watch the animal trainer, finally managed to pull him out of the habitat, by which time Rocha had suffered a minor concussion and two broken ribs.

Rocha did not give up. Over the next six months, he entered the gorilla habitat no less than ten times, and the animals continued to greet him with the same volatility and aggression. The gorillas took the food he offered them, lived in the habitat he created for them, and in that habitat, they were peaceful. Once he entered their world, however, as if they had been trained for it, the gorillas circled him, trapped him, ignored him as he spoke, and then, after five or ten minutes, Rocha needed to be pulled from the cage, with a broken arm, broken fingers, broken ribs, badly bruised skin, cuts, contusions, abrasions, or minor concussions.

When the fire started, Rocha was with the gorillas, standing outside their habitat talking to them from a safe distance. He hooted and chirped and howled at them for a full fifteen minutes before leaving to attend to the other animals in the park. By the time help had arrived and the other animals had been freed from their cages and environments, the fire raged out of control, burning until dawn, when the last embers snuffed out and all that was left—the zoo, the howler monkey, the chimp, and the gorillas—was ash.

At present, Rocha lives in Mexico City, where he teaches zoology and animal husbandry at Universidad Nacional Autonoma de Mexico.

OMNIPRESENT
AND UNCERTAIN

by DARIN STRAUSS

THE SOUTHERN WOMAN has lipstick the color of blood on the sharps of her teeth, and she tells me I'll be lynched. "I'm sincere about that," she says—and it troubles her whole face. If this were a cartoon she'd be an explosion from the neck up. "Some of us are very not happy with you, Mr. Strauss."

The woman approached me at my book signing in Durham, North Carolina. Her family is planning to gather the following weekend in the nearby country town of Mt. Airy—and this is her way of cautioning me not to attend. She knows I will anyway.

My novel *Chang and Eng* is based on the lives of this woman's ancestors: the 19th century brothers, united at the chest, for whom the term "Siamese twins" was coined. Chang and Eng Bunker fathered twenty-one children and have 1,800 descendants—and every July many of them come together in Mt. Airy, where the twins settled after escaping certain death in Siam. This year I've been invited, by way of the tabloids. ("Tell that Darin Strauss to come," one of Eng's great-grandsons said to a newspaper reporter who'd written a profile of me.)

After phone calls to make sure the invitation is legitimate, I swerve my book tour South to include Mt. Airy—which is the town Andy Griffith's Mayberry was based on—to visit a get-together of people I don't know, understanding I'll be disliked. Why go, why inconvenience myself only to face possible scorn? For some reason I keep coming back to a line from *The Sun Also Rises*: "Tell them I'm ashamed of being a writer." Maybe the writing of the book and the trip South are acts that in some way cancel each other. Even though the book is something I'm proud of, I feel that I need to defend it, and myself.

As I finish signing books in Durham, a second descendant comes up to me. His name is Fred Bunker. "Just explain to us it's fiction and not biography, and maybe it won't be so bad," Fred says. "Nearly all of us are hillbillies about that question of fiction versus non." Actually, he's not the only one. Though my book is clearly marked *a novel*, one not-so-untypical review on Amazon.com was: "I loved this book until I found out it was a fake." Likewise, a TV news reporter went on the air with this scoop: "The author of a new book on the Siamese twins admits to making some stuff up."

Fred Bunker is nine-tenths WASP, but his face is an echo of Eng's. Maybe you've seen the photograph of the Siamese twins in the Guinness Book of World Records. The brothers are caught standing arms over each other's shoulders, like two rummies trying to support each other. Eng is the one whose eyes give you the perception that he knows you'll be gawking at his picture a hundred-and-thirty years after his death. His eyes say: "I know, it's dreadful, isn't it?"

Fred is eager to point out that his family is widely misunderstood. His sister once visited Thailand, he says. People in Bangkok had thought that all the Bunkers must be rich, descended as they were from such celebrated twins. "But the thing is," Fred tells me, "most of us are not rich at all."

*　　*　　*

BEFORE I ARRIVE in Mt. Airy, a reporter from the *Atlanta Journal-Constitution* calls to ask if she can tag along. "If a hot-shit New York writer gets strung up by the Southern descendants of the characters in his book," she says, "then the *Atlanta Journal* should cover it." She's from New Jersey, originally.

*　　*　　*

THE DAY OF the reunion the famed Carolina breeze is asleep on the job. By noon the heat is a string of firecrackers going off inches from your ear. Now, this part of the world is thick with foliage, just as green as I imagined it, but the meeting hall is found on a dirt lot—an acre of peanut-brown earth worn out under its own dust, the dead land plunging around the hall as if the building sits atop a huge sucking straw.

I hadn't known what goes down at Southern reunions (my people call them seders), so I'd decided to bring some fried chicken. On line at the local Long John Silver's, in a moment of sweaty optimism, I'd imagined that maybe people would kick up their heels as I entered the meeting hall, every descendant gracious and affectionate, fans of my book. I had it wrong. But then not completely.

Inside I meet Tanya, Eng's great-granddaughter, a fine-looking local woman of upmarket blouse and efficient hair. "It's not your writing I have a problem with, Mr. Strauss." Her smile's a show of nothing more genial than the muscles of her cheeks. "It's your ethics I don't like." She holds a copy of my book between two fingers as if it's gone to rot.

What could I say in defense of my ethics that wouldn't come off as a base rhetorical overstatement? That I surrendered the facts to the voluntary hallucination that is artistic creation? Doesn't that sound like bullshit?

I should explain that *Chang and Eng*, while based on true characters, is purely a fiction. It's presented as a meditation on what the brothers' truth might have been—not least because the facts of their biography were lost to sideshow embellishment even while they lived. In certain pamphlets they sold during their tours, for example, Chang and Eng were said to have lived lives unbound by any conflict or hardship; or to have had the benefit of Herculean powers; sometimes they were said to have lived forever—none of which says very much about what it meant to be Chang and Eng. Still, we do know: Chang and Eng came to America and great celebrity, sustained a coupled life as farmers during the Civil War, marrying Southern belle sisters and owning slaves. This is Bunker family history. And as a novelist I've discarded and finessed and invented certain details of this history. Thoughts, feelings, conversation—and, I hope, the way this all illuminates realities of *our* time—that is what a novelist (or, *this* novelist) adds to the historical material to try to make it more resonant. And apparently this has made some of their people angry and other people confused.

Another descendant to approach me is a tall Carolinian named Woody Haynes. "I've seen you written up in magazines, I know all about you," he says. He thinks my name is "Daris." He says, "I'm a descendant of Chang, the one you said was dim-witted in your book."

"I'm sorry you felt that I—" Even as my mouth releases some stale explanation, I'm thinking: maybe I shouldn't have come? The reporter from the *Atlanta Journal*—Jill—sidles up beside me, scribbling notes.

Hundreds of people have shown up, eyeing the jerk who has rejiggered their family secret into a bestseller. I'm asked to sign a few books, and I feel sort of vulgar doing it. When I'd been writing in the early mornings before heading off to the job I'd had, the last thing I thought was that "my characters" might have flesh-and-blood descendants, people who'd be affected by decisions I'd made in my underwear at sunup. And now they look puzzled to have me here, a stranger with a reporter trailing him.

I carry my box of Long John Silver's to the great table where people have put their food; I arrange it among the legion of china plates of home-cooked chicken—the air smells like Kentucky Fried drippings—when a woman taps me on the shoulder. "Mr. Strauss, you brought some lunch for us," she says. In a white pants-suit, she moves with such deliberate carefulness that I get the feeling her body is fixed together with packing tape.

"Yes, I did bring some lunch," I say, smiling. (Wanting to make the best impression on these people, despite the heat I'd worn a button-down shirt and a fairly prim pair of pants. But I forgot to pack a belt, and so now I'm conscious of my trousers drooping.)

"Well," she says, "I'll bet you didn't even cook the chicken yourself." Then she walks off.

What I want to say is: guess what, my room in the Hampton Inn doesn't come with a kitchen. Or: Actually, I did cook it—my name is Long John Silver, do you like the box I made?

"No, ma'am, I guess I didn't." I'm saying this to her departing back.

After about an hour, I'm asked to stand before a microphone and address everyone. I want to tell them that I hope I've done their plucky forefathers justice, because the story I did my best to tell involved heroism and tragedy—the great courage that Chang and Eng demonstrated by striving toward their notion of what it took to lead normal, happy lives, and the great sorrow that they suffered when finally they were unable to rise above the sad circumstances of their odd birth. That the best way I knew to portray Chang and Eng's story was with the immediacy and vitality of fiction —that's why I've written a novel and not a biography. That Art is omnipresent and life is uncertain. "Uh, hi, everyone," I say, feeling like a centipede with a stretch of ice under his feet.

By writing my book in the first-person, from the point of view of one of the twins, I'd hoped to bring the brothers nearer to the reader; by trying deferentially to depict Eng's thoughts, I wanted my depiction to be more affecting than some dry biography that would be unable to cover all of the many factual unknowns. Isn't mine a truer picture than that cold, hole-filled biography would have been—or at least an example of the kind of truth that takes into account the never-documented emotional verities, along with the known facts?

*   *   *

"THANK YOU VERY much for having me." I'm speaking into the microphone, which shocks my lips. My shirt sticks to my sweaty chest like papier-mâchét. "I just want to thank your family and your wonderful ancestors." I can't think of anything else to add. "And for your kindness for inviting me here. Thank you," I say. And for good measure: "Thank you." I can't stop myself: "Thanks."

As I sit down, a woman named Loraine Haynes touches my sleeve and shows a toothy grin. "It's really great that you came, Darin." And it's all over her gentle eyes that she means it—and it's as if I'm being pulled up out of a hundred feet of ocean into a different world.

At once people are coming up to shake my hand and pat me on the back. I'm not sure what has happened. My own smile is unsteady, a face of someone trying to keep friends he doesn't deserve. Tanya, the woman who'd questioned my ethics, invites me back for the "Mayberry Days" festival that celebrates Andy Griffith each year. My earlier flash of optimism hadn't been far off-base. The descendants are kind people, I guess they simply want to make sure I've understood and respected my obligation to their family. With one awkward speech I've convinced them that I have. I'm just not sure I've convinced myself.

It's an odd thing making a living mining other people's stories. The differences between biography and novel might be construed as somewhat esoteric, and while I hold them precious, a book is merely a book; a family history is sacred. It's out of my respect for the history of this one rural family that I've come to North Carolina to honor.

Several 1860s newspaper accounts called the twins "The monster." I've tried to show them as men. I'd like to think that speaks well of the ethics of my project. But that doesn't change the fact that I've profited by transforming the story of the Bunker family. I still can't say for sure that I don't agree with Tanya's original assessment of me.

One young guy, a breakable, hollow-chested teenager, thanks me while enjoying a glass of his mother's iced tea. "I learned so much about my own family from what you wrote," he says. "Well, I—made a lot of stuff up." And now the boy looks hurt.

*   *   *

AT THE END of the reunion the entire family proceeds out of the meeting hall into the muggy sunshine, but not before most of them stop to find the writer. They thanked me as if I'd done them a favor. Woody Haynes puts his hand on my arm and says, "You're part of our family now, Daris."

HOAXES WITHOUT END

AN INTERVIEW WITH JOEY SKAGGS, ABOUT MAKING UP NEWS

ON APRIL 13, 1844, the *New York Sun* published a special edition, called *The Extra Sun*, on the strength of a front-page story announcing that a hot-air balloon had successfully crossed the Atlantic Ocean. With no fewer than eight exclamation points and a series of bold headlines, subheads, and kickers that filled one-third of the column, the Sun trumpeted its astounding news. The balloon had crossed the Atlantic in three days! The "Flying Machine!!!" had just arrived and landed in Charleston, South Carolina. The article promised "full particulars of the voyage!!!" The article, as it happens, was fictional. It was written by Edgar Allan Poe and published knowingly by the *Sun*. New York newspapers were far more numerous then and competition for readers was fierce, and so Poe's story was a sure-fire way for the *Sun*'s editors to boost their circulation. They were right; the paper sold 50,000 copies of the special edition. Poe was amazed and, even stranger for him, genuinely overjoyed at the enthusiasm that greeted his story. He wrote:

> On the morning (Saturday) of its announcement, the whole square surrounding the Sun building was literally besieged, blocked up—ingress and egress being alike impossible, for a period soon after sunrise until about two o'clock p.m.[...] I never witnessed more intense excitement to get possession of a newspaper. As soon as the first copies made their way into the streets, they were bought up, at almost any price, from the news-boys, who made a profitable speculation.

Today, Poe's fictional news article appears in most of the major collections of his writing, as a story called "The Balloon-Hoax." His story came to mind as I was preparing to interview Joey Skaggs, an artist who has, since 1976, made up stories that are the contemporary equivalent of Poe's and managed to get them published in newspapers and on the Internet and broadcast on television and the radio, all without editors and reporters suspecting a thing. Most recently Skaggs created The Final Curtain, a fake company and its requisite web site, promising to do for cemeteries what Walt Disney did for theme parks, and do so tastefully. The company got quite a bit of attention in the media before Skaggs revealed it as his latest hoax. Thinking about Skaggs and Poe, I wondered about the 50,000 people who bought that issue of the *Sun*. Were they just hoodwinked? Was it that simple? Or did they also come away with a story, albeit fictional, about progress, human achievement, and risky adventures, all of which they happened to want to believe in? And could the same be said for those of us fooled by a Skaggs hoax today, or tomorrow?

Q: Now that you've revealed the Final Curtain, I'd like you to talk about some of the logistical nitty-gritty that goes into one of your productions.

A: The Final Curtain took about two years of work from when I first started putting it together to when I released the exposé. Having come up with the concept to satirize the funeral industry, I decided to create a bogus company and web site to promote the concept. I wanted to use the Internet because while fact and fiction are so easily manipulated and blurred, it has also become an ubiquitous and supposedly reliable source for information. It gave us an instantaneous and constant presence, with the illusion of having a history. I registered a domain name and put together a team of volunteers. In this case over fifty people helped perpetrate the hoax—businesspeople, writers, architects, web designers, programmers, ISP providers, and the artists who provided concepts and sketches for their monuments.

. We created the Final Curtain web site complete with architectural renderings, a development proposal, biographies for the management team, information about investment opportunities and the time-share program for the deceased, a monument gallery of iconoclastic and satirical grave sites and urns, and a tour of the memorial theme park.

To be successful, this project had to appear completely real. I needed a mailing address, letterhead, telephone business listing, and a staff. One volunteer agreed to let me use his home/office address in New Jersey and we installed a telephone line under the name of Investors Real Estate Development d.b.a. the Final Curtain.

All calls and mail were forwarded to my New York City studio. Our web master created e-mail addresses for all the staff members which were also routed to me. They were real people, but since none had the time to deal with the day-to-day correspondence once the piece took off, I played all the roles.

Then I placed ads in twenty alternative newspapers around the country. The ad read, "Death got you down? At last an alternative! www.finalcurtain.com."

Q: What initial reactions did you get from the ads?

A: As soon as the ads came out, the hits to the site spiked into the tens of thousands per day for several weeks. However, only a few people responded directly.

Q: Then what happened?

A: I let the Final Curtain percolate. Over the next six months, we added artists' submissions to the Monument Gallery. This helped it look as if it had caught on and that more people were becoming involved.

When I felt the site was sufficiently populated with creative, emotionally poignant monuments, I launched a major PR campaign announcing the concept and soliciting artists' monuments for a scholarship program. The winners would receive free 10' x 10' plots for their memorials or urns at one of our soon-to-be-created memorial theme parks.

Q: Satire always seems to require at least some of the audience to completely miss what's funny and accept it as real. Were these very serious, earnest submissions from artists who took the web site at face value?

A: The responses I got seemed genuinely sincere. Some artists embraced the concept and were happy to participate. Others saw it as a business opportunity. For example, one artist who did tombstone engraving for people and pets wanted to put her work up in the gallery as a way to get more work through the Final Curtain.

Q: So next the Final Curtain starts to get early attention from the media.

A: The media response kept me extremely busy granting interviews. I played various staff members and appeared on radio shows, in newspapers and magazines, on the Internet, and on TV shows. Thankfully no one asked me to come in to the studio.

After an article appeared in the *Los Angeles Times*, the legal challenges began. A lawyer for Uncle Milton Industries Inc., owner of the registered trademark "Ant Farm," sent a formal complaint to both the writer at the *Los Angeles* Times and our company claiming trademark infringement because one artist's monument emulated an ant farm.

It pays to have a *pro bono* lawyer friend with a sense of humor. In response we changed the language on the site to "ant habitat," and all was well with the world again. But I couldn't pass up the opportunity to stir up a little more trouble. I sent a second press release out about the ant farm controversy to keep the Final Curtain in the news.

Q: I like how the fact that Uncle Milton's attorneys took the Final Curtain seriously can become justification for journalists just hearing about the Final Curtain to take it seriously, too.

A: When something seemingly adverse happens, I use it as an opportunity. Controversies help to distract reporters from questioning the original premise.

Q: Then what happened?

A: Months went by and I maintained nine-to-five business hours, pretending I worked in a real office. I handled a flood of interviews by phone and e-mail. I had an answering machine with a secretary's voice on the message, so I could occasionally leave "the office."

I tape recorded and logged all the calls, and kept track of the articles and stories through print and electronic clipping services. I had to keep everything going long enough for numerous magazines, with very long lead times, to publish their stories.

Q: In order to create a fictional business you had to behave like an actual business. You kept business hours, you held meetings with your volunteers, you did all those standard business things. It's as if some semblance of reality can't be imitated accurately without recreating reality completely. Running a business that's supposed to appear real could even be harder than running a real business.

A: When I create a false reality, I always try to create a plausible structure to help convince people.

Q: When and why did you decide to reveal the hoax?

A: After many months of running this non-existent company I was satisfied with the success of the piece. I composed and mailed an exposé press release. I canceled the auxiliary telephone line and mounted a disclaimer on the Final Curtain web site. But releasing an exposé doesn't mean the piece is over. Since a majority of the media that had fallen for it chose not to do a follow-up and never revealed it was a hoax, many people weren't exposed to the truth. Consequently some serious inquiries continued to come in. Even with a disclaimer on the web site, I receive letters of inquiry, commentary, and offers.

Q: As you watch the news or read newspapers, what do you notice about journalism that you then take into account in your hoaxes? Are there types of stories reporters tend to go for that you then try to replicate?

A: Sometimes it's a matter of being topical and outrageous. Other times you can use a calendar to predict the kinds of stories the media is looking for. Celebrations of anniversaries of disasters, such as nuclear power plant meltdowns or political assassinations provide opportunities, as do holidays. And then there are the ubiquitous animal or pet stories. There's one every day.

Most important to any fake story is a plausible, realistic edge with a satirical twist that is topical. I want people to be amused or amazed but fooled. I want them to say, "Unbelievable!" but believe it. Satire and believability are irresistible to the news media. Sensationalism gets them every time.

Q: Sensationalism is something that people regularly accuse some journalists of. What must be alluring about your hoaxes is that you present journalists with a sensational story. That is, they don't need to cover the cathouse for dogs or the cockroach vitamin pill in sensational ways. They're already sensational. Your hoaxes allow them to be thoughtful, objective journalists while covering something that's completely outrageous.

A: I'm willing to play the buffoon or the wacko and let them laugh at my expense, knowing I'll have the last laugh.

Q: How did you get started doing this?

A: I loved painting and sculpting, but realized how difficult it was for a young artist to be taken seriously by the art establishment. Also, I was impatient. So I began doing confrontational, iconoclastic performances, bringing my artwork into the public arena, like the Easter Sunday Crucifixion in 1966, which started when I dragged a 200-pound ten-foot-tall sculpture depicting a decayed figure on a cross into Tompkins Square Park on the Lower East Side.

These were the early stages of using the news media as an integral part of my work. These performances usually ended up badly for me and anyone associated with me. They were not humorous. I was scorned, chased, and arrested. But I learned first-hand how the news media operates by watching how they interpreted, changed, and misrepresented my intentions.

Q: How did the news media report on those early projects?

A: As a news story, I'm just a subject, not a person. My early performances were provocative, so I was stereotypically portrayed as a counter-cultural figure by the mainstream media. Not much has changed.

Q: Then the media became much more integral to your work.

A: I began to experiment using the media as my medium rather than just a vehicle to report on my performances. I learned more complex ways to manipulate the manipulators, to bring attention to issues about which I felt passionate. My performances became, rather than simple political or social statements, more sophisticated theatrical productions, like the Vietnamese Nativity in 1968, where I constructed a life-sized Vietnamese village in Central Park on Christmas Day and had actors representing American soldiers with weapons attack and destroy it.

I combined advertising art and public relations techniques with theater, film-making, set design, research, writing, character development, acting, photography, and, of course, sculpting and painting. And I added hoaxing to my repertoire, where I would fool the media into believing total fabrications. I called these my plausible but non-existent realities. I was inspired by the need to be cunning enough to fool intelligent journalists, while leaving clues and challenging them to catch me. I'd given up the control a painter might have, but I was dealing with issues, with irony, and with worldwide media attention. It was no longer necessary to have a gallery in order to be seen.

Q: You've written that when reality as reported on the news gets as strange as it sometimes is, "pranks are needed more than ever to jolt us into reexamining our values." What values and what sort of reexamination do you have in mind?

The issues of my performances vary, but most of the questions buried in the work remain the same: What do we believe? Why do we believe it? This is true whether we're talking about questioning the authority of the media or questioning deeper personal beliefs, such as political, religious, moral, or ethical concerns.

My challenge as a satirical artist is how to present ideas to people to enable them to question and reexamine their beliefs. My hope is that my work provokes people to look at things in a new way.

Q: What sort of reexamination do you have in mind for the Final Curtain?

A: The theme is life and death. It's about as heavy as you can get or as light as you can try to make it. Hopefully, the Final Curtain has inspired people to think about how they respond to the death of a loved one. I tried to create an inspirational framework around an absurd premise to jumpstart the process. As it turns out, the premise of a cemetery theme park mall with a time-share program for the deceased may not be that absurd after all. Many people thought it was a great idea.

Q: How reliant are the reporters who write about the Final Curtain on the press releases you feed them?

A: Most reporters who come to me get their stories directly from press releases. Very few do what one would consider to be their professional duty. I count on this to a degree.

If I'm successful in fooling a wire service, I don't really have to do anything else to promote the story, because the media will feed off of itself. They all assume the original author did his or her homework.

The Final Curtain web site contained a lot of information including contacts for the staff. So even if a journalist considered the concept over-the-top, there were people to talk with to get verification. Some journalists did call, which allowed me to have fun elaborating on the concept in order to convince them. Most did not question the premise but would focus on getting clever material for their stories. They asked about the artists' submissions. So I made up answers I thought they'd like.

Q: What sort of questions did reporters ask you?

A: The questions were quite typical: Where did the idea come from? When and where will the first theme park open? Tell us about some of the artists and their concepts. Is there anyone famous? How much will it cost to be buried there?

Q: Did any reporter want to pry into the story a bit?

A: A few journalists dug deeper. Some had questions about the backers and potential investors. But I'd answer probing questions with, "I'm sorry but what you are asking is proprietary in nature and I'm not at liberty to disclose this information." Very few continued to pry after that.

Also, I could always try to manipulate the conversation and feed them other aspects I thought might interest them. I'd tell them we were being besieged by the public, that we were really filling important needs. I'd speak of economic development for the areas in which we planned to build. If it was a radio interview, I knew they wouldn't spend much time. If it was a print journalist I'd ad-lib as long as they wanted. But it was relatively easy to answer their questions and keep them engaged.

Q: Did any reporters contact you, ask a few questions, and then not run a story?

A: A journalist from the *Bergen County Record*, in New Jersey, called several times. Each time he called he tried to dig deeper. Finally he called to say his editor was not satisfied with the information, and he needed more. I told him I could understand the editor's hesitancy since we had not yet broken ground on the first park. And since I couldn't tell him exactly where the first park would open, "for fear that the information would drive up prices of surrounding properties," I suggested he wait until we announced a groundbreaking. He sounded disappointed that his editor was holding him back, but agreed that maybe it was best he wait.

His calls were particularly challenging. The Final Curtain office was not far from his office. I feared he'd take a short trip to our headquarters only to find it was a private home. But he never brought up the subject of visiting us and he never wrote the story.

Q: Before you revealed the hoax, *The Boston Herald*, *Mother Jones*, National Public Radio, and many others reported on the Final Curtain. Have any of those organizations run retractions or stories explaining the hoax?

A: Disappointingly no. Yahoo! Internet Life, *Mother Jones*, NPR, Fox TV, Associated Press, Flash News, and the *New York Daily News*, etc.—none of them ran retractions. Only the *Boston Herald* ran a retraction, but it was a put-down. And they were joined by the Boston Globe, which hadn't fallen for it. But then, I'd hoaxed both repeatedly.

Follow-up stories by those who have been fooled are rare. When it does happen, it isn't necessarily an explanation, apology, or examination of the issues brought forth by the hoax. They don't want to give the story any more attention for fear of further embarrassment. They don't want the public to question their credibility as an investigative news source.

Q: So your hoaxes typically get more coverage than your subsequent revelation that they are hoaxes?

A: The news media mostly choose to focus on the aspects of the story that concern their having been fooled, not the issues brought forth in the hoax. So the follow-up story is usually an admission that they "among many other journalists" were fooled by a hoaxer. They try not to mention my name. And if they do, they usually put me down. Not that I expect them to praise me.

Q: You ever have any close calls with reporters almost discovering you hiding behind their story?

A: I'm sure, well, at least hopeful that there have been suspicious journalists who, thinking the story was bogus, decided it wasn't worth their time to investigate and let it go. But my experience has shown me that most journalists don't want to screw up a good story with reality, and they will talk themselves out of questioning the story to death.

I remember the first time I fooled *UPI*, this was with my Cockroach Vitamin Cure Hoax. When asked by another journalist for a statement, a *UPI* senior editor said, "The information was correct at the time." I never forgot that. That comment was the excuse he used to justify their incompetence. Incidentally, I've fooled *UPI* numerous times since.

Q: Has the Final Curtain received any media attention since, as the *UPI* editor would have it, the information about it now appears to be incorrect?

A: Even though the site has an exposé announcement on the home page, the site still receives thousands of hits from all over the world everyday. And the servers those hits are coming from keep changing. For example, last week I started getting hits from Poland. So apparently, someone somewhere is writing about it.

Also, I'm still getting e-mails from people interested in financing or mounting their memorial, or offering planned giving opportunities. Obviously people don't read very carefully. If I removed the hoax disclaimer, the hoax would continue on. It would be an interesting test, and I'm tempted to do it.

Q: Your Celebrity Sperm Bank, a plausible but non-existent reality circa 1976, has recently become a plausible, existent web site that auctions model's eggs to the highest bidder. In "Writing American Fiction," Philip Roth wrote, "The American writer... has his hands full in trying to understand, describe, and then make credible much of American reality. It stupefies, it sickens, it infuriates, and finally it is even a kind of embarrassment to one's one meager imagination. The actuality is continually outdoing our talents, and the culture tosses up figures almost daily that are the envy of any novelist." As a satirist, do you ever feel you're in a high-stakes race against reality?

A: Sure, but it also reminds me not to get old or culturally stuck, and not to be disappointed when reality beats me to the punch. It's a wonderful challenge. Not just to keep up, but to guess ahead of the crowd.

Q: Do you consider yourself at all gullible?

A: It is the fool who thinks he cannot be fooled. I hook lots of journalists because of this attitude. Especially Europeans who say, "You couldn't get away with that here." I say, "Excuse me, but I have."

But I'm as susceptible as anyone else. At the same time, I'm highly skeptical. It would make life much easier if I could have total faith and not question everything all the time, but I can't do it and I won't do it.

Q: What would you do if a Joey Skaggs impersonator began making hoaxes in your name, in effect adding counterfeit hoaxes to your real body of fake work in much the same way that van Gogh's oeuvre, say, is today swelled by a number of careful fakes?

A: Are you trying to create more trouble for me here? Actually I thought a lot about continuing my work even after I'm dead. So I've been designing hoaxes that can be executed when I'm no longer alive. For example, hoaxes that my friends can drop in the mail. I actually can still continue working, and no one will be the wiser.

Q: So you might create a hoax that's never revealed, that forever remains a plausible but non-existent reality? That would be a fitting memorial for you, to leave behind some complex, undisclosed puzzles, a bunch of hoaxes without any end.

A: It makes the thought of dying a little more amusing.

THESE THINGS NEVER
HAPPEN OVERNIGHT

by CHRIS COLIN

From a series of letters received by Oakland, California resident Mary Nelson, between February and June 1999. Nelson corresponded with Andy Knudsen, Assistant Co-Director of the West Oakland Transit Village Study, a group formed to develop plans for a retail and living center adjacent to West Oakland's Bay Area Rapid Transit station. The letters first appeared in the December 9, 1999 issue of the Brown Argus, *published in Fruitvale, Oakland.*

Dear Ms. Nelson:

I'm sorry you received two of our form letters. We've been incredibly busy here, as you can probably imagine, and we don't always have time to reply to each community member from whom we hear.

 To answer your questions, our aim is to begin construction by or after July. The Transit Village will be built in installments. We have identified Opportunity Sites (p. 2, fig. 2 on the mailing), and these will be maximized into the Key Project Areas discussed in the mailing. Once the KPAs are underway, renovation of the BART station, and augmentation of the ParkingThorp, will occur. Finally, we will authorize construction of the Transit Village Towers.

 We are sensitive to the history and needs of the West Oakland community. Notice I say "community." Alternate proposals failed to consider the varieties of issues that circulate in the West Oakland neighborhoods. We chose to hear those issues, and believe that the growth of the Village will translate directly into pride in this developing city.

Please do not hesitate to write, should you have further questions.

Best regards,
Andy Knudsen
West Oakland Transit Village Study

* * *

Dear Ms. Nelson:

I appreciate the second letter! What are "The Colonials"? Oh, I guess that was the name of your son's team in Madison(?).

Moving forward, I'm glad you're paying attention to the particulars of the project here. We respect the paying of attention—it behooves us as West Oaklanders to take nothing for granted as we embark on this voyage. For it's a voyage that takes us no further than our own (new, and in qualifying cases, newly painted!) front doors.

Are we building a utopia? A reinvention of clouds? No. We are building a transit village, which will mingle condominium living with a convenient retail experience. Historically—and we are all history—this type of retail community has specifically involved low-priced electronics shops, thrift stores, storefront fast-food restaurants, discount sneaker outlets and personal beautification centers.

Regarding your inquiry into procedure, the site designations were selected by a committee convened from the central committee. The smaller committee reviewed proposals and experimented with thoughts such as: 1) I am an astronaut; 2) You are an astronaut; 3) We enjoy radio; 4) We enjoy SOCIAL; 5) Things are _____; 6) Man (and woman) is adaptable. These "mind realization" techniques may sound amusing, but we believe they encouraged a certain creativity while proposals were on the table.

Best regards,
Andy Knudsen
West Oakland Transit Village Study

* * *

Dear Ms. Nelson:

Thank you for the thoughtful comments. Even in a fairly brief note, you got me thinking a little more closely about specifics of the project:

A poet once said, Look at the spaces in between. In the case of the

WOTV, those spaces are lined with California poppies and non-intrusive sodium-vapor lamps. This project is about walking and, whether or not you believe the 1969 moon landing was a hoax, surely it's true that small steps and giant leaps can occur simultaneously.

As for the mind realization techniques, I appreciate your word of caution. I assure you these are harmless exercises, and at no point were we in danger of inflicting psychic injury. (I'm not even sure there is such a thing.)

Best regards,
Andy Knudsen
West Oakland Transit Village Study

*　　*　　*

Dear Ms. Nelson:

I appreciate your perceptivity. It's true—the West Oakland Transit Village does mean something to me personally. I'm a bureaucrat, true, but I'm also a citizen who believes in convenience. And yes, I'd be happy to talk a little about how I became interesting in the project. Suffice it to say I spent several years in Virginia in my twenties and there I developed a garden-variety but upsetting confusion over what to do with my various notions. I was clomping around like a Sasquatch—I was trouble! These things never happen overnight, but in my case they pretty much did: In one evening I quit a decent landscaping job, drank my last paycheck, and woke to my own voice telling my grandmother to take me to a "monkastery." A monkastery! I was in Oakland two weeks later and, as we say around the WOTV office, "Don't look down—or back!"

Regarding your other question, we have received many letters expressing the same puzzlement. The painting in our lobby above the water fountain is of a cloud formation resembling a majestic lion, in the eyes of the children gazing at it. The artist is Oakland's own Marsha Dgrent, and she describes her art as "whimsical." We apologize for the confusion.

Best regards,
Andy Knudsen
West Oakland Transit Village Study

*　　*　　*

Dear Ms. Nelson:

No apologies please! It was *my* error. My impression was that you had inquired as to my motives for joining the WOTV effort. I now realize you were inquiring in a more general, and less detail-oriented, way. Again, my mistake! I look forward to continuing our normal correspondence.

Best regards,
Andy Knudsen
West Oakland Transit Village Study

*   *   *

Dear Ms. Nelson:

Thank you for sharing the interesting information regarding India's rhesus macaque monkeys. I was unaware that these creatures grow enraged upon seeing people smoke cigarettes. Imagine a monkey grabbing a cigarette from your mouth and stamping it out! I suppose they feel like I do about smoking: No smoking.

As far as Topic 31.1794, from the "Gains" segment, goes, your concern(s) have been noted. Obviously de-inclusion is a step we aim to avoid here. If we had a plaque, it might read, "Include All Topics If Possible"! The process of amending Board agenda—particularly when segments such as the "Gains" segment are involved—is, as we sometimes say, disfortunately fraught with complexity. Topic 31.1794 touches the community and in many ways, you're right to regret its "elimination." But in other ways, we haven't "eliminated" anything, and have merely expanded opportunity by creating an exciting, previously filled "hole." After all, we don't look down or back, only up/forward, and ultimately we must begin the process of moving on.

Right?

Best regards,
Andy Knudsen
West Oakland Transit Village Study

MARCHE FUNÉBRE

by CURTIS WHITE

"What miserable rogues fill the market place while that beautiful soul burns out!"
—Delacroix

1.

THE SOLDIERS OF the Czar have come to the home of Mikolaj Chopin and his wife Justyna, an apartment at the Saxon Palace in the Saxon Gardens in Warsaw, Poland. The Russian imperialists had ruled in Warsaw and Poland since the defeat of Napoleon in 1812. Mikolaj Chopin was actually considered by most Poles to be a collaborator with the Russians. He taught at their lyceum, presented his child prodigy Frédéric at the Russian palace, and refrained from participating in the periodic "uprisings" against the Russian status quo.

So he was surprised, in the winter of 1830, when the soldiers arrived at his door. He of course opened it for them anyway, surprised or not.

"What can I do for you?" he asked.

Four grim, crimson-coated soldiers stood before him. "We have orders to burn the bed of your son, Frédéric."

"What? Burn his bed?" He called to his wife. "Justyna, the Russians have come to burn Frycek's bed."

Justyna Chopin came to her husband's side looking over his shoulder, her hands on his arm. Chopin's parents had a long, successful, mutually caring marriage, something their son would never have.

"What? Has the world gone mad? Why would they want to do such a thing? The boy no longer even lives here. And where will he sleep when he returns to us?"

The officer in charge replied, "We have our orders. We are to burn his bed. Please step aside."

They stepped aside, of course, and the soldiers entered and climbed the stairs to the bedroom where Chopin spent his youth. Justyna and her husband followed, confused but persisting in their complaints.

"I tell you, the boy has done nothing wrong. Nothing to deserve that his bed should be burned. And he has left the country. He is a musician. The Czar himself loves Frycek. Please, explain to us what you are doing and why."

At the top of the stairs, the officer stopped, although his men continued forward, into the bedroom. They didn't even need to ask where the room was, or which was the bed in question. But the officer paused and explained their purpose for a last time.

"Madame, sir, we do not know why we have been required to do this thing. We have orders to burn the bed of Frédéric Chopin. It is that simple as far as we are concerned. We do not press beyond that fact. And we will burn his bed. You would be well advised not to interfere or to ask too many questions. I do not wish to be obliged to include your name in my written report."

The parents of Chopin paled. Mikolaj turned to his wife and said, "Did you hear that, dear? There is to be a written report about the burning of Frycek's bed! It is beyond question an important matter."

The soldiers lifted the bed and were carrying it down the narrow wooden stairs when the officer returned to them. "No," he said to them, "there is no requirement that we burn the blankets or the pillows. Throw them to the floor."

The soldiers hesitated and looked at him with some concern.

"Don't worry. I'll take full responsibility for the decision." He turned to the Chopins and nodded as if in fact he wished them to understand that he understood their position and truly cared for them. They could be his own parents.

"And the bed is small enough that we can simply throw it from that balcony window to the street. Don't bother with the stairs."

So, they threw Chopin's bed from the balcony over the narrow Warsaw street. It landed awkwardly with the legs at the foot of the bed striking first and causing the bed to buckle and break with a loud snapping of tearing wood and ripping pegs.

The soldiers rapidly and noisily descended to the street, their boots thudding as the boots of soldiers do when descending wooden stairs. Some kerosene was thrown on the bed and the sad, broken thing was ignited. It blazed quickly, the flames climbing the crazily tilted headboard. A crowd gathered and muttered stormily. Perhaps Chopin's bed would be the cause of the next uprising.

"The filthy Russians have gone too far this time ... they're burning our beds ... even Chopin! ... serves him right, the dirty collaborator ... but why would the Russians do this if the Chopins are with them? ... I'm going home to see if they're burning anything at my house."

2.

FRÉDÉRIC CHOPIN, AS is well known, had tuberculosis from a very young age and was sick and feverish off and on his entire life. Most troubling for both Chopin and his friends was, naturally, his intense cough, a cough through which, he once complained, he would "cough up my soul." But Chopin's cough was also, oddly, a part of his charm the women in Paris society, especially the great George Sand. This was, after all, the era of Romanticism, and genius was thought to be coterminous with "consumption," as it was then called. Consumption was the "fever of the Romantics." According to Dr. Jean-Claude Davila, "thinness and a pale face were an extreme distinction: women loved thin and fragile men, considering it symbols of virility." According to the "cult of consumption," the disease gave its victims "an exalted inner life" as a sort of compensation for their ravaged bodies.

The most notorious period in Chopin's famed relationship with the novelist and ur-feminist George Sand was the winter of 1838 that the two spent with Sand's children on the Spanish island of Majorca. Sand sought an idyllic retreat from the intense life of Paris. She also argued that the southern climate would be good for the delicate Chopin's health. The reality of Majorca, however, was anything but salutary. First, upon their arrival in Palma, they discovered that there were no hotels. And as soon as the word about Chopin's condition spread, there were no private rooms available to them either. Ultimately, the beleaguered family was obliged to live above a barrel makers shop while waiting for rooms to be made available to them in an abandoned medieval Carthusian monastery at Valldemosa. According to Chopin, the very walls sweated with an antique decay. A fine place for a tubercular man to take a cure.

While the near-indestructible Sand and her children enjoyed the romantic ruins of the monastery and even enjoyed the daily deluges of rain to which they were subjected during their stay, Chopin found that the infectious walls of the monastery leaked all-too-familiar anxieties about death.

As Sand wrote in her *Story of My Life*, "He became completely demoralized....For him the cloister was full of terrors and phantoms, even when he felt well....I would find him at ten o'clock at night, pale at his piano, with haunted eyes, and hair standing on end....He then made an effort to laugh, and he played sublime things he had just composed or, better said, the terrible or heart-rending ideas that had captured him, despite himself, in that hour of solitude, sadness, and fear."

In general, that winter, "death seemed to hover over our heads to seize one of us." So, Sand decided to cut short their stay, and on February 11, 1839, they left the monastery with all of their belongings, including the Pleyel piano that had only just arrived after several months en route from France. It was none too soon. Chopin was suffering "a frightening expectoration of blood."

When they boarded the ship, *El Mallorquin*, bound for Barcelona, the piano had to be shipped above deck. (They would have preferred to simply sell it, but the good people of Palma believed that the tubercular Chopin had infected the instrument and they would not offer to buy it.) It was strapped to the deck and covered over in canvas. Chopin would not leave the piano's side, despite the "basins full of blood" he was spitting up. It even appears that at one point he asked to be strapped to the piano. A strange idea, perhaps, but not when compared with the alternative: being transported below deck with a herd of pigs being shipped to the mainland.

But the horror of this trip did not end in Majorca. Sand writes, "When we left the hotel in Barcelona, the manager wished to make us pay for the bed in which Chopin had slept, under the pretext that it had been infected, and that the police regulations obliged him to burn it."

Sand had no choice but to pay for the bed they would burn, and try though she did to hurry her loved ones from the scene, they witnessed the peasants—who seemed, oddly, to be the same dark little men they had seen in Majorca—bring the detested bed into the street before the hotel and set it ablaze. As their carriage pulled away, headed for the ship, which would finally return them to France, Chopin stared out the back window at the conflagration. Humiliated. Appalled. Ashamed to live.

The peasants danced about the bizarre pyre.

3.

THE GREAT FRÉDÉRIC Chopin, virtuoso pianist and consummate composer of the romantic style, had just settled back in his seat on the train bound for

Paris. It was the fall of 1846. He was humming to himself the melody he had created for one of Mickiewicz's ballads. At just that moment, a delegation of farmers arrived at the home of the great French writer, she of the beautiful soul and fat ass, Madame George Sand, in rural Nohant. We will not disappoint you, she was smoking a cigar when she came to the front door, summoned by her maid.

"What do they want?" asked Madame Sand.

"Excuse me, Madame, but they say they have come to take Chopin's bed."

The cigar dropped from her mouth. "Damn! His what?"

"His bed, Madame."

The spokes-farmer for this delegation tried to clarify the situation. "In fact, if you will, we don't want to take the bed. We are here because we are obliged to burn it."

"Well," Sand replied, "that is some clarification." There was a despairing look of recognition in her face. This again. Familiar and awful. It was really the farmers themselves who were most confused about what exactly they were doing. For Sand, it was awful life-business as usual.

"Our apologies, Madame Sand, but we must take Mssr. Chopin's bed and burn it. We would prefer to burn it outside and away from the house. But burn it we will. It occurs to us as in the nature of a sad and strange necessity."

Sand stared at this mopish delegation sternly. She retrieved her cigar and puffed aggressively. "You farmers never really liked the poor, suffering, angelic man, did you?" No response.

Sand was nonplussed. "Sad and strange it is; you are right about that. Listen, Mssr. Chopin is a sick man. He needs a bed. He spends a lot of time in it. Just where is he to sleep when he returns?"

The farmers looked one at the next, as if mulling this question over as a group. "Excuse us, but you could perhaps afford to buy him another bed."

"Why? So that you could come back and ask permission to burn it too?"

"Again, our apologies, but we do not ask permission. We will take and burn the bed. If it's not clear to us which of the beds is Chopin's, we will have no choice but to burn all of the beds in the house."

"Oh, a fine idea! I'll be the first French woman driven into poverty through the burning of beds! Sad and strange indeed!"

Just then, the farmer who functioned as some sort of spokesman put out his hand and gently touched Sand's wrist. "Madam..." he said, *"si vous plaît."*

Sand sighed deeply. "Oh, of course, come in." And she moved aside.

The farmers walked through the house carefully, quietly, apologetically, with a certain melancholy. It was as if they were coming to move the corpse of Chopin and not his bed. Four of them lifted the bed at its corners and in a stark procession moved gravely out of the house and into the yard, beneath a group of fruit trees. They set the bed down with extreme care. The maid came running after them to take the blankets and sheets from the bed before they ignited it. The farmers kept her firmly away, a burly farmer's forearm across her chest.

"Gentlemen, Madame Sand had this quilt made as a gift for Chopin. There can't be a need to burn it, too."

The farmers discussed the issue. The quizzical, rough expressions on their farmer faces. The throwing of hands in the air. The dolor of the wrinkles, and graying beards. These were not young impetuous farmers but the oldest, wisest men in the area. They did what they did with all due deliberation.

"Our profound regrets, mademoiselle, but you must inform Madame Sand that since we are unclear on the fate of the blankets, but we know that we may not delay in our chore, we have no choice but to burn them with the bed. We would not wish to make a mistake here. The consequences would be grievous for the entire agricultural region."

This rather stunned the poor young woman. Her bewilderment leapt to yet higher levels. "Oh, my God, what can you mean? Agriculture? Are you afraid your pigs will catch his disease?"

The farmers sighed and returned to their awful business. How could they expect this young maid to understand what big, strong French farmers could not. It was a necessity and a mystery and therefore a solemn obligation. That was all there was to say about it.

A small fire of sticks and newsprint, Sand's own journal *La Revue Indepdente*, was started beneath the bed, but it did not grow quickly because the air could not circulate well with the blankets hanging down on both sides. Eventually, though, with much flapping of arms, the fire did blaze and catch the mattress and soon the poor small bed with its fiery headboard looked like a comet scorching through the yard. The farmers had to cover their faces from the heat.

Already, George Sand had gone to her desk and was beginning a letter to Chopin.

Dear Chopinet:

I have most disturbing news for you....

And at just that moment, Chopin sat bolt upright in his seat, as if his intestines had been connected to an electric current. He sensed that something had happened, something awful. He was very receptive to such psychic presentiments, especially where Sand was concerned. He recalled the time the peasants had burned his bed in Spain. He saw it burning, floating in space, a universal emblem of some depressing kind. But then the tune for the *ballade* returned, winding about the burning bed in a pleasing and blissful way. Chopin thought, "The sky is beautiful and my heart is sad." In his mind the *note bleue* resonated and there he was in the azure of transparent night. And nothing else mattered.

4.

AT THE END of his life, back in Paris, impoverished after the Revolution of 1848, permanently estranged from the "vampire" Sand, surrounded strangely by "Scotchwomen" who were "so good, but so boring, so help me God," Chopin retreated to die to an apartment in the Passy hills overlooking the Seine. He was now "an arch-delicate insect" that could be touched only very carefully lest a dry wing should snap off.

His death scene has been recounted by many, including a majority who were not there at all. The "mucosities" in his lungs made him feel as if he were suffocating. It had been a short life, surely, but hugely productive from a musical standpoint. It had also been a sad life in many ways—the tumultuous burlesque of the relationship with the omnivorous George Sand was at the top of that list—but not so oddly, perhaps, in those last moments Chopin's thoughts turned to the happy things, the little jewels in the pig shit of life. In particular, he recalled that when he lived with Sand at Nohant they spent many evenings with the children creating their own puppet theater. They had one-hundred-twenty puppets, all dressed by Sand. *Le Théatre des marionettes de Nohant* was a little world over which they were Gods intensely glad of what they had created. Chopin's part was to improvise at the piano while the young people performed different scenes together with comical dances.

At first, Chopin was most struck by how ridiculous his own deathbed agony made him feel. The Scotswomen were sniveling around and offering to pay for everything. The musicians were trying to figure out the most appropriate last things for the immortal one to hear as he passed through the Great Wringer. Something from Mozart's *Requiem*? Of course, a fine choice but a bit on the obvious side. "Hymn to the Virgin" by Stradella? An air by Pergolesi? A psalm by Marcello? Yes, yes, fine, but sing something, quickly, his belly is swelling with death. He is more than a candidate for the next world, he is half-inaugurated! In the end, it hardly mattered what they played for no sooner would they begin than Chopin would suffer a loud coughing fit and interrupt the tableau.

Dying people make for a very poorish audience.

And then, naturally, every aristocratic lady to whom Chopin had once given piano lessons was there determined to be witnessed by the rest of the *haute monde* achieving a successful faint beside Chopin's bed. The one "Lady" who was not allowed near his deathbed was the highest of them all, Madame Sand. Her apparition, cigar at mouth, enveloped in purling smoke, was felt at every window looking in on the last pathetic moments of her dear, vulnerable Chopinet.

But of course the only thing Chopin himself wished for, as he had wished all his life, was simply not to be disturbed. He said, "God shows a man a rare favor when He reveals to him the moment of the approach of death; this grace he shows me. Do not disturb me."

When at last he died, his heart was cut from his body, placed in alcohol, and given to his sister, Ludwika, who smuggled it back to Warsaw hidden beneath her dress. She feared that the filthy Russian czarists would confiscate the great heart. The body was interred at Pére Lachaise, the ersatz destinations of American tourists. It is said that women still like to faint before his headstone.

But the deathbed itself had to be burned, *bien sûr*. And the musicians, artists, ladies and benefactors lifted it high upon their shoulders and passed through the front door into the courtyard, the lugubrious opening chords of Chopin's own *Marche funébre* from the B-flat minor sonata echoing behind them. They moved through the Parisian suburb of Chaillot, on the Passy hills overlooking both the city and the Seine. On a long hillside they paused and set the bed afire, still raised high on their shoulders. Then with an enormous shrug they sent it down the hill over which it seemed almost to flow, brightly, like lava, on unearthly wheels, flames arcing back.

"*Bon voyage*, Chopinet," they cried. "*Au revoir* you who first made us completely human, through your universal tears. *Bonne chance*. Your triumph is the beginning of our long failure."

THE BLUE GUIDE TO INDIANA

by MICHAEL MARTONE

THE WORLD HEADQUARTERS OF WORLD HEADQUARTERSES

Given its central location geographically and its abundant supply of fresh water, the municipality of Indianapolis, which also serves as the state's capital, has become an attractive location where various corporate entities, trade associations, and fraternal organizations have established a significant number of world headquarterses, home offices, and central distribution warehouses. What follows is an abbreviated list of such sites, many open for tours and often containing museums, libraries, company cafeteria, dioramas, animated displays, and/or gift shops, all available to the public. The vast majority of world headquarterses may be found along the city's principle paved motor artery, Meridian Street, which runs north and south through the center of Indianapolis, tracing exactly the geographical 86° west meridian for thirty-seven miles.

The Glutinous Maximus Corporation
8317 North Meridian Street
Adjacent to the United States Postal Service's National Center for Affixation of Post-Addressed Postal Labels and Notices (USPS-APAPLN), the world headquarters of The Glutinous Maximus Corporation (GMC)—the nation's third-largest producer of adhesives, pastes, glues, putties, sealants, and caulking—houses the financial offices as well as the chemical research laboratories. On the site of the original abattoir, the grounds still include the historic

stockyards, re-visioned, by the architect Michael Graves, as an extensive topiary garden and, at the rear of the property, a small Museum of the Tongue.

Gramm's Globes
On the island in the middle of the 8000 block of
North Meridian Street
Designed by the architect Michael Graves, the spherical president's office and astronomical observatory on the roof of the thirty-seven-story tower rests on a titanium gimbal and is motorized in a such a manner as to replicate the rotation of the earth. In 1999, the entire production of globes was moved to unrevealed locations overseas, leaving thirty-five of the other thirty-six floors vacant and a picket line of cashiered members of the International Amalgamated Brotherhood of Globe Workers, Local 27, circling the ground floor continually since the layoffs. However, the bank of twenty-four glass lifts fully exposed on the building's north facade will still serve as the site for the summer's World Elevator Surfing Championships, sponsored by the company's hydrology and atmospheric departments and broadcast on ESPN2.

The Association of Normals
6250 North Meridian Street
Administrative offices share space with a conference center and convention hall in this ranch-style house, renovated by the architect Michael Graves and operated by a coalition of cities named "Normal." The association publishes a newsletter, *The Thermostat*, and, each year, during its annual banquet, presents its annual award, The Golden #2 Pencil, acknowledging an individual who most exemplifies the group's tenets and principles. With the money it generates during this event, the association continues to fund research into the design of squirrel-resistant birdfeeders and for the technology needed to compress further the segment of the radio band spectrum allocated to automatic garage door openers.

League of Basketball Managers and Officials
5932 North Meridian Street
Indianapolis's renascence has been the result of a community and governmental strategy which actively pursued amateur and professional athletic events and organizations, making the city a necessary destination for competitors and competitions alike. The offices of the League of Basketball Managers and Officials relocated here from Martinsville, Indiana, in 1973. Among its many projects, the League provides the seat of the Court of Final

Technical Appeals, where games played under protest receive their ultimate adjudication, and the Grand Union Hall, where the world's pool of referees and timekeepers competitively bid their weekly games based on seniority. The Hall of Fame, built from plans based on sketches rendered by the architect Michael Graves, hosts an active program in the archiving and preservation of whistles, analgesic balm, and shoes.

The Hellenistic Consultancy
4444 North Meridian Street
Housed in the Gattling Homestead and refurbished by the architect Michael Graves, this research and design firm works exclusively with the world's Greek letter social sororities and fraternities in the development of their graphic and cultural identities. Field representatives report here on the continuity and the degradation of the millions of secrets utilized or compromised on campuses while, at the same time, generating, during special brainstorming sessions in the Brainstorming Room, a fresh supply of handshakes, passwords, and ancient rituals. The Map in the Map Room tracks every active or probationary chapter by means of a blinking display. The Hellenistic Consultancy also acts as the official depository for the proprietary branding of the various organizations. In its ongoing effort to maintain the integrity of this process, the firm employs the use of the largest Cray computer in the state.

The Society of Mary Gravida
Square Mary, North Meridian and 38th Streets
In addition to the geodesic domed chapel, the architect Michael Graves's master's thesis project when at Ball State University, the grounds also include The Grotto, The Home for the Unwed Mother, and The Chancellory Office for this excommunicated heretical holy order. The Grotto features the fifty-foot limestone statue of Mary Expectant. The clients of The Home, during their residency, manufacture, in a variety of media and in several scales, reproductions of the statue in the hope of fulfilling the prophecy, delivered by The Virgin Mother on this site in 1872, to propagate only representations depicting Our Lady as pregnant with the Son of God. The Gift Shop is open 24 hours a day, everyday, throughout the year.

LOVE Incorporated
3628 North Meridian Street
Operating out of an "L" shaped building that is the architect Michael Graves's homage to Richard Meier, LOVE Corp. administers the assets of the estate

derived from the LOVE work by the artist Robert Indiana, including the management of all royalties derived from the ongoing sale of the postage stamp and the .000005 cent fee levied on the everyday use of the word. The LOVE Foundation, located on the mezzanine, supports, philanthropically, the proliferation of benday and pantone to the Third World. The Gallery on the first floor displays the artist's early drafts, sketches, models, and alternate versions of the masterpiece, which include a galvanized "V," an "LE" in India Rubber, a series of "O" studies in aspic, a feldspar "LL," and the adobe "OVL," the top two horizontal strokes of the "E" having deteriorated over time.

The Great States Company
1510 North Meridian Street
The only remaining manufacturer in the world of push lawn mowers, the Great States Company utilizes the former Stutz Bearcat automobile plant, originally designed by Kurt Vonnegut, Sr., to produce a gross of machines each day. The twelve-acre roof of the factory has been converted into the test track, planted in stripes of varietal grass strains, which are kept viable throughout the year with heat and moisture disbursed by a subterranean system of tiling and pipes. The steam the system transports is created by a co-generation process derived from the world's largest compost heap, located in the company's adjacent parking lot. During the Memorial Day festivities, the company sponsors push mower races at the facility, which are televised locally by means of cameras mounted aboard helicopters hovering overhead.

The Re-reinsurance Insurance Company
1300 North Meridian Street
In this nondescript building, reminiscent of the early work of the architect Michael Graves, the actuaries of the Re-reinsurance Insurance Company calculate the risk of insuring insurance companies which insure insurance company. The company offers to these corporate clients, through its sales staff, a variety of re-reinsurance policies that are said to set the industry standard. The daily Re-Re Index, scoring the twenty leading re-reinsurers, is published in *The Wall Street Journal* and on a blackboard propped on an easel in the small front lobby. A vestibule off the lobby contains a Depression-Era soda fountain and grill run by the Marion County Association for the Blind.

Mikes of America
22 Monument Circle
The oldest nominal club in the country, Mikes of America boasts that it is

also the world's largest organization of same-named individuals with an active membership of over twelve million "Mikes," "Michaels," "Micheles," and "Michaelas" according to the most recent available figures. This total, it must be said, also includes the auxiliary of "Micks" and "Mickeys." The Italianate campanile, designed by club member Michael Graves, pays homage to the nearby state monument honoring Indiana's soldiers and sailors, which dominates the circle's center. The spire's interior circular ramp is lined by a constantly circulating gallery of portraits depicting the club's more recognizable members, such as Michael Graves, Leonard Michaels, and David Michael Letterman.

FC2
South Meridian and McCarthy Streets

In a second-floor suite of offices above a laundry and Shapiro's? Delicatessen in Indianapolis's famous Chinatown, FC2, the publisher of the *Blue Guide to Indiana* series of travel books, makes its corporate home. Staffed entirely by temporary employees who must demonstrate they are at least second-generation Hoosier natives, the media conglomerate constantly updates its several outlets of tourist information, including its real-time internet videofeed, its errata chain letter network, and the 300-foot crawl light display which wraps around the building. On the roof, the famous PoMo dovecot and carrier pigeon roost, based on a design that appeared to the architect Michael Graves in a dream, stands next to the sand and platform volleyball courts, where employee teams, routine competitors on the I States Semi-pro Tour, practice during their half-hour lunch breaks.

The Need for Some Home Assembly Furniture Institute
3245 South Meridian

Located in a Quonset hut designed in the manner of the school of Michael Graves, this think-tank reports to the eponymic producers of portable home furnishings. Its testing laboratories simulate conditions for domestic construction and do-it-yourself finishing of the merchandise as well as authenticates and verifies the time estimates given for the various tasks. Its literary office translates English translations into the English found on enclosed package instructions and is a leading contributor to the International Signage Initiative. There is an interesting collection of veneer in the sculpture garden along with Claus Oldenberg's monumental *Allen Wrench*.

Central Beetle Breeding

South Meridian and County Line Road

This family-owned enterprise has been raising free-range Scarabaeid on this site since 1901, when patriarch Hiram "Hi" Hinga domesticated his first wild "doodle bug." The intermodel transhipping terminal, the plans for which were discovered in the trash of the architect Michael Graves, has the capacity to handle up to six boxcars of live insects each day while off-loading liquid manure from a like number of dedicated tankers. In addition to supplying the farm market with a reliable source of dung beetle, the concern also provides certified beetle semen for private use in small scale artificial insemination programs as well as a collection of hybridized carrion, *scarabaeus sacer*, for use by natural history museums, taxidermists, and religious organizations.

THE SITE OF THE FIRST OBSERVED HUMAN FEMALE ORGASM IN AMERICA

FORT WAYNE

Editor's Note:

The photograph that was to accompany this segment of The Blue Guide to Indiana *was not available at the time this issue went to press. The editor apologizes for this inconvenience. The reader who is curious about the missing photo may write to the rare books department at the Dale McMillen Library, Indiana Institute of Technology, 1600 E. Washington Boulevard, Ft. Wayne, Indiana, 46803, stating his or her desire for it, and attach to this request a stamped, self-addressed, business-sized return envelope. The library will return a copy of the intended photograph suitable for pasting into the article's body copy at the indicated area. It will be necessary only for the reader to moisten the adhesive on the photograph's reverse with his or her own tongue.*

Pictured below (figure 1) is the marker erected by The National College of Sex Researchers and Sex Therapists to commemorate the centennial of the first American observations of the human female orgasm by Dr. Joseph R. Beck at the home of his patient, Mrs. H. L____ , on August 7 and 8, 1872.

fig. 1

Dr. Beck first published his findings in the St. Louis Medical and Surgical Journal the following month and delivered the same paper to the American Medical Association two years later when an expanded version was published in the November 1874 edition of the American Journal of Obstetrics and Diseases of Women and Children.

Mrs. L_____ who was, at the time, thirty-two years old and living with her husband of eight years at their middle class home on the corner of Spy Run and Tennessee Avenue, now the parking lot of a mortgage and loan company, was suffering from a severe "falling of the womb" or retroversion of the uterus. When fitting her with a pessary offering mechanical support, Dr. Beck, having already observed his patient was "an intelligent and appreciative lady," also noted, in the course of the examination, signs of sexual arousal if not possibly orgasm. Dr. Beck continues:

> In making my visit to the residence of the patient the next day, for the purposes of adjusting the supporter, I made a second examination by touch, and upon introducing my finger between the pubic arch and the anterior lip of the prolapsed cervix, I was requested by the patient to be very careful in my manipulations of the parts, since she was very prone, by reason of her nervous temperament and passionate nature, to have sexual orgasm induced by a slight contact of the finger, a fact which I believed had been manifested in my office examination of the previous day, and which she afterward admitted having been the case. Indeed she stated further that this had more than once occurred to her while making digital examination of herself.

To Dr. Beck, the possibility of observing Mrs. L_____'s cervix while she actually experienced an orgasm was of the very greatest scientific interest. The raging medical controversy of the day centered on explaining how spermatozoa entered the uterus from the vagina. A possible theory involved a sucking or aspirating action of the cervix as the principle conveyance. This was disputed by others. Mrs. L_____'s cervix was visible through her labia and hence offered Dr. Beck the opportunity to lay the controversy to rest.

> Carefully, therefore, separating the labia with my left hand, so that the os uteri was brought clearly into view in the sunlight, I now swept my right forefinger quickly three or four times across the space between the cervix and pubic arch, when almost immediately the orgasm occurred, and the following was what was presented in my view——
>
> Instantly after that the height of excitement was at hand, the os opened itself to the extent of fully an inch, as nearly as my eye could judge, made five or six successive gasps, as it were, drawing the external os into the cervix each time powerfully, and, it seemed to me, with regular rhythmic action, at the same time losing its former density and hardness, and becoming quite soft to the touch. All these phenomena occurred within the space of twelve seconds of time certainly, and in an instant all was as before. At the near approach of orgastic excitement the os and cervix became intensely congested, assuming almost a livid purple color, but upon cessation of the action, as related, the os suddenly closed, the cervix again hardened itself, the intense congestion was dissipated, the organs concerned resolved themselves into normal condition, and their relations to each other became again as before the advent of the excitement.

Dr. Beck's observation held sway for more than half a century, finally being eclipsed by the work of Dr. Robert Latou Dickinson in 1949 and his use of a transparent glass phallus equipped with a headlight, demonstrating that the inch-wide gasping entrance to the cervix was thus, at best, a rare and perhaps imagined phenomenon. But this happened in Rhode Island.

Dr. Beck's papers and surgical instruments are on display in the rare book room of the McMillen Library.

BRISTOL

Here, in 1875, Albert Einstein, while filming another instructional movie explaining his theory of general relativity, visited a local tourist curiosity called "The Blue Hole," where an enterprising local charged two bits to observe an azure opening in the air. For his film, Einstein used the Doppler effects of the New York Central's crack streamliner, The Twentieth Century Limited, as it tore across the state. Professor Einstein realized that Bristol's "Blue Hole" was simply another anticipated rip in the fabric of time and space. The savvy reader will have realized as well, at this point, that the Professor, in 1875, had yet to be born (nor had the motion picture and the train, named for a century that hadn't happened yet, been invented). The actual filming took place in a barely existing 1939. Now, today, whenever you read this, Bristol is the site of a factory manufacturing aspirin for exportation. The disruption in the continuum continues and contributes to the phenomenon, reported by many, of residents being stricken by a series of excruciating headaches and migraines and other debilitating cerebral electrical disruptions. These include perceptual disorientations of all the senses and of all kinds, including, especially, the phenomena of serial déjà vu whose déjà vu-ed images of this place's particular history often overwhelm the victim, rendering him or her spastic and disoriented. A visitor quickly senses an uncanny pattern of sameness to the days here and reports sensations of dread and despair surrounding the phrase, "The Good Old Days," and upon innocently entering the cafe on the town square.

FOUR FACTUAL ANECDOTES
ON FICTION

by MICHAEL MARTONE

1.

At the end of the Second World War, my grandfather responded to a radio appeal broadcast by General Mark Clark, governing occupied Austria, for Americans to send packages of food and other vital necessities to the refugees, displaced persons, and homeless civilians of a devastated Europe. That very day, my grandfather sent his first care package. He told me, years later, that he tried to imagine what a family, in circumstances he could not imagine, would want or need. He sent potted meat, paper and pencils, chocolate bars and gum, evaporated milk, a pack of playing cards, a can opener, flour and sugar, envelopes, needles and thread and buttons and zippers, coffee and tea. He also sent peanut butter.

His monthly charity was assigned to a family in Vienna, the Gabauers, who wrote back using the equipment supplied by my grandfather, thanking him and meticulously inventorying the contents of each subsequent package. I have read the letters. The exchange of goods and the receipt of letters went on for three years after the end of the war. The Gabauers were initially confused by the peanut butter. "What is 'peanut butter?'" At first they used it as a cooking oil and then as leavening in their baking. The letters, in German, had been translated by a friend of my grandfather's, the English penciled in between the lines of German, a layered sandwich of languages.

Eventually, the family figured out what to do with the peanut butter. They wrote—a daughter usually wrote—of their evolving life in recovering

Austria, their growing but meager prosperity. They sent detailed renderings of local color and narratives about their attempts to learn English. There are eighty-three letters, most written on the paper sent by my grandfather. I have them still, inheriting them when he died.

I used the above anecdote in a story once, changing a few of its details to make it, well, fiction, of course, and a better story. I elaborated on other details and added new ones. In the story, the narrator, a young man, a college student, is encouraged by his grandfather to learn German in school. Once he learns the language, his grandfather reveals that he had sent care packages to a family in Austria after the war. They, in turn, had sent letters to the grandfather who can now, years after their composition and with the help of his educated grandson, translate their thanks, their daily observations, their confusion about peanut butter. The letters, in my story, had lain dormant for thirty years, awaiting the fictional scene in which a character very much like me reads them for the first time to his grandfather. The final letters, when translated, wonder why the grandfather has never written back. The family begs him to stop sending packages, indicates they are back on their feet. The very last letter in my story is written in English by the daughter who has now learned the language. Her letter remained unread, unopened and undisturbed for thirty years, until the story's very end.

I wrote the story not long before my grandfather died. I read it to him. The story ends with the scene where the grandson is reading a letter to the grandfather in the kitchen of the grandfather's apartment, which was very much like the one where I sat reading my grandfather the story. He said, as I finished, using my diminutive pet name to address me, that, yes, I had got it exactly right, that the story was exactly as he remembered it.

How curious, I thought. I was quite conscious at that very moment that the story I had written and had just then read, with its made up particulars and invented circumstance, had just that moment overwritten the actual memory in my grandfather's mind. It was as if my dream of the story had infected my grandfather's dreaming of his own life. I had never learned German. He had given me the letters a long time ago to read and admire. Since high school, I had known the story of the Gabauers, reading the mortar of English between the blocks of solid German. "You got that right, Mickey," he said.

I didn't say anything to dissuade him of his belief. He was, I could see, delighted to remember these events of his life. Perhaps he was simply delighted to remember any events of any life. In a few months, he would be dead and all his memories erased. In the meantime, he avidly told any of the other residents of his building who cared to listen, the story, only recently, from his point-of-view, recalled. There was the war, Mark Clark, the packages, the Gabauers, their letters at long last translated by his grandson, and the sad and funny search found within them for the uses of peanut butter.

2a.

The Gideons usually work in pairs, holding down a strategic corner or crosswalk at the gateways of the campus. They show up twice a year. Boxes of the little green, gold-trimmed Bibles are at their feet. They dip into the boxes, scooping out a handful of books. They hand the books to the students as they shuffle past. I have a collection of these Gideon Bibles. Twenty-five years of Bibles. They are all exactly the same. The leather like wrapper, the pocket size, the prohibition against selling this book.

Many students, as they put some distance between themselves and the Gideons, seek to dispose of their gifts. I always like it when the result is the spontaneous decoration of a nearby shrub or bush, the Bibles trimming the branches, scattered like presents on the carpet of needles beneath the lowest limbs.

The Gideons never seem to pick up the discards as they depart. Theirs is a mission of mine laying. It is the distribution that matters. One day, the little package will find its mark, or, more exactly, the mark will stumble upon it by accident at a vulnerable moment. The Bible as crisis intervention, a 1-800 number on a refrigerator magnet. The Bible's first pages feature a handy directory, called "Where to Find Help When," that lists a series of afflictions and the corresponding verse. Where to Find Help When—Afraid, Anxious, Backsliding, Bereaved, Bitter, etc. Boom, boom, boom. I am reminded of the entomologist who imported the Gypsy moth parasite and released it into the infestation and nothing happened. He went to his grave thinking his efforts had been a failure when, only recently, after years and generations, the parasite has just now reached a critical population and begun to do its work.

2b.

Also appearing seasonally on campuses are itinerant preachers who, in the middle of the quad or yard, accost the students, pestering, proselytizing. The strategy is to get the students to stop. You do that through accusation, condemnation. You want them to heckle, argue, and hence attract a crowd.

Once, I wrote a play about an itinerant preacher who comes to a college campus and, using the above techniques, engages students as they mill about the campus. I didn't know much more of what would happen or how it was going to end since it was to be performed out on the quad with only a few actors who would perform the roles of the preacher and students. The rest of the play would proceed improvisationally through audience participation of real students thinking that they were witnessing an ordinary appearance of an actual itinerant preacher. Attending every performance would be two audiences, one innocent of the fiction and a second completely aware.

That was several semesters ago. Every year since, in the fall and the spring when the weather is fine and the preachers appear, I go out to watch the performance. I even participate, calling out some lines I have composed for the occasion. I never know now what I am watching. I have to, finally, make up my mind about what I am seeing. Am I watching my play or is it a play written by someone else. Sooner or later, I go ahead and see it one way or the other, an illusion I switch back and forth in my head.

3.

I went to a circus. It was an old-fashioned circus, with one ring and wood bleachers in a battered canvas tent set up in a city park. The members of the circus company all did many jobs. The ringmaster sold tickets. The lady on the trapeze, when she finished her act, came back down to earth and sold popcorn in the stands. Clowns came out between the tumbling or wire acts to distract the audience while the trampolinist-turned-roustabout re-rigged the ring. The only animal act, appropriate to the scale, was a dog one. The dogs, dressed in dog tuxedoes, walked around on their hind legs.

One of the intervening clown acts made fun of the circus's lowered expectations. This clown act was a parody of an equestrian performance, consisting of one horse and its trainer. The horse was a two-piece affair, head and tail sections, a burlap get-up. The clown trainer wore the red riding tails and top hat and repeatedly injured himself with his own whip. The horse did a lot of business in which the front and tail end disagreed. The front end was the straight man, naturally, its legs crossed casually as the unruly ass end danced around behind. The clunky head would snap around to stare down the revolting rear half which, when spied, would freeze and act nonchalant, shuffling its droopy hooves casually. The clown played to both ends, appealing to each to perform the tricks he was eliciting.

I was thoroughly convinced that I was watching men dressed up like a horse. Yet the disguised pair was talented enough to, at moments, make me believe I was seeing, even though the costume was so shabby, a real horse. And, at that moment, they would do something to remind me, lift the fake tail, say, that I was really watching an elaborate and full-sized puppet. I am allergic to real horses, and, suddenly, I felt allergic as I watched this performance. I remember thinking, this is marvelous, the illusion so convincing at times that I am behaving as if I was in the presence of the actual animal. Even as I began to sneeze, I thought it must be a reaction to the burlap or the hay the horse refused to eat.

The interlude drew to a close, and the clown trainer took his bow. The horse, too, awkwardly genuflected its front legs, bowing while tossing its hollow head. The clown moved toward the seam in the fabric at the horse's waist. He tugged at the burlap and the disguise fell away, not to reveal the team of operating clowns, but instead another horse. This horse was not a costume of a horse. It was a real horse that had just finished performing a counterfeit of men who are dressed up like a horse. My immune system, the one making me sneeze, had not been fooled, but every other sensing system, all of them completely shorted out by this revelation, was now taking a very pleasant second or two to come back on line.

4.

A woman I know wrote her geography dissertation about places in the world that had become real once they had been read about in a story. These places were now destinations for tourists. Green Gables, The House of Seven Gables, Sunnybrook Farm, The Bridges of Madison County, W.P. Kinsella's and Kevin Costner's Field of Dreams. People went to see the fence Tom Sawyer painted, walk the street Ishmael walked on his way to the sea. The insurance company occupying the offices of Sherlock Holmes assigns an employee to answer the detective's mail. In the Mediterranean there are tours that follow the course of *Odyssey*. In Dublin, there are organized odysseys as well.

I recently wrote a fictional travel guide for visitors to Indiana. I published parts of the book, called *The Blue Guide to Indiana*, in some local newspapers. Their publication did nothing to indicate their fictional nature. The newspapers simply presented them as places to see and things to do in the state. I like the idea of a fiction without character or plot, a fiction that instead provides costumes and props, things for the reader to use. The book is, after all, a travel guide, presenting a collection of places and objects that you can pick up or put down by turning the page. Let's do this, the tourist says. Let's go there. Tourists can, with a travel book, select their destinations and bring their trips to life. Most fiction provides character and plot; with most fiction you get the travel book as well as the travelers and the trip they take. In my travel guide the story is left partially complete. Much is missing. Perhaps what remains is enough for the reader to construct the story anyway.

Another woman I know wrote her dissertation on the use of labels in museums. She was all for them. It turns out to be a big debate in museum school, labels. I'm all for museums without labels, a museum where the clientele is let loose with artifacts to make heads or tails of the junk on their own. I like the idea of someone coming upon my fiction, not knowing it is even fiction, and having to ask, What is this? We all are constantly sifting through the detritus of the world trying to make sense of it.

One day I got a call from a reporter from *The Washington Post*. He told me he was doing a story on little-known federal facilities and programs. I knew what he was about to ask. One part of my travel book detailed a tour of sites having to do with death: The Tomb of Orville Redenbacher, The Cemetery at Naked City, The Monument for Those Killed by Tornadoes in Mobile Home Parks. There was also the Federal Testing Facility for Coffin and Casket Standards. The reporter was interested in the testing facility. Did I know anything about that? He had been led to believe I might know something about it. I thought about maintaining the illusion or at least remaining deadpan. But I told him I had made it up.

"I made it up," I said.

"Oh," he said, "that's too bad. This was one of the more interesting ones. I wanted this one to be for real."

JONATHAN AMES is the author of two novels and a memoir. *My Less Than Secret Life*, a collection of short fiction and essays that includes the essay published in this issue, will appear May 2002.

AMIE BARRODALE is a writer living in Brooklyn.

JOSHUAH BEARMAN is a journalist who likes to write about science. He lives in Los Angeles.

SANDOW BIRK's book, *In Smog and Thunder: Historical Works from The Great War of the Californias*, is available from Last Gasp, of San Francisco. An exhibit of his paintings of California prisons opened in November, at the Catharine Clark Gallery, in San Francisco.

JANET L. BLAND lives in Denver and is at work on a novel.

PATRICK BORELLI is a stand-up comedian. He lives in Brooklyn.

STEPAN CHAPMAN is the author of *The Troika* (Ministry of Whimsy Press, 1997), a surrealistic novel that received the Philip K. Dick Award. Creative Arts Book Company recently published *Dossier*, a collection of his short stories.

RACHEL COHEN's essays have appeared in *The Threepenny Review*, *DoubleTake*, and *Parnassus*. She is currently at work on a book based on "A Chance Meeting," from *McSweeney's* no. 4.

CHRIS COLIN is an editor at Salon.com. He lives in Oakland.

KARYN COUGHLIN lives in Somerville, Massachusetts and runs Toscanini's Ice Cream in Cambridge. She is currently collaborating on *Volume 13: M*, a fictional encyclopedia.

MICHEL DESOMMELIER is a professor at the University of Basel specializing in twentienth-century Anglo-American literature and Peter Handke.

RIKKI DUCORNET is the author of six novels, most recently *The Fan-Maker's Inquisition*. She is currently writing *The Kosmétérion*, a novel set in Cairo.

MONIQUE DUFOUR is Monique Dufour.

BEN DRYER is the editor of *Volume 13: M*. He lives in Somerville, Massachusetts.

JEFF EDMUNDS is a painter, musician, and writer-translator. He edits *Zembla*, a web site devoted to Vladimir Nabokov that he created in 1995.

ERIC P. ELSHTAIN's writing has appeared or is forthcoming in *Fence*, *The Denver Quarterly*, and *New American Writing*. He is poetry editor of *Chicago Review*, and his chapbook, *Seventy-two Malignant Spirits*, is available at www.beardofbees.com.

AMY ENGLAND's book of poems, *The Flute Ship Castricum*, will be released by Tupelo Press this fall. Her work has appeared in *New American Writing*, *TriQuarterly*, *Volt*, and *Fence*.

BRIAN EVENSON is the author of five books of fiction, including *Altmann's Tongue* (to be reissued in 2001 by University of Nebraska Press), *Father of Lies*, and *Contagion*. His translations include work by Rafael Cadenas, Eduoard Maunick, Jean Fremon, Ludovic Janvier, and C. Stelzmann.

DAN GOLDSTEIN is a writer and theater producer. He lives in New York City.

J. MANUEL GONZALES is working on a collection of short fictional biographies. He lives in New York.

KEVIN GUILFOILE of Chicago is a regular contributor to mcsweeneys.net, and the co-author, with John Warner, of *My First Presidentiary: A Scrapbook by George W. Bush*.

ALEKSANDAR HEMON is the author of *The Question of Bruno*.

JOHN HODGMAN is a former literary agent whose writing can be found in *The Paris Review* and on mcsweeneys.net.

MARK HONEY is a writer and attorney in Houston.

CARLA HOWL is writer living in Denver.

GABE HUDSON's story collection, *Dear Mr. President*, will be published by Knopf in August 2002.

CHRISTINE HUME is the author of *Musca Domestica* (Beacon). She teaches at Eastern Michigan University.

SAMANTHA HUNT is completing two books of fiction. Other stories by her can be found in the *Iowa Review*, *Western Humanities Review*, and *Colorado Review*. Her story "Bathymetry" appeared in the last issue of *McSweeney's*.

MICHAEL M. JEROMINSKI lives in Carlisle, Pennsylvania, where he studies law. He is a distant relative of Edna St. Vincent Millay.

CATHERINE KASPER's chapbook, *Blueprints of the City*, was published by Transparent Tiger Press. She is an assistant professor at the University of Texas at San Antonio, and her writing recently appeared in *Chicago Review*, *Volt*, and *Mid-Amerian Review*.

ERIK P. KRAFT is the author of the children's books *Chocolatina* (Bridgewater Books, 1998) and the forthcoming *Lenny and Mel* (Simon and Schuster Books for Young Readers, 2002).

CYNTHIA KUHN's writing has appeared in *Muddy River Poetry Review* and *The Edge*.

PAUL LAFARGE's new novel, *Haussmann, or the Distinction*, is about Georges-Eugène Haussmann, the urbanist who rebuilt Paris in the 1850s and 60s. It was published in September.

J. ROBERT LENNON is the author of three novels, most recently *On the Night Plain*. He lives in Ithaca, New York.

BEN MARCUS's novel, *Notable American Women*, will appear in spring 2002. His book *The Father Costume*, with images by Matthew Ritchie, is also forthcoming. He is the author of *The Age of Wire and String*, and the fiction editor of *Fence*. He lives in Maine.

JILL MARQUIS lives and works in New Orleans. Her writing has appeared in *Mississippi Review*, *Cutbank*, *Teacup*, *Litrag*, and I Can Learn© educational software.

MICHAEL MARTONE is the author of several books, including *The Flatness and Other Landscapes*, a book of essays, and, most recently, *The Blue Guide to Indi-*

ana, a travel book. Michael Martone was born in Fort Wayne, Indiana, and was educated in the public schools there. His first published work, a poem titled "Recharging Time," and a character sketch, "Tim, the Experience" about his brother, appeared in *The Forum*, an annual literary magazine produced by the school system featuring contributions by its students. His mother, a high school freshman English teacher at the time, in fact, wrote the poem and the character sketch signing her son's name to the work and sending it to the editor, another English teacher at a south side junior high school who had been her sorority sister, Kappa Alpha Theta, in college. Indeed, most of his papers written for school were written by his mother. Examples included: English research papers, history term papers, translations from the Latin, speeches, and lab reports. It began innocently enough, with his mother writing his essays, the prose supposedly dictated by the son to his mother, whose penmanship was far and away more legible. This arrangement, her son sitting across the kitchen table in a sense thinking out loud as she transcribed his thoughts with the same pen she used to grade her own students' papers, engendered in her a very active editorial intervention which began to shape the spontaneous utterances emanating from her son. Soon this situation evolved to the point where her son sat silently while she wrote an original response to his initial prompt. Once she finished the first draft, she read it back to her son who made a few minor suggestions as to form, style, and content. It was at this time and under these conditions that Martone, understandably, began thinking of himself as a writer. His mother promoted that view in other ways, announcing to her friends at the local chapter of the educational honorary that her son had an aptitude for writing. The collaboration continued through college where assignments were mailed home and returned or, in some extreme cases, the prose response was communicated via a telephone and copied out in a rather cramped and illegible long hand in the dormitory phone booth. Most of Martone's first book of stories and his occasional essays on the subject of writing and published under his own name were written by his mother who learned, finally, to type in 1979, the year she wrote his graduate thesis. Today Martone receives microcassette recordings his mother has made of his future work with the hard copy arriving by fax or courier with little or no interaction between the collaborators prior to the work's appearance. Martone is hard-pressed to tell you what exactly of his published work could truly be said to be his original contribution, if any, including this contributor's note and the contribution published elsewhere in this magazine.

EDNA MAYFAIR is a character in a novel by Curtis White.

WHITNEY MELTON is a writer and performer in New York City.

EUGENE MIRMAN is a New York City-based stand-up comedian. He has appeared in the HBO U.S. Comedy Arts Festival, and has been featured on "Late Night With Conan O'Brien."

RICK MOODY is the author of the novels *The Ice Storm* and *Purple America,* and, most recently, a collection of stories, *Demonology.*

ROBERT NEDELKOFF's writing has appeared in *GQ, The Baffler, Raygun,* and elsewhere.

GARY PIKE is a writer living in Syracuse, New York.

CEDAR PRUITT studies education and cyberlaw in grad school at Harvard.

CHRISTY ANN ROWE has work published or forthcoming in *Salt Hill, The Alembic, North Dakota Quarterly, Denver Quarterly,* and other journals.

MATT SAUER is an architect living in Philadelphia.

KEVIN SHAY is a writer and computer programmer who has been involved with the online arm of *McSweeney's.* He is working on a play about a professional drowner.

JOEY SKAGGS lives in New York and Hawaii and is working on something that he is not at liberty to talk about at this time.

GILBERT SORRENTINO's *Gold Fools,* a burlesque boys' Western was recently published by Green Integer. His fifteenth novel, *Little Casino,* is due from Coffee House Press in spring 2002.

BRIAN SPINKS is a writer, performer, and graphic designer in New York City.

C. STELZMANN lives and works in Munich. His works include a complete bibliography of his grandfather's travel writing and a collection of occasional essays. "Moran's *Mexico*" is his first essay to be translated into English.

DARIN STRAUSS is the author of *Chang and Eng*, and the forthcoming *The Real McCoy and Old Women & Boys*, a collection of stories. *Chang and Eng* is being made into a film, directed by Julie Taymor, and is scheduled for release in 2002.

LYNNE TILLMAN's most recent novel is *No Lease on Life*. A collection of her short fiction will come out in 2002 from DAP.

STEVE TIMM has recently had poems in *American Poetry Review*, *Skanky Possum*, and *Shampoo*. He is a member of Dyna-Music, a quartet that performs music and poetry around Madison, Wisconsin.

STEVE TOMASULA's fictions have appeared most recently in *The Iowa Review* and *Fiction International*. Recent essays on body and genetic art can be found in the *New Art Examiner* and *Leonardo* (M.I.T. Press).

DAVID RAY VANCE's writing has appeared or is forthcoming in *Sniper Logic*, *Denver Quarterly*, *Private Arts*, and the *Chicago Review*.

JAMES WAGNER was born in Fond du Lac, Wisconsin, in 1969. A former editor of *Salt Hill* and a founding editor of *3rd Bed*, his poems have been published in *The American Poetry Review*, *Denver Quarterly*, and *Grand Street*.

EARL WANG is a freelance journalist currently based in Astoria.

BILL WASIK is an editor at *Harper's*.

COLLEEN WERTHMANN is a writer and performer living in New York City. She can be seen in the upcoming independent film "Make Pretend" and the season premiere of "Law & Order."

LAWRENCE WESCHLER is a contributing editor at *McSweeney's* and the author of numerous books, including *Calamities of Exile* and *Mr. Wilson's Cabinet of Wonder*.

CURTIS WHITE is the author of *Memories of My Father Watching TV*, and most recently *Requiem*. He is also the editor of *Context*.

JOHN WILLIAMS works for a book publisher in New York, and is a freelance writer. He lives in Brooklyn.

SEAN WILSEY, an editor at *McSweeney's*, is at work on a book about his experiences in and out of reform schools, to be published by Random House. This is his first published short story.

RANDALL WILLIAMS lives in Durham, North Carolina and writes for *The Independent Weekly*.

MARCEL DZAMA lives in Winnipeg, Manitoba. His work is exhibited widely and has been seen in many publications. McSweeney's will publish a new collection of his work late this spring.